The Girl Who Came Home to Cornwall

Emma Burstall

The Girl Who Came Home to Cornwall

First published in the UK in 2019 by Head of Zeus Ltd
This paperback edition first published in the UK in 2020
by Head of Zeus Ltd

9 7 5 3 1 2 4 6 8

A catalogue record for this book is available
from the British Library.

ISBN (PB): 9781786698889
ISBN (E): 9781786698865

Typesetting: Silicon Chips
Map: Amber Anderson

To Yael, Jonathan, Alex, Fia, Gloria and Monica.
Thank you for sharing your beautiful Mexico
with me.

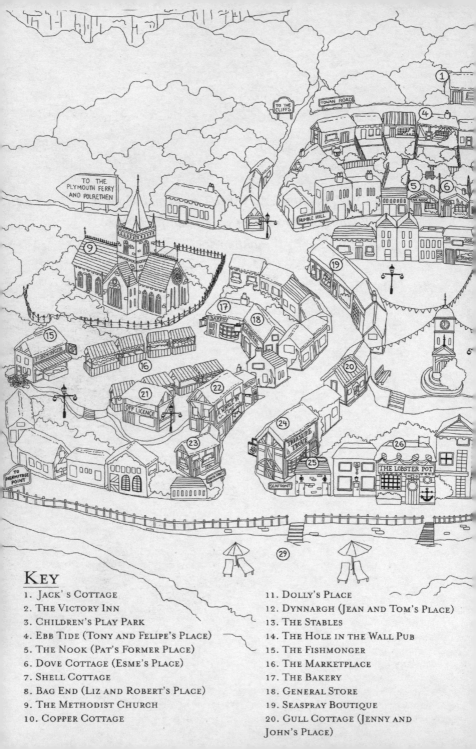

KEY

1. JACK'S COTTAGE
2. THE VICTORY INN
3. CHILDREN'S PLAY PARK
4. EBB TIDE (TONY AND FELIPE'S PLACE)
5. THE NOOK (PAT'S FORMER PLACE)
6. DOVE COTTAGE (ESME'S PLACE)
7. SHELL COTTAGE
8. BAG END (LIZ AND ROBERT'S PLACE)
9. THE METHODIST CHURCH
10. COPPER COTTAGE
11. DOLLY'S PLACE
12. DYNNARGH (JEAN AND TOM'S PLACE)
13. THE STABLES
14. THE HOLE IN THE WALL PUB
15. THE FISHMONGER
16. THE MARKETPLACE
17. THE BAKERY
18. GENERAL STORE
19. SEASPRAY BOUTIQUE
20. GULL COTTAGE (JENNY AND JOHN'S PLACE)

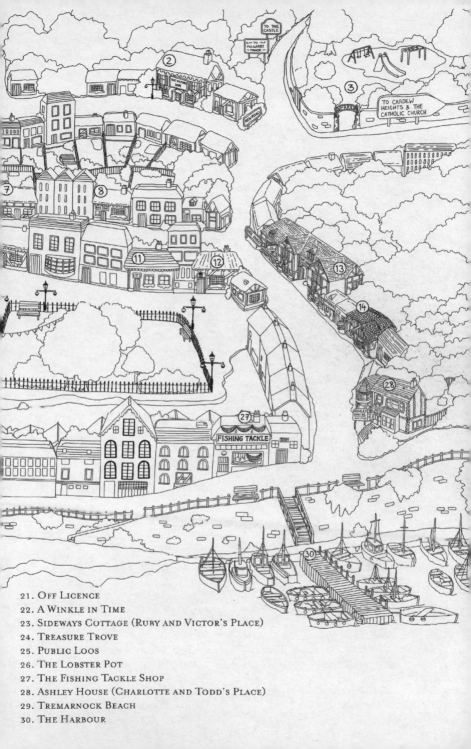

Chapter One

RICK ADJUSTED THE POSTCARD DISPLAY outside his gift shop, wondering idly if customers would mind about the odd dog-eared corner and dirty smudge. He hoped not. Some of his cards had certainly seen better days but there was nothing wrong with the photos on the front of the stunning Cornish coastline, whitewashed fishermen's cottages and quaint cobbled streets.

Trouble was, folk didn't seem to send so many cards these days; they stuck their pictures on Facebook and the like instead. Shame.

He could still remember how his mother, long since gone, had given pride of place on her mantelpiece to the cards she'd received; she'd read them over and over, sometimes out loud with an annoying running commentary thrown in: 'Uncle Graham and Auntie Maeve have gone to Mallorca this year. Fancy that! It was the Costa Brava last year, and the year before. I expect they wanted a change of scenery…'; and, 'The hotel looks nice. I hope that pool's heated, otherwise if I know Maeve, she won't be setting foot in it!'

A sudden gust sent the multicoloured windmills in a bucket by Rick's feet swirling around and light caught the shiny foil, making him blink. It was the first Saturday in June, sunny and bright, but the air was still cool, especially at night when you needed a sweater.

A few postcards fluttered off the rotating display stand that he carried from his shop, Treasure Trove, every morning, and placed on the uneven cobbles. As he knelt down to gather them together, something made him turn to look over his shoulder up narrow, winding South Street past the rows of shops and cottages that led to Humble Hill.

At first all he could make out was a moving mass of colour – canary yellow with splashes of emerald, pillar-box red and royal blue. He narrowed his eyes and as the image came into focus, he started, nearly knocking the display stand flying, and had to steady himself against the wall. 'What the…?'

Sashaying towards him, in a swishing yellow skirt with a bright green pattern, was the most attractive woman that he thought he'd ever seen. From his squatting position he scanned quickly upwards, taking in her strappy red espadrilles, shapely calves, slim waist and generous bust, encased in a tight blue cardigan. He had to pinch himself to make sure that he wasn't daydreaming.

She paused for a moment, bending down to retie the laces on her shoes. She was flesh and blood, for sure, no figment of his imagination. When she stood up again, his gaze settled on her face, but from this distance all he could really see was red lipstick, a creamy-brown complexion, dark eyebrows and thick, wavy, shoulder-length black hair.

He whistled under his breath. She was getting nearer now, just a few metres away. There was no one else in the street and fearing that she might notice him bent double and gawping, he looked away quickly and stood upright, pretending to rearrange his postcards. Every now and then, however, he couldn't help darting furtive glances in her direction and the closer she came, the more his heart pitter-pattered. He didn't know what had come over him.

Rick, who was in his early sixties, had lived for most of his life in the little seaside village of Tremarnock. Although the place was very quiet in winter, in summer, tourists flocked from near and far to enjoy the beaches, water sports and spectacular local scenery. It wasn't unusual to see groups of all different nationalities sauntering in and out of the pubs, rental houses and shops, including his own.

This woman, however, was different from the usual crowd. With her chin raised, shoulders back and arms swinging loosely by her side, she was alone, yet didn't appear lonely; on the contrary, she looked quite confident, as if she were accustomed to her own company and, indeed, rather enjoyed it.

Although she was walking quite fast, she didn't seem to be in a hurry. Instead, she was taking her time, looking left and right, absorbing her surroundings and savouring the moment – the feel of the wind in her hair and the sun on her back. She looked like a free spirit, Rick decided, which he found interesting and strangely moving, too.

A small brown and white dog ran out of one of the houses a little way up the street, yipping wildly: Sally, the Jack Russell belonging to Jenny and John Lambert, who owned Oliver's, the fishing tackle shop on the seafront.

Jenny, who was short, blonde and in her late forties, hurried out soon after, grabbing the dog's collar and clipping her firmly on the lead. Sally was always escaping; she was known for it. Many were the times that Rick and the other villagers had had to join in search parties, scouring the beach and nearby countryside for clues.

Luckily, so far they'd always managed to locate the dog in the end, usually down a rabbit hole or rootling in the undergrowth of the neighbouring woods, but everyone feared that one day she might be gone for good.

Once Rick had established that the dog was safely tethered, he glanced again at the stranger, who was now almost alongside him, and unintentionally caught her gaze.

A pair of large, round, greenish-brown eyes stared back and seemed to smile at him mysteriously. His heart beat louder in his chest; it was all he could do not to gasp. His own eyes must have been popping out on stalks, he couldn't help it, and when he finally tore his gaze away, he noticed that her red lips were turning up slightly at the corners, as if in amused recognition, and two little dimples had appeared in her cheeks. At that moment, he was well and truly hooked.

'Good morning,' the woman said in a foreign accent, pausing for a moment in front of the postcard display, behind which he was lurking.

Rick, who was normally quite voluble, felt the blood rush to his face and could only muster a muted, 'Morning,' back.

'Beautiful day,' she went on, craning her neck slightly so that she could see him more clearly.

He nodded, noticing for the first time the fine lines running horizontally across her brow and around her eyes. She wasn't quite as young as he'd assumed. Mid thirties, perhaps? He wasn't very good on ages. His pulse quickened. Perhaps he was in with a chance.

Silly old fool! He gave himself a mental shake. She was only being friendly. Someone like her could have anyone she wanted. Besides, she was probably happily married with three kids!

She seemed to hesitate, maybe hoping that he'd strike up a conversation.

'The sun's nice and warm but there's a chilly breeze,' he commented, wishing even as he spoke that he was the sort of bloke who always had a witty comment up his sleeve.

She hugged her arms around her, as if to acknowledge the nippiness in the air, before reaching out, taking a postcard and examining the scene on the front.

'I'll have to come back another time,' she said after a moment, popping the card back. 'I don't have any cash with me now.'

Rick wanted to say that she could have any of his cards – all of them, in fact – for free, if only she'd stay and tell him everything there was to know about her. But he was in such a state that he could only manage a grunt.

She smiled again before bidding him goodbye, then turned on her heel and walked off, raising her chin and swinging her arms again as she headed past his shop to the seafront.

It required an almost superhuman effort not to stare after her, and Rick was still trying to compose himself when someone coughed loudly, making him jump.

'She's very colourful!'

Jenny Lambert smiled cheekily at Rick, who acted as if he hadn't noticed.

'Who? Oh her,' he said fake-nonchalantly, when Jenny signalled in the stranger's direction. He couldn't help adding, 'Who do you think she is?'

Jenny, in a green Barbour jacket and stout walking shoes, was still hanging on to Sally, who was straining at the lead, keen to be off. Jenny never needed much of an excuse to stop and gossip.

'There's a foreign lady staying at Polgarry Manor for several weeks. Mexican, apparently. Maybe that's her.'

Polgarry Manor was the large, rambling guest house on the cliff above Tremarnock, which the owner also rented out for weddings and other big events.

Rick pulled thoughtfully on his bushy grey beard, which almost met up with his whiskery sideburns.

'She's foreign all right. Could be Mexican with that dark hair and complexion. A few weeks, you say?' His eyes widened.

'That's what I'm told.'

'Here for quite a spell then?'

Images of those red espadrilles and scarlet lips, that tight blue cardigan and those greenish-brown eyes swam into his mind, like a vivid dream.

'I wonder what's brought her to Tremarnock?'

CHABELA SMILED TO HERSELF AS she left behind the man with the funny grey beard and sideburns and strolled towards the beach.

She'd made quite an impression on him, that much was obvious, but it didn't surprise her. She was accustomed to male admiration as well as female stares, though these weren't always quite so friendly.

She was well aware that she was beautiful and it had certainly come in handy down the years, but she'd never allowed it to define her. Rather, she regarded her good looks as just one of many elements that combined to make Isabela Adriana Penhallow Maldonado, or Chabela for short, the woman that she was. Penhallow was her paternal surname, Maldonado, her mother's, and she used both, as was the custom in Mexico.

There was no rush, in fact she had all the time in the world, and after strolling past the public loos on her left, she stopped to admire the hanging baskets outside the Lobster Pot pub, which were stuffed with trailing blue lobelia and pink geraniums, just coming into bloom.

The pub door was closed and propped up against a wall inside the porch was a blackboard, on which someone had chalked: 'Moules Frîtes – Hand Baked Cornish Pasty and a Pint – Potted Shrimps – Village Scrumpy. Come on in!' Alongside was a rough drawing of a jolly farmer on a haystack.

Before long, Chabela guessed, the sign would be placed outside on the pavement and folk would start to wander in but for now, all was quiet.

It was so different from the dusty, densely populated street in the Colonia del Valle neighbourhood of Mexico City where she'd grown up, lined with tall, modern apartment buildings and row upon row of parked cars.

There, people gathered in cafés and restaurants from early in the morning till late at night, talking and laughing in loud, excited voices. Instead of hanging baskets, there were giant tubs of bougainvillea and violet-blue jacaranda, as well as palm trees, rubber plants and cacti.

Nostalgia nibbled at her insides, until she remembered that she'd come here to escape her old life, at least for a while. Savour the differences, she told herself. Enjoy the foreignness. You'll soon be treading those familiar streets and seeing those same old faces again...

Her thoughts were interrupted by a series of loud bangs and she swivelled around sharply. A youngish, dark-haired man inside the pub appeared to be pounding on the frame of a small, lead-paned window, which suddenly flew open, nearly coming off its hinges in the process.

As the man stuck out his arm to pull the window back in and secure the metal fastening, he spotted Chabela just a few feet away and his jaw dropped. He looked so funny that Chabela couldn't help smiling and his face lit up in a delighted grin, which made her smile even more.

It felt good to spread a little happiness, she thought, as she gave a wave and continued on her way. However, having had a mother whose beauty had bowled men over, but who'd been quite incapable of taking care of herself, Chabela had worked out long ago that you couldn't get by in this world on looks alone. After all, a car with great bodywork but poor suspension, an unreliable engine and defective steering was no use to anyone, and even as a child she'd known that she wanted to contribute something to the world, although back then she wasn't sure what.

While her mother had worked through a string of husbands, popping pills and drowning her sorrows in tequila in between, the young Chabela had focused more on her mind than her appearance. She'd strived hard at school, gained top results and won a scholarship to a good university in Mexico City.

After graduating with a First, she'd stayed on to do a PhD in Latin American studies, then 'Doctora Penhallow Maldonado', as she became known, took up the post of junior lecturer at the same institution.

Much respected by students and colleagues alike, she'd loved her job and could happily have spent her entire working life there, so it was quite a shock when she was headhunted by Mexico City's most prestigious university and offered a promotion. She might even have turned it down, had not her peers warned her against committing career suicide.

She was thirty-two years old when she accepted her new position, still single and vaguely aware that her biological clock was ticking, but not unduly bothered by the fact. She'd dated plenty of boys and men down the years, but her mother's disastrous track record with relationships had made her wary of commitment.

She thought that she'd like to have children, but not at any price, and the truth was that she'd never been properly in love – that is, until she met Professor Alfonso Hernández Soler.

His name seemed to dangle tantalisingly in the air before her and her stomach tightened into a hard, painful knot. She hadn't thought of him for, what, at least half an hour? That must be a record. And now here she was again, about to go down the same old path that led precisely nowhere.

Angry with herself, she crossed the road and walked briskly along the track by the sea wall before descending some stone steps on to Tremarnock Beach, which was small, horseshoe-shaped, and sheltered on both sides by rocky promontories.

After bending down to untie her espadrilles and remove her shoes, she wiggled her toes on the shingly sand, enjoying the feel of roughness beneath her feet.

It was low tide and some way off, near the water's edge, a man in a brown jacket and wellington boots was walking his golden retriever. Every now and then he'd throw a stick and watch the dog plunge joyfully after it into the waves before hurtling back, brandishing its trophy between its jaws. Then it would deposit the stick at the man's feet and he'd hop back smartly before the animal shook itself vigorously, spraying water high into the air and all around.

Further out, some orange buoys were bobbing in the choppy waves and beyond them were a couple of small fishing boats with dark nets dangling over the sides.

Picking up her shoes, Chabela walked a little way towards the grey-blue ocean, inhaling the scent of fresh, salty air. A clock struck ten a.m. in the distance and as she closed her eyes, the chimes mingled with the piercing cries of seagulls, drowning out the nagging chatter in her head.

Then Alfonso's handsome face and intelligent brown eyes flooded her consciousness again. Was there no escape? Something seemed to press down hard on her chest, compressing her lungs and making it difficult to breathe.

It was no use. Having lost control of her thoughts, she gave up trying and allowed them to drift where they wanted – which was straight back to him, of course.

Everywhere she looked, she could picture his features. His profile was there in the patterns of the waves and as she glanced up, every passing cloud reminded her in some way of him.

A low groan escaped from her lips, but there was no one to hear and it was soon whipped away by the wind. 'Alfonso, Baby, Alfa,' she whispered, for this was what she used to call him, and sometimes just, 'My love'.

She couldn't begin to imagine life without him.

The man with the dog clambered over some rocks and she watched them disappear from view, the hound's fluffy yellow tail being the last thing to vanish. Alone on the beach now, she padded down to the water's edge, still carrying her espadrilles, picked up her skirt and dipped her toes tentatively in the foamy surf.

The water felt like ice. Nothing, she thought, would induce her to go all the way in, though she'd seen bikinis and swimsuits for sale in the window of the local dress shop.

For a few moments, she watched with fascination as ripples lapped around her feet, making shapes in the sand below that vanished as soon as the tide retreated, before re-forming into something else entirely. Then all of a sudden a bigger wave whooshed up her calves and caught the end of her skirt.

She squealed and hopped back smartly. No matter. Her feet and skirt would soon dry off, but what to do next? It felt strange and rather unsettling not to have any firm plans. Her working life had been so structured that sometimes she'd longed for more flexibility, yet here she was twiddling her thumbs at just after ten in the morning.

Of one thing she was certain: she needed to be among people today. Thinking that a cup of coffee would both warm her up and give her an excuse to be out longer, she decided to go in search of a café. She was out of cash but hoped to be able to use her debit card to pay.

After climbing the steps back to the seafront, she sat on one of the wooden benches overlooking the ocean and dusted the sticky sand off her feet before replacing her shoes.

When she stood up and spun around, she saw two young men outside Oliver's, the fishing tackle shop, one in white overalls smoking a cigarette, the other in a blue uniform holding on to the saddle of his bike, with bulging sacks of post on either side.

They were deep in conversation, their backs half turned, then the man in white overalls noticed the stranger and nudged his friend, who cast a furtive glance in her direction.

'Look at that!' she heard the first man whisper in a local accent.

'In your dreams, mate!' his friend replied, with a laugh. 'She's way out of your league!'

Chabela was half amused, half appalled by their cheek, because they were almost young enough to be her sons. Fishing some sunglasses out of the pocket of her skirt, she plonked them firmly on the end of her nose and headed swiftly around the corner, pretending not to hear.

Chapter Two

SHE WASN'T AFRAID OF GETTING lost in the village because it was so small and besides, there were quite a few folk about and she could always ask the way.

As she strolled up cobbled Fore Street, she thought she could remember noticing a little coffee shop on her brief visit the previous day, but it seemed to have disappeared. Perhaps she'd imagined it.

About halfway up the road was a pub, with a distinctive, painted sign above the entrance saying, 'The Hole in the Wall'. Beside the name was an amusing picture of a villainous-faced smuggler, complete with flowing black hair, beard and a tricorn hat.

The door was open and when she peeped into the dark interior, she spotted a tallish man with a ponytail behind the bar, stacking glasses on the shelves behind.

The place looked very cosy, with wooden floors, a low, oak-beamed ceiling and a big stone fireplace against one wall. In the centre of the room and dotted around the edges were round tables with iron legs and mismatched metal chairs with striped cushions to sit on.

She was almost tempted to pop inside and ask if they did coffee, but something told her that she'd be out of luck and besides, the man seemed very preoccupied.

Just past the pub was a long, squat building called The Stables, which had been painted white and looked very old, with eight small, black timber-framed windows on the top floor and four on the bottom.

Chabela paused again to examine the heavy oak door, which was surprisingly low, and found herself wondering if people in those days were midgets, or were just used to stooping.

The village must be steeped in history, she mused, thinking that she'd like to know all about the individual buildings and who had once lived here. There must be books about the place – maybe a museum somewhere. Luckily, she knew exactly whom to ask.

Turning left after The Stables she entered Humble Hill, which had a Methodist church at the top, near where she'd parked her hire car. On the corner of the hill, just before the incline, was a cottage with an odd name above the door that she couldn't pronounce – Dynnargh – and she found herself stopping again to take a look.

The house was quite modern and not as pretty as its neighbours – mostly old fishermen's cottages painted yellow, pink and blue. She was struck, however, by how much love had gone into it. There were sparkling white lace curtains in the windows and the neat little front garden was bursting with colourful flowers and surrounded by a freshly painted white picket fence.

In the middle of the garden was a miniature stone wishing well and beside it, a metal statuette of a comical boy on a bike in blue dungarees, carrying a flowerpot filled with blooms. Chabela would have liked to pick some and take them home with her.

'Mornin'!'

She glanced up and saw a round woman of sixty-odd, with short fair hair, opening the front door and walking purposefully down the path towards her.

'I was just admiring your beautiful garden,' Chabela said, hoping that it didn't seem odd.

The woman didn't appear to be suspicious, and on reaching her gate, gave Chabela a broad, friendly smile, revealing big, strong front teeth. She was obviously out in the fresh air a good deal because her cheeks were ruddy and her lower arms, beneath the rolled up sleeves of her pink blouse, were quite tanned.

'Folk often stop and look,' she said comfortably. 'The garden's my husband's pride and joy. I'm Jean, by the way,' she went on, proffering a hand, which Chabela took, noticing how warm and soft it felt. 'Are you on holiday? I don't think I've seen you round here before.'

They were soon chatting like old friends. Jean explained that 'Dynnargh' meant 'Welcome' in Cornish, and that she worked as a childminder during the week. Her husband, Tom, was retired now and helped out with the babies and toddlers, when he wasn't pruning his roses or raking his borders, that was.

The couple, who had grown-up children of their own, had lived in Tremarnock all their married lives and wouldn't dream of moving anywhere else.

'It's more than just a place,' Jean said, suddenly serious. 'We've been through things together, you see – big things.' She gave Chabela a meaningful look, which she didn't understand. 'We don't always see eye-to-eye but when the chips are down, we stick together. It's just the way we are.'

Chabela was surprised. Tremarnock seemed so sleepy to her, the kind of out-of-the-way spot where nothing much ever happened. She wanted to ask what 'big things' Jean was referring to, but didn't get the chance.

'It's been pretty peaceful lately, though, thank the Lord,' the older woman continued. 'I'm not too keen on drama, to be honest with you. Give me the quiet life any day!'

Without warning, she turned and hollered over her shoulder, 'Tom!' – which made Chabela jump. Soon Jean's husband appeared at the front door. He was so quick, he must have been watching them from inside the house.

'This lady here was admiring your handiwork!' Jean cried, as her husband, a short, sturdy, weather-beaten chap with grey-white hair, came towards them.

Jean leaned over the gate and whispered in Chabela's ear: 'You'll make his day. Spends hours here, he does.' She winked. 'Keeps him out of mischief.'

The couple must have had time on their hands because Tom opened the gate and insisted that Chabela come in, so that he could give her a guided tour of his flowers: purple puffballs of tall-stemmed allium, white aquilegia with delicate green tips and bright red oriental poppies. He was very knowledgeable and seemed to love every single one of the plants. He clearly liked an audience, too.

Chabela mentioned that she was staying at Polgarry Manor, up on the cliff, and Tom said that he knew the owner, Bramble, and her partner, Matt.

'Gorgeous garden they've got, magnificent. Must be a lot of work, mind. The place was a wreck when they moved in. Amazing what they've done. It's transformed.'

He had a strong Cornish accent and Chabela, though pretty much fluent in English, had to listen closely. She explained that she'd only arrived from Mexico the day before yesterday.

'I've been so busy unpacking and catching up on sleep, I haven't had the chance to explore the grounds properly yet. I can see the ocean from my bedroom window. It's a stunning view!'

Jean then asked what had brought her here, and Chabela hesitated.

'I needed a holiday and I've always fancied visiting Cornwall,' she said carefully, before adding, 'I think some of my ancestors may have come from here.'

'Oh?' Jean's ears pricked up and Chabela wished that she could take the words back. She was afraid of having to answer questions, especially from folks that she'd only just met, that might lead her to mention Alfonso by mistake.

'I may have my facts wrong, I'm not sure,' she went on, quick as a flash.

Opening the gate swiftly, she stepped back on to the narrow street, which had no pavement. 'I'd better go and find my car. I hope I can remember where I parked it.'

If Jean and Tom were surprised by the sudden hurry, they didn't show it. Tom snapped a pale pink rose from a bush and gave a gallant bow as he handed it to Chabela before she departed.

'I'll put it in a vase when I get back to Polgarry Manor,' she said, touched. 'It'll make my room smell nice.'

'I'm sure we'll bump into each other again,' Jean commented, as they shook hands once more and said their goodbyes. 'This village is so small, you can't hide away for long!'

As she climbed into her pale blue Polo and switched on the engine, Chabela found herself reflecting on the couple. They seemed like lovely people, and there was something appealing about the community spirit that Jean spoke of.

Back home, Chabela had good relationships with students and staff at the university, and a small circle of women friends whom she saw from time to time and whose company she greatly valued. The city was so big, however, and the pace of life so hectic, that it was quite easy not to connect much with those around you, not really, and besides, for the past seven years, she had devoted herself mainly to Alfonso.

That name again. What was he doing? Was he thinking of her? Missing her? Feeling sad? She couldn't know what was going on in his head, and it was none of her business anyway. He was no doubt getting on with his life and so must she – but how?

She thought of Jean's open, curious, smiley face and Tom's evident pleasure in his surroundings. Chabela had been outward-looking once, but somehow Alfonso had given her tunnel vision. Perhaps she could learn, or rather relearn, something from these people about living in the moment, the here and now; about how to just *be*.

She had forgotten all about coffee and as she left the village behind and took the narrow, winding road that led up towards the cliff, she tried to focus solely on her environment: the tall, lush green hedgerows, the ever-steepening climb, the occasional glimpses through farmyard gates of grassy fields dotted with sheep and glossy brown cows.

Lowering her window slightly, she caught a whiff of manure, which reminded her that she was well and truly in the countryside, miles from any city and as far, she thought, from her old life as she could possibly be. If a complete change of scenery couldn't cure her broken heart, then nothing would.

There was a sharp zigzag in the road, then a pair of tall, smart, black iron gates came into view, that opened automatically as Chabela drew up so that she could drive straight in. Once inside the grounds, the car lurched on the bumpy drive flanked on either side by overgrown fields, until she finally came to a halt in front of her temporary new home.

Polgarry Manor was imposing by any standards: large and grey, with mock battlements and stone steps leading up to a heavy, panelled wooden door. The central section looked older than the lower wings on either side, and in front of the house was a terraced garden, with squares of neatly cut box hedges, that sloped down to a squat stone wall.

The sun was warmer now and it seemed the perfect opportunity to explore the grounds behind the manor that she hadn't yet seen properly.

Pushing up the sleeves of her blue cardigan, she skirted around the edge of the building before ascending some steps onto a stone terrace, surrounded by a white balustrade.

On the far side, there was another set of steps leading to a gravel path, some flowerbeds, and then a large patch of land divided into two sections by metal railings. This area looked more unruly than the front part of the manor and when Chabela stood on tiptoe, she could just make out what appeared to be the remains of a brick gazebo. Covered in ivy and missing its roof, it was peeping over the foliage at the far end of the left-hand section.

She was about to go in search of it when a shriek made her turn and she saw her tall, blonde hostess, Bramble, hurtling out of some French doors, brandishing what appeared to be a wriggling brown mouse by its long, skinny tail.

Hot on her heels was a short, elderly woman with iron-grey hair and steel-rimmed glasses, wearing a stiff white blouse, brown tweed skirt and a stern expression: the housekeeper, Maria, who had brought Chabela her breakfast earlier in the day.

'Out of my way!' Bramble screamed unnecessarily, for Chabela was already hopping to one side, anxious to get as far from the mouse as possible.

'Give that to me, Miss Bramble,' the older woman commanded, in a strong Eastern European accent. 'I will dispose of it.'

She sounded so fierce that Chabela would have done exactly as she was told, but Bramble had other ideas.

Chabela stared in amazement as her hostess ran to the balustrade, hurled the creature through the air, its little legs splaying like spaceship feet, and watched it land with a plop into one of the flowerbeds.

'What did you do that for?' Maria was flat-backed and furious, her hands firmly on her hips. Despite her small stature, she managed to make Chabela quake, but Bramble didn't flinch.

'You'd have chopped off its head,' she said. 'Poor little thing. It won't do any harm out here.'

She turned to Chabela, who was still cowering.

'Sorry for the fright,' Bramble said, with a sheepish smile. 'Maria and I have an ongoing disagreement about rodents. She likes to execute them – preferably with her bare hands – whereas I take a more lenient approach.'

Chabela laughed; she couldn't help it. 'I think I'm with Maria. I can't stand mice and rats, but I couldn't kill them myself. I'd have to set a trap.'

'Miss Bramble is lily-livered,' Maria muttered, knitting her dark eyebrows. 'If she is not careful, we will be overrun.'

'Oh, it's not *that* bad.' Bramble must have noticed Chabela shudder because she added: 'Jesus! What must you think of us? I hope we haven't put you off staying here!'

In truth, it had crossed Chabela's mind that perhaps this mightn't be the right place for her after all. She was a bit scared of mice – and Maria, too, come to that. But she was too polite to say so.

Before she knew it, Bramble was taking her by the arm and leading her into the sumptuous drawing room, which Chabela had seen only briefly on the day she arrived.

A large, rectangular room with a very high ceiling, it had a grand piano at one end, with two intricate tapestries on the side walls. One depicted female figures bathing by a river, surrounded by rocks and trees, and the other, a white heron in a wooded landscape with buildings on the horizon and a large house, not unlike Polgarry, on the hill.

At the opposite end, near the French doors where they were standing, a chaise longue, a couple of tall armchairs and a faded crimson velvet sofa were arranged around an impressive marble fireplace, above which hung a gilt mirror.

All the remaining wall space seemed to be filled with gold-framed oil paintings of crusty-looking gentlemen on horseback and crinoline clad ladies.

'Most of them are ancestors of my grandfather,' Bramble said, noticing Chabela gazing at them. 'I suppose that makes them my ancestors, too. It doesn't feel like it, though, because I didn't know him.'

Chabela raised her eyebrows. 'Oh?'

'It's a long story. Have you got time for coffee?'

It was the best idea that Chabela had heard all day. While Maria fetched the drinks, the two younger women sat side by side on the velvet sofa, looking out of the open French doors onto the terrace and gardens beyond.

Sunlight streamed in, warming their feet and knees, and Chabela listened intently while Bramble explained about her very grand grandfather, Lord Penrose, and his doomed love for her much younger grandmother, Alice. A baby had been conceived – Bramble's mother, Mary – but Alice had refused to marry Lord Penrose, and her bitter, angry and controlling parents had forbidden him access to the illegitimate child.

Mary, who had a troubled childhood, had died tragically when Bramble was very young, and Bramble had been raised, knowing next to nothing of her ancestry, by her father Bill and his new wife, Cassie, whom she adored.

'So, as you can imagine, it was quite a surprise when I got a letter from the solicitor saying that Lord Penrose had died, leaving his whole estate to me. I honestly thought it was a joke at first. I came to see the manor and it was a total wreck. Dad, Cassie and my boyfriend, Matt, tried to talk me into selling up. I nearly did, but the place sort of got hold of me and I found I couldn't.

'The first year of living here was really tough. I had no money and the ceiling was falling down and I thought I might have to give up after all. Then amazingly, I found a painting that was worth a lot of money. I sold it at auction and the cash enabled me to do the refurbishment. It's an extremely expensive house to maintain, which is partly why I started the bed and breakfast, but actually I love doing it – and putting on big events. They're my favourite part.'

It was an extraordinary story and Chabela was enchanted, all the more so because Bramble seemed so young, at twenty-eight, to have taken on such a big responsibility, yet appeared to be coping remarkably well.

Tall and willowy, she had round blue eyes, a slender, arched nose and pale English skin, very different from Chabela's own creamy-brown complexion. Bramble's mouth was also quite large and there was a pronounced dimple in her chin. You couldn't call her classically beautiful but she was attractive all the same, in a quirky kind of way.

'Matt refused to come at first,' she went on, tucking one long leg underneath her while the other stretched out in front. She was wearing a pair of old, pale blue denim dungaree shorts and a faded red T-shirt. 'He didn't want to leave London but he changed his mind, thank God. He loves it here now.'

Maria arrived with a silver tray, which she set on the table in front of the women. On it was a dainty antique silver coffee pot, as well as two porcelain cups and saucers decorated with tiny violet flowers, two matching plates, a jug of hot milk, a dish of sugar with a set of tongs and another, larger, plate of home-made chocolate brownies.

The smell of food made Chabela's mouth water and she was glad when Bramble leaned forwards, picked up the plate of brownies and passed it to her.

'What about you? Do you have to work or are you just here on holiday?' she asked, as Chabela helped herself.

She noticed Maria pause, as if wanting to hear the answer, and was relieved when Bramble dismissed her: 'Thank you, Maria. I'll pour the coffee.'

Now, Chabela could relax properly and after a couple of bites of brownie and a sip of her drink, she set her plate, cup and saucer on the table and took a deep breath.

'Well,' she said, tipping her head to one side and feeling surprisingly bold all of a sudden. 'I'm mainly here for a holiday – I really need one – but I've come to do a bit of research, too. You might have noticed my surname?'

Bramble nodded. 'I wanted to ask you about it, actually. There can't be many Penhallows in Mexico.'

Chabela smiled. 'You're right. I always knew it was a Cornish name when I was growing up, but that's about all. My parents divorced when I was very young. My late mother cut my father out of our lives completely and she never talked about his side of the family. I suppose it was a bit of a forbidden topic, so I never asked and wasn't particularly interested, to be honest. But then a few months ago, I was contacted out of the blue by a stranger...'

She went on to explain how she'd been at the university where she worked when a letter had arrived from a man called Simon Hosking.

'I know him!' Bramble cried. 'Not well, but he lives on the outskirts of the village. I met him properly for the first time last Christmas, at a party.'

Chabela's dark eyebrows shot up. 'Oh? What's he like?'

'Quite quiet. Intellectual. Serious. In his forties and single, I think. He was quite friendly but we didn't talk for long and he left early. I see him in the village occasionally. He always says hello but rarely stops to talk. I think he's a bit of a loner. He prefers his own company.'

'That figures,' Chabela replied. 'His letter was quite short and formal, though not unfriendly. He told me he's head of modern languages at a school in Cornwall in the UK, and he knows Mexico well. By chance, he picked up an academic journal in the library and read an article that I wrote some time ago about the schooling experiences of bilingual children in my country. He noticed my name – Penhallow – at the bottom.

'He said the Penhallows, like his family, the Hoskings, came originally from a little village called Tremarnock, which was where he still lived.'

'Interesting!' Bramble leaned back, her arms folded across her chest. 'Go on.'

Chabela took another sip of coffee before clearing her throat and resuming.

'He said he'd been researching his family history and had discovered that in the 1840s, one branch of the Penhallow family had moved to the Camborne-Redruth area to find work. A man called Joseph Penhallow had got a job at one of the tin mines but there'd been an accident and he'd been killed. He had one child, James, then about eight years old, and soon after, James's mother had died, too, leaving him orphaned.'

Bramble tutted. 'Poor kid. Life must have been so hard in those days.'

'Indeed.' Chabela leaned forwards and rested her elbows on her knees. 'Now here's the really fascinating bit: after James Penhallow's mother died, he moved back to Tremarnock to live with some family friends – the Hoskings.'

'Goodness!' Bramble's eyes widened. 'How on earth did Simon Hosking find that out?'

Chabela put the question to one side, because she didn't want to lose her train of thought.

'Simon told me that James Penhallow decided to leave Tremarnock in 1854, I think it was, when he was about seventeen. And guess where he went to seek his fortune?'

Bramble shook her head.

'Mexico!' Chabela said triumphantly. 'He got a job in one of the silver mines and eventually made a lot of money. And there's more. While there, he met and married a Mexican woman and they had several children.

'Apparently, Simon has a letter in his possession that James wrote to the Hosking family to tell them about his wedding. Simon said he hoped I didn't mind the question, but Penhallow is an unusual name and he wondered if I'm a descendant of James.'

'Wow!' Bramble was impressed. 'And are you?'

Chabela shrugged. 'That's just it. I have absolutely no idea and now my mother's dead, there's no one to ask.'

'Oh!' It was a bit of an anticlimax and Bramble looked disappointed. 'How can you find out? Maybe Mr Hosking can help?'

Chabela nodded. 'I'm hoping so. I thought about trying to do some research myself, but I wouldn't really know where to start and besides, I've too little information to go on. Even if Simon can't shed much light on it, I'll be interested to see the letter. Whatever happens, it won't have been a wasted journey to come here.'

'I'd be curious, too, if I were you,' said Bramble. 'It's amazing to think there might be a link between you and this village. It seems so unlikely.'

Chabela grinned. 'It does, doesn't it? But even if it turns out to be rubbish, it's given me a great excuse to get to know a new part of the world. I've never been to Cornwall before.'

Bramble took a strand of blonde hair and twisted it around her finger. 'So, when are you going to meet Simon Hosking? Have you made an arrangement?'

The door creaked and they both turned to see Matt, Bramble's boyfriend, making his way across the room towards them. Of medium height and solidly built, he had a small nose, soft grey eyes and fair hair that was just beginning to recede at the sides.

Bramble had told Chabela that he was general manager of a gym in nearby Plymouth and that he worked unusual hours, sometimes going in and coming home late, or the other way around. He looked very clean, smart and businesslike, in a navy pinstriped suit, white shirt and a thick blue tie that was knotted rather tightly at his neck, giving him a slightly flushed complexion.

Chabela had the urge to jump up and loosen the tie, but managed to resist, and after the introductions, Matt removed his jacket and sat down in the armchair opposite, his legs splayed in that way that men have, his feet, encased in shiny black lace-ups, set at a quarter to three.

While he helped himself to a brownie, Bramble filled him in quickly on the reasons for Chabela's visit and he mentioned that he, too, was acquainted with Simon Hosking.

'Clever as hell, always got his nose stuck in a book,' he said, brushing some crumbs off his chunky thighs and onto the floor. Bramble didn't bat an eyelid.

It was clear from Matt's tone that he wasn't much of a reader himself.

'The kids like him at school 'cause he's a bit eccentric and makes them laugh. He's a good teacher, too, apparently. Gets great results.'

'Has he ever been married?' Chabela wanted to know. 'Children?'

Matt put the plate back on the table before scratching his head.

'He's married to his work, by the sounds of things. Doesn't socialise much. Rick – he owns the village gift shop – he knows him a bit because they both like local history, but he doesn't seem to have many friends of either sex.'

'Oh dear,' Chabela said, sighing. 'It doesn't sound as if we'll have much in common.'

'Except your ancestors, perhaps,' Bramble replied, with a wry smile. 'But don't worry, if you can't stand him you won't have to see him again.'

The subject changed to places of interest in the local area, and Matt invited Chabela along to his gym for a free trial.

'Plymouth's worth a visit. I'm driving that way now. I can give you a lift, if you like? You could do a class, have a mooch around the city and come home by bus.'

Chabela thanked him, but said she was keen to stay away from busy places for the time being.

'Mexico City's so huge and the traffic's a nightmare. It's wonderful to come here and be close to nature. I think I'll go for a long walk this afternoon to clear my head. '

Sensing that her hosts might want to be alone for a few moments before Matt left, Chabela rose.

'Thanks for the coffee and the chocolate brownie.'

'Same again tomorrow?' Bramble said, smiling. 'My stepmother always talks about having her elevenses. I never thought I'd get into the habit but since I've lived here, it's become a bit of a ritual – and Maria does bake the best cakes and biscuits.'

As soon as she was out of the room, Matt joined Bramble on the sofa.

'Come here, you.'

He put an arm around her shoulder and she snuggled into his side, resting her head on his chest.

'She seems really nice,' Bramble said, and he agreed.

'Quite chilled. Her English is brilliant.'

'She didn't mention a husband or partner or anything. D'you think she's single?'

Matt shrugged. 'No idea.'

'It must be weird, travelling on your own. Quite brave, don't you think? I wouldn't fancy it.'

Matt gave her a squeeze. 'Since when have you gone all girly? Have you forgotten how you packed in your job and came here? That was pretty brave – or stupid.' He grinned. 'I'd hardly call you a shrinking violet.'

Bramble laughed. 'True, but the difference is, I had a friend with me. I wouldn't have come if Katie hadn't agreed to tag along, too.'

'Well, our Mexican lady seems quite independent and sorted. I don't think we need to worry about her.'

Bramble considered this for a moment. 'Mm,' she said at last. 'But I get the feeling she's not happy.'

'What do you mean? She seems cheerful to me.'

A rustling outside on the terrace caught their attention and they both turned to look. A grey squirrel scampered from one side of the flagstones to another before darting up the nearest tree.

'I'm not sure, I mean, there's a sort of wistful look in her eye,' Bramble commented. 'Sometimes, when we were talking, it was as if she was here but not here, if you know what I mean.'

Matt laughed. 'Give the poor woman a break! She's probably still jet-lagged.'

Bramble tipped her head to one side as if attempting to view the problem from a slightly different angle. It didn't seem to work, however.

'No,' she said, placing a hand on her partner's knee and giving it a playful smack. 'You're wrong. She's running away from something. Trust me. I wonder what it can be.'

Chapter Three

CHABELA SLEPT BADLY THAT NIGHT, despite having had a long, blowy walk along the cliffs, followed by a hearty supper in a local pub and a couple of glasses of red wine.

She couldn't fault her room or bed either – a grand old four-poster in one of the manor's front wings, with ivory silk drapes and a matching, deep-buttoned chaise longue at the foot, just asking to be curled up on with a good book.

The place had obviously been refurbished only recently, as the white walls and sand-coloured carpet were immaculate, as was the en suite bathroom, complete with freestanding, roll-top bath with dainty little claw legs. Chabela found it enchanting. Behind it stood a cast-iron fireplace with a mirror on top and beside that, a wooden rocking chair.

She could just imagine what bliss it would be to turn the lights down low and lounge in the warm bath, watching the flickering flames dance up the chimney, but the hearth was empty and had clearly not been used for some time. There was no need, after all, as the house was centrally heated.

She'd sat on the rocking chair after her bath and before going to bed, drying herself with a soft white towel, already looking forward to diving beneath the clean white sheets, closing her eyes and sinking into blissful oblivion.

Instead, however, she'd tossed and turned, listening to the owl hooting in the distance, the occasional creak and groan of a floorboard, like an old man getting up out of his chair, the gurgling of a bathroom pipe next door.

She didn't feel spooked by being in a strange old house; what haunted her far more was a painful sense of severance. Once, she had felt so connected to Alfonso that she'd imagined she knew if he was thinking about her even when they were miles apart.

Now, as she lay wide awake in the dark, try as she might she couldn't find a direct link; it was as if the lines between them had become scrambled. Like a bad phone call, his voice seemed to fade in and out and she couldn't grasp his tone or what, if anything, he was trying to communicate to her.

The worst part was that she was straining so hard to hear, it almost hurt. She knew that it would be best to put down the receiver, so to speak, and walk away, but instead, she had it pressed so close to her ear that it seemed to burn.

The idea that he might not be at the other end at all was just too much to bear. She had to picture him mouthing words to her, whispering messages that couldn't get through, otherwise she might go mad.

STOP! No matter how hard she tried, her thoughts kept swirling in concentric circles, always settling back into the exact same spot where they'd started, like a falcon returning to its perch. She wanted so much to break away and be free. It was torture.

Snapping on the light beside her bed, she picked up the novel that she'd brought with her for the plane. It was a psychological thriller – quite gruesome in places.

For some reason she'd recently taken to reading dark, sinister books for relaxation, instead of her usual diet of light, funny fiction. She couldn't decide if it was masochism or catharsis. Either way, the horror seemed to jolt her out of her normal state, providing temporary relief from her ruminations.

It was almost three a.m. when she finally fell asleep with the light still on, and she could hardly believe it when the alarm on her phone buzzed, because it felt as if she'd only just dozed off. Could it really be seven forty-five already?

When she leant across to grab the mobile from the table beside her, she was astonished to discover that it was. Normally an early riser, she often set her alarm late, knowing that she'd most likely beat the clock and wake naturally. Now, there was barely enough time to shower and get down to breakfast.

Flinging off the cotton duvet, she padded over to the floor-length taupe curtains and pulled them open. Bright sunlight flooded the room and it took a moment or two for her eyes to adjust.

Once they'd done so, she took a deep breath and gazed out, feeling just as awed as on her first morning here. The manor was perched on a headland and below her lay the neat front garden filled with shrubs. Stretching out behind it were green fields dotted with minuscule purple, yellow and white flowers that swept all the way to the cliff edge. And beyond that, as far as the eye could see, was the turquoise ocean, which seemed to glitter like diamonds, while seagulls circled overhead, wheeling and crying.

Whatever else was happening in her life, she thought, nothing could take away the glory of this vista and for a few, blissful moments she felt happy just to be alive.

Opening the window wide, she leaned out and filled her lungs and nostrils with the sweet scent of damp grass and salty morning air. She might have stood there for ages, but could hear noises coming from down below – pans clattering, a cutlery drawer, perhaps, being opened and shut, a kettle being filled – and she guessed that Maria, the housekeeper, was making breakfast.

In truth, Chabela would have preferred to help herself to a bowl of cereal or some toast and jam, but she had already gleaned that this was not the Polgarry Manor way.

Yesterday, when she had been five minutes later down for breakfast than expected, Maria had rapped quite crossly on her bedroom door and told her that her eggs were getting cold.

Chabela couldn't remember having asked for eggs, but didn't dare say so. What Maria wanted around here, it seemed, Maria generally got. It wasn't how the boss–servant relationships in Mexico normally functioned, but who was Chabela to try to change things?

'When in Rome…' she told herself, turning from the window and hurrying into the bathroom for a speedy shower. There was no way that she was going to give Maria cause to knock on her door again.

She managed to find her way to the dining room – a big, square, wood-panelled space with a long rectangular table in the centre and windows looking out onto a neatly cut lawn.

Maria was already there, standing rather stiffly in front of a heavy sideboard, on which were placed two antique silver breakfast dishes, a toaster, an uncut loaf of brown bread and a jug of orange juice.

She was a small, thin, elderly woman with a slight stoop. Her iron-grey hair was styled in a shapeless bob while her thick fringe, unusually short, had probably been cut by herself.

She had sharp little black eyes, framed by rectangular, steel-rimmed spectacles, and was wearing a brown tweed skirt, a white blouse buttoned up to the neck and sensible, mannish brogues.

Despite her age, Chabela decided that she could most likely walk the length and breadth of Britain if she had to, without complaining, and put younger women to shame.

A strong scent of cooked eggs and bacon filled the air and the table was laid for just one person with silver cutlery, a linen napkin and pots of honey and jam. Chabela didn't mind being the only guest – she was used to eating alone – and she was relieved when Maria disappeared to fetch the coffee, closing the door firmly behind her.

Having helped herself to a generous pile of scrambled eggs on toast, Chabela sat down, placed the napkin on her lap, pulled a letter out of the pocket of her trousers and spread it on the table beside her plate.

'*Querida Señorita* Penhallow,' she read – Dear Miss Penhallow – and at the bottom: '*Cordiales saludos*, Simon Hosking' – Kind regards, Simon Hosking.

Her stomach fluttered and she wasn't quite sure why. The letter was polite and formal, with nothing in it to raise doubts about its provenance or authenticity, yet still the prospect of meeting the Cornishman for the first time made her anxious.

Taking a forkful of eggs, she idly scanned the script for the umpteenth time. Small, pointy and quite difficult to decipher, it seemed to her to come from the hand of someone private and insular, just as Bramble and Matt had suggested.

Picking the letter up, she held it to the light, noticing with what heavy pressure the writer had applied the pen. There was something intense about the dense black letters and narrow spacing between each word, as if he had been concentrating very hard, totally focused on the task in hand and unaware of what was going on around him.

He was most likely an introvert, she decided, and perhaps quite rigid in his thinking. No, they almost certainly wouldn't get on.

The eggs were delicious – pale yellow, light and fluffy, though she would have preferred them done the Mexican *huevos rancheros* way, with tortilla, refried beans, hot chilli sauce, feta and guacamole on the side.

Right now she rather wished that she had brought her own supply of chilli, although that would have gone against her intention to immerse herself in the Cornish way of life.

The food here wasn't bland, but it wasn't spicy either. Bramble had told Chabela that they sourced most of it locally and you could tell. The wholemeal toast was dense, hearty and packed with nutritious seeds, as if every bite would do you good, while the butter, straight from the farm, was thick, yellow and creamy.

Chabela loved eating, but often did so on the go during the week and didn't give as much thought to her diet as she might. Who knew? Perhaps a spell in Tremarnock would change all that and she'd arrive back home super-fit and bursting with vitality.

Maria returned with a pot of coffee and a jug of hot frothy milk and left Chabela to pour it for herself. Three cups and the entire plate of scrambled eggs later, she felt positively bloated; it was just as well that she had an appointment or she might have been tempted to sneak back to bed with her book and wait for the uncomfortable fullness to subside.

After cleaning her teeth and collecting her coat and bag, she headed out into the crisp morning air. Her feet crunched on the gravel as she walked across the drive to her jolly, rented Polo, and the bright blue sky overhead seemed to lighten the weight in her stomach as well as her spirits.

The winding road leading down to Tremarnock was empty, save for a lean, Lycra-clad male cyclist on a racing bike who pedalled past in the other direction, helmet lowered, legs pumping furiously to propel him up the hill. He was clearly in tip-top condition and Chabela was impressed; there was no way that she'd make it up to the summit without having to stop and push.

Bramble had advised her to leave the car in the centre of the village and walk the final section of the journey; there was very little room for parking near Simon's cottage and besides, the road was perilously steep and narrow. Clutching a battered map that Matt had given her, Chabela strolled along the seafront and turned left along Fore Street, before taking a sharp right just past a big white building called Ashley House, and up a narrow set of steps that she hadn't noticed before.

The crumbling brick walls on either side were very tall and silky-looking, with dark green moss growing between the cracks. The light faded as she started to ascend and there was a damp, musky smell. She held tight to the wobbly iron rail and kept her eyes focused on the ground, fearing that she might stumble on a wet or uneven tread and fall.

Once or twice, when she did look up, all she could see ahead was a formidably sharp incline with a tiny, round, but very welcome circle of light at the top.

She was panting hard as she climbed and her thigh muscles started to protest, but she didn't stop. Descending soon became a more daunting prospect than continuing in the same direction and she managed to distract herself by imagining that she was on a magic ladder. What awaited her at the summit? A giant, a fairy, or the secret, perhaps, to her Cornish ancestry?

Up and up she went until she reached the very last step, where the walls came to an abrupt end. She passed through a short row of gnarled, dense trees before finding herself back in the open air, where she paused to catch her breath and scan her surroundings.

She was quite high up now on what appeared to be a rocky promontory. To her right was the wide, grey-blue ocean and to her left, a row of higgledy-piggledy cottages, perched sideways in a slightly awkward manner, as if they were struggling to keep their balance. A pebbly, weed-strewn path lay ahead.

After pulling the map from her back pocket, she put her finger on the spot where she believed herself to be and followed the track for some little way until it appeared to peter out and come to an abrupt end at the cliff edge.

She was wearing trainers, comfortable red trousers, a cream sweatshirt and padded navy gilet, but still she felt chilly and exposed; the wind was stronger up here and although the sun was shining, it was still only half nine in the morning and she hadn't yet acclimatised to Cornish temperatures.

It crossed her mind that if anyone wanted to commit the perfect murder here, it wouldn't be difficult. One big shove and she'd probably teeter, fall and be dashed on the rocks below. There'd be no witnesses and most likely no one would hear her either, as the wind and waves would drown out her cries.

A welcome waft of woodsmoke coming from the chimney of one of the nearby cottages calmed her down. She'd been reading too many scary books, she decided, picking up her pace again now that her breathing had returned to normal. Folk were minding their own business and no one was remotely interested in murdering her; she was just being silly.

The ground was uneven and she had to take care not to catch her foot on a stone or root or slide on the loose pebbles. The low, scrubby bushes on either side were prickly too, and once or twice she had to raise her arms above her head so as not to get scratched.

Simon Hosking had certainly chosen a remote dwelling place. She would much rather live in the thick of things, close to the shops and pubs, but he probably preferred nature to people.

The path started to narrow even more and soon, just as she was beginning to feel anxious that she'd misread the map, she found a gap in the bushes to her left with a track leading downhill. It was fairly steep and flanked by high rocks, which she leaned on occasionally for support. She couldn't fathom where it might end other than on the beach. *Hombre*! Did the man live under an upturned rowing boat or in a cave?

Thinking that she must surely reach sea level again soon, she was surprised and relieved to come to a fork on her right, which opened into a smooth, curved trail that was cut into the lower half of the cliff.

Not too far below was the mighty ocean, while on her right was a row of darling little mismatched cottages that seemed to demand the best of both worlds – snuggled as they were into the craggy rock face whilst enjoying magnificent views in front.

A sign outside the first house said Karrek Row. Chabela took a deep breath. By hook or by crook, she'd reached her destination. She was quite proud of herself, a city girl more familiar with satnav than a map, and more accustomed to driving than going on foot.

Each cottage had its own name – Gwel Teg, Seabank, Wild Rose, Crafty, Farthing, and finally, on the very end of the row, Kittiwake. This was it.

Before arriving in the UK, Chabela had studied online images of Cornish cottages as well as local beauty spots. The picture that she'd formed of Simon's house was of a once delightful, now distinctly dilapidated bachelor residence, perhaps with a leaky thatched roof and an unkempt garden.

It was thus a pleasant surprise to behold a modest but charming, solid, whitewashed stone property with a smaller outhouse attached that could once have been the stable. There was a neat wooden porch, with a pair of green wellington boots tucked inside, a bright blue front door and blue-painted windows that almost matched the colour of the sky.

Just to the left of the door, beneath the front window, was a wooden bench positioned in a perfect, sheltered spot facing the ocean. On either side were tubs filled with lush, spiky plants and the garden itself was a riot of colour – vivid yellows, pinks, purples, whites, oranges and reds.

The roof wasn't thatched, but slated, with patches of rough, orangey lichen growing across, and a row of washing hung on a line, flapping furiously, like a crowd of angry protesters.

Amidst the browns, tans and greys, Chabela was amused to see three flimsy white sleeveless vests, presumably to put on under shirts. She thought that such items had gone out of fashion; certainly Alfonso didn't wear one.

Instead of opening the garden gate and going straight in, she skirted around the bend, where she hoped that she wouldn't be seen, and paused for a few moments, taking in the scenery and collecting her thoughts.

The grassy headland on which she was standing sloped rapidly down between rocky outcrops before reaching the curved, sandy beach. The tide had retreated quite far out, exposing long trails of seaweed and interesting-looking rock pools that must be teeming with crabs and other sea creatures.

To the right, some way off, the crescent shore came to an abrupt end when it reached a stack of huge boulders, which seemed to loom large, grey and formidable over the rest of the cove, stretching long, bony fingers far out to sea.

Chabela shivered. Although the house and its neighbours were quite protected from the elements, she thought that if you lived here you might never feel completely safe. When the wind whipped and the sea roared, you might fancy that the cliff was in a bad mood and you'd better watch out.

As her eyes slid left to right and back again, she found herself thinking of some of the other awe-inspiring places that she'd visited around the globe – Venice, the Grand Canyon, Niagara Falls, not to mention home-grown beauty spots such as Tulum, Chichén Itzá and Oaxaca.

How come she hadn't heard of this? If it wasn't already a World Heritage Site, it should be. Wild, raw and dramatic, it almost took her breath away.

'Miss Penhallow?'

She was jolted from her thoughts by a low voice and spun around to find a man of medium height and build standing on the other side of a low hedge.

At first glance he looked very *brown*: he had short brown hair, brown tortoiseshell glasses, a beige sweater and sludge-brown trousers. Chabela couldn't see his shoes but was certain that they'd be brown too.

Self-conscious suddenly in her red lipstick and bright red capri pants, she could only nod and smile at him tentatively.

'Simon Hosking,' said the man, extending a hand. 'I saw you out of the window and then you disappeared. I thought you might be lost.'

'Oh no, I was just admiring the view. It's so beautiful.' Chabela swept her arm across the panorama and he grunted something that might have been agreement in return.

'That's Old Charley,' he then said, pointing to the imposing cliff on their right. 'Legend has it that he's a giant who was put under a spell thousands of years ago by a wicked witch. He went to sleep and never woke up. He sometimes has bad dreams and when he rolls over, the sea becomes rough and restless, but he's not a malevolent sort. He mostly protects the locals from the worst of the weather and he doesn't mind children and adults climbing over him.'

Chabela tipped her head to one side and frowned. 'He looks fierce to me, but maybe it's all show.' She sounded doubtful. 'I wouldn't want to mess with him.'

Simon scratched his scalp quite hard, as if he wasn't sure how to respond. Either that, or he had nits. She hoped it was the former.

'You should go up there sometime,' he went on, still scratching. 'That is, if you like walking. Do you walk in Mexico?'

She was about to answer when he slapped his forehead a few times with the fleshy part of his palm. 'Silly question. I mean, of course you walk. Everyone does. Unless they have some sort of disability.'

His eyes widened in dismay, then he shrugged one shoulder several times, seemingly involuntarily, and jerked his chin in the other direction. It was quite alarming to watch and, unsure if he was aware that he was doing it, she pretended not to notice.

'Not that there's anything wrong with having a disability...' he went on, giving another shrug and then a jerk, quite a violent one this time. 'I'm not suggesting... I mean...'

He seemed to be tying himself in knots and Chabela came to his rescue. 'It's all right,' she interrupted. 'As it happens, yes I do walk, though not so much in Mexico City. I walked here today.'

'Ah.'

To her relief, the fret lines on her host's forehead smoothed out and the shrugging and jerking stopped.

'That's good,' he said. 'Glad you arrived safely. It's not easy to find us, not easy at all.'

Quite whom he meant by 'us' was a mystery, but Chabela didn't have time to ask because before she knew it, he was attempting to push down the stumpy hedge in front so that she could climb over.

'Shall I use the gate instead?' she suggested, looking doubtfully at the sharp, bristly twigs and leaves, but he was insistent.

'No, no, this'll be quicker.' He proffered a helping hand, which she took, whilst stepping gingerly across the divide. 'Come inside. I've got something for you that I think you'll find rather interesting.'

Chapter Four

Soon, she was following him across the lawn, through the porch, past the wellington boots and into a small, low-ceilinged room at the front of the cottage. A very tall person would have had to stoop, but both she and Simon could move about freely.

'Will you have tea – or coffee?' he asked, as she unzipped her gilet. He hesitated, scraping his fingernails back and forth again across his scalp. Scritch, scritch scratch. She wished he wouldn't do that; it made her itchy, too.

'How rude of me!' He shrugged involuntarily again. 'How presumptuous! I just assumed we'd converse in English. Would you prefer Spanish? I'm happy with either.'

Chabela, who was doing her best not to appear unnerved by his strange spasms, shook her head. 'No, I like talking in English. I need the practice. In fact it's my aim not to speak a word of Spanish all the while I'm in Cornwall!'

She was only joking, but he took her comment at face value.

'Very well,' he said seriously. 'I'll do my best to make sure no word of Spanish crosses my lips.'

While he went to make coffee, she seized the opportunity to have a good look around. She loved exploring strange houses and was hoping for some clues about this one's owner, as she hadn't yet worked him out.

He was odd, certainly, just as she'd expected. He spoke just as he wrote – in a rather formal, uptight way – and he looked as if he'd walked straight out of the pages of a slightly old-fashioned men's clothing catalogue.

In fact, if someone had asked her to imagine what an unmarried schoolteacher from a remote corner of provincial England would look like, she might have described Simon Hosking exactly, complete with nervous tics.

But he seemed friendly enough in his stiff, awkward way. He'd hurried from his house a moment ago to find her, and he'd welcomed her in like a long-lost relative or an old pal.

Another upside was that his cottage was lovely, inside as well as out, and not at all the sort of dishevelled place that she had feared. In fact, if anything it was almost *too* tidy, the sort of home where, if you put something in the wrong place, it might just get whisked away before you knew it.

The room she was in had clean, parchment-coloured walls and a polished wooden floor with a hessian rug in the middle, on which sat a big old pine chest with wooden handles. Now used as a coffee table, there was a heavy, dark blue book on top with the words, 'The Compact Edition of the Oxford English dictionary, Volume 1, A–O' written in gold letters down the spine.

She supposed that her host had been browsing through it before she arrived, otherwise it would surely have been put back with its sister, Volume P–Z, on a shelf.

On either side of the chest were two plain but comfortable-looking sofas, one grey, one blue, with matching standard lamps beside them topped with pale, wide shades. On the far wall was an unlit, cast-iron wood-burning stove with a basket nearby stacked with neatly cut logs. She could imagine that the place must feel very cosy in winter.

To the left of the wood burner was a smallish oil painting of some half-cut melons with green skins, sweet, orange flesh and glossy black seeds. She liked the image, which added a welcome splash of colour to its otherwise understated surroundings, and the fruit looked good enough to eat.

Tall shelves on either side of the chimney breast were laden with books of all different shapes and sizes, and the sea was clearly visible from the smallish, ocean-facing window.

This was framed by heavy, floor-length cream curtains with a pattern of fine, ink-drawn seashells, like something from a Victorian geologist's sketchpad.

More books ran across the sill, the biggest carefully stacked together at one end and the shortest at the other. There was an atlas, a thesaurus, a book of Buddhist teachings, some Persian poetry, James Joyce's *Ulysses*, Gabriel García Márquez's *One Hundred Years of Solitude*, *To the Lighthouse* by Virginia Woolf and a selection of nonsense verse; his tastes were clearly eclectic.

On top of the thesaurus was a small brass pocket telescope, which looked as if it were in constant use. The brass had long since lost its shine and the leather handle was worn. Chabela was tempted to pick it up and try it out, but resisted the urge, sensing that there was something rather personal about it.

In one corner of the room was a battered pine storage unit with a neat, black flat-screen television on top and alongside it, a portable Bluetooth speaker.

All in all, there was plenty of comfort and interest, enough to keep you occupied for a very long time. In fact she thought that if she lived here, she mightn't need anything else at all, other than some seriously bright colours to cheer things up.

A sudden feeling of sadness swept over her. Hadn't she made her apartment in Mexico City exactly as she wanted? It was comfortable, vibrant and there were books galore. Yet somehow, without the prospect of any visits from Alfonso, it had lost all its charm.

The rich colours of the sofas, blinds and paintings that she had chosen so carefully seemed to have become bleached and ugly. She no longer kept the place particularly clean and rarely opened the sliding doors or stepped out onto her shady balcony, which overlooked the busy street below.

Until he'd gone, her life, despite its imperfections, had seemed mostly fulfilling. She simply hadn't realised how much of her happiness had been invested in him. She had been unwise, to say the least, more likely downright foolish. Now, despite her intellect and all her interests, she struggled to find true meaning in anything.

Simon came back carrying a wooden tray, which he set down carefully on the pine trunk. On it there were two cups of coffee in matching blue and white striped mugs, two small, blue and white striped plates, a dish of scones and two little glass bowls, one containing dark red jam, the other a dollop of thick, yellowish clotted cream.

He'd clearly gone to some effort and Chabela was touched; Alfonso was in many ways an unreconstructed male. His doting mother had done everything for him, then his wife, and Chabela suspected that he wouldn't know where the jam in his house was kept, let alone think of transferring it from a jar into a dainty bowl.

'How pretty that looks!' she said, settling down on the sofa facing the window. She noticed the tips of Simon's ears go pink.

'Here, do have some coffee,' he said, swivelling the handle closest to her around the right way before sitting down on the sofa opposite. They were now some way apart, with the wooden chest acting like a barrier between them.

'Well I must say,' he went on, rubbing his palms up and down his thighs as if that might somehow help to bridge the gap, 'it's nice to meet you at long last.'

Now that they were square on for the first time, she was able to look at him properly. He wasn't unattractive: he had quite thick, slightly wavy hair that could have done with a trim, dark eyebrows and hazel eyes behind roundish tortoiseshell glasses, a straight nose, firm jaw and surprisingly full lips that lent him a slightly boyish, vulnerable air.

He was naturally pale skinned, you could tell, with a light tan and a sprinkling of freckles across his nose and cheeks. The morning sun had started to warm up the room and when he took off his sweater, placed it on the back of the seat and rolled up the sleeves of his light brown checked shirt, she could see freckles on his forearms, too.

Although he wasn't a big man, he looked strong. He didn't seem like the gym type and Chabela guessed that his fitness most likely came from brisk, solo walks up and down the cliffs and chopping his own logs for the fire. She couldn't imagine him jogging or playing team sports.

Pushing his glasses up his nose, he coughed awkwardly and she looked away quickly, hoping that her gaze wouldn't have set off another volley of shrugs and jerks.

'I was really happy to receive your letter,' she said, reaching for her mug and blowing on the coffee to cool it down. 'Were you surprised when you saw my name on the bottom of the article? What did you think?'

Simon crossed one leg over the other and she clocked for the first time that his shoes were, indeed, brown. She almost laughed.

'I was intrigued. It's unusual to see a Mexican name juxtaposed with a Cornish one like that and I felt it couldn't just be coincidence; there must surely be a link with that friend of my ancestors who had gone to Mexico – James Penhallow. I wanted to find out more but I didn't know if you'd ever write back. It was worth a try, though. Nothing ventured, nothing gained.'

He caught her eye, gave a small, tight smile and she smiled broadly back. She wanted to put him at his ease; she was sure that they'd both have a much more enjoyable time if she could only get him to relax.

'Well I'm very glad you ventured,' she replied, taking a sip of her coffee, which was now cool enough to drink. 'I wouldn't be here otherwise and I'd never have seen Cornwall.'

This was his cue to ask politely about her flight, and he wanted to know if she had settled in at Polgarry Manor and was comfortable there.

'I understand the owners have done a lot of work on the place. They're quite a young couple, too, I hear? From London. It's a big undertaking.'

Chabela was both surprised and amused. He spoke as if he'd never met them, yet Bramble had expressly said that she and Simon had talked at a party and that they acknowledged each other sometimes in the village.

His mind was probably always elsewhere, stuck in his Oxford English Dictionary, perhaps, or some historical tome about the ancient Mayan civilisation. Chabela decided not to point out the error, switching instead to what she hoped was the safe topic of his cottage.

'How long have you lived here? It's got one of the most idyllic views I've ever seen.'

He said that he'd bought the place more than twenty years ago, after he left university and teacher training college and started his first job.

She did a quick mental calculation and reckoned that he must be in his early- to mid-forties, though he didn't look it.

'It was virtually derelict,' he explained. 'It had been a holiday let but the owners hadn't bothered to maintain it and no one had come for years. It was extremely cheap, or I'd never have been able to afford it. I pulled it apart and rebuilt it bit by bit with my own hands.'

She was impressed and said so, complimenting him on his skill and vision. But he seemed to find her praise embarrassing, so she quickly moved on to his job at the large comprehensive school that most of the local children attended from the age of eleven.

This topic made him much more comfortable.

'They're great kids,' he said, almost animatedly. 'I like teaching the older ones best, because they've chosen to study languages; they're not doing it under sufferance. But the younger ones can be very rewarding, too. They're full of energy and so curious, well, most of them.' He frowned. 'Some are a real handful but when you find out about their backgrounds, it's hardly surprising.

'We have an exchange programme with a school in Valencia, which I organise. The children stay with Spanish families over there and vice versa. We've been doing it for years. It seems to work very well.'

'You should bring a group to Mexico one year,' Chabela suggested. 'I'm sure I could put you in touch with a suitable school.'

Simon visibly perked up, but then shook his head.

'The flights would be too expensive. Most of our parents wouldn't be able to afford it.'

His gaze slid to the painting of watermelons to the left of the wood burner and her own eyes followed.

'I bought that about ten years ago in a little town near Cuernavaca.' He sounded wistful. 'I haven't been back to Mexico since. The artist was selling his paintings at the side of the road. He wouldn't accept much for it. He looked hungry, so I ended up taking him for tacos in the market, then we drank tequila in a bar up the road. I have no idea what time I got home. Late, anyway. I don't suppose he sold any more paintings that day, but I think he enjoyed himself. I certainly did.'

The story surprised Chabela, because she had had her host down as the cautious type, not given to spontaneous acts and certainly not ones that involved talking to strangers.

She could imagine that Simon would have thought long and hard before even sending her the letter, probably ruminating over the pros and cons and deliberating carefully over each word once he'd resolved to go ahead.

Perhaps there was another, less restrained side to his character that only emerged on holiday, or maybe it had got lost somewhere in the mists of time.

'Have you been to Mexico often?' she asked, and he nodded before qualifying himself.

'Well, on a few occasions, three I think, to be precise. I always had an interest, ever since I was a boy. I used to hear my father talk occasionally about his dead relatives and their relationship with the Penhallow family. I had no idea where Mexico was but I thought it sounded very exciting and far away.

'I think I was intrigued by the idea of a young man from round here, someone a little bit like me, setting off to a completely unknown country and starting a new life.'

'Did you ever do it yourself?' she wanted to know. 'I mean, did you ever live abroad, in Mexico or anywhere else?'

At this, his shoulder shot up and his head jerked in that most uncomfortable looking way, which made her regret asking the question.

'Oh no. I'm not very adventurous,' he replied, staring hard at his hands.

She was about to approach the subject from a different, perhaps less obtrusive angle, but he jumped in to deflect her.

'Would you like a scone?' He rather clumsily passed her an empty plate, knife and a paper napkin. 'I bought them from the village bakery this morning.'

After her enormous breakfast, Chabela wasn't remotely hungry but food always cheered her up. In any case, she felt that it would be rude not to accept. Plus, she'd read about Cornwall's famous 'cream teas' and had been curious to try one. Now was her chance.

Leaning forward, she helped herself to a scone from the large plate still sitting on the tray, along with a generous dollop of jam and cream. The scone was bulging with plump, juicy raisins and she cut it in two before spreading the dark red jam, complete with little chunks of raspberry, over both halves with a knife.

Next, she slathered on the rich, buttery cream which had a crusted, grainy surface. It sat comfortably on the raspberries, blending slightly at the edges to create a pretty pinkish colour.

Her mouth watered and without more ado, she sank her teeth into the food and closed her eyes, wanting to savour fully the combination of sweet, floury scone, slightly tart fruit and nutty cream, which had the texture of soft cheese.

'Delicious!' she pronounced after she'd finished the first mouthful. 'It's what heaven would taste like, if it had a taste.'

After breathing a sigh of satisfaction, she opened her eyes again and would have repeated the experience straight away. Glancing up at Simon, however, she realised that he was staring at her rather hard.

His plate was balanced on his lap and when she caught his eye, he looked away quickly, lifted his scone with both hands and nervously nibbled the edge, like a squirrel with a nut.

Chabela was confused. 'Aren't you having jam or cream?'

She tried to pass him one of the little bowls, but he shook his head, and a troubling thought crossed her mind: perhaps you were supposed just to look at the toppings, not eat them. Had she committed a terrible faux pas? But if so, why did people go on about these famous cream teas – and shouldn't her guidebook have warned her?

Putting down her plate quickly, she wiped her mouth with a corner of the napkin and gave an embarrassed little cough, but he didn't seem to notice.

'I avoid sugar as a rule,' he said seriously, 'and I don't eat cream or butter.'

Chabela, who loved both, was genuinely shocked. 'But they're so delicious!'

He gave a small shrug. 'I don't normally have scones or cakes either, but I thought I'd make an exception today.'

'Don't you like them?' She couldn't imagine what anyone could possibly *not* like about them.

'I do, but I try to eat healthily.'

'So do I! Well, sort of.' She gave a wry smile. 'But you've got to indulge sometimes. I mean, we only live once, don't we?'

Instead of replying, he took another nibble from the corner of his scone, and this time she felt an unexpected prickle of annoyance.

'Well I'm not giving up anything,' she pronounced rebelliously, before chomping again into her own food. Then, with her mouth still half full, she added in a most unladylike fashion, 'In fact, I think I'll buy a big tub of cream on the way home and eat the whole lot in one sitting all by myself!'

Chapter Five

SIMON LOOKED TAKEN ABACK AND Chabela felt slightly ashamed. Just because she was greedy didn't mean that he had to be, too. Some people were into self-denial; it seemed to give them pleasure in the same way that a little hedonism from time to time suited her.

'I wouldn't really – eat a whole tub of cream in one go, I mean,' she said apologetically. 'It would probably make me sick – and imagine how fat I'd be! I'd go home looking like a great big *churro de cajeta*.'

At this, she blew out her cheeks, guessing that he would be familiar with the popular Mexican dessert, consisting of flat fried dough stuffed with caramel sauce and laden with calories.

She was right. His eyes lit up and he gave a loud, deep laugh, like a mini explosion.

'That wouldn't be good! No one would recognise you!'

So he did have a sense of humour! Chabela had been starting to wonder. His amusement didn't last long, however.

'I haven't had churros for years.'

He looked quite mournful and without thinking, Chabela said she'd make some for him. She liked cooking, when she had the time to do it properly, that was; she found it relaxing.

'My mother's housemaid showed me the recipe. Lots of families have a maid in Mexico, you know,' she added quickly, not wishing to sound grand. 'It's much more common than over here.'

Simon nodded. He seemed a little doubtful about the churros, however.

'I shouldn't—' he started, but she ignored him.

'I hope the housekeeper at Polgarry Manor won't mind me using the kitchen. Bramble won't, anyway, and she's the boss.'

'I'm not really—' Simon began again, but Chabela was so thoroughly taken with her idea that she scarcely heard him.

'I won't add too much sugar, I promise. Anyway, one or two churros won't hurt. I wonder if I can remember how to cook the caramel sauce...'

She was already thinking that she would make enough for Bramble and Matt, too, and Maria, if she behaved. Chabela liked the idea of giving her hosts a little taste of Mexico. They seemed to be lovely people and they'd already made her feel so welcome.

Simon seemed to know when he was defeated and stopped protesting, offering instead to show Chabela one of the letters that he had in his possession from James Penhallow to the Hosking family, some years after James had moved to Mexico.

So caught up had she been in the thrill of their meeting that Chabela had quite forgotten the real reason why she was here.

'Ooh, yes please!' she said, wriggling in her seat with enthusiasm.

He got up and went into another room, returning shortly after with a see-through folder containing a flat, yellowing page of writing in one hand, and a large piece of white paper in the other. Chabela gave a little whoop of excitement, which made his shoulder jerk violently and shoot up almost to his ear.

'This is a digital copy,' he explained once he'd recovered. He waved the white paper in the air. 'And this other one's the original. It's in pretty good condition. I've got two other letters but this is the clearest.

'For years, the letters were shoved in a drawer in my father's bureau, along with all his other correspondence. Eventually, I persuaded him to let me look after them. I took some advice and bought an acid-free archive box to protect them from light, dust and pests. It seems to be doing the trick.'

She could just imagine him eyeing his father's messy drawer with distaste; Simon himself would no doubt have a neat, logical filing system for everything. In fact she'd bet he even had a special way of organising his pants and socks, and she was certain that he'd change his bed linen on the same day each week.

But orderliness had its advantages, not least it meant that he'd been able to lay his hands on the precious letter immediately.

Chabela herself was woefully untidy. Her main filing system consisted of a large folder emblazoned with the words 'VERY IMPORTANT STUFF'. She wasn't proud of it but there again, she didn't seem to lose things very often; there was a certain order in the chaos.

'Can I have a look?' She stood up, expecting Simon to hand her the original letter, but he swung his arm above his head, so that it was well out of reach.

'You need to wash and dry your hands first,' he said fiercely, 'or you might transfer oil from your fingers onto the paper; it's very fragile.'

Feeling like one of his naughty pupils, Chabela apologised profusely, and when he told her where to find the nearest loo, she scuttled off without a murmur, tail between legs.

The small cloakroom was at the end of the hallway, and she was relieved to find a sturdy hand soap dispenser by the washbasin, proudly boasting its organic, environmentally friendly credentials.

After helping herself to a generous squirt, she lathered her hands thoroughly and then repeated the procedure all over again, imagining Simon watching, beady-eyed, to make sure that she was doing it properly.

The soap had an unusual, peppery scent, which only a man would go for, perhaps mixed with bergamot. It wasn't particularly pleasant, but it wasn't nasty either and it did leave her hands feeling very soft and clean.

Having dried them carefully on his beige towel, she was about to re-join him in the front room but couldn't resist poking her head in the kitchen first.

Like the rest of the cottage, this was shipshape and orderly, with a small, square wooden table in the centre, just big enough for two people, plain, tan-coloured cupboards and walnut worktops that were remarkably free from crumbs, gadgets, cookery books or unopened letters.

A rectangular window above the sink looked out onto a smallish, grassy back garden with a gnarled old apple tree in the centre. This seemed to lower its branches, stooping respectfully towards the rocky cliff that was guarding the house from beyond the fence.

Some wooden shelves to the right of the window were laden with large jars containing different varieties of pasta, brown and white rice, green and red lentils and yellow split peas. Above these was an impressive assortment of spices: cumin, cardamom, cinnamon, fenugreek, garam masala, ginger, mustard seeds, saffron, turmeric and so on, all neatly labelled and in strict alphabetical order.

An old black Aga dominated the other side of the kitchen, with a cast-iron pan on top, and beside it was a large wooden knife block, which must have contained at least nine or ten knives with serious-looking black handles.

The only other piece of equipment on show, save for a heavy wooden chopping board, was an electric bread maker, which would probably account for the warm, slightly yeasty aroma that she'd noticed when she first entered the cottage.

He must do a lot of cooking, she thought, presumably just for himself, and she found herself wondering if he ever felt lonely. She had trained herself not to pine when Alfonso was away, and she'd managed to find a way of being happy, mostly, in her own company. But it was always with the knowledge that her lover would come back to her eventually.

Did Simon have a girlfriend waiting in the wings? She very much doubted it. He struck her as the confirmed bachelor type, who preferred being alone. She was rather envious; it would be so much easier never to have fallen in love or needed anyone.

When she returned to the front room, he had migrated to the sofa where she had been and put the plastic folder and the other piece of paper on the adjoining seat. There was no room for her. She wondered for a moment whether he meant her to take the opposite sofa, but then he picked up the papers, slightly testily she thought, and beckoned to her to sit beside him.

'You need to be very careful,' he said, easing the original letter out of its plastic folder and placing it on the coffee table. 'Perhaps you'd rather look at the digital copy first?'

Having been ticked off about her dirty hands, Chabela was keen not to be reprimanded again and decided there and then that she wouldn't risk touching the original at all.

Picking up the copy, she quickly scanned the words, which were written in a large, slightly childish-looking script.

The address at the top of the page was in Real del Monte, Hidalgo, Mexico, and it was dated 3rd March, 1867.

Dear Fred and Dolly, and of course, the rest of the Hosking clan,

I'm writing to tell you the wonderful news – I'm a married man! I wed my beautiful bride, Jacinta, last Saturday at the Methodist church in Pachuca. So what do you think of that!

The work on my hacienda was completed just in time and we are at last man and wife, living together in wedded bliss. Jacinta has brought her little cat, Elodia, with her from her mother's house, and so we are three.

I hope you will one day meet my Jacinta. I'm certain you'll love her. She's beautiful, kind, funny, gentle and sweet. She speaks little English, so I have arranged for her to have lessons with the wife of one of our foremen. However, her lack of words hardly seems to matter. Her eyes are the windows to her soul and we understand one another perfectly. I truly believe that I'm the luckiest fellow alive…

There was then a section on the weather – extremely hot and uncomfortable, apparently – before he went on to talk about his work.

On another subject, I have persuaded people with money to invest in a third abandoned mine that I came across some time ago on my travels and have wanted to open up. I feel certain that we shall be lucky again and strike a good vein.

Soon, I hope to be able to put aside more money, some of which will find its way to you, my dearest friends. It is the least I can do after all the kindness you have shown me.

I enclose a photograph of me with my beloved Jacinta on our wedding day. It was taken in the drawing room of our hacienda, which overlooks the main square. As you can see, it's quite grand! My mother and father would have been amazed to think of their Jimmy living in such a place. They wouldn't have believed it.

I trust that you are well and that Fred's cough has cleared up with the better weather. I expect the daffodils are out by now and the hilltops are a blaze of yellow.

How are the Penrice lot? And Annie and Christopher Dawes and old Ma Hopkins? How I miss you all! I would give anything for a pint of Walter Hicks' ale. God willing, one day I will return to Tremarnock with my wife. I know that you will take her to your hearts as she will take you to hers.

Until then, I send you my warmest good wishes.

Your ever grateful friend and surrogate son,

James Penhallow.

Simon must have been following Chabela's gaze, as he waited until she got to the bottom of the page before speaking.

'The photograph is lost, unfortunately,' he said. 'It's pretty extraordinary that we've still got the letters. In one of the others, James mentions how he and Jacinta met. He was playing football with some of his friends in the village square. The Cornish tin miners brought football to Mexico, you know, in the eighteen twenties. It had never been played there before.'

Chabela nodded. 'I believe there's a plaque in Real del Monte which marks the spot.'

'Indeed,' said Simon. 'Jacinta was out with her sister and they stopped to watch the lads. They must have seemed very strange and foreign to the girls, with their pale skin and light hair and the odd language they spoke. It would have been quite incomprehensible.

'James himself was red-headed. We know because he mentions how amazed Jacinta was. She caught his eye and he went over to talk to her, presumably in his broken Spanish, and he said she was fascinated by his "*cabello rojo*".'

'May I see them – the other letters, I mean?'

Simon got up and left the room to fetch them.

Once again, Chabela touched only the copies that he had made, and was charmed by James Penhallow's almost childlike enthusiasm. In one letter, where he talked about meeting Jacinta for the first time, he mentioned that he'd managed to save enough from his earnings as a miner to buy himself a mule.

It seemed clear that the two events were connected; he must already have been thinking about marrying the beautiful Mexican señorita and was hoping to make enough money through his own enterprise to be able to provide for her.

On my days off, I intend to travel on my mule to abandoned mines in the area. There are many of them and I'm convinced that some could be worked again lucratively.

Of course I shall have to persuade rich people to invest. That won't be easy, but if I succeed then one

*day, God willing, I hope that I might have the means
to marry and start a family of my own.*

In the second letter, he mentioned that while he was
working down the mine, a large rock fell on his head.

*Fortunately I was saved by my hard hat, but I lost two
teeth in the process. I am not quite so handsome now,
to be sure, but I'm grateful to be parted only with some
teeth and not my life!*

'I'm quite surprised he could read and write,'
Chabela commented, when she'd finished. 'He sounds
so articulate, but his father can't have earned much
money in the mines, and then he was orphaned so
young. Would he even have gone to school?'

Simon pulled an 'I don't know' sort of face. 'He
might have attended a charity school of some sort for
a while. There were quite a few around at that time,
specifically for poor children. He could have learned the
basics there. He was obviously an intelligent, ambitious
chap, so maybe he taught himself after that, or took
night classes. Later on, of course, once he'd made his
fortune, he could have hired a private tutor and bought
all the books he wanted.'

It all happened so long ago but having seen the letters,
Chabela found that her interest had only been further
piqued. Whether or not she and James were related, she

realised that she wanted to know more about this man whose surname she shared.

'Do we know what happened to him and Jacinta?' she asked. 'Did they stay in Mexico? Did they have any children?'

'I'm afraid I can't tell you,' Simon replied. 'I've always wanted to do some research but so far I haven't got round to it. I rather hoped you might have some information, but I gather that's not the case?'

She shook her head apologetically. 'My mother was a strange, difficult woman. For whatever reason, she cut herself off from family and hardly had any friends, either. The only thing I do know is that my father's father was called Rodrigo Penhallow Aguado. He once sent me a birthday card with a little note inside. My mother normally refused to allow me to read any letters from him or any other member of the family; she'd tear them up. This one must have slipped through the net.'

Simon looked thoughtful. 'Rodrigo? OK. Well that's something, anyway. I don't suppose you know the name of his wife – your grandmother?'

Chabela shook her head again.

'I'm sorry I can't tell you more,' Simon went on. 'I hope you don't think I've brought you here under false pretences.'

'Not at all.' Chabela tucked a strand of hair behind an ear and pushed up the sleeves of her sweatshirt. The sun had moved around and was shining right on her, making her quite hot.

'To be honest, your letter came at just the right time. I'd wanted a holiday and it gave me a great excuse to visit somewhere new. I'm curious about the Penhallow link, but if I don't ever find out anything more, I won't be too bothered.'

Simon removed his glasses for a moment and rubbed his eyes. He looked even younger without them, almost boyish. Perhaps not having a spouse or children to worry about kept the wrinkles at bay.

Folk sometimes said the same thing to Chabela, which made her smile. 'You look like a teenager!' they'd marvel. 'How do you do it?' Then the penny would drop and they'd nod knowingly, as if they'd just unearthed some great truth. 'Ah! Of course! No children…'

When she looked at herself in the mirror she could never really see what they were talking about. In any case, she thought that she'd rather have Alfonso and a family than an unlined complexion, but of course she took the compliment with good grace and kept schtum.

'I may know someone who can help,' Simon said now, referring back to the Penhallow link, and Chabela's ears pricked up.

'He's called Rick. He runs a rather shabby gift shop in the village. Don't tell him I said that, though,' he added as an afterthought.

'I think I met him! Lots of hair?' Chabela made an exaggerated beard shape around her chin with her hands.

'That's the one.' Simon gave a small smile. 'He's an amateur historian. He might have a suggestion or two.'

For some reason she rather liked the idea of joining Simon in a spot of sleuthing; if nothing else, it would be a good excuse for them to meet again. Otherwise, she suspected that he might go back to burying himself in his books and she'd never set eyes on him again.

She started to ask him about his own family now, taking care not to sound too nosy. He had, it seemed, been born just outside Tremarnock. His father was a farmer and his mother had stayed home to raise him, an only child. Both parents were now dead.

She didn't dare enquire if he had ever been married or even if he had any children. His tics and spasms appeared to have subsided and the last thing she wanted was to stir them up again. In the event, however, he gave the information voluntarily.

'If I'd married and had a family, I might have wanted to live somewhere a bit livelier. Not London, maybe Bath or Bristol. But this place is perfect for antisocial old me. In the school holidays, I can go for days without speaking to anyone at all if I don't want to,' he added, without a hint of irony.

Something about his expression – slightly wistful, perhaps – made her wonder if he did have some regrets but was doing his best to hide them. He soon put her right on that score, however.

'I'm not at all the marrying type.' He screwed up his nose as if there were a bad smell. 'I like my own space.'

There was silence for a moment when she couldn't think of anything to say. She wondered if he might ask about her own personal circumstances, but he didn't. Instead, he leaned forwards and picked up the coffee pot, which was still half full, and topped up both their cups without asking.

When he reached for the milk jug and peered inside, though, he found that it was empty.

'I'll get some more.' He started to rise but she was quicker on her feet and nearer to the door, too.

'I'll go. Presumably it's in the kitchen?'

By the time he answered she was already halfway there. It didn't take her long to locate the fridge or the milk on a shelf just inside the door.

The interior was sparkling clean, but there seemed to be very little fresh food – just a small wedge of hard, yellow cheese, carefully wrapped in plastic film, a ceramic butter dish, half a cucumber, two spring onions, also carefully wrapped, a few potatoes and a carton of orange juice.

In a glass drawer at the bottom, she noticed two breasts of chicken, a cauliflower and some sprigs of broccoli, but that was all.

Her own fridge, by contrast, was usually bulging. Jars of half-eaten jam, mayonnaise and assorted condiments wrestled for space with leftover meals. They would most likely never get eaten, but she couldn't quite bring herself to waste them.

Having remnants lying around didn't bother her unless the food went mouldy, at which point she would finally throw it out. Simon was clearly much more disciplined. He probably bought only as much as he could consume and never had to throw anything away.

Although she could see the merits in such an approach, it seemed a bit too frugal for her liking. Where were the naughty half-eaten bars of chocolate and comforting packets of cookies? Where were the tasty soft drinks and bottles of beer and wine?

If a monk or a nun possessed a fridge, this is what it would look like, she decided, resolving there and then to tuck into a very large dinner tonight complete with starter and pudding. All this evidence of abstinence was making her feel hungry again.

At that moment, an idea popped into her head and stayed put. Closing the fridge again quickly, before Simon could accuse her of snooping, she returned with the carton of milk, which he poured into the jug.

She waited until they'd finished their second cup of coffee before making her proposal.

'Well,' she said, rising and pulling down her sweatshirt at the same time. 'I really think it's time to go.'

'Must you?' he replied, rising also, but he didn't look too upset. In fact, she suspected that he was really rather relieved. He was probably looking forward to getting back to his books. After all, they'd been talking for at least two hours, which was probably quite a lot for him.

'I wondered...' she said, feeling suddenly uncharacteristically shy, 'if I could come here and make the churros? Instead of doing them at the manor, I mean?'

She watched his face for signs of dismay or panic but couldn't see any. Emboldened, she carried on.

'I could cook you a whole Mexican meal, if you'd like that? Of course—'

Knowing his penchant for tidiness, she was about to add that she would be sure to do all the clearing up, too, but he interrupted her.

'That would be nice, thank you.'

He looked genuinely quite pleased and her face broke into a huge smile.

'*Muy bien*!' She clapped her hands while he stood with his arms hanging awkwardly at his side, looking for all the world as if he'd never witnessed such a startling display of enthusiasm. 'I'll wait for you to tell me which day would be most convenient,' she went on. 'You have my phone number?'

He gave a small, restrained nod. 'And I'll speak to Rick the amateur historian.'

It was after one o'clock when she set off for the village once more, having responded to his rather stiff farewell handshake with a kiss on his surprisingly smooth cheek.

By his expression, you'd think that she'd gone for his lips instead, which made her giggle inwardly, and she was still laughing as she climbed back up the cliff, going over their conversation and remembering all his little peculiarities.

The nervous twitches, the almost military-style neatness, his fondness for brown and beige, his frugal eating habits; he could hardly be more different from most of the Mexican men she knew, including Alfonso.

And yet, despite all this, she found being with Simon quite reassuring in a way.

For one, he had taken her mind right off her problems and secondly, it was clear that he wanted nothing from her at all, other than that which she might choose to give.

If he never saw her again, she thought, he wouldn't be too bothered, yet on the other hand, he was perfectly happy for her to cook him a meal if that's what she wanted to do.

Such self-reliance in a man was a revelation to her. At the height of her affair with Alfonso, he had been so needy, expecting her to drop everything the moment he was free, calling her any time of the day or night when he wanted her advice, or just to be reassured how much she loved him.

He could sulk for days if she cancelled a date or failed to respond to a message. And he was so jealous, he thought that every man she ever spoke to was a rival whether she met him at work or in a social situation, so she did her best not to mention any names.

It was exhausting, but it was all she knew, and the husbands, brothers and fathers of her friends were equally demanding in their different ways. What's more, as far as she was aware, not one of them knew how to iron a shirt or put on the washing machine, let alone cook themselves a meal or use a vacuum cleaner.

As she headed over the brow of the cliff, retracing her steps along the narrow path that would lead, eventually, to the village, she found herself thinking that Simon and the Penhallow link might prove to be just the diversion that she'd been hoping for.

An oddball he certainly was, but he also seemed gentle, genuine and kind. And right now, after all that she'd been through, these three qualities seemed to draw her instinctively, as a cooling lake draws the weary, footsore traveller.

Chapter Six

LIGHT WAS ONLY JUST STARTING to peep through Liz's bedroom curtains when she was woken by a loud screeching overhead.

She snapped open her eyes.

TAP-TAP-A-TAP-A-TAP-A TAP-BANG-BANG! And again, TAP-TAP-A-TAP-A-TAP-A TAP-BANG-BANG!

It sounded as if Michael Flatley and a troupe of Irish dancers had taken up residence on her slate roof.

'Robert?' She turned and touched her husband's bare shoulder. He had his back to her and was breathing in and out slowly and heavily, his head creating a deep dent in the white pillow.

How on earth could he slumber through this?

'Robert?' she repeated, more loudly now, and she shook him quite firmly.

'Uh?' He twisted around and sat bolt upright, his eyes wide and staring. His brown hair was sticking up at right angles, as if he'd stumbled into an electric fence.

She nearly laughed out loud. Serious bedhead.

TAP-TAP-A-TAP-A-TAP-A TAP-BANG-BANG! That noise again, repeated over and over in a series of rhythmic cracks and thuds.

'What the hell *is it*?' She sat up, too, hugging the duvet around her naked body and fixing on the closed door. At any moment she half expected to see it burst open and an army of... she didn't know what... charge into the room, waving their bayonets high in the air and roaring.

'Sounds like something on the roof.' Robert swallowed and two pairs of eyes floated skywards in unison.

'I'm scared,' said Liz, putting on a silly girly voice, but she was only half joking. She snuggled into her husband's side and he wrapped an arm around her shoulder and squeezed. She rather wished that he had a big chunky weapon in the other hand.

Their attention was diverted by a loud squawk at the window. Through a chink in the curtains, they spotted the fat, feathery body of a very large white and grey seagull perched on their sill.

'Shoo!' Liz shouted instinctively, waving her arms in its general direction. The bird, however, seemed quite unperturbed. It paused to peer at them beadily through the gap before flapping lazily away, as if it hadn't a care in the world.

Meanwhile, the screeching and banging carried on above them; it was giving Liz a headache.

'Will you go and have a look?' She got up and padded across the wooden floor to fling open the curtains. There was clear blue sky above, and the pink geraniums in the neighbour's window box opposite were in full bloom. It was going to be a glorious day.

'Sorry, babes.' She could hear Robert stretch and throw off the duvet while she scanned up and down Humble Hill, searching for clues. 'I'm meeting Ryan at the shack in half an hour. I need to get in the shower.'

Ryan worked at the village fishmonger's in Market Square and supplied fresh fish for Robert's successful restaurant, A Winkle in Time, as well as for his more recently acquired seaside café, the Secret Shack.

Business there was slow in winter but now that the weather had picked up, more folk were strolling on the beach and some were even venturing into the water. Come the school holidays, the place would be heaving and he'd need to employ extra staff to cope with the rush.

'I can't see anything,' Liz commented. The street was deserted and most of the blinds in the windows were still shut. However, she did notice some seagulls flying in the general direction of her beloved cottage, Bag End.

Two left the flock and settled on a chimneypot just across the way while the rest flapped on. Soon the noise above ramped up several decibels. TAP-TAP-A-TAP-A-TAP-A TAP-BANG-BANG!

'I think it might be herring gulls,' she hissed, as the penny started to drop. 'Why are they making so much noise?'

There was no response and when she spun around, she caught sight of her husband's naked bottom disappearing into the shower room. It was a very nice bottom – round and firm with cute little cheeks like sculpted apples.

The rest of him was tall and thin and she liked the fact that she could grab onto his bum, that and his beefcake biceps, like tennis balls, formed through years of lugging heavy crates of wine, food and kitchen equipment.

Water whooshed and steam soon started to waft through the open bathroom door. It was no use expecting him to investigate the disturbance now.

What was the point of having a husband if he wasn't available to shin up roofs when required?

She felt a flush of irritation, then she remembered that unlike her, he was afraid of heights. It was one of his pet hates, along with grapes, rice, tomatoes and swimming.

Mostly she found it endearing, except when she needed him to check the gutters, fix a light bulb in the ceiling – or investigate strange noises overhead. Back when she was single, she'd had to do all these jobs herself, of course. Now, she couldn't help feeling that they were *man's work*.

As she viciously plumped the pillows and threw them back on the bed, she decided that Ryan was probably just an excuse to avoid getting out the ladder.

She was tempted to be immature and only smooth her side of the sheet and duvet while leaving his rumpled, but then her mind flitted back to last night when Robert had returned late from the restaurant. She'd been asleep and had woken to find him doing something unusual and really rather delicious with his big toe.

A little smile curled the corners of her lips while she pulled on her dressing gown, and there was a new-found spring in her step when she strolled along the landing to check on her daughters.

Rosie, who had recently turned fifteen, was extremely difficult to rouse and it often took stern words to get her to school on time. It was a different story with Lowenna, however, who'd be three in August.

She generally rose with the larks and Liz could hear her chattering further up the corridor. She was probably playing with her pretend plastic people, who lived in a large Lego house, complete with beds, tables, chairs, a grandfather clock and even some soft furnishings. They had tremendous adventures.

'Bad girl! Go to your room! NOW!'

Uh-oh. Lowenna's voice had risen to a fierce, high pitch. It was funny how strict she could be with her toys given that Liz, to her knowledge, never spoke to her own daughters like that. But her youngest was a sweetheart – mostly, anyway. Rosie had been once, too, but she was more complicated now.

Her bedroom door was closed and Liz opened it tentatively, rather fearing what she might find inside.

'Morning, darling!'

She paused for a moment while her eyes adjusted to the darkness. The air smelled stale and she wrinkled her nose as she stepped gingerly over a pile of clothes, an open school bag, several mugs and a half-eaten bowl of dried out cereal. Frustration tugged at her insides and she had to force herself not to bark.

Fifteen was a difficult age, after all, plus Rosie had an awful lot more to cope with than most. She'd been born with mild cerebral palsy and everything was that bit harder for her.

Liz was so used to her daughter's quirks that she sometimes forgot about her slight limp and tricky arm, which didn't work as well as it should. On top of all that, she'd been diagnosed with a brain tumour at ten years old and had needed a major operation to remove it, followed by proton beam therapy.

She was doing amazingly well, but her sight had suffered and she needed thick glasses to see properly, which, of course, she hated.

The whole experience had been terrifying and Liz's instinct, still, was to wrap her daughter in cotton wool and generally overcompensate. But sometimes, like now, Rosie would take the mickey and push her mother just that bit too far.

'Time to get up!' Liz said, opening the blind and blinking as light flooded into the gloomy interior.

The place looked even worse when she could see properly. Clothes were strewn over every available surface, including a pile of school shirts that Liz had ironed only the previous day. Prickles of annoyance ran up and down her arms and back, into the base of her neck and right across her scalp.

The wastepaper basket was overflowing and shoes were scattered about, along with the odd bra and pair of knickers. Whether these were clean or dirty, it was impossible to tell. How could Rosie bear to live like this?

'Time to get up,' Liz repeated, more loudly this time.

'Noooo!' The girl's voice rose up from beneath the duvet, which she'd thrown over her head. She was awake, then.

'You need to get dressed.' There was an edge to Liz's voice, which Rosie picked up on immediately.

'Stop being a nag! I've got five more minutes. My alarm hasn't gone off yet.'

Liz took a deep breath. Rosie's 'five minutes' usually turned into fifteen as she kept hitting the snooze button. Then she'd tear downstairs and stumble out of the door to catch the bus, without having had any breakfast and probably having forgotten several crucial textbooks and bits of equipment.

Still, there was no point having a row; experience proved that it didn't make Rosie any quicker and would only leave them both feeling miserable for the rest of the morning.

'See you later!' Robert hurried past, his footsteps heavy on the wooden floor, and after a few moments Liz heard him slam the door behind him. He could move like the wind when he wanted to.

More clattering and banging overhead made her jump, but Rosie didn't seem to notice. Vertigo or no vertigo, the seagulls, or whatever that noise was, would have to wait till Robert returned. Liz certainly wasn't venturing up there on her own.

Lowenna was crouched on a cream sheepskin rug in front of her toy house when Liz entered her room. She was clutching two little figures in her chubby hands and looked very intense as she leaned forwards and tried to prop them both on miniature chairs, which promptly fell over.

'Bother!' she said crossly, before trying again. Liz was rather relieved; she'd heard her daughter say far worse.

The little girl had dark, straight, shoulder-length hair like her mother, and big round brown eyes that drew you in. She was in a short-sleeved, pink nightdress with Cinderella on the front, and a large chocolate milk stain down the side that Liz hadn't noticed last night.

'Shall I do it?' She stepped forwards to help but on hearing her mother's voice, Lowenna jumped up and promptly dropped the figures, which clattered to the ground. Then she rushed over to Liz, throwing her arms around her legs.

She was irresistible. Liz bent down and scooped her daughter up, burying her nose in her soft hair. She smelled of flowery shampoo and fabric conditioner and sweet, dewy baby skin.

Her bare legs were twisted around her mother's waist, her arms tight around her neck, and like a limpet, she wasn't letting go. She was quite heavy but Liz didn't mind, and together they made their way downstairs in a messy jumble, with Liz laughing and hanging onto the rail to keep them upright.

There was no playgroup that day and it was quite some time before they made it back upstairs after breakfast to get washed and dressed. Then Lowenna wanted a story, then Liz's father rang from London for a chat and before they knew it, it was almost ten thirty and Esme was knocking on the door and calling through the letterbox: 'Cooee!' Liz would know that voice anywhere.

'Goodness!' she said, hurrying down the hallway with Lowenna hot on her heels. 'She's early, isn't she? I haven't even put on the kettle.'

The women embraced on the step before heading into the kitchen. They went back a long way. Esme, a potter, lived in the upstairs flat at Dove Cottage, just along the road, and Liz and Rosie had once occupied the chilly ground floor.

This was well before Liz and Robert had married, in the days when she had needed two jobs – cleaning and waitressing – just to make ends meet and was still sore after her break-up with Rosie's father.

Esme, who was single and in her early sixties, was a talented potter with a studio in the next village. Everyone now knew that she and her former school friend, Caroline, had been secretly in love for years, and that they had rekindled their passion on a recent Cornish walking trip.

However, Caroline had reluctantly decided to return home to Paris to nurse her sick husband and be with her pregnant daughter, leaving Esme heartbroken.

Since then, she had thrown herself into her work to try to take her mind off her unhappiness, and Liz and the other villagers had been doing their best to cheer their friend up.

It seemed to be working – to a degree at least. Today, Esme looked really rather beautiful, in a long, navy fisherman's smock, a flowing purple skirt, almost down to her ankles, and dozens of coloured crystal beads in her ears and around her neck and wrists.

Her long, salt and pepper hair was tied up in a messy bun, and there was a smudge of clay on her cheek and a sparkle in her eye that Liz hadn't seen for a long time.

'You look well,' she commented, and Esme smiled rather mysteriously.

'I had an email from Caroline.'

'Ah!' From the look on the older woman's face, it had to be good news. 'What did she say?'

'She's missing me.'

'Of course she is,' Liz cried, with some exasperation. It had been so obvious to all who cared about Esme that she and Caroline were made for one another.

The pity was that Caroline's husband, Philip, had Parkinson's disease and during her stay in Tremarnock, he'd taken a turn for the worse. Their daughter, Helen, had blamed it on Caroline's absence and the pressure on her to go home from Helen, her brother Andrew and Philip himself, had eventually proved too much.

Still, Liz held out hope that Caroline and Esme might one day be reunited, and Esme certainly looked pleased to have heard from her lover today.

'How is she?' Liz asked now, and Esme made a so-so gesture with her flattened hand.

'Bearing up. The baby's due any day and she's very excited, but Philip's being difficult. He can't stand being so immobile. He takes his frustration out on Caroline, I'm afraid. She really doesn't deserve it.'

'Perhaps she can come here for a holiday after the baby's born?'

It seemed like a good idea; after all, Philip, Helen and Andrew already knew that Caroline and Esme were friends. They didn't need to be told anything more. But Esme shook her head.

'Philip can't be left alone for a minute and he won't have anyone other than family looking after him. Helen can't help and Caroline wouldn't dream of asking

Andrew; she says he's far too busy with his job. So that just leaves her.'

'Oh dear.' Liz filled the kettle and fetched two mugs and a cafetière from the cupboard. She could well imagine how powerless and desperate Esme must feel and what a struggle it must be to accept Caroline's self-sacrifice. It wasn't as if she still loved Philip, after all; according to Esme, he had been a bit of a beast and betrayed his wife spectacularly.

'She's going to ring me tomorrow while he's with the doctor,' Esme went on, brightening again. 'We tend to use Facetime. It's lovely being able to see her when we talk.'

She was perched on a wooden chair at the battered old pine table, scored with chips and scratches through years of use. She hadn't even noticed Lowenna, pulling on the corner of her skirt. Esme didn't know much about the ways of children, not having had any herself.

In desperation, the little girl yanked on Esme's necklace, finally grabbing her attention.

'Careful!' she said quite sharply, 'you might break it.' Then, more softly, 'Is there something you want to show me?'

Relieved, Lowenna nodded and taking Esme by the hand, she led her purposefully into the sitting room at the front of the cottage, where there were more toys.

Meanwhile, Liz made coffee and put some biscuits on a plate.

'Alexa, play Norah Jones on Spotify,' she commanded, and the voice-controlled device on the worktop sprang to life. It had been a birthday present from Robert, and Liz often used it to check the weather, play music or tell a silly joke.

Robert and Rosie teased her for adopting a special, haughty voice when she barked her instructions at the speaker, but she ignored them. Now, she couldn't imagine how she'd ever lived without it.

When Esme and Lowenna returned with a truck of coloured bricks, Lowenna settled on the floor to play with them while the women resumed their talk.

Esme enquired after Robert, and Liz said he was extremely busy with work, as ever, and had had no time to investigate the strange squawking and banging on the rooftop this morning.

'I didn't notice anything.' Esme took a sip of coffee before arching an eyebrow. 'Perhaps you have bats in the belfry?'

'Surely not?' Liz looked alarmed, which made her friend laugh.

'I'm rather partial to bats myself.' Esme had a funny, slightly old-fashioned way of speaking and sometimes used long, baffling words that most folk couldn't understand.

After helping herself to a biscuit, Liz nudged the plate across.

'But you wouldn't want them in your attic, would you? Bats, I mean.'

'Perhaps not.' Esme tipped her head to one side and wrinkled her long, thin nose. 'But they're insectivores, you know. They can be rather a useful form of pest control.'

'You mean they gobble up flies and mosquitoes?' Liz shivered. 'I'm not sure I wouldn't rather have gnats than bats.'

Esme was pondering a suitably witty riposte when she remembered something else.

'I say! It's good news about Max, isn't it?'

Liz's stomach did a sickening flip. An image flashed into her mind: Max at a fireworks party last November. His lips on hers, his hand between her thighs.

'What?' Her mouth felt dry and it sounded odd and rasping.

She'd wanted him so badly yet been horrified at the same time. She and Robert had been going through a bad patch. It was no excuse but… After that kiss, she'd told Max never to contact her again.

She tucked her hands under the table so that her friend wouldn't see them shaking.

'You haven't heard?' Esme helped herself to a chocolate finger biscuit, holding it up and examining it between thumb and forefinger before popping the end in her mouth and snapping it off with her teeth.

Liz was grateful for the pause. She became transfixed by Esme's lips, moving in and out, the muscles in her cheeks flexing and extending, the jaw clenching and relaxing. The sound of crunching seemed unnaturally loud, like ice cracking underfoot. Such a lot of effort for one small bite.

When she swallowed at last, Liz did the same, wincing slightly because it hurt.

'Heard what?' she said now. Her heart pitter-pattered in her chest.

'The plaque unveiling next month. Max is coming after all.'

The blood seemed to drain from Liz's head, making her dizzy. She was tempted to use an excuse to leave the room.

Max, from Germany, had visited the village after Rosie had discovered a message in a bottle from his grandfather, who had been a prisoner of war in Tremarnock during the Second World War.

Much to the villagers' delight, Max had stepped in to save the local playground from developers who wanted to turn it into a housing estate.

There was to be a grand ceremony in two weeks to commemorate his grandfather, who had remained grateful throughout his life to Tremarnock's inhabitants for the kindness they had shown him. But after what had happened with Liz, he had said that he couldn't make it.

'Audrey told me,' Esme went on. The remaining portion of her finger biscuit was still suspended rather elegantly between her fingers.

Audrey owned a dress shop and a bed and breakfast in the village. She also ran a small but thriving catering business, which delivered food to their rental properties, sometimes for up to twenty people. Her boeuf bourguignon was a particular favourite, as was her luxury Eton mess, made with local strawberries and clotted cream from the nearby dairy. She always seemed to know everything about everyone.

'That's nice! I wonder what made him change his mind.' Liz tried her best to sound pleased but she must have done a bad job because Esme fixed on her with her clear grey eyes.

'I thought you'd be happy. You and he got on well, didn't you?'

'I haven't spoken to him for ages, to be honest. I've almost forgotten what he looks like.'

Esme's gaze remained steady. 'He's not staying with Audrey this time. She's a bit put out, to be honest.'

Liz recalled an amusing conversation between her and Max when he'd complained about Audrey's nosiness and incessant talking. It had made her giggle. Later, they'd kissed, and it was after this that he'd spoken of his strong feelings for her.

She hadn't forgotten his features at all, of course; she could picture him here right now, standing before her, his face close to hers. His short dark hair, tinged with silver, his close-cropped beard, broad, athletic shoulders and wide neck, those intense blue eyes...

That kiss was never supposed to mean anything, but somehow it had.

'I expect he's found a nice hotel,' she said, pulling back her shoulders and attempting to gather herself together. 'More up his street than a B and B.'

'You're probably right.' Esme's gaze shifted at last and she took another sip of coffee. 'Anyway, it'll be good to catch up with him. I'll certainly pop along to the unveiling ceremony.'

There didn't seem to be much to say after that and there was silence for a few moments while the two women watched Lowenna build a tower of bricks, which soon toppled down.

When the hush started to feel awkward, Liz racked her brains for a safe topic and settled on Esme's latest commissions. It seemed that she was in the process of making a set of urns for a wealthy client with a weekend home in Fowey.

'I'd better get back to my studio,' she said at last, rising and pushing back her chair, one leg of which almost skewered Lowenna, who was sitting right behind. Esme was always doing things like that, not deliberately, of course, but she tended to forget about the presence of children.

Once she'd left, Liz tidied away their mugs and plates and fetched Lowenna's jacket and shoes from the hallway. There was just time for a short stroll before lunch.

As she slipped the little girl's feet into her red sandals, she found her mind drifting back again to Max and anxiety, guilt and fear nibbled at her insides.

Robert, of course, knew nothing of what had occurred at the party. There used to be no secrets between them and now, it was as if she had buried a body in the sand, knowing that it was only a matter of time before the wind and tide would inevitably expose it.

After all, it hadn't been just a kiss for her either, had it? She'd been so drawn to Max and had felt a connection so powerful that from the moment she'd picked him up from the airport, it was almost as if she'd known him all her life.

And yet she loved her husband and the family that they'd created together and dreaded the thought of hurting him. So what on earth had been the matter with her? And why did her stomach still do somersaults at the mere mention of Max's name?

She'd been planning on going to the plaque unveiling, believing that he wouldn't be there. But now, as she walked with Lowenna into the hallway and started to unfold the pushchair, she found herself inventing reasons not to show up.

Illness? A visit to her father and stepmother in London? It really didn't matter, so long as it worked and she never saw the German again.

It was the only reasonable course of action open to her. It was the only way that she could be one hundred per cent sure of staying safe.

Chapter Seven

As she stepped out of the cottage and bumped Lowenna and her pushchair down the doorstep, Liz was startled by a tremendously loud shriek. Glancing up, she saw the underside of a large, feathery gull just above her head.

Ducking instinctively, she caught a glimpse of the bird's pink webbed feet and fearsome talons as it swooped up, up and away, carrying something in its razor sharp beak.

Her heart was hammering and blood whooshed in her ears; the creature couldn't have been more than a foot from her scalp and three feet from her daughter's precious knees; definitely too close for comfort. She couldn't help thinking that it was no accident and that she'd been the target.

'Are you OK?'

She straightened up and turned around to find a dark-haired woman standing in the road just outside her gate.

Liz didn't recognise her but she looked friendly, her big greenish-brown eyes wide with concern.

'I'm fine, thanks.' Liz patted the top of her head just to make sure it was still there. 'That's never happened before. They don't normally attack unless you've got food.'

'I think they're building a nest on your roof.'

The woman indicated with a forefinger. She sounded foreign and looked it, too, with her dark, wavy hair, olive skin, slim, pointed nose and wider than usual nostrils.

'Really?'

Liz swivelled around and looked skywards, shielding her eyes with a hand to protect from the glare. When she couldn't spot anything, she left the pushchair, stepped into the road and stood on tiptoe, craning her neck to try to see beyond the wonky gable.

Two big herring gulls were perched on her chimney pot, and two more on the slate tiles around it, seemingly surveying the scene. That in itself wasn't unusual; the birds were as much a part of the fabric of the village as the inhabitants themselves and landed whenever and wherever they pleased.

What was out of the ordinary, however, was that a fifth gull – perhaps the one that had almost dive-bombed Liz – appeared to have a pile of twigs, grass or leaves in its bill. It vanished behind the chimney for a few minutes, then reappeared with an empty beak and flew off again, to a cacophony of squawks and stamps from the other birds.

'Cheeky thing!' cried Liz. She could swear that the remaining gulls were mocking her. 'You never asked my permission!'

The stranger laughed. 'I think you'll be sharing your home with some feathery friends for a few months, whether you like it or not.'

'Bloody hell!' Liz wasn't altogether keen on the idea, but suspected that there was nothing she could do about it. She knew that it was a legal offence to injure or kill any wild birds or interfere with their nests or eggs. Perhaps Robert could frighten the mother and father off before it was too late. She'd have to talk to him about it later.

'Well,' she said, turning back to the stranger, 'that explains all the loud noises this morning. I thought there was an elephant in the attic.'

After that, it seemed rude not to introduce herself and the other woman did likewise, adding that she was on her way to the local restaurant, A Winkle in Time, to see if the owner, a man called Robert, needed any temporary staff. She'd heard that his business did very well, especially in the tourist season.

'That's my husband!' Liz replied, pleased. 'He should be there now. I'll take you.'

Soon, they were walking side by side up Humble Hill, past the rows of brightly painted cottages, all with their own names, that Liz had come to love.

Chabela explained that she was staying at Polgarry Manor, and that it was the owner, Bramble, who had suggested speaking to Robert about employment. Before leaving Mexico, Chabela had gone to the trouble of obtaining a one-year business visa, which would allow her to undertake academic work in the UK. Although she had no idea how long she'd want to stay, it had seemed like a sensible precaution. Now, she was rather hoping that the visa would come in handy for working at the café. If Robert were worried about being prosecuted, they could always say that she was doing some research for a book and who knew? Perhaps one day she would write about her experiences here so they wouldn't be telling a lie.

'I originally thought I might only be in Tremarnock for a few weeks, but I've decided to stay for the whole summer now, if I can. It's such a lovely village.'

She didn't say what had made her change her mind, but Liz felt herself increasingly warming towards the stranger, who seemed lively and easy-going. She also appeared to be single and, perhaps, a wee bit lonely, just as Liz had been when she'd first arrived in the village with a then very small Rosie.

With this in mind, she resolved right there and then to persuade her husband to find Chabela a job; it shouldn't be too difficult, after all, with the summer season fast approaching.

'Here we are,' she said, feeling a shiver of pride when they finally stopped outside the restaurant at the bottom of South Street. 'Welcome to the best fish joint for miles around!'

The place certainly looked smart and attractive, particularly in the morning sunshine, painted white, with bright blue shutters across the windows and its name – A Winkle In Time – emblazoned in swirly white letters on a matching blue board above the door.

The building was once a well-to-do sea captain's home and the restaurant itself was on the ground floor, while the top floor had been converted into a flat, owned by a wealthy couple from Truro.

They normally rented it out and Robert had the keys and kept an eye on it for them. It rarely caused him any problems, although he had once had to complain about some tenants who were dumping their rubbish in the street. The roof had also leaked when no one was living there and caused a mini waterfall in the restaurant kitchen.

Liz wheeled the pushchair inside and Chabela followed. It was quite dark within, owing to the low, oak-beamed ceiling and the dinky, lead-framed windows that looked out on to the narrow, cobbled street.

Two of the eight stripped wooden tables were occupied by early lunch guests and Robert was standing behind the bar at the back, tea towel in hand, polishing glasses.

He looked surprised and not altogether pleased to see his wife and daughter arriving unexpectedly, and he quickly ushered them and the stranger into the busy kitchen at the back, so as not to disturb the diners.

When Liz explained their mission, however, his eyes lit up.

'It must be fate!' he said, smiling at Chabela and shaking her by the hand. In his enthusiasm, he leaned back against the stainless steel worktop, only for one of the staff to yell at him not to upset the freshly prepared plates of salad that were waiting to be taken into the other room.

'Sorry,' he muttered, raising his hands in mock surrender. Then he focused again on the foreigner, who was hovering just behind Liz, looking slightly overwhelmed by the noise, smells, heat and general hubbub.

There were four members of staff in there, not including Robert, so with Chabela, Liz and Lowenna, that made eight – far too many bodies in such a small space.

'I'm going to need extra people to run my beach café, the Secret Shack,' Robert explained, fixing Chabela with an appraising eye.

Liz could imagine what he was thinking – smart appearance, tick; attractive smile, tick; fit, healthy and on the ball, tick. So far so good.

'It's an upmarket snack bar, essentially,' he went on, 'and it'll get very busy. I think I can rotate my existing chefs. My teenage stepdaughter, Rosie, and her friend,

Rafael, will also help out at weekends and in the school holidays. They can wash up and clear the tables and so on, but I need a manager. Do you have any experience?'

'Not really, no.' Chabela sounded confused. 'I'm really a university lecturer, you see—'

'She'll be a quick learner,' Liz interrupted. 'I don't mind giving her a hand to start with and showing her the ropes.'

She hardly knew the woman, of course, but could see that Robert's eyes were already starting to glaze over and he was losing interest.

He ran his fingers through his messy brown hair and frowned. Liz knew that look. He was so generous and kind, his instinct would always be to help out if he could. But he was in charge of two businesses, about which he worried constantly, and he couldn't afford to employ time-wasters.

Liz had a hunch, however, that Chabela would be quite capable of rising to whatever challenges he set her.

'You could take her on for a trial period,' she suggested in her sweetest voice. Then, turning to the Mexican: 'You wouldn't mind doing, say, a week for starters, would you? Just to see how you get on?'

Chabela nodded enthusiastically.

'Sounds all right in principle,' said Robert, still frowning.

There was a crash, which made them all jump. Jesse, the blond, curly-headed sous-chef, had dropped a large china bowl and an extremely rude word burst from his mouth.

'Sorry, guv,' he said, noticing Robert's glare, before bending down to pick up the pieces of broken crockery.

'Can you come back tomorrow morning around ten?' Robert asked, turning back to Chabela. 'Bring your CV and we'll take it from there.'

It was clear from his expression that the interview, if you could call it that, was over and besides, Lowenna had started complaining and it was only a matter of time before she would explode.

As she pushed her daughter back out into the sunshine, Liz found herself wondering if her husband would find some excuse tomorrow not to employ Chabela after all.

There were always plenty of local people without visa problems looking for work – students home for the summer holidays as well as those who relied on seasonal jobs to top up their meagre earnings the rest of the year.

'Tell him you worked in bars and cafés when you were younger,' she whispered to her new friend, pulling a little box of raisins out of her handbag to give to Lowenna.

'But I didn't!' Chabela looked alarmed.

'Did you help your mother prepare meals?' Liz asked now, and Chabela nodded.

'And clear up the dishes afterwards?'

Another nod.

'And do you sometimes cook for friends, as well as for yourself?'

'Of course!' came the reply.

'Well then,' said Liz triumphantly, 'you *do* have experience. Running a café isn't rocket science, you know. You'll pick it up dead fast.'

Chabela wrinkled her brow. 'Why are you helping me like this? You hardly know me.'

Liz thought for a moment before replying.

'Because you're alone in a strange place and for whatever reason, you want to stay. That's enough for me.'

'Thank you.' Chabela was smiling now. 'If I get the job, I'll prove that you've made the right decision. You won't regret it.'

After that, they parted company. Chabela said that she was going to walk along the cliffs to explore in a new direction, while Liz took Lowenna to the play park. They didn't last long, though. There was no one for the little girl to play with and she soon started getting tired and whingey. Liz decided to cut her losses, thinking that it was a good thing it was almost time for her daughter's afternoon nap.

They strolled slowly home, stopping once to stroke a fluffy white cat that curled itself around Liz's ankles. Lowenna watched, transfixed, until it tried to jump on her lap, causing a shriek of dismay.

'Off!' said Liz, gently shooing away the animal, which slunk off behind some bins where it sat, examining them sulkily through narrowed eyes.

As she picked up the pace again, watching out for cars and potholes in the road, Liz became aware that her most pressing problem right now was what to cook for dinner. Spaghetti carbonara or mushroom risotto? Rosie would prefer the former and Lowenna wouldn't mind either way. Robert, on the other hand, probably wouldn't want anything.

Long gone were the days when he would come home as regularly as clockwork for an early supper with the family before his evening shift started. Now, with two businesses to run, he was far too busy and he would generally grab something on the go.

Liz would always leave out a plate of whatever she and the girls had eaten in case he was hungry when he returned from work around midnight. Nine times out of ten, however, she would find the food sitting untouched in the fridge when she went downstairs in the morning. She didn't know why she bothered.

Realising that her mind was occupied with nothing more interesting than tonight's menu rather shocked her. In her previous life as a single mum juggling two jobs, she had worried constantly about how to pay the bills and whether she could afford this or that school trip for her daughter.

Looking back, she wondered how she had coped. She had felt permanently exhausted and then when Rosie had fallen ill with her brain tumour, the strain had been so immense that she had almost reached breaking point.

So how come she was suddenly struck with a sneaking suspicion that in some ways, she and Rosie had been happier back then, at least before the tumour was diagnosed? It didn't add up.

It dawned on her that in those days, she'd had a strong sense of purpose; her sole reason for existence was Rosie and the only thing that mattered was ensuring that she, Liz, could earn enough to keep a roof over her daughter's head and that she was content and well cared for.

The fact that there were just the two of them had made them extra close, and even in some of their worst moments, when they'd felt so anxious and isolated, they'd managed to laugh and have fun.

Money may have been tight, but walking along the cliffs and building sandcastles on the beach had cost nothing, and Liz was always able to find a few pence for an ice cream or lolly to put a smile back on her daughter's precious face.

Things were certainly easier now, she mused. Thanks to Robert's success, she'd been able to give up work and devote herself to the girls. They had a cosy home, food, a car and plenty of cash for clothes and treats. Yet she and Rosie had never been further apart and Robert, well, he was always working.

An unpleasant, niggling sensation settled in her gut. At first she couldn't identify it, then she realised with a jolt what it was – dissatisfaction – and the words *Is this all there is?* seemed to hover before her, like a pantomime ghost.

Enough! She pulled herself up sharp. She should be grateful for what she had and stop imagining that there was something better just around the corner. She'd once been so good at making the very best of things. Prosperity had made her greedy.

With Max, she'd come face to face with the reality of what she stood to lose and it had terrified her: Robert, her home, their family life and cherished friends, Mitzi the cat, even.

Ever since then, she'd been like an Olympic oarswoman, rowing with all her might to get safely back to shore. She thought that she'd made it but now, she wasn't quite so sure.

It was Max who'd unsettled her, Max whose fault it was for deciding to come to the unveiling ceremony after all. Damn him. She wished to God that she'd never set eyes on his beautiful, handsome face.

LOWENNA WENT TO SLEEP STRAIGHT after lunch and after tidying away the dishes, Liz sat at the kitchen table and opened her laptop. Along with cleaning and waitressing, she'd once run a small online business making and selling hair accessories, but she'd wound it right down and now only made things occasionally for friends and family.

It was months since she'd looked at her website and it crossed her mind that should either update or close it altogether. Curious to see it again, she Googled the name, RosieCraft, and was surprised by how appealing the homepage looked; she'd forgotten how much thought she'd put into the design, which she'd done on a shoestring with a little help from an arty friend.

At one point, her home-made velvet scrunchies, flowery headbands and quirky slides, decorated with beads or semi-precious stones, had sold like hotcakes. She'd never earned much from them because she didn't charge a lot, but it had been enough to make it worthwhile.

For a time, she'd enjoyed it, and it had helped to take her mind off Rosie's illness. She still kept a big box of fabric, elastic, wool, ribbons, beads and suchlike at the bottom of her wardrobe, which she hadn't looked at for at least two years.

Perhaps she should revive the business – or even start something new? Soon, Lowenna would be at nursery school and she, Liz, would need a project to get her teeth into. Everyone needed a mountain to climb, after all; for too long, she'd been meandering pleasantly but idly across the plains.

Her gaze fell on a photograph of one of Rosie's school friends, modelling a pair of particularly cute hair slides with rhinestones and pearls. Liz could still remember making them; they had taken longer than usual because the rhinestones were so small and fiddly and she'd had to do most of the stitching at night, while Rosie was asleep, when the light wasn't so good.

She could recall taking the photo, too, and the sense of satisfaction when Rosie's friend had proudly worn the slides to school. Soon all the other girls had wanted some as well.

This unfamiliar discontent that she'd been feeling was surely a sign that she needed to change something. Reviving the business might give her the sense of purpose that seemed to be missing, and bringing in some cash would take a bit of pressure off Robert, too.

He'd never ask her to get a job; quite the opposite, in fact. When she was pregnant with Lowenna, he'd insisted she should feel free to devote herself to motherhood if that's what she wanted, knowing how hard she'd had to struggle when Rosie was little.

Thankfully, she knew that he'd also support her if she chose to return to work. She made a mental note to show him her appreciation more often.

After browsing through the other pages, she closed the website down and clicked on her email inbox. It was a while since she'd checked it, and she scrolled through the unread messages now, deleting all the nonsense.

To her dismay, there was one from a potential customer to which she'd never got around to replying. The woman from Norwich wanted two dolly bow bands for her daughters, Iris and Daisy, and wondered if Liz could decorate them with special flowers appropriate to their names.

The message was dated 15 December, nearly six months ago. Ashamed, Liz closed it quickly. The bands had probably been intended as Christmas presents. How rude the woman must have thought her! Well, it was too late to redeem herself now.

Once she'd tidied up her inbox, she started on the junk folder. It contained more than two thousand bits of spam, which only went to show how preoccupied she'd been with other things.

She was about to delete the lot without another glance when her attention was caught by a particular name about halfway down the page. Her stomach lurched for the second time in just a few hours and she had to reread the words to make sure that she hadn't dreamed them up.

Max Maier

Subject: Hello again

There it was in bold letters, clear as day. A coincidence, given the conversation with Esme earlier – or not?

Quickly clicking on his name, she realised that he'd used a different, business address, which would no doubt explain why the email had been rejected.

Her fingers trembled slightly as she scrolled down further, seeing his name crop up again and again. She counted seven messages, all unopened. The first one dated back to last November, soon after he'd left the village for the final time.

Just delete them, a little voice told her; he'd probably think that she'd done so already. But then another, louder voice drowned out the first and before she knew it, she was opening up that first email and starting to read.

Dear Liz,

You asked me not to contact you, but I couldn't bring myself to leave things like that between us.

I meant what I said about my feelings for you. It was hell going back to Munich and, trite as this may sound, I miss you.

Maybe I'm imagining it, but I sense you care a little for me too. If I'm wrong, I apologise. Just tell me the truth and I promise you'll never hear from me again.

If, however, you feel anything at all, please put my mind at rest and let me know how you are.

Can we at least be friends?

Max x

His words seemed to set off a chain reaction in her: joy followed by confusion, fear, anger, despair and finally, a giddy sense of recklessness.

Unable to contain her curiosity, she read his next email, and the next until she'd seen them all, the last one dated only two days ago.

Most of them said much the same thing – how he missed her, how he wished they could be friends, and so on, interspersed with a little information about his life in Munich.

He was very busy at work, it seemed, and the publishing company he owned had recently acquired three new titles. He and his daughter, Mila, had been on holiday to Dubai, where she'd learned to water-ski, and her mother, his ex-wife, was getting remarried.

As she imagined him going about his day, meeting up with family, perhaps having dinner with friends, Liz felt a pang of regret. Maybe he went on dates, too. He was handsome and single; she was certain that other women would have their eye on him.

One might take his fancy and help him forget about her, which would be a good thing, wouldn't it? So why did it feel like a stab in her heart?

Telling herself not to be silly, she read on until the final email, when the tone suddenly became more formal and less friendly. Max confirmed that he had changed his mind and would be coming to Tremarnock for the plaque unveiling after all.

I think it's important for me to honour my grandfather. It wouldn't feel right for me not to be there.

And in conclusion:

I'll be arriving late on the Thursday and leaving on the Saturday morning. I won't be staying in the village. As I haven't heard from you, I don't expect to see you but I thought it would be courteous to let you know.

I hope you're well and that you have all the joy in your life that you deserve.

Max.

There was no kiss this time.

When she'd finished, Liz sat back and took a deep breath. The last line had stung her, there was no doubt about it, though whether it was meant to or not, she wasn't sure.

Was her life filled with joy? Right now, not really. Hadn't she just been complaining to herself that she lacked purpose and, if she were honest, a bit of excitement, too?

But how much joy did she really deserve? How much did anyone, for that matter? Deserve was a strange, subjective word, suggesting worthiness and entitlement, rather narrow, old-fashioned concepts which didn't seem to fit with what she knew of Max's easy-going, liberal personality.

Perhaps that was the point and he was berating her for being self-limiting.

She certainly had plenty of blessings, but who was to say that there should be a cap on how much happiness one person was allowed? Wasn't life to be lived and enjoyed? Seize the day, and all that – so long as you didn't hurt anyone in the process.

And there was the rub. Although she'd only kissed Max once, she knew that Robert would be desperately hurt if he found out, as she would be if he'd done the same to her.

She could pretend all she liked that the kiss had been nothing more than a moment of madness, a flash of lust, fuelled by wine and soon extinguished. But she'd be kidding herself – and Robert – and she owed him more than that.

Perhaps she owed Max something, too, for having stolen a little piece of his heart, even if it could quite easily be replaced.

Sitting upright, she pulled back her shoulders and pressed reply.

Dear Max,

I'm sorry I haven't answered your emails. I've only just found them in my junk folder. I think they must have gone in there because you used a different address.

I'm glad you're well and I think it's good that you're coming to the ceremony. It would have made your grandfather very happy to watch you unveiling the new plaque.

Unfortunately, I'm going to be away that weekend so I won't see you. I hope it's a terrific event, I'm sure it will be, and I know the other villagers will look after you.

With very best wishes,

Liz

She thought about it for a moment before deciding to add a small x on the end; it looked too stark without. Then she pressed send.

A warm glow of virtue spread through her body, followed by relief. She'd done the right thing by Max and Robert, thank goodness, and could surely wipe the slate clean.

It was with a skip in her step that she went upstairs to check on Lowenna, who was just beginning to stir. And later, when she went into the back garden to bring in the washing, she even gave the seagulls, peering at her from the safety of her roof, a friendly, 'Good afternoon' as if they were old friends.

Chapter Eight

WHAT ON EARTH DID YOU wear for your first day at work as a snack bar manager? Chabela had absolutely no idea. She had plenty of suits and smart shirts, skirts and trousers for her university job, but she hadn't brought them with her and besides, they'd look totally out of place in a beach shack.

As she looked out of her bedroom window, she could see spots of rain pitter-pattering on the gravel drive at Polgarry Manor and the sky overhead was ominously grey.

This was not an auspicious start, she thought, taking off her pyjamas and delving into the chest of drawers for knickers, bra and socks. Not only was she pretty clueless about what she was supposed to be doing at the café, but she was also likely to get wet and cold in the process. Great.

For the first time since she'd formally accepted the job from Robert four days ago, she began to have doubts about her course of action.

Friends back home already thought she was mad for having come to Cornwall in the first place. If she wanted a holiday, they'd said, why not choose London, Paris or Rome instead? As a single woman, surely she'd be safer in a big city, and wouldn't it be more fun?

She'd argued them down, insisting that she wanted somewhere a bit wild and different and that she was used to solo travel. Right now, however, the thought of being in a bustling capital seemed extremely appealing. At least there would be plenty of indoor entertainment and warm, comfortable places in which to hide away from the rain.

As for working in a beach shack, those same friends would think that she'd gone quite mad.

It was Saturday morning, and she found it hard to believe that she'd only been here for just over a week. She'd already met Simon, found herself a job and Tremarnock was beginning to feel quite familiar, although of course she'd seen just a fraction of the area so far.

Rather quaintly, Simon had sent her a note in the post to say that he was 'on the case' with the Penhallow story and that he'd come back to her soon. In the meantime, could he be so bold as to suggest that she start trying to source the ingredients for the Mexican meal she was to cook, and to which he was greatly looking forward?

Some items, such as black beans and cilantro, may be hard to get hold of here in darkest Cornwall, although I think you will find them in the best supermarkets. If you have any problems, do let me know and I'll see what I can do.

She thought he must surely be joking – who 'sourced' ingredients for supper before a date had even been set, for God's sake? – but then she decided that he wasn't. From what she knew of him so far, he seemed like the sort of man who believed in doing things correctly. If a recipe specified black beans, any other colour simply wouldn't do. She made a mental note not to try to palm him off with improvisations.

Time was getting on and she was due to start work at ten a.m. Without more ado, she settled on some jeans, white trainers and a blue and white striped Breton top. Simple and comfortable. And she wore a red and white spotted scarf to keep her hair out of her face, tied at the front with a jaunty bow.

Checking herself in the mirror above her chest of drawers, she decided that the outfit had a good beach vibe, but that she'd need to take an extra sweater or two. Given the weather, wellington boots might be more suitable than trainers, but as she didn't have any, they were out of the question. In any case, the café would at least be dry inside, though not especially warm, given that the front serving hatch was permanently open to the four winds.

It hadn't seemed like such a problem when she'd met Robert there for another chat the day after she'd called in on him at the restaurant with Liz. Now, though, she was beginning to wonder whether she might need to invest in thermal underwear if she were to survive a whole British summer.

What would her students think if they saw her dishing out cups of tea and lobster rolls? She almost laughed out loud at the idea. And what of Alfonso?

A cloud seemed to settle just above her head, grey, damp and heavy with rain. She could imagine his look of incredulity, dismay and probably disillusionment, too. After all, she had once been his protégée, destined, he insisted, for great things.

The fact that she'd chosen instead to hide away in a village in the middle of nowhere, serving ice creams and French fries to tourists, would no doubt appal him. How the mighty had fallen!

She took a deep breath and gave herself a mental shake. What Alfonso might or might not think was no longer any business of hers; this was her life and she alone was mistress of her destiny.

She turned around to check her reflection in the mirror one more time before grabbing her bag and coat off the bed, marching swiftly to the door and closing it firmly behind her.

*

IT WAS ONLY A TEN minute drive from Tremarnock to Polrethen beach, which was situated at the bottom of a steep, winding, tree-lined lane. Robert had told Chabela not to use the gravel car park, which you had to pay for, but to pull up instead on an area of hard standing at the back of the café, which was especially reserved for members of staff.

The shack itself was a long, low, wooden hut atop a gentle mound, surrounded by sand and sea grass. Robert said that it had been in a terrible state when he bought it, with broken slats and windows and a gaping asphalt roof that let in the rain.

Now, it was painted white with pillar-box red window frames and a door to match. All across the front was a red and white striped canvas awning that would look very jolly in the sunshine. Today, however, it was flapping angrily in the breeze and seemed in danger of flying off its wooden supports.

Beneath it stood a patio heater, which was turned off, and some damp wooden tables and benches, optimistically laid with salt and pepper, ketchup, mayonnaise and glass jars of fresh flowers, weighed down with stones in the bottom to stop them blowing over.

It all looked a bit windswept and uninviting, but it was easy to see why Robert had chosen to buy here and also why he'd opted to retain the original structure rather than knock the building down and start all over again.

Even in this weather, there was a simple charm to the place, which seemed to blend into its surroundings so that you'd hardly know it was there. On a hot sunny day, when the crescent-shaped beach was filled with people, the awning would no doubt look like just another brightly coloured parasol or windbreak.

If you stood with your back to the wide, rectangular window-cum-serving hatch, all you could see ahead was sand interspersed with little rock pools and miles and miles of ocean.

What's more, apart from a small surfing school to the left and a breeze-block shop selling body boards, towels, buckets and spades and suchlike, there was scant other evidence of human activity and, most importantly, nowhere else to buy food. On hot, sunny days, Robert would no doubt have a large, potentially very hungry and thirsty captive audience. He was clearly no fool.

'Mornin'!'

Chabela spun around to find a round-faced young woman with rather extraordinary pink hair sticking her head out of the open hatch.

'I'm Loveday, Robert's niece,' she said in a strong Cornish accent, flashing a wide smile. 'You must be Marbella.'

'Er, Chabela,' Chabela said, leaning through the window to shake the girl's hand. 'It's really Isabela, but no one calls me that.'

The girl bit her lip and frowned.

'D'you mind if I just say Bella?' she replied at last. 'Cha... Chab... whatever you said, I'll never remember it. I'm not very good with languages.'

She seemed so friendly that Chabela couldn't take offence, and soon Loveday was joined at the hatch by a tall, thin teenage boy with dark skin, brown eyes and orange flesh plugs in his ears.

'This is Rafael. From Brazil,' she explained, giving Chabela a meaningful look as if to say 'you're foreign, he's foreign so you're bound to get on'. 'He's doing weekends with his girlfriend, Rosie, Robert's stepdaughter.'

'She's not my girlfriend, it's just a *thing*,' Rafael replied, quick as a flash, which seemed a little ungallant, especially as the girl in question had appeared now, too, and was eyeing Chabela up from behind a pair of thick, pale blue glasses.

'I'm certainly *not* your girlfriend,' Rosie said angrily, crossing her arms and glaring at the boy, who seemed to lose a few inches in height. 'In your dreams. I wouldn't go out with you if you begged me.'

He looked hurt all of a sudden and opened his mouth to respond, but Loveday interrupted.

'Quit arguing!' she said, raising her eyes heavenward. 'Bella's only just arrived. She'll think she's come to a madhouse!'

She wasn't far wrong and it was with some trepidation that Chabela accepted an invitation to enter the café to be shown what was what.

Now she understood that she was to be working with a pink-haired girl and two sulky teenagers, at least at weekends, she was beginning to have even greater doubts about the new job. But there was no going back now.

The café was small, clean and crammed with expensive equipment, all neatly stacked and stowed, like a ship's cabin. The walls were decorated with plain white, brick-shaped tiles and there were white cupboards and stainless steel worktops.

A serious-looking black coffee machine took pride of place beside the serving hatch, and there was also an industrial-sized oven, a microwave, a sandwich toaster and a handsome square pie cabinet.

There was absolutely no room for tables and chairs, which meant that everyone would have to sit outside.

'The bathroom's at the back,' Loveday explained, pointing to an open door leading into a narrow corridor. 'You can put your stuff in the cloakroom beside it. We always keep it locked during opening hours, so it'll be quite safe.

'By the way, that toilet's only for staff. Everyone else has to use the public one on the beach, by the surf shop.'

Now that she was indoors out of the wind and drizzle, Chabela was able to take a proper look at the girl, who was tall and big-boned, with an enormous bust that you couldn't ignore, encased in a tight white T-shirt.

She must have been in her early twenties and her pink hair was tied into two messy bunches, which stuck out at right angles and made her look like a naughty schoolgirl.

Her dark brown eyes were heavily rimmed with kohl and she had numerous piercings in each ear, a silver ring in her nose and a stud just above her top lip.

Despite all the metal, however, there was something rather endearing about her, as if she were trying very hard to look cool but couldn't quite mask the goofy, vulnerable kid within.

She tried several times to pull down her short, tight denim skirt but it kept riding up, and one of the silver buttons that went up the front was hanging by a thread. The top one, at the waist, wouldn't fasten, so she'd used a safety pin instead.

Glancing down, Chabela noticed that she was wearing a pair of very loud, white and pink trainers with enormous wedges that would make them quite impossible to exercise in. In fact, from Loveday's slightly wobbly and uncomfortable-looking stance, it was clear that they weren't particularly good for doing anything in, not even standing still.

'What time do we open?' she asked, glancing at a big brass ship's clock on the wall.

'Eleven,' Loveday replied, fiddling with one of her pink bunches. 'Only till the end of the month, though. After that it'll be nine, and we won't close till seven.'

Chabela was a bit shocked. '*Dios mío*, that's a long day! Robert didn't tell me that.'

Loveday raised one badly plucked black eyebrow. 'He's a sly one, my uncle. Comes across all nicey-nicey, like he wouldn't hurt a fly, but he's a slave-driver, really. He makes me work every other Sunday at the restaurant and it's going to be the same here.

'He knows I go drinking on Saturday night and on Sundays I've always got a hangover. Doesn't make any difference to him, though. He says if the other staff have to do it, I do too or it wouldn't be fair.'

It sounded reasonable enough to Chabela, but Loveday had gone quite red and the last thing Chabela wanted was to upset her on Day One.

'Oh dear,' she said instead. 'Well, I won't be doing much on Saturday nights, seeing as I don't know anyone. I can get here first if you like, and start setting up?'

Loveday's brown eyes sparkled and her sulky pout turned into a smile as wide as a watermelon.

'Would you? Cheers! Maybe don't mention it to my uncle though,' she went on, lowering her voice. 'Let's keep it just between us, eh?'

She went on to explain that there was to be a severely reduced menu today, as the place wasn't likely to be busy. Rafael was charged with food preparation, which basically consisted of fetching some preprepared home-made chips from the freezer, heating up the deep-fat fryer, warming a vat of lentil soup and fixing some sandwich ingredients.

There was also a range of freshly baked cakes, biscuits and scones, which Rosie set out on pretty red and white china plates under a glass display case on the serving counter.

On the back wall, clearly visible through the open window, was a giant blackboard on which someone had already written out the menu and prices in a bold italic hand. A smaller board to the right had a list of artisan ice creams in a variety of flavours including vanilla, pistachio, raspberry and pear.

Just thinking about ice cream today made Chabela shiver and she rather wished that she'd brought a woolly hat and scarf with her as well. The busiest job that day was likely to be making hot drinks, which sounded very appealing, but Loveday said that as she was a trained barista, she'd be in charge of the coffee machine while Rosie would make the mugs of tea and hot chocolate.

With Rafael on food, Chabela was to assume the role of general dogsbody, which would include keeping the kitchen clean, the floor swept, clearing the outside tables and helping with anything else that needed doing.

It could have been humiliating to have to take orders from Loveday, who was so much younger, but Chabela had made up her mind to swallow her pride and just get on with it. Café work was so far out of her range of normal experience that it felt like quite a novelty and in some ways more daunting than writing a five thousand word thesis on Mexican geopolitics.

Rosie fetched some clean red and white striped aprons from the cloakroom and once Chabela had hers on, she felt quite the part. Gazing out of the hatch, however, she wondered whether they would have any customers today at all.

The sky was still murky grey and the wind was playing games with the sand, whipping up the grains which hopped, leaped and scurried along before blending into flurries of shape-shifting fabric.

Sometimes, the gustiness would turn into a gale and the flurries would become continuous sheets, hurtling across the beach like a marauding army of dust. Surely no one in their right mind would venture here today?

'Can we have some music?' Chabela said suddenly, noticing a red, retro-style radio in the corner of the kitchen. 'Is that allowed?'

'Good idea!' Rafael glanced hopefully at Loveday, who nodded, and he swiftly removed his plastic sandwich-making gloves, wiped his hands on some kitchen roll and strode towards the radio.

Soon, country and western was blasting out and Chabela felt her spirits lift a little, even more so when an Elvis track came on and Rafael started doing a silly impersonation of him in the middle of the room, until Loveday shouted at him to stop.

'I hate Elvis,' she said angrily. 'I'd rather have silence.'

'How about some Mexican music instead?' Chabela suggested, and before anyone could object, she had fished the phone out of her pocket and found Rodrigo Amarante's '*Tuyo*'.

'*Soy el fuego que arde tu piel...*' came the familiar, haunting voice. I am the fire that burns your skin...

Immediately she was transported back to her apartment in Mexico City on one particular summer's evening. The balcony doors had been open, letting in the warm night air. She could hear the gentle hum of voices outside, the occasional car rumbling by. There was a sweet scent of jacaranda in the air and the sky had been filled with stars. She had danced to this very song with Alfonso, just the two of them, hand to hand, cheek to cheek, heart to beating heart.

A stab of regret and longing almost took her breath away and without thinking, she closed her eyes and found herself raising her arms high, swinging her head and swaying slightly as she sang along to the music. She'd always loved dancing.

'*Tú el aire que respiro yo...*' You're the air that I breathe...

A painful lump formed in her throat and a tear dribbled down the side of her nose and onto her chin, which she wiped away with the back of her hand.

'*Tuyo será, y tuyo será…*' Yours it will be, and yours it will be…

'Are you all right?'

The sound of Loveday's voice jolted her back to the present.

'Yes, absolutely,' Chabela said briskly, taking hold of the broom again, which she had been using to sweep sand off the floor. 'I love that song so much, especially the lyrics.'

She flashed Loveday a smile as if to say there's nothing whatever the matter – but she could tell by the girl's expression that she wasn't fooled.

'Have you always lived in Mexico?' she asked shyly, tipping her head to one side.

Chabela said that she had.

'Does your family live there, too?'

'I don't have much in the way of the family,' she replied truthfully. 'My parents divorced when I was very young and I barely knew my father. I don't have any brothers or sisters and my mother died a few years ago. I have a few cousins, but we're not close.'

'And…?' Loveday swallowed. Chabela could guess what she was thinking but didn't quite dare to ask.

'I'm not married,' she said quickly, to put the girl out of her misery. 'And I don't have children.'

'Oh!'

Loveday looked stricken. If Chabela had told her that she had terminal cancer, it wouldn't have been more of a tragedy. Her eyes even started to fill up.

'I'm... I'm so sorry...' she stuttered, but Chabela interrupted her flow.

'I'm married to my work, to be honest with you.' She flashed a wide smile. 'And I never really wanted children, I'm not the maternal type.'

This seemed to reassure Loveday, whose compassion quickly morphed into incredulity.

'Really? I never met anyone before who didn't want kids. My mate Lauren's got two and she's only nineteen! I think I'll wait till I'm quite a bit older, though,' she added sensibly. 'Maybe twenty-one. I don't really want to be a young mum. I want to experience life first.'

Rafael had his back turned to the women but he'd obviously been listening in.

'My mum has eight kids,' he announced suddenly. 'And she was one of fourteen. Women have to start young if they want that many.'

He had a slight Cornish burr, mixed in with Brazilian Portuguese, which made it quite hard for Chabela to understand.

'I'm definitely not having fourteen kids!' Loveday declared and Rosie looked appalled.

'Me neither. I only want two – a boy and a girl.'

She glanced at Rafael, who remained resolutely facing the other way.

'I don't want any, not till I'm at least twenty-six anyway.'

'Positively middle-aged,' Chabela said with a wry smile, but the joke went unnoticed. She wondered what these three must make of her, a woman of thirty-nine. Perhaps they imagined that she'd come to Cornwall to retire.

For over an hour, the beach remained deserted and for a while the rain drove down so hard that Chabela wondered if they'd be washed away.

She felt a bit like Noah on his ark, with no one for company save a few strange fellow human creatures, clinging to her and each other for comfort, trying hard to keep up their spirits by jigging to the music which was now turned up full blast to drown out the deluge.

She was bent double, wiggling her hips to the beat as she peered under the fridge for a teaspoon that she'd dropped, when she heard a deep voice behind her.

'Any chance of a cuppa?'

Ay caramba! Her cheeks shot into flame. She'd had no idea that anyone was there.

Rising quickly, she turned around and saw a tall, hefty man standing at the hatch, wearing a green waxed jacket and wide-brimmed hat that was literally dripping wet. Twisting rivulets were slipping and sliding onto the brim before splashing off the edge like water from a garden sprinkler.

It was quite difficult to make out any features, because the hat came down so low, but you couldn't miss the man's large, bushy grey beard and sideburns that trailed down his cheeks like damp seaweed.

There was something strangely familiar about them and Chabela racked her brains to remember why. Then it dawned on her: wasn't he the man who ran the gift shop on the corner of South Street, with whom she'd chatted briefly on her second day in the village? Simon's friend. She was pretty certain that they were one and the same.

He seemed to recognise her, too, and politely removed his soaking hat to unveil an impressive pair of shaggy eyebrows, complete with ill-disciplined strays that shot out at right angles like daddy-long-legs.

'Haven't we met before?' he said in what sounded like a rather awkward attempt at nonchalance. 'I believe I failed to sell you one of my postcards.' This was accompanied by an ironic smile.

Chabela smoothed down her apron and smiled back.

'Actually, I know who you are,' he said quickly, which rather undermined his earlier comments. 'Simon Hosking told me about your mission and I'm looking into it for you.'

'How kind of you!' she replied, walking swiftly over to the radio to turn down the volume. For some reason the others hadn't seemed to notice that you could hardly hear the stranger speak. 'That's better.'

Rick, as she now knew him to be, looked relieved and started to talk a little bit about his interest in amateur local history.

'I collect old books on the subject – mostly out of print. I must have hundreds. I run a local history group on a Thursday evening at the Methodist church hall.

Why don't you come along to the next one? A lady called Florence is giving a talk on sanitation through the ages. She's done a good deal of research. It should be very interesting. It's called "Living with the smell" and it starts at seven thirty. The admission fee is two pounds, but I'm happy to waive that as you'll be a first-timer.'

Chabela was aware of a volley of snorts coming from somewhere nearby and, turning to look, she unintentionally caught Rafael's eye. The bad boy was shaking with laughter.

She flashed him a stern look and he bowed his head and covered his mouth with a hand, but his shoulders were still quivering and to her dismay, her own started to wobble, too.

'That sounds fascinating,' she said to Rick, digging her nails hard into the palms of her hands. 'What can I get you? Tea? Coffee? A nice piece of cake, perhaps?'

For some reason this seemed to amuse Rafael even more, and he tried to involve Rosie by calling to her on the opposite side of the kitchen and asking if she fancied going to the smells talk, too.

Luckily, Chabela didn't hear the reply because Rick asked for two cappuccinos to take away, one with chocolate sprinkles and one without.

It soon became clear why, when he was joined by a very tall middle-aged lady in a long, billowing, bright yellow waterproof jacket like a traditional fisherman's mac, and a matching sou'wester hat.

'Here you are! I thought you were never coming back,' she complained, grabbing him proprietorially by the arm. 'I've been waiting in the car for ages.'

Loveday, who was standing by the coffee machine, leaned over and whispered rather loudly in Chabela's ear.

'Uh-oh, that's Audrey, the nosy old cow. She and Rick have known each other for ever. They're just friends, though. He wouldn't go out with her. No one would.'

If Audrey heard, she pretended not to, instead leaning forward and peering closely at Chabela, eyeing her up and down. It made her feel quite uncomfortable, and even more so when the older woman gave a disconcerting sniff and turned away, as if she'd seen quite enough, thank you very much.

'Um, would you like anything else?' Chabela asked Rick, as he handed her some coins. After checking the amount, she gave them to Rosie, who put them in the till, because Chabela wasn't very good at operating it yet.

Rick shook his head and picked up the drinks, in eco-friendly disposable cups. Audrey had now walked off and he seemed rather sorry to have to follow.

'Let me know about the talk,' he said to Chabela. 'Just pop into my shop anytime and I'll reserve you a ticket.'

He seemed very keen; perhaps he was low on numbers. She hadn't the heart to turn him down.

'I'll do that,' she promised, ignoring Rafael's further snort of derision. 'And thanks again for looking into the Penhallow family history.'

THE DAY SEEMED TO GO quite quickly after that, despite a distinct lack of customers. Loveday's boyfriend, Jesse, dropped by with a fresh stock of coffee beans, bread for the freezer and suchlike, and when he found them all dancing, he joined in.

The atmosphere was so jolly that he didn't want to leave, but he had to get back to A Winkle in Time or he said Robert would 'blow his top'.

'It's much more fun here,' he grumbled, running a hand through his blond corkscrew curls and flashing Chabela a winning smile. 'Must be the Mexican influence.'

Jesse could be a bit of a flirt.

Loveday frowned. She could be very jealous, but she soon melted when he gave her a big snog by way of goodbye.

Just before closing time, when the rain had finally stopped and patches of watery blue sky were peeping through the clouds, Chabela heard her phone ping.

After wiping her hands on a tea towel, she checked her messages and saw that she had one from Simon.

Made a bit of progress on the Penhallow front. Would
you be free to pop over tomorrow at 6.p.m.? All best.

There was no mention of the Mexican meal; perhaps
he'd gone off the idea. It wouldn't surprise her.

In any case, she was keen to know what he'd found
out and if she didn't go tomorrow, which was Sunday,
her visit might have to be delayed until the following
weekend. She typed back in her politest English.

I'm most grateful. Thank you. I have a new job and I'll
come straight from work.

For some reason, there was a slight fluttering in her
stomach, which she put down to curiosity about his
findings. Then she remembered that she was really only
mildly interested in her family tree anyway, and the
butterflies quickly vanished.

Chapter Nine

THE LOBSTER POT PUB on Tremarnock's seafront was always full on Saturday evenings, and tonight was no exception; in fact Liz could hardly get through the door.

She could see Barbara, the landlady, behind the bar, chatting with one of the local fishermen who was bending forwards so that his nose was practically in her cleavage. Whether this was deliberate or not wasn't clear, but neither seemed uncomfortable with the situation.

Barbara, a widow in her fifties, ran an extremely successful business and was also a great organiser. When it came to raising funds for the village hall, for example, or organising a search party for a missing dog or person, she was your woman.

With her halo of dark-blonde hair, her tight tops, high heels, pillowy bosom and friendly, open demeanour, it was easy to see why she was so popular with the local men of a certain age. As far as anyone knew, however, she'd not dated a single one since her husband had died.

'I'm like a swan, I mated for life,' she was once overheard saying to a fellow who had taken to propping up the bar on the nights when he knew that she'd be there. 'I love men, but Gareth was the only chap for me.'

That didn't stop her taking more than a passing interest in the lives of her customers, however, who flocked to her for advice about all sorts of issues, ranging from relationship worries to work and even health problems.

She would always lend a friendly ear and offer advice, too, without ever overstepping the mark. No wonder her tills were always ringing. Spending time in her pub was like rest, relaxation and therapy all rolled into one.

As she scanned the room, Liz saw quite a lot of people she didn't recognise. Some might be tourists, although it was still a bit early in the season, while others had probably caught the ferry across from Plymouth.

Tremarnock was popular with Plymothians, as well as folk from the surrounding towns and villages, because of its cobbled streets, quaint architecture and, of course, its proximity to the sea.

It had a certain holiday feel at weekends, even in the depths of winter, and the Lobster Pot was famous for its lively atmosphere, local beers, fine wines and warm welcomes.

It wasn't the only pub, of course. The Hole in the Wall, around the corner, was also popular but catered mainly for teens and twenty-somethings, who flocked to its live music nights. Meanwhile, the Victory Inn on Towan Road was considered rather staid, being mostly frequented by elderly pensioners.

Nudging her way through the bodies, Liz finally made it to the far side of the pub, near the fireplace. In winter there was always a roaring blaze, but the grate was empty now.

Sitting on a tall wooden bench, with his back pressed to the wall, she soon spotted the familiar, whiskery face of Rick, in a bright pink shirt, open wide and displaying quite a lot of curly grey chest hair.

He was nursing a pint of warm ale, his large, meaty hands cupped around his three-quarters empty glass almost reverentially. Beside him sat Jean the childminder, and opposite were Audrey and Jean's husband, Tom. Liz would know them anywhere – even by the backs of their heads.

Her heart sank ever so slightly, because she hadn't realised that Audrey would be present. She should have guessed. Rick had only recently split from his latest girlfriend and was somewhat bereft. He didn't like being single and, indeed, it was pretty unusual. An avid online dater, he generally enjoyed a great deal of success with the more mature ladies of the region and was rarely without someone on his arm.

Now, however, he was having to endure a hiatus and Audrey, whom he'd known since childhood, had stepped into the breach. No one doubted that their relationship was purely platonic and they seemed to enjoy a love-hate sort of bond. Each appeared to find the other intensely irritating, yet somehow they couldn't ever be apart for long.

Liz had hoped to stay for just one or two drinks before hurrying back to collect Lowenna, who was at Tabitha's house, playing with her son, Oscar. Liz had only agreed to come here at all because Jean had pressed her, insisting that Rick needed company, but this clearly wasn't the case tonight.

'Liz!' he cried, catching sight of her and rising abruptly, almost knocking over the table in his enthusiasm. 'What can I get you?'

'My round,' she replied, noticing that Jean's glass was almost empty, as was his. 'Same again?'

Battling her way to the bar and back took ages, and when Liz finally sat down, Jean was halfway through a long and tedious story about her daughter's mother-in-law's niece. It was quite hard to follow, and Liz found herself zoning out for a while, listening to the buzz of voices, the clink of glasses and the occasional scrape of chairs on the wooden floor.

She was brought back to the present by a sharp dig in the ribs from Audrey.

'Well?' the older woman said bossily, clearly enjoying Liz's evident confusion. 'What do you think?'

'Er, about what?' Liz felt her cheeks heat up. 'Sorry, I was miles away.'

'About the plaque ceremony,' said Audrey with exasperation, as if she were speaking to a naughty, inattentive pupil. 'Jean thinks we should get the local children to perform something for Max at the reception afterwards, a poem or something. Any ideas?'

Liz racked her brains and remembered how Max enjoyed music. 'What about singing some sea shanties?' she said at last. 'Things like "Trelawny" and "Robbers Retreat"? It wouldn't take the kids long to learn. They probably know most of the lyrics already.'

Everyone thought this was a marvellous idea, even Audrey, who generally vetoed any suggestions that she hadn't made herself.

'They'll have to start rehearsing pronto,' Rick commented. 'They've only got a couple of weeks.'

'Alex can accompany them on the accordion,' Tom suggested. 'I'm sure Ruby won't mind giving up a few hours to teach them the tunes.' Alex was the head chef at A Winkle in Time while Ruby, a grandmother in her sixties, was a competent pianist.

'You've got a lovely singing voice, Liz.' All eyes turned to Jean, in a lilac sweater decorated with little yellow flowers. 'You can be choir mistress.'

Liz's heart beat a little faster. 'Actually, I can't—' she started to say, but Jean wasn't listening.

'I'll come along, too,' she said. 'I can keep the kiddies in order.'

Tom suggested that the children should all wear blue and white, like sailors, and maybe someone could search online for some cheap nautical hats. 'I can see Lowenna in a cute little doughboy cap.'

If Liz had had her wits about her, she'd have interrupted him right there to explain that she and the girls were away that weekend and wouldn't be able to attend the ceremony at all.

For some reason, however, she was struck dumb, and before she knew it, she had been appointed the official director of singing, to be accompanied on the piano and accordion by Ruby and Alex, while Jean was tasked with contacting the local mums to invite their children to take part.

By the time they'd all finished discussing their favourite sea shanties and Rick had treated them to a few lines of each in his booming baritone, the whole pub, it seemed, was in on the idea and Liz hadn't the courage to back out.

'Will you ask Ruby if we can rehearse at her house?' Jean asked, and Liz nodded meekly, cursing herself for being so weak.

All her good intentions, it seemed, had come to nothing and whether she liked it or not, she would be seeing Max again after all.

Her stomach flip-flopped at the prospect, but she told herself not to worry. His visit would be brief and for most of the time he'd be surrounded by people, both at the ceremony and the reception afterwards. There'd be no opportunity for them to speak alone and as soon as the day was over, she could go home and put him out of her mind.

The subject moved on after that to other forthcoming village events, including the annual summer barbecue at Polgarry Manor. Tom mentioned 'the Mexican lady' who'd stopped to admire his garden, at which Rick's ears pricked up and he told them that he was helping to research her family tree.

He made it sound rather as if he were in charge of the whole project and didn't refer to Simon Hosking once.

'With a surname like Penhallow she's got to be part Cornish,' Rick commented. 'The question is, does she come from the Penhallows of Tremarnock, or from another branch of the family?'

Liz remarked that Chabela was working at the Secret Shack for the summer, not realising that Rick and Audrey had been there earlier in the day.

'Be careful,' Audrey said suddenly. 'She's trouble.'

Liz raised her eyebrows. 'Whatever do you mean?'

'I reckon she's a man-eater,' the older woman added darkly. 'A flirt. Most likely a gold-digger, too.'

'You can't say that!' Jean spluttered. 'You don't even know her!'

Liz agreed. 'She's only been in the village a week!'

But Audrey was having none of it.

'Check out the way she dresses. And how she holds herself. She thinks she's the Queen of Sheba, craves male attention – can't get enough of it. I've met her type before.'

She shot a look at Rick, who was too busy twiddling his moustache to notice and seemed lost in thought.

'She's a good-looking woman,' he said at last, with a faraway look in his eyes.

'And she knows it!' Audrey barked. 'She was even flirting with Rafael. Disgusting! He's young enough to be her son!'

Tom said he didn't believe it; Chabela was very pleasant and not at all coquettish with him.

'You see!' Audrey cried triumphantly, 'That's exactly what I mean! She makes you think she's all sweet and nice and then, bam, she's trapped you in her web and there's no getting out.'

'You only saw her briefly!' Rick sounded wistful, as if he'd rather like to be caught in Chabela's silken strands. 'How can you possibly judge a person in that time?'

'It was long enough,' Audrey replied, tapping the side of her nose mysteriously. 'She's a Jezebel, mark my words. The wives round here had better watch out.'

Later that night, Liz strolled to Tabitha's house to collect Lowenna, leaving the others still drinking in the pub. It had stopped drizzling but there was a chilly wind and as she headed uphill, she could hear the waves thrashing against the sea wall, dragging the pebbles back down the beach as they receded.

Her footsteps clattered on the cobbles and her shadow made strange shapes in the lamplight. At one point, a white cat darted across her path, making her jump, and she wrapped her coat more tightly around her.

It had been wrong of Audrey, she reflected, to speak of Chabela in that way. Liz tried her best to think well of people and not jump to hasty conclusions, but in Audrey's book, it seemed, you were guilty until proven innocent.

Even so, Liz couldn't help thinking that it was a good job Chabela would be working such long hours in the café; she didn't like to think of a dangerous female let loose in Tremarnock, although from the look on Rick's face, he for one would be more than delighted to offer himself up as prey.

And as for Max, well, he was a problem for another day. Tonight, Robert had promised to come home in good time, leaving Alex and Jesse to close the restaurant.

A Saturday night in with her husband was a rare treat for Liz. They'd probably open a bottle of wine and snuggle on the sofa in front of a film.

He'd be tired, no doubt, but hopefully he'd be able to stay awake for a couple of hours at least to give her his undivided attention. She intended to make the most of it – and him.

*

CHABELA ARRIVED EARLY AT THE Secret Shack the following morning, which was just as well because Loveday didn't roll up until nearly eleven o'clock and Rafael wasn't much before her.

Rosie was more punctual but still, it fell to Chabela to open up, turn on the lights, update the menu board and heat the deep-fat fryer. When Rafael finally arrived, Rosie had made the sandwiches and Chabela was serving a group of customers who were out for a Sunday morning walk with dogs and children.

She might have been a quick learner but still managed to get in a flap when one of the women walkers asked for a double macchiato with soya milk. She couldn't remember whether to pour the foamed milk directly on top of the espresso or whether to spoon it in and stir. Fortunately, Rafael came to the rescue.

'I'll do it,' he said, removing his black jeans jacket and throwing it in a cavalier fashion on the counter behind.

His skin was a slightly strange putty colour and an angry red spot had sprung up on his unshaven chin. There were also dark circles under his eyes, and his hair, which had yesterday been styled into a dashing Mohican quiff, was looking distinctly flat.

'Did you have a good night?' Chabela asked wryly.

He nodded rather too vigorously and his face contorted in pain.

'Do you have a headache pill?' he called hopefully to Rosie, who scowled back.

'Plonker! I bet you were drunk as a skunk last night, weren't you? You should have come to the cinema with me instead.'

Her sharp tone made him wince again and he lowered his eyes and focused on pouring the coffee. At that moment, Liz glanced out of the hatch and saw a dishevelled Loveday walking gingerly across the sand towards her.

Yesterday's rain and wind had given way to sunshine and blue skies and it was really quite warm. Even so, Loveday was wrapped in a swishy black coat that nearly reached her ankles, her arms hugged around her as if for protection.

She was wearing the same chunky platform trainers as yesterday, and her pink hair was scraped into a ponytail perched on top of her head. She was frowning hard and even from several metres away, Chabela could see that she hadn't washed her face properly. Last night's black kohl and mascara were smudged around her eyes and her thick white foundation was streaked.

'*Vengaaaa!*' Chabela muttered to herself in exasperation. 'Oh come *on!*'

To have to suffer one co-worker with a crippling hangover was bad enough, but *two* simultaneously? This was going to be a long day.

By the time she set off for Simon's cottage in the car, her legs were aching from standing for so long and really all she wanted was to return to the manor for a long, hot bath.

Once she'd left Loveday and Rafael behind, however, she started to feel better and decided that it had mainly been their sallow faces and gloomy moods that had dragged her down.

After leaving her hired Polo in the car park at the top of South Street, she strolled towards the steep, well-hidden set of steps that she'd taken previously. This time, the walk seemed less far and before she knew it, she was opening the garden gate at Kittiwake and rapping loudly on the front door with the brass knocker shaped like a scallop shell.

It took Simon a little while to answer and when he finally appeared, she was disconcerted to find him looking surprised and, frankly, not especially pleased to see her.

'Oh!' he said, scratching his head, shrugging one shoulder and jerking his chin in the opposite direction, all at the same time. 'It's you!'

He was in an old brown sweater with a couple of large moth holes on the front, creased beige trousers and well-worn tartan slippers. His thick tortoiseshell glasses were smudged and his chin was covered in dark stubble.

Chabela guessed that he must have been reading or doing other close work because behind the spectacles his eyes seemed to have disappeared into the sockets and his black pupils had shrunk to pinpricks.

'Sorry, am I early?' she asked, unsettled by the less than ecstatic reception.

Simon was standing very stiff and upright, like a Buckingham Palace guard, but then all of a sudden a look of recognition crossed his features, his shoulders relaxed and the frown melted away.

'Of course! I invited you!' he exclaimed, as if it were a revelation, and he stepped back and motioned for her to go inside. 'I've been marking Year 11 French homework. I'd completely forgotten about our arrangement.'

Chabela offered to return at a more convenient time, but he wouldn't hear of it, instead leading her into his kitchen at the back of the cottage. There, he filled the kettle and popped some teabags into a large green ceramic teapot.

He didn't ask her to sit down but she did so anyway, pulling out a chair and settling at the table, which was strewn with red exercise books, some in neat piles while others were open and covered with red pen marks.

'That's Rafael Oliveira's,' Simon commented, noticing her gaze falling on one particularly battered book that seemed to have a muddy footprint on the open page. There were so many red corrections that the original handwriting was scarcely legible.

She started. 'Rafael? I know him! I was working with him today!'

When she explained about his job at the café, Simon clicked his tongue.

'If he spent a bit more time studying instead of earning beer money, he wouldn't get so many detentions. Look at the state of that homework. It's a travesty!'

Simon's face had turned quite red and he sounded so outraged that Chabela wanted to laugh, but managed not to. She decided that she wouldn't mention Rafael's hangover, not wishing to get him into any more trouble.

Once Simon had made the tea, she took her mug into his front room while he went to fetch something from next door, returning shortly after with a large, dark blue, hardback notebook. Then he sat down opposite her, as before, and started scanning silently through the first few pages.

Chabela sipped her tea and tried to wait patiently, hoping that he wouldn't notice her leg jiggling up and down with frustration. It was a relief when he finally looked up and cleared his throat.

'I spoke to Rick yesterday,' he said ponderously. 'As I suspected, he was very helpful. He gave me the name of a woman in Redruth, who runs the Cornish-Mexican Society. That sounds grander than it really is. In fact it's just her and a few distant relatives of miners who emigrated from Cornwall to Hidalgo in the nineteenth century.

'The society was founded some years ago by this woman's father, whose relative had lived for a period in Real del Monte. The father wanted to keep alive the connection between the two mining communities, here and in Mexico. When he died, his daughter took up the baton.'

Simon went on to explain that he had managed to contact the Redruth woman and by a tremendous stroke of good luck, it turned out that her father had heard of Rodrigo Penhallow from Mexico. They had even shared some correspondence in the 1990s.

Chabela felt her pulse quickening because, of course, Rodrigo was the name of her grandfather on her father's side. She had a million questions but Simon was on a roll and she didn't want to interrupt.

'This Redruth woman – Yvonne, her name is,' he continued. 'She sounds quite elderly but she's all there, mentally I mean. Anyway, she went off and dug out a letter from Rodrigo. It transpires that he was the grandson of one James Penhallow, originally of Tremarnock, who emigrated to Real del Monte in 1854 and made a fortune in mining.'

'Goodness!' Chabela's eyes were like dinner plates. 'I can't believe it!'

Simon looked up briefly and nodded before consulting his notes once more.

'This much we now know,' he went on seriously. 'James Penhallow married a Mexican girl called Jacinta and they had two children, Helen and James Junior, born in 1865. When the children were still quite young, tragedy struck. James Senior was accompanying a wagon train carrying silver bars to Mexico City when he was set upon by a large group of bandits and killed.

'That's terrible!' Chabela, who was beginning to feel quite invested in the story, felt a catch in her throat.

Simon nodded again. 'And there's more.'

Not long after James Senior's death, he said, Jacinta, now a wealthy woman, had married a Mexican called Santiago Gonzalez. According to Rodrigo, Gonzalez had insisted that from then on, his stepchildren be known as Iliana and Jaime Gonzalez, the Spanish versions of their forenames.

'Gonzalez forbade them or their mother from mentioning James Senior or Cornwall ever again. It was only after their stepfather died that the children reverted to their original surname of Penhallow.'

'He sounds mean,' Chabela said darkly, thinking about the selfish way her own mother had behaved when she had divorced Chabela's papa, preventing any contact between father and daughter.

'I suspect he wasn't very kind,' Simon agreed. 'Rodrigo said that the marriage wasn't happy. I don't know what happened to Jacinta, but James Junior went on to have three children, one of whom was Rodrigo...'

Chabela let out a squeak; she couldn't help it. She could sense the net closing in and her pulse started to race again.

'And Rodrigo had a son?' she said breathlessly.

Simon looked pleased with himself. 'Indeed he did, called Hector. And Hector, as we know, married a woman called Catalina and they had a daughter – Isabela.' His eyes twinkled as he spoke the name.

'Rodrigo said it was a source of regret that when Hector and Catalina separated, she forbade him from having any contact with Isabela, or Chabela, as she was known. Rodrigo only met his granddaughter one time, just after she was born.'

This news, coming all at once, so surprised and moved Chabela that for a moment she was speechless. It felt to her like a grand reunion, filled with joy but also tinged with regret and sadness for the time lost. Perhaps this was what adopted children experienced when they finally met up with their birth mothers. It felt a bit like coming home.

All through childhood, through her whole life, really, she'd felt alone, with no father or paternal grandparents, no siblings and precious little contact even with her mother's side of the family.

By hook or by crook she'd carved out a good existence for herself, but there had always been something lacking, some space in her soul that nothing and no one seemed able to fill, not even Alfonso.

Although she'd never meet Rodrigo, James Junior or any of these other ancestors, still, she felt that already they provided some insight into who she was and why.

Now that her appetite was truly whetted, she wanted to know more.

'I can't believe Yvonne has all this information about my family that I never even knew existed.'

All of a sudden, tears welled up and before she knew it, they were dribbling down her cheeks. Soon, the dribble turned into a deluge. It was as if all the sadness, isolation and longing that she'd kept buried for so long had come rushing to the surface and nothing and no one could keep it down any longer.

Her shoulders shook and she was so racked with sobs that she didn't even notice Simon get up and move over to her side of the room, where he stood like a spare part, staring at her in dismay and confusion.

So lost in sorrow was she that it was only when she felt a tentative pat on her shoulder and a desperate voice whispering, 'There, there,' that she remembered where she was.

'I'm sorry,' she managed to blurt, in between the tears. 'I don't know why it's upset me so much.'

Opening her swollen eyes just a little, she noticed Simon's feet, in tartan slippers, shuffling this way and that, as if he didn't know what to do with them.

'Do you have a hankie?' she managed to ask at last, wiping her wet nose with the back of a hand. It didn't do any good, because the weeping wouldn't stop.

She was vaguely aware of the slippers vanishing and when they reappeared, a large box of man-size tissues was thrust onto her lap. Grabbing a wodge, she blew her nose unceremoniously.

'Sorry,' she said again, managing to peer up at her host at last. Her face burned as if she'd been stung by nettles and she could barely see out of her sore eyes.

All she could tell was that he was excruciatingly uncomfortable, hovering over her anxiously and looking for all the world as if he'd rather be anywhere but here.

'Can I get you a drink – whisky or something?' he asked desperately. He looked tremendously relieved when she nodded.

Alcohol seemed to do the trick because after taking a few sips, she felt slightly better and, little by little, the crying abated.

As she sat there, huddling over her glass and contemplating what had just happened, she felt exposed. It was as if she'd lost several layers of skin after baring her soul to this relative stranger.

For the first time, he settled next to her, perching uncomfortably on the edge of the sofa as if he might need to bolt at any minute. She thought that he might start to probe a little, to try to find out what lay behind her outpouring of seemingly disproportionate distress – that's what she would have done – but he didn't.

Instead, he fiddled with the cuff of his sweater, pulling at a loose thread, and she wondered idly if the whole garment might start to unravel, which would be strangely symbolic, somehow.

THE GIRL WHO CAME HOME TO CORNWALL

'Um, do you feel better?' he asked hopefully after a few moments and she said she did, more to put him out of his misery than because it was the truth. Emotional literacy clearly wasn't his forte.

'Look at the sunset!' he said suddenly, and she turned and followed his gaze out of the window that faced the ocean.

She almost gasped, because in the time that she'd been weeping, the sky had turned from pale blue, studded with clouds, to an orangey red so bright that it almost hurt her eyes.

'Wow!' Without thinking, she rose and walked over to the window, aware that he was following close behind. It was as if they were both being pulled by an invisible force.

Beyond the garden, the cliff edge and the darkening beach, it was hard to tell where the sky ended and the water began. There was a kaleidoscope of colour, like a tangerine dream, that seemed to hit all the senses and leave her reeling.

'This is what it's all about,' he said quietly, 'don't you think?'

'What do you mean?' She was puzzled.

'I mean, the past is gone and who knows what the future holds? All we have is this moment, right now. Enjoy it.'

Something in his words resonated with her. Taking a deep breath, she let her eyes, her whole body melt into the scene and the warmth and beauty of the blood reds, golds and burned oranges seemed to touch her soul.

For a few blissful minutes she felt fully connected to the earth below her feet, the air around and the sky above. Alfonso seemed like nothing but a distant irrelevance.

When the colours finally started to fade and darkness encroached, she turned back towards the room and watched Simon move swiftly away. Shadows fell over the walls and furniture and as he stood by the door, waiting for her, she shivered suddenly, aware only of a feeling that it was time to go but that she didn't want to leave.

'Thank you for your help,' she said, picking up her jacket and her bag and trailing behind him down the hallway.

For some reason, she thought that this might be it; that he'd done all he could for her.

'I still owe you a meal,' she said, scrabbling around for an excuse to see him again and kicking herself inwardly for sounding a bit desperate.

'You do.'

To her relief, when she looked at him his eyes were troubled but gentle.

'I'll have a think about where we go from here with our Penhallow investigation.'

She was glad about the 'we'; it reassured her.

He offered to walk with her across the cliff to the steps that led into the village, at least, but she didn't need it, now; she was all right on her own.

When he opened the garden gate for her, he hesitated for a moment and she wondered if, this time, he would kiss her on the cheek. But he shook her hand instead and strode back into the house so fast that anyone watching might have thought that he couldn't wait to say goodbye.

Chapter Ten

Liz stood with her foot on the bottom of the extension ladder while her husband started to climb. Their cottage wasn't very tall, which was just as well considering Robert's aversion to heights; he'd managed to conceal it from most people, but Liz knew the truth.

'Well done, not much further,' she said encouragingly, as he gripped the sides of the ladder so hard that his knuckles turned white. Around his waist was a belt to which he'd attached a black pistol.

It was actually a BB gun, firing plastic pellets, but it looked like the real deal. It had been purchased especially, the aim of the mission being to scare, not kill.

'I feel like I'm scaling Everest,' Robert moaned, stopping for a moment to take a few deep breaths. Then, 'Shit!'

He leaned back suddenly, causing the ladder to wobble, and Liz's heart flew into her mouth.

'What's happened?' she started to cry, but the question died on her lips because a big fat gull appeared from nowhere and swooped almost across his path, its wings spread wide. From where Liz was standing, it looked positively prehistoric, like a feathered pterodactyl complete with razor sharp talons.

While it was diving, its friends, invisible behind the chimney pot, launched into a cacophonous screeching. Robert ducked, then started to descend rather more quickly than he'd managed to go up.

'Jesus!' Liz said, once he'd safely reached the bottom. Her heart was beating loudly in her chest. 'That was scary. How many of them do you think there are?'

Robert, who'd turned quite pale, narrowed his eyes and glanced up.

'No idea. Quite a lot. The buggers saw me coming and prepared to attack, I know they did.'

Just as he spoke, another bird, high above, let out a squawk and a gooey splat landed on the toe of his boot, followed by a second, a few feet from Liz's shoe.

'Right, that's it!' Robert was incandescent. 'This is war!'

He marched back into the cottage, leaving Liz alone for a few moments, and reappeared in a bright yellow hard hat, which he'd bought for safety reasons when the Secret Shack was being ripped apart and renovated.

On his hands were some strong leather gloves and he'd also found his thick, green, military-style jacket.

All he needed was some camouflage face paint and he'd be ready for combat.

'Are you sure you want to go up again?' Liz asked anxiously, because she knew that this was his worst kind of nightmare. 'Maybe we should call the council? They might frighten them off for us instead?'

Her words fell on deaf ears, however, and Robert shook his head.

'I'm angry now,' he muttered, pulling back his shoulders and jutting out his chin. 'I'll show them who's boss.'

His bravado didn't fool her for a second.

'Be careful,' she begged, as he started to ascend once more, this time with the BB gun wedged in his jacket pocket. 'I'm too young to be a widow.'

A Winkle in Time was closed on Mondays, which meant that, technically, Robert was off duty. In the early days of marriage, he'd kept this time free for Liz. She'd treasured their walks along the cliffs, pub lunches and lazy afternoons, while Lowenna napped and before Rosie returned from school.

Sometimes they'd draw the curtains and hop into bed themselves, giggling like naughty children as they dived under the covers. Now, though, Robert usually went over to the Secret Shack on Mondays or did his paperwork. At least he left Bag End a little later than normal, though, which was why he'd picked today for Operation Seagull.

Up he went, rung by metal rung, while Liz looked on in trepidation. When he finally reached the last few steps, he was able to rest his knees on the edge of the guttering and lean across the slates, which had been warmed by the sun.

Craning his neck in the direction of the chimney pot, he gave a shout.

'I can see it!' He turned his head slowly towards Liz and called again, 'There's a nest! It's big!'

'Any eggs yet?' she shouted back.

'No!' came the reply.

That was one good thing, anyway. Liz didn't like to think of upsetting any offspring, hatched or not. She'd rather shoo the prospective parents off before they could reproduce.

She wanted to know how many gulls Robert could see, but her yells were drowned out by another volley of screeches, which seemed to go on and on. When they finally died down, she tried again.

'Can you see the husband and wife? It sounds like they've got the whole family up there – uncles and aunts and everything!'

Robert didn't respond, but raised a hand in the air to indicate that he wanted hush. Then, very carefully, he ascended two more steps, until he was almost on the very last one. Even Liz, who didn't mind heights, felt giddy.

She held her breath as she watched him lower himself flat against the roof, elbows first, followed by his trunk and tummy, so that he was almost spread-eagled. Then he reached around to pull the BB gun out of his pocket.

If it hadn't been for the yellow hat, anyone watching might have thought that there was a trained sniper in their midst. Unlike Liz, they probably wouldn't have noticed the way that Robert's limbs were shaking and his hand, holding the gun, was trembling, too.

After a few minutes, he composed himself enough to take aim. Dropping his gaze, he extended his arms as far as he could, with the gun pressed tight between both palms, and flipped the de-cocking lever. His intention was to fire close enough to scare the creatures away, but not so close that any of them would get hurt.

Liz could imagine him whispering, 'One, two, three... steady now – shoot!'

She squeezed her eyes shut and straight away a series of sharp bangs, like firecrackers, ricocheted around the small garden. This was soon followed by some high-pitched screams, then a flurry of gulls left the roofs of Bag End as well as all its neighbours round about, and launched themselves into the heavens. For a short while, their wings blotted out the sun and the whole world seemed to turn black.

Liz's arms shot up instinctively to protect her head and it crossed her mind to run for cover. But Robert shinned down the ladder double-quick and soon had his arm around her shoulders to give her a reassuring squeeze.

'Mission accomplished,' he said proudly. 'I looked a few of them in the eye and I reckon we came to an understanding. I don't think they'll be back.'

'Well done!' Liz went up on tiptoe to kiss her husband's cheek. 'You're a hero!'

As they strolled back into the cottage, however, she had the strange sensation of being watched and when she turned her head, she saw that one gull had already returned and settled on the garden fence, from where it was examining her beadily.

'Pesky thing,' she muttered under her breath, giving it her most withering look. It merely cocked its head cheekily to one side and ruffled its feathers.

'Squawk,' it went, and 'Eeeeeeee!'

She could swear that it was laughing at her.

She didn't tell Robert – it would drive him mad.

WHILE HE WAS STILL WARRING with the gulls, Rosie left for school, meeting up with Rafael at the bus stop on the way. The pair usually travelled there and back together, unless Rafael was late, in which case she went on without him.

He knew the score – he had five minutes' grace and after that, he was on his own. She was very strict about it.

In their absence, Chabela and Loveday had to run the café on their own; it wasn't a problem, though, as they weren't exactly inundated with customers. All this would change in a few weeks, of course, but by then they hoped that Robert would have lined up the extra helpers.

It was a warmish day but there wasn't much sun, and Chabela felt a bit dreary as she stared out of the serving hatch at the deserted, windswept beach.

Digging out her phone, she searched for some Mexican guitar music and turned the volume up loud. It perked up both the women immediately.

'Fancy a coffee?' Loveday called over the din, and Chabela did a thumbs up.

Something occurred to her then and she told Loveday to prepare two mugs half filled with black coffee and a jug of hot, frothy milk. Disappearing into the cloakroom, she reappeared not long after clutching a miniature bottle of alcohol.

'Tequila,' she said with a wink, holding the bottle up for Loveday to see. 'It's delicious in coffee with a bit of cream, sugar and cinnamon. I brought it with me specially. I thought we might need a little boost!'

Loveday glanced furtively out of the hatch to check if anyone was there, but all was quiet.

'I don't think Robert would approve!' she said with a wicked laugh. 'Make mine a double!'

'Nonononono.' Chabela waggled her index finger and clicked her tongue. 'No doubles, just a tiny dash – see?'

She walked over to the counter, where Loveday had put the half-filled mugs, and poured not much more than a thimbleful of tequila in each. Then she added some hot milk, a soupçon of whipped cream from the fridge, a spoonful of sugar and some cinnamon sprinkles.

'Here,' she said, picking up one of the cups and handing it to Loveday, who sniffed the drink appreciatively. 'Tell me what you think.'

Without any further encouragement, the girl put her lips to the mug and took a tentative sip.

'Mmm!' she said, glancing up, with foam still around her mouth. 'It's delish!'

Chabela was pleased. 'Isn't it?' She closed her eyes and took a swig herself, savouring the taste, which reminded her so much of home. 'You wouldn't think the ingredients would go together, but they do.'

'I've never had tequila before,' Loveday commented, dipping a finger into the froth and licking it off. 'Lush!'

They stood side by side for a little while gazing at the ocean, silently communing with their drinks, each other and their surroundings while Mexican guitars strummed in the background.

Every now and again, Loveday would make an appreciative slurp or suck, and once or twice, when the strumming reached a particularly rousing crescendo, either she or Chabela would break into a sort of flamenco jig.

Loveday especially liked to click her fingers and drum her feet on the floor because her heavy trainers made a satisfying thud, which seemed to resonate around the interior and make the walls and ceiling quiver.

When she grew tired of the music, she switched to the radio instead and listened intently with Chabela to the weather report. Out here, all alone in a glorified hut on a vast, inhospitable beach, the forecast was suddenly particularly interesting.

'Thick cloud and a forty per cent chance of rain later,' came a woman's voice.

Her clipped English was quite unlike the accents of most of the folk around here and Chabela realised that she was becoming accustomed to the Cornish burr and even learning to like it.

'Ugh,' said Loveday, pulling a face. 'I hate it when it rains. I wish we could close early.'

Already, it seemed, the cheering effects of the tequila were wearing off and Chabela didn't dare give the girl any more in case it made her tipsy.

'It rains a lot in Mexico City in the summer,' she said, hoping to distract her. 'At about three in the afternoon it's torrential and everyone runs for cover. But it only lasts an hour or two, then the skies clear and the sun comes out again.'

'I'd quite like to visit your country,' Loveday commented. 'But it's not top of my list.'

There was something so open and artless about her that it was difficult to take offence. She was only telling the truth, without the usual social politeness filter turned on.

'What's number one on the list, then?' Chabela asked with a smile.

'Zante,' came the reply, 'in Greece. My friend went there last summer. She had a right laugh. The clubs were open all night and she slept all day. She came back whiter than before. Hardly saw the beach at all!'

Loveday seemed to regard this as an impressive achievement, and Chabela decided not to challenge her.

'Mexican girls and women stay out of the sun, too,' she commented drily. 'It's not fashionable to have a tan like it is here.'

'Really?' Loveday looked astonished. 'My friend was hoping she'd come back black, but she never woke up in time to see the sun!'

The good news, she went on, was that the friend had met a lad from London out there and they were still texting each other.

'He keeps saying he's going to come to Cornwall to see her, but he never does.'

'Men!' Chabela raised her eyebrows. 'They're an unreliable lot.'

Loveday bit her lip and seemed to think about this for a moment.

'I know what you mean,' she said at last, her head on one side, 'but Jesse's not like the rest. Usually, if he says he'll meet me somewhere or do something, he does.'

'You're lucky. You should hang onto him.'

There must have been something about Chabela's tone that made Loveday take notice.

'Have you ever had a boyfriend?' she asked, quite shyly.

Maybe it was the tequila, or perhaps it was the girl's straightforwardness, but for some reason Chabela found herself opening up a little about Alfonso. It was a subject so raw and close to her heart that she hadn't mentioned him to anyone since arriving in Cornwall, and hadn't intended to.

'I was in love with someone once,' she said, with a sigh. 'I thought we had a future together, but it turned out we didn't.'

Loveday's eyebrows shot up. 'Why not?'

'It's a long story.'

'Tell me!'

Chabela shook her head.

'Oh go on,' Loveday wheedled. 'You can't start and stop like that. It's not fair!'

She looked so cross that Chabela laughed, despite herself.

'Well, he's married,' she said carefully, watching Loveday's face to gauge her reaction.

The girl's pupils grew very large. 'Ooh! Naughty!'

Chabela nodded.

'It went on for many years – seven, to be precise. I adored him. I'm not proud of it.'

'Did he finish with you?'

'The other way round.'

'Why?'

Chabela swallowed. Already she'd said too much. She felt that she could trust Loveday, but didn't know for sure and in any case, how could a girl her age be expected to understand? What experience did she have of real life? She'd hardly even been out of Cornwall.

'I'm sorry,' Chabela said, lowering her eyes to the floor, 'I shouldn't have mentioned it. I came here to try to get over him.'

'And is it working?'

The directness of the question caught Chabela by surprise.

'Um, not really.' She gave a sad smile. 'A little, perhaps.'

'Well, that's a start!' Loveday clapped her hands. 'Maybe you'll be swept off your feet by a handsome Cornishman.' She pulled a face. 'Mind you, there aren't many round here. You get more choice in Truro. It's a proper city, with shops and cinemas and that.'

The conversation switched to the safer topic of films and hot actors. Loveday admitted that she fancied men with ginger hair, which cheered Chabela up no end, especially when she discovered their shared passion for Damian Lewis.

They were giggling so much that at first they didn't notice Rick hovering by the serving hatch, but when Chabela glanced up, she became aware that he was staring at her, seemingly transfixed.

'Oh!' she said, self-consciously smoothing back her hair. 'Sorry. Have you been waiting long?'

He didn't reply, in fact he seemed a million miles away, so she tried again.

'What can I get you?'

This time, he coughed with embarrassment and slid his gaze away.

'Er, coffee please,' he said, staring down and shuffling from one foot to another. 'White, no sugar.'

While Loveday made the drink, Chabela talked politely with him about the weather. She had already discovered that this was a favourite topic among English people and seemed to put them at their ease.

Rick was wearing a smart, woollen navy reefer jacket with black anchor buttons and his grey hair, previously quite long and unkempt, had had a trim.

'I wanted to ask you something,' he said at last, wincing slightly as he spoke, as if it caused him pain.

Chabela had no idea what was coming next and felt slightly nervous for some reason.

'I wondered if you'd be interested in visiting the tin miners' museum?' he went on. 'I thought it might be useful for your research. You can go right down underground. There's also some information up top about the Mexican migration. I can drive you there if you like? It's not too far.'

Chabela exhaled loudly. She hadn't realised that she'd been holding her breath. She realised that at the back of her mind, she'd been worried he was going to ask her on a date, but this sounded like nothing of the sort.

'That would be great, thanks,' she said with a smile and Rick's face lit up.

'Cracking! I mean good,' he added quickly, checking himself. 'When are you free?'

They settled on a week on Wednesday, when Chabela would have the day off. Rick said he wouldn't mind shutting the shop at lunchtime.

'I'll put a notice up soon as I get back, then no one can say they haven't been warned.'

He left with a spring in his step and as soon as he was out of earshot, Loveday dug Chabela in the ribs.

'Watch out!' she hissed. 'I think he's got the hots for you.'

At first Chabela didn't understand. 'The hots?' she said innocently, but then the penny dropped. 'No, no, you're wrong,' she insisted, appalled. 'We're going to a *museum*, for goodness' sake. He's just being friendly.'

'Don't you believe it,' Loveday replied with a scoff. 'You'd better keep an eye on his hands down that mineshaft!'

This made Chabela shudder and she rather wished that she'd refused. But Rick was a nice person and it would be interesting to see a real tin mine. She might even learn something more about her ancestor's historic journey.

After that, customers came in dribs and drabs and the women took it in turns to have a short lunch break. During hers, Chabela sat in her car with the heating on, eating a prawn sandwich.

She'd parked in her usual spot behind the café and it wasn't much of a view, but she didn't care. Loveday's questions about Alfonso and then Rick's unexpected invitation had set off a train of thought that she wanted to pursue, no matter where it led or how uncomfortable the journey.

Why had she been drawn to Alfonso, when he was so clearly attached to someone else? Back then, there had been countless admirers knocking on her door. Yet from the moment she met him, she had eyes for no one else.

She'd always assumed that she was simply swept away by his good looks, intelligence, experience and charisma. She wondered now, though, if there was something about his very unavailability that had been irresistible.

She found herself returning to their very first meeting, when she had no inkling of the fact that the course of her life was about to change dramatically and for ever.

He was director of the Centre of Latin American Studies when she took up the post of senior lecturer and researcher, and although she hadn't met him before, she knew him well by reputation.

A political scientist and world expert in the field of US and Latin-American relations, he had written a number of highly acclaimed books, sections of which she could recite by heart.

Fifteen years older, married and with two teenage children, he wasn't exactly good boyfriend material, but she was instantly hooked. She tried her best to disguise her attraction and at first, he seemed hardly aware of her presence. As time went on, however, he began to take more of an interest in her, stopping to chat when they passed in the corridor and asking how she was getting on.

Once, he offered to lend her a book that he said might help with a research paper that she was writing, and she went to his office to pick it up.

She could still remember how nervous she felt knocking on his door and how her legs almost gave way when he gestured to the chair on the opposite side of his vast wooden desk and invited her to sit down.

The room was high up, with views of the tall buildings that dominated the city's skyline. A bright light shone through the windows that ran along the entire length of the wall behind him, illuminating his broad shoulders and head of thick, silvering hair, that was cut short at the sides and slightly longer on top, almost curly.

He was handsome by any standards – smooth-shaven, shortish in height and athletic-looking, with thick dark brows, a slim, straight nose, a full lower lip and clever, intense brown eyes behind a pair of distinctive, retro, black-framed glasses.

The sleeves of his pale blue shirt were rolled up and he'd undone a couple of buttons and removed his tie, while the jacket of his navy suit was laid carefully across the arm of the small black sofa to his right.

'Would you like some coffee – or water, perhaps?' he asked, leaning back and stretching, his arms behind his head, so that she could see the outline of his chest and taut stomach, the way his biceps seemed to be struggling to get free.

She could picture the moment as clearly as if it were yesterday, and desire licked at her insides all over again and seemed to burn through her gut, making her feel quite sick.

There was an open can of Diet Coke in the car's cup holder beside her and she took a sip, remembering how, back then, she had declined his offer of coffee, thinking that she couldn't trust herself not to spill it down her front.

After that, she'd watched him push the book that he'd mentioned across the desk to her with his fingertips, so overcome that she could barely raise her eyes far enough from her lap to take it from him.

He was clearly in no hurry and invited her to summarise the main arguments that she intended to put forward in her paper on the effects of the Cold War on gender and women's rights in Latin America.

Panicking, she'd launched into a half-baked summary of her ideas, realising too late that she was making a fool of herself and that it would have been far better to stay schtum.

After a few moments of listening to her waffle, he removed his glasses, tucked them in his shirt pocket and bent forwards, his elbows resting on the table.

This caused her to lose her chain of thought entirely and as she paused to collect herself, she noticed to her dismay that his eyebrows had shot up. At the same time, he'd lowered his chin almost to his chest and was fixing her with a disconcerting look.

'I'm sorry,' she blurted, before she could stop herself. 'I haven't—'

'Dr Penhallow Maldonado,' he interrupted, with a devastating smile, 'if you don't mind my saying so, I've never heard such a pile of shit in my life.'

Her mouth dropped open, tears sprang to her eyes and it was all she could do not to bolt from the room. Fortunately, however, he took pity on her.

'I'm joking. Forgive me,' he said, leaning forwards now, his arms folded across his chest. 'I realise your project is only in its infancy. I shouldn't have put you on the spot.'

Relieved, she was able to breathe again. 'I've barely begun, to be honest,' she gabbled. 'I know what I want to say, it's just that I haven't worked out how to say it yet.'

'I'm sure you'll do a very good job,' he replied reassuringly. Then, 'I'm sorry for my bad behaviour. Can I take you out for a drink tonight by way of apology?'

Chabela was so surprised that it took her a moment or two to respond. He had a smile on his lips and seemed to be teasing, but maybe he wasn't.

'Really, there's no need—'

But he insisted. 'I'll meet you at the car park entrance at six thirty. I can drop you home afterwards and you can pick up your car in the morning.'

She stumbled from the room in a daze of excitement and confusion and then delivered such a bad lecture to her students that she had to apologise and pretend that she was feeling unwell.

She took a bite of prawn sandwich, which was delicious but quite messy. A blob of mayonnaise fell on her lap but luckily, she'd put a napkin there and had brought another one for her face.

Coincidentally, the first food that she and Alfonso ate together had been prawns, or *cocteles de camarones*, a classic Mexican dish with shrimp, lime juice, tomatoes, hot sauce, celery, onion, cucumber and avocado.

He had chosen a quiet bar in the Roma district and led her to a table at the back, with comfortable seats directly facing each other. To begin with, the conversation had been purely work-related, but after a couple of drinks, things got a bit more personal.

He told her that he and his wife had married in haste and were profoundly unhappy. She was only interested in parties, gossip and fashion and they were staying together purely for the children's sakes.

That such a great man should be miserable and unappreciated seemed like a tragedy to Chabela, who took it as a great compliment that he had chosen to confide in her. It was clear that he needed her, or so she decided back then, and several more dates followed in out-of-the-way restaurants. Before long, they became lovers.

That was almost a decade ago and in all that time, Chabela had scarcely looked at anyone else. So deep was her love that she was willing to make do with the one or two nights a week when he could get away from his family to spend a few blissful hours with her.

Sometimes she'd cook for him, but more often they'd make love straight away, then lie back against the pillows on the king-sized bed in her apartment, entwined in each other's arms.

The relationship wasn't purely physical, though. After that, they'd talk quietly about all manner of subjects including their work, the politics of the day and the books they were reading. How she missed those discussions! They had been her lifeblood.

They seemed to share so many of the same views and when they didn't see eye to eye, they would listen quietly to each other's opinions, both valuing greatly the different perspectives that this brought.

During the summers, when Alfonso went abroad with his family, sometimes for two or three months at a time, Chabela would cope with the loneliness and longing by working even harder, writing books and academic papers that were translated and published around the world, as well as taking on extra tutoring.

Her bank balance grew along with her reputation, and although money was never her motivation, it felt good eventually to be able to buy a bigger apartment in a better area of the city and decorate it exactly as she wanted.

Occasionally she would talk wistfully to Alfonso of sneaking a weekend away together, or even a week, to make up for all the times that they were apart.

'One day, Chabelita,' he'd say, gently stroking her cheek. 'I can't risk my wife finding out and upsetting the kids. Not yet. Not until they've left home.'

And so the years had rolled on until something happened that made Chabela realise she must finally give him up, or risk annihilation. But how was she to do it, when they lived in the same city, worked in the same building and one word from him, one look, was enough to bring her running to his side?

She dithered and dallied until that morning when Simon's letter had arrived out of the blue in her in-tray. In different circumstances she would probably have

THE GIRL WHO CAME HOME TO CORNWALL

shoved it to the bottom of the pile and forgotten about it. But she was looking for a way out and this, she'd decided, could be it.

Feeling too hot all of a sudden, she opened the window halfway and a gust of wind almost blew what was left of her sandwich, and the napkin, on to the floor.

Quickly, she swallowed the remaining bite before shoving the rubbish into the glove compartment to dispose of later.

Around and around her mind went, chewing over everything that he'd ever said to her, all that they'd shared. But it was over. Finished. Did she really believe it, in her heart of hearts, or was she still clinging on to some vain hope that he'd come running after her?

The sight of Loveday, hobbling from the shack towards her in clunky platform trainers, flipped her back to the present. The girl must be wondering where she'd got to as she'd promised not to take long.

Winding down the window fully, Chabela stuck her head through the gap and called out, 'I'm coming!'

Loveday, who wasn't looking where she was going, tripped on an uneven paving stone and almost fell flat on her face.

'Oh dear,' Chabela muttered, opening the car door and hurrying out to help, and, 'Oh God!' when Loveday wobbled precariously again and threatened to topple over.

After flicking the switch to lock the vehicle, Chabela grabbed Loveday's arm and led her back inside; she wasn't safe on those heels, that was for sure. She could do with a pair of crutches.

'Thanks,' the girl muttered, plonking down on the nearest chair she could find once they were safely indoors. 'I thought I was a goner!'

'You're welcome.' Chabela checked the girl's exposed knees, which were intact, which was just as well as she supposed that neither of them had much in the way of first aid skills. 'But please don't wear those shoes to work again,' she added. 'They should come with a safety warning!'

Chapter Eleven

FROM HER BEDROOM WINDOW, CHABELA watched the small, metallic-blue car making its way slowly up the drive towards Polgarry Manor.

Rick had said that he'd pick her up at two p.m. and it was exactly five to; he liked to be punctual, clearly.

Ever since she'd made the arrangement to visit the old tin museum with him, Chabela had felt slightly nervous. It was mainly Loveday's fault, for suggesting that Rick might have wandering hand trouble down the gloomy mine.

Now that Wednesday had come, however, and he'd arrived on her doorstep, excitement took over and Chabela found herself looking forward to finding out more about the 'Cousin Jacks' – the Cornish migrants to America – to whom she now knew that she was related.

While Rick opened his car and started to climb out, she hurried down to meet him. She was wearing practical jeans, white trainers and a navy sweatshirt, but he had gone smart, in a Gatsby-style pale pink striped linen blazer, an open-necked shirt and tan trousers.

On his feet was a pair of two-tone, suede deck shoes that looked brand new. She found herself hoping that they wouldn't get dirty.

'Good morning!' he said in a cheery voice, before opening the passenger door for her with a flourish. He made sure that she was comfortably settled, with her bag on her lap, before shutting her in and moving around to his side of the vehicle.

Once seated, he produced two small silver thermos flasks from a carrier at his feet and passed one to her.

'I thought you might like some coffee for the journey. I made it with hot milk, I hope that's all right?'

He was very gallant and seemed anxious that he might have done the wrong thing, but Chabela put his mind at rest.

'Perfect,' she said, unscrewing the lid that doubled as a drinking cup and pouring herself a few mouthfuls. 'How thoughtful! Thank you.'

To her relief, Rick was a careful driver, sticking to the speed limit and checking in his mirrors frequently, which meant that she could sit back, relax and enjoy the trip.

As they buzzed along country lanes, he was quiet while she did most of the talking, commenting on her new job, the people she'd met and her general impressions of the area so far.

Every now and again she'd drop in a personal question, and his answers were quite stilted, until she got onto the subject of his interest in local history, when he became positively animated.

'You should have come to Florence's talk on sanitation through the ages,' he said. 'It was fascinating.'

Chabela had forgotten to buy a ticket and when she remembered, it had been too late as the talk was already under way.

'I'll try to make the next one,' she promised.

They came to a junction and he paused, checking this way and that before taking a sharp right. Soon, they were on a major road flanked by tall trees on either side, with little traffic in either direction.

While he kept his eyes firmly ahead, she found herself glancing at him surreptitiously, and she was struck once again by the bushiness of his long grey beard and sideburns, and the way in which his moustache curled at the ends, as if he'd used heated rollers.

His lips, protruding from all that fuzz, were quite full and surprisingly pink, almost indecently so, while his fingers, gripping the steering wheel, were like the plump pork sausages that she'd seen for sale in the Tremarnock village store.

She looked away quickly. He was kind and charming, for sure, but she couldn't ever imagine him as anything other than a friend.

Alfonso, by contrast, was olive-skinned and smooth all over, with little in the way of body hair. How she'd loved to run her flattened hand across the contours of his chest!

Him again. Everything always led back there. She clenched her fists and forced herself to focus on the road ahead until her eyes started to sting and go blurry.

It took about forty minutes to arrive at their destination and they swung into a car park with a big sign in the corner saying, WELCOME TO WHEAL CHESTEN. COME AND LOOK INSIDE!

To their left, a tall, thin, granite chimney rose high into the sky. Once, it would have been fiery hot and belching out smoke but now, pale green ivy grew up the sides and it was flecked with orangey-yellow lichen.

Beside it were the remains of what must have been the square-shaped engine house. Towering behind that was the old pithead winding gear machine, for lifting and lowering men and materials into the shaft.

Still and silent now, Chabela thought that she could nevertheless still picture the great wheels turning and the men with their hats and candles huddling together as the metal cage went down, down into the bowels of the earth.

Rick led the way to the ticket booth and was adamant that he wanted to pay for them both.

'My treat,' he insisted, pushing away Chabela's proffered twenty pound note. 'You can buy me a drink later.'

Soon, they were making their way through the gate into the main enclosure. This was a large patch of grass dotted with picnic tables and surrounded by a number of purpose-built chalets housing assorted exhibits.

The entrance to the mine itself was on the far side of the lawn, where they could see a sign saying, NEXT TOUR IN TEN MINUTES.

There was already a small queue of people lining up to be fitted with hard, yellow miners' hats, complete with a torch on top. It wasn't long before a short, amiable-looking man in old-fashioned miners' gear was handing one to Chabela.

'I'm your guide for today,' he said in a strong Cornish accent. He was wearing loose, grimy trousers, held up with a leather belt, an open shirt and a filthy cotton jacket down to the knees, 'I hope you're not frightened of the dark!'

Chabela had never been down a mine before, and her stomach rotated anticlockwise as they descended some steep steps into the tunnel. It went clockwise again when they arrived at the bottom and she found that she could stand up straight, see a few metres in front of her and, most importantly, breathe.

She was enthralled by the guide's explanations of the extreme conditions that the men had to work in hundreds of feet below.

Temperatures, it seemed, could reach up to sixty degrees Celsius, and the air was so polluted by dust and fumes from detonated explosives that it could barely sustain the candles that the men brought with them, glued to their hats with molten wax.

In fact, some miners would choose to snub their candles out and work in complete darkness in order to conserve the air. Not surprisingly, there were many injuries and life expectancy was short. If you didn't fall off a ladder or blow yourself up by mistake, the guide said, you were likely to die of TB, bronchitis or silicosis, caused by particles of mica dust puncturing the lungs.

Mindful of Loveday's warning, Chabela tried to keep a little distance between her and Rick as they made their way along a network of more tunnels, sensing the dark closing in.

She needn't have worried, however. He was the perfect gentleman, pointing out the places where the ceiling was low and she should stoop, and helping her to switch on her torch when it got so black that they couldn't see so much as a metre ahead.

'Watch out for the knockers,' the guide said at one point, explaining that these were the mischievous folkloric spirits of caves and wells and denizens of the mines. Miners claimed to be able to hear the imps tapping as they worked alongside them, and would often leave a small portion of their beloved pasties as peace offerings.

Children were often employed at the mines, the man went on, initially working above ground with the women, or the bal maidens, as they were known, breaking up rock. Once past the age of twelve, however, the boys would join the men below the surface.

Chabela was moved to think of her own ancestor, James Penhallow, toiling away in the darkness, until he made his decision to join the Cousin Jacks and seek his fortune in Mexico.

He would most likely have been short, she speculated, because the height of boys was stunted and their bodies were often crippled from working in thin seams where they couldn't stand up straight.

The fact that he survived at all, then made it safely by ship, train and on foot all the way to Hidalgo seemed, to her, to be a miracle. It was a cruel blow that he should have died at the hands of bandits after making such a success of himself and finding happiness with his beloved Jacinta.

When Chabela and Rick reached the surface again, they made their way to the nearest chalet, which contained an exhibition on migration. Cornish miners, it seemed, were considered to be the finest hard-rock miners in the world.

From the 1800s, thousands went abroad, taking their skills and technological advances with them, to places as far flung as South Africa, Australia, New Zealand, Spain and Cuba as well as Mexico.

'Today,' Chabela read, 'numerous migrant-descended Cornish communities flourish around the world.

Cornish-type engine houses, Methodist chapels, industrial housing, male voice choirs and pasty shops proliferate in many of the former mining communities.'

There were various enlarged black and white photographs of miners and their families in old-fashioned clothing. Some were at the train station at Redruth, waiting to join the weekly exodus to South Africa. Others were pictured after their return home.

Chabela was particularly taken by one image of a man named Arthur Jenkins from Chacewater, Cornwall. He was standing with his wife and their small daughter, who was perched on a chair between them.

The photograph had been taken soon after their return from Mexico, and despite the graininess of the image, you could tell that the man was quite tanned.

He had grown a Mexican-style moustache and was wearing a wide hat, white jacket and a *guayabera*, the typical white cotton or linen pleated shirt favoured by Mexican men for weddings and in very hot weather.

There was a certain swagger about his stance, one hand on hip, the other arm around the back of the chair where his daughter was standing, in a frilly white, sleeveless dress and straw bonnet. His wife, meanwhile, was in a long, pale dress with a high neck and voluminous sleeves, her hair piled on top in an elaborate plait.

The man looked pleased with himself and proud to show off his prosperous, attractive family. He even had a little lap dog at his feet with fluffy ears and white paws. Clearly Mexico had been kind to him.

Chabela would have dearly loved to find photos of her ancestor, James Penhallow, but that would have been an extraordinary coincidence. In her mind's eye, however, she now had him down as similar in looks to this Arthur Jenkins, with the same moustache and easy, contented bearing.

The next chalet contained numerous artefacts, including historic items made from tin such as tin-plate, telephones and pipe organs, taken from Methodist chapels both in the area and abroad. There were also examples of early mining hand drills, dairy items, teapots and other paraphernalia.

These were of only minor interest to Chabela, who whizzed through the collection before heading for the ninety-five-year-old steam engine, originally from Falmouth Docks, which was housed in a large, adjoining building.

'She's a beauty,' Rick commented, coming up behind. 'They don't make 'em like that any more.'

'Someone loves her,' she replied, pointing to the glossy green sides and shiny, copper-capped chimney. 'She's very beautiful.'

'Like you.'

Chabela started. Had she misheard? She fervently hoped so, and pretended not to have caught the quietly spoken comment.

EMMA BURSTALL

'Shall we have some coffee?' she asked brightly, making purposefully for the café that she'd spotted on her arrival. Rick walked alongside her and if he were disappointed that she'd ignored him, he didn't show it. Perhaps her ears had deceived her.

Even so, she was careful not to catch his eye when he sat down opposite her and sipped his drink thoughtfully.

'I hope you've enjoyed yourself,' he commented. 'I hope it's not been a waste of time?'

'Oh no!' Chabela meant it. She mightn't have learned anything new about the Penhallows, but she had a more general feel now for the lives of migrant miners.

'I'll do some more digging around for you,' Rick promised. 'See what I can come up with. It's a shame Pat's gone. She was the village's oldest inhabitant. Lived in The Nook on Humble Hill. If anyone had any knowledge of a family named Penhallow, it would have been her. She's dead now, more's the pity. Wonderful woman, she was. There's a gravestone for her in the Methodist churchyard.'

By the time they got up to leave, it was almost six o'clock and they were virtually the last visitors remaining on the site.

Rick suggested stopping off for a pub supper on the way home. Chabela was quite hungry but said no, not wishing to send out wrong signals.

'It's been a wonderful afternoon,' she said, when he drew up outside the manor.

She could see Maria through the ground-floor kitchen window, watering plants on the sill with a little copper can. The old woman looked up briefly when she heard the car, then turned away without acknowledgment.

As soon as the engine was off, Rick hopped out and hurried around to Chabela's side to open the door for her.

'Thank you so much.' She put out a hand to shake his, but he ignored it.

'It's been my pleasure,' he replied, bending down to plant a whiskery kiss on her cheek instead. 'I hope you'll allow me to take you out again?'

'I'd like that,' she said, 'but I'm going to be doing long hours at the Secret Shack. I don't think I'll have much free time.'

Rick waved a hand in the air as if he were swatting away a fly.

'Oh, you don't need to worry about that,' he said airily. 'I'll have a word with Robert, tell him not to overwork you.'

Chabela frowned. The last thing she wanted was Rick interfering with her schedule, however kindly meant. He might put up Robert's back and besides, she liked working at the café and didn't particularly want to reduce her hours or go out with Rick again for a while.

She was about to say something of the sort, as diplomatically as possible, but he turned on his heel and got back in his car before she had the chance.

As he started to reverse, checking in the mirror to see what was behind, she caught his eye by accident and his bushy brows shot up in a rather suggestive manner.

She frowned a little and gave a polite wave back.

'Gerroffof me! Shoo! Arrgh!'

Liz was rounding the corner out of South Street when she heard someone shouting at the top of his voice.

The noise seemed to be coming from the other end of Humble Hill. Startled, she quickened her pace and soon, a very tall man came into view, waving his long arms in the air and hopping from one foot to another, as if he were stepping on hot coals.

He was right outside Bag End, and above his head was a circling seagull.

'Robert!' Liz cried, hurrying down the hill and hanging on tight to Lowenna's hand. 'What is it? What's going on?'

The sight of her father in such apparent distress was too much for Lowenna, who started to howl.

'DADDEEEE!' she screamed, breaking away from her mother and racing towards him as fast as her legs would carry her.

She was wearing pink shorts and white sandals and Liz's heart was in her mouth as she followed on helplessly, praying that her daughter wouldn't fall and cut her knees or stub her toes.

At the sound of the little girl's high-pitched voice, or perhaps it was at the sight of her bright pink shorts, the seagull appeared to reconsider its position. After hovering for a moment, perilously close to Robert's scalp, as if preparing to dive, it began to flap off.

Liz breathed a sigh of relief, but then it appeared to have second thoughts, flying back towards Robert, who took off a leather shoe and threw it as hard as he could in the bird's general direction.

This seemed to do the trick. The gull swooped up, up and away, landing on the rooftop of Bag End, from where it surveyed them smugly.

'It's all right, darling,' Robert said, wrapping his arms around Lowenna as she flung herself towards him, and lifting her up. 'Daddy's OK. Daddy's not hurt.'

But as soon as Liz was alongside, his tune changed.

'They've got it in for me,' he muttered ominously. 'Those bloody birds. Ever since I used that BB gun, they've been lying in wait for me. They watch until I get right up close to the garden gate, then pounce.'

He pointed towards the offending gull and shook his fist.

'That one would have attacked me if you hadn't come. I'm sure of it. It knew exactly what it was doing. I could have been seriously hurt.'

'Oh dear!' Liz was concerned for her husband but couldn't quite believe that he'd been deliberately targeted. 'I don't think it's got a personal grudge. It was probably protecting its nest. Maybe it thought you were a predator or something. I wonder if there are any eggs yet.'

Robert growled. Needless to say, his attempt at frightening off the birds had failed dismally. Not only were they still in residence, they also seemed determined to cause as much inconvenience as possible. Every morning at daybreak, they'd wake up Liz and Robert with their drumming feet, and she could no longer hang washing in the garden, in case they pooed on it.

'I'll ring the council in the morning, without fail,' she said, cursing herself for not having done so sooner. 'I'm sure they'll help when I tell them the birds are getting vicious.'

'I wouldn't count on it.' Robert kissed the top of Lowenna's dark head and frowned. 'From what I hear, gulls have more rights than humans. It's absurd!'

He picked up his shoe, unlocked the front door and they all went indoors. It was only then that Liz thought to ask why he'd come home at all; she hadn't expected to see him until the restaurant closed.

It seemed that Jesse had accidentally tipped hollandaise sauce on his boss's trousers, which needed to be changed. Being reminded of this, though, only seemed to put Robert in a worse mood.

'He smashed some plates last week and now look what he's done,' he grumbled, taking off his baggy trousers in the middle of the kitchen, scrunching them up and flinging them through the utility room door. 'He's getting careless. I need to have a proper word with him.'

Robert seemed completely unaware of how funny he looked, standing there in nothing but a cream shirt, brown socks, one shoe and his red and white striped boxers.

Liz raised an eyebrow. 'D'you need to change your underpants, too?' She took a step forwards. 'Shall I take them off for you?' She was hoping to make him smile, but it didn't work.

'No,' he snapped. 'There's nothing wrong with them.'

And with that, he stomped off upstairs. He never used to have a foul temper, Liz reflected. She blamed overwork. She'd begged him not to buy the Secret Shack but he wouldn't listen to her. Now look at him! He could do with a month off, but there was no way that he'd take even a week.

She turned to Lowenna, who was plonked on the floor with her thumb in her mouth, staring into space. The poor little thing was obviously exhausted. She'd been with Liz this evening to the penultimate choir rehearsal prior to the plaque unveiling ceremony on Saturday.

For an hour and a half, the little girl had sat, good as gold, on a beanbag in the church hall, watching the older children practising their sea shanties. Then, right at the end, when Liz had said they could all leave, she'd gone quite mad, giggling hysterically as she raced around the hall and the garden outside, chased by some of the other children. It seemed that they were all full to bursting with pent-up energy that needed releasing somehow.

No wonder Lowenna looked now as if she were ready to fall asleep right there on the floor.

After a quick bath and a story, Liz tucked her youngest into bed with her favourite teddy bear, and she'd drifted off before her mother had even left the room.

Robert was long since gone again. He'd called a hasty 'bye' before slamming the door. Liz imagined him running for his life down the garden path like an ambushed soldier, his arms over his head to protect it from flying bullets or, in his case, dive-bombing seagulls. She hoped that he'd made it safely.

Tiptoeing next door into Rosie's room, she was dismayed to find her eldest glued to her laptop, watching an episode of her favourite reality show.

'Have you done your homework?' Liz asked rather sharply, and immediately wished that she hadn't.

'Nice to see you too, Mum,' Rosie replied sarcastically. Then she softened a little. 'How was the rehearsal?'

'Good,' came the reply. 'Or good enough, anyway. We've only got one more practice session, so it'll have to be.'

Back downstairs, Liz put on a wash and tidied away the remains of what must have been one of Rosie's snacks. She was very health conscious these days, and went in for things like hummus, chopped up carrots and wheat-free crackers, the remains of which were sprayed across the worktop.

Once all the jobs were done, the light outside had faded and shadows had started to dance across the walls and floor, Liz realised that she could put it off no longer. Sitting at the kitchen table, she opened up her laptop and logged on.

Ever since agreeing to be choir mistress for the plaque unveiling ceremony, she'd known that she must write to tell Max that she would be there after all. It was only fair to give him time to prepare. It would be far worse just to turn up; he mightn't be able to hide his surprise, or someone might notice a funny atmosphere between them and make comments. Her stomach fluttering at the mere thought of his name, she typed an email.

Dear Max, I just wanted to let you know that I'll be there on Saturday after all. I was asked to lead the choir so I'll be there just for the ceremony, then I'll have to leave…

She stopped short and erased the last sentence. No need for lengthy explanations or excuses. Keep it simple.

I hope you have a good flight. See you at the ceremony.

Love, Liz x

She reread it once to check for mistakes, then pressed send. At least now she could turn up with her head held high, knowing that she'd been as straight and honest with him as possible. He couldn't ask for more than that.

Chapter Twelve

THE SUN WAS SHINING AND there was barely a cloud in the sky as scores of villagers left their cottages and started to make their way slowly from all directions along the narrow, cobbled streets of Tremarnock to the playground.

It was eleven thirty a.m. and Liz was holding Lowenna with one hand, while her other arm was linked through Rosie's. Just ahead, at the bottom of Humble Hill, they could see Jean outside Dynnargh, waiting for Tom, who was fiddling with the latch of their white picket gate.

In front of them, a gaggle of children in blue and white striped sailor outfits were starting to disappear around the corner. The choir. Some were singing raucously while others pushed and jostled with each other. They weren't exactly an orderly bunch and Liz hoped that they'd calm down in time for their performance.

She was feeling nervous and wished in some ways that Robert were at her side. He'd kindly drafted in temporary staff to cover the lunchtime shifts at his two establishments, so that his regular employees could attend the ceremony. But he himself was to remain at A Winkle in Time until the very last moment.

He might only catch ten minutes or so of the fun at the end, he said, but it would be better than nothing, and Liz had decided not to put up a fight.

Whilst she would have liked his support, she was also quite relieved that he wouldn't be there to witness her reunion with Max. She wasn't at all sure that she was going to be a good enough actress to conceal her sense of unease, which, of course, Robert would pick up on immediately because he knew her so well.

Rosie would be meeting Rafael there and she was looking very pretty in blue jeans and a skimpy white top with spaghetti straps. Her long fair hair was newly washed and hung, thick and glossy over her thin shoulders. Liz had always loved her daughter's hair; it reminded her of a horse's mane.

Liz herself had chosen a simple navy cotton shirt dress with a tie at the waist, and her black Birkenstock sandals, while Lowenna had on a pink, sleeveless A-line dress, white sandals and a cream cardigan.

Her dark hair, the exact same colour as her mother's, was tied up in two pigtails, which looked incredibly cute, while Liz had a ponytail. Strangers would often smile as the pair went by and say they looked like twins. Although Liz couldn't see it herself, she did understand why, for they were both small and slight with big, round brown eyes and black lashes.

As they turned left into Fore Street, they heard a shout. Spinning around, Liz saw Tabitha and her partner Danny, sporting a beard and a man bun, with Oscar on his shoulders.

Tabitha waved and Liz, Lowenna and Rosie waited for them to catch up. Behind them were John and Jenny Lambert with Sally on a lead, and even further back was Rick, in a bright red flannel shirt. Beside him was Audrey. You couldn't miss her either because she was almost as tall as Rick and broad, too. Her dark hair, cut pixie-short and artfully mussed, was tipped with platinum streaks, which seemed to twinkle in the sunshine.

She had on a striking sugar pink and white striped top and big gold earrings, and she was peering down and talking animatedly to a much shorter woman, whom Liz didn't recognise.

'Hello, friend!' Tabitha said to Liz, once she'd caught up properly. Meanwhile, Oscar bobbed up and down on Danny's shoulders, grinning at Lowenna and pulling on Danny's man bun until, wincing, he told the boy to keep still or he might fall.

'Looks like there's going to be quite a crowd,' Tabitha commented, and indeed, there was a queue for the car park at the top of the road and several drivers appeared to be rather stressed, winding down their windows to shout at the vehicles in front and beeping their horns.

In the field opposite, in the middle of which the play park was situated, folk were already milling around, chatting amongst themselves and setting up portable chairs in what they hoped, no doubt, would be prime viewing positions.

They were a colourful sight, in summer blues, white, pinks and yellows and someone was selling metallic gold and silver helium balloons, which bobbed gaily in the breeze.

Dotted around the perimeter were several blue and white striped canvas gazebos as well as white plastic chairs and tables. There was to be food and drink available after the ceremony, which Barbara had been charged with organising, assisted by, among others, her son, Aiden.

If it had been raining, they'd planned to move everyone into the Methodist church hall for the reception but luckily, the weather was set fair. An al fresco feast was what the whole village had been hoping for and their wishes, it seemed, were about to come true.

Beneath a very large oak tree on the far side of the field stood the village brass band, complete with trumpets, trombones, tubas, drums and euphoniums. What the players lacked in skill, they made up for in enthusiasm, and they struck up just as Liz and crew wandered through the main gate.

Instantly, Lowenna's hands shot out to cover her ears.

'Ouch!' said Liz, feeling her daughter's pain. 'That's a bit shrill. I hope they warm up!'

The playground itself had been recently renovated, thanks to Max's generosity, and the council had installed new swings, a climbing frame, assorted roundabouts, a sand and water area and the pièce de résistance – a large, thrilling, wood and stainless steel structure resembling an ocean-going ship.

This had two slides, a scrambling net, a sort of suspension bridge, a tempting bright blue talking tube and a big red ship's wheel. It was the first time that anyone had been allowed anywhere near the new equipment, and Lowenna's eyes were on stalks.

'Me, me!' she shouted impatiently, pointing at the galleon, but the gate into the asphalt-covered area was locked and no one was allowed in until Max had officially cut the ribbon.

Some children in leotards from a local gymnastics club were limbering up on the grass outside, doing stretches and handstands in preparation for their demonstration. Even they hadn't yet been permitted into the enclosure, and one or two were poking their noses longingly through the gaps in the green bow-top fencing, their fingers curled around the metal bars.

Liz glanced around, scanning the sea of faces for Max, but there was no sign of him. She guessed that he would probably arrive with Reg Carter, the pompous leader of the parish council.

Reg had been dead keen on selling the land to housing developers, right up until the moment when Max had stepped in. After that, Reg had swiftly changed his tune, pretending that he'd been rooting to preserve the playground all along.

No one was fooled, but as he lived in the village and was constantly in and out of the local shops, it seemed easier just to suffer him and try to turn a blind eye rather than engage in an unpleasant, long-running dispute.

Nevertheless, he rarely got invited to people's houses these days and few offered to buy him drinks in the pubs. Liz was almost starting to feel a little sorry for him, though he was so thick-skinned that he didn't seem aware of the hostility.

Rosie had wandered off, presumably to find Rafael, and soon Esme trotted over to say hello. She was smiling widely and Liz noticed that her eyes were particularly bright.

'You look—' she started to say, but Esme interrupted.

'Guess what?' she cried breathlessly, grabbing Liz's upper arm and squeezing tight.

She wasn't much given to public displays of emotion and Liz felt slightly anxious.

'Helen's had her baby – it's a girl!'

'Oh that's wonderful!'

Esme's enthusiasm was infectious, and Liz became giddy with delight.

'Are they both OK?'

Esme nodded happily.

'Does the baby have a name yet?'

'No. Apparently Juliette's a hot contender but nothing's decided.'

'And how's Caroline?' Liz studied Esme's face, for this, she knew, was really the most important question of all.

To Liz's relief, her friend's features lit up.

'Unbelievably happy! Helen wanted her there at the birth, along with Helen's husband, of course. Caroline said it was the most amazing experience of her life.'

'I'm so glad.'

Liz was, indeed, delighted for Esme, but at the same time she was aware of how much the older woman would have loved to be with Caroline now, sharing in her joy.

'I know what you're thinking,' Esme said, as if reading her friend's mind. 'Of course I miss her like mad, but this is Helen's time. She needs her mum. I wouldn't dream of getting in the way, even if I could.'

'That's very generous of you. I'm not sure I could be as unselfish.'

'I have to be,' Esme replied simply. 'There's no other choice.'

'Hello, darlings!'

Liz swung around to find Tony right behind, with his Brazilian husband, Felipe, who was Rafael's older brother. In desperation, their mother had sent Rafael to live in England with the two men when she could no longer keep the boy under control at home in Rio.

So far, the experiment seemed to have been a big success. No longer hanging out with minor criminals and druggies, Rafael had slotted well into the local community and went to school every day.

Although he wasn't exactly a diligent student, he was popular with the other pupils, having helped to set up monthly Friday night discos in the school hall, at which he was the deejay.

Somewhat grudgingly, the teachers had had to admit that they quite liked him, too, not least because he hung out with Rosie, for whom they had a soft spot. And although his homework was atrocious, he made everyone laugh and didn't seem to stop Rosie from working either. Indeed, her marks had recently gone up.

'My favourite girl!'

Tony crouched down to Lowenna's level and stretched his arms wide.

The little girl looked uncertain for a moment, before plucking up courage and running straight in. He picked her up and swung her around in a circle, making her squeal with pleasure.

He was dressed in jeans and a loud, paisley-patterned shirt, which was bursting at the seams. A few months before, he'd hit the gym and lost a lot of weight, but it appeared to have all gone back on, and more.

Felipe, who was tall and thin, didn't seem bothered, though. He'd once told Liz that he loved his partner for his mind, not his body.

He was grateful to be married to someone who adored food as he was a very good cook and preferred an appreciative audience. Tony, a real gourmet, fitted the bill perfectly and all in all the pair, who had been together for quite some years, seemed ideally suited.

The group were distracted by some particularly loud honking and watched a large white van trying to get past the queue of cars. Eventually, enough disgruntled drivers mounted the verge for the van to squeeze through, and it drew to a halt right outside the gate.

Soon, a gang of men were unloading crates of food and booze and staggering across the field towards the main gazebo, where they were greeted by Barbara and her team of helpers.

'Lunch!' Tony said, patting his round stomach. 'I hope it's good. I'm ravenous!'

Liz smiled. 'With Barbara in charge, it's bound to be. I think she's using a catering company from Looe. She's had them before, for pub events. She said they were great.'

Before long, delicious smells began to waft through the air as a part-cooked hog roast started to warm up on a giant spit. The band was still playing while someone on a loud speaker moved amongst the crowd, urging folk to gather around the edge of the playground.

'Our German friend is on his way,' the man announced in a tinny voice. 'Please wait quietly and make room for the procession.'

Liz felt her heart lurch, as if she were on a roller coaster, waiting for the off.

'There they are!'

It was Esme who shouted in Liz's ear and involuntarily, her head twisted to look. Coming across the field towards them was a handful of people, one of whom she recognised as the portly Reg, in a flapping brown suit.

He was flanked by the local MP, in a smart dark skirt and jolly yellow jacket, and the town mayoress. She was wearing full ceremonial dress, including a scarlet robe with a white lace jabot at the neck, a gold badge and a heavy gold chain of office. On her head was a black tricorn hat.

She was smiling broadly and waving a regal, white-gloved hand at the onlookers as she made her way slowly towards the playground. Meanwhile, the brass band blasted out the opening of the main theme of Jerome Moross's *The Big Country*, which certainly grabbed everyone's attention.

Straining her neck, Liz could make out a few extra heads behind the mayoress – more councillors and local dignitaries, probably. Then all of a sudden she clocked Max, who, though surrounded by bodies, appeared strangely alone.

It was as if he had a spotlight on him, drawing her gaze ever closer, sucking her in. Her mouth went dry and it was just as well that all eyes were on the procession rather than her, because she was sure that she must have gone pale.

To her, he looked the same but different, and at first she wasn't sure why. He had the same broad, athletic shoulders and wide neck that she remembered, and that had once made her think he might be a rugby player. His beard was as closely cropped as before, and his short dark hair was still flecked with silvery streaks.

His skin was slightly tanned, just as it had been when they'd first met. She knew now that he had a weekend home on a lake near Munich, where he kept a boat, and also took his daughter, Mila, on frequent foreign holidays. Back then, though, she'd just assumed that he was naturally dark-skinned.

He was walking quite purposefully, his arms swinging loosely at his side. He was wearing a navy suit – she hadn't seen him in one before – a white shirt and no tie, and his smile made him look friendly and approachable.

However, Liz noticed that all the time she gazed at him, the smile didn't change or move at all. It remained fixed in the exact same position while he stared straight ahead, not engaging with anyone or even seeming to notice the faces in the crowds.

She had the strange sensation, though, that all the while his eyes were focused on his destination – the playground – he was actually staring at her. Not literally, of course, but it was as if every cell in his body was acutely aware of her presence, seeking her out and searching for clues.

Perhaps she was imagining it and, in reality, she was the only one looking for signals, but she didn't think so. Call it animal instinct, but she was convinced that he knew exactly where she was.

This made her uncomfortable, so much so, in fact, that she probably would have bolted, had she not committed herself to conducting the children's choir.

She started. 'Oh my God!'

Esme glanced around. 'What's happened?'

Checking her watch, Liz saw that it was eleven fifty. She had agreed to meet up with Jean, Ruby the pianist, and all the children at a quarter to eleven by the oak tree.

The idea was that they would stand together during the ribbon cutting and make their way as a group when it was time to sing. But Liz had completely forgotten about the arrangement; she really was at sixes and sevens today.

Grabbing Lowenna by the hand, she started to extract herself from her friends.

'I have to find the choir. I'll see you a bit later,' she told Esme, who nodded briefly before returning her gaze to the processing dignitaries.

There were ten children in all standing beneath the tree, ranging in age from six to eleven. Lowenna had been considered just that little bit too young to sing.

Jean, in a flowery shirt and beige trousers, was holding on to two of the littler ones and looked immensely relieved when she spotted Liz.

'Thank goodness!' she said, nudging Ruby, who turned and pressed her palms together in mock prayer. 'We thought you'd abandoned us!'

Liz apologised for being late and asked if they'd seen Alex, who was to accompany them on the accordion. Alex was Robert's head chef, who had a penchant for fifties music and sported an Elvis-style quiff.

Rather surprisingly, perhaps, he also played the accordion for the local morris men.

'He's over there by the fence with Loveday and Jesse,' Jean replied, pointing, and Liz noticed Loveday's pink hair first, followed by Alex's black quiff and Jesse's blond curls. She was pleased to see that they were with the Mexican visitor, Chabela, who might otherwise have been on her own.

Rick was hovering close by with Audrey, but she had her back turned to Chabela. After the mean things that Audrey had said about her in the pub, Liz doubted that Audrey would be quick to involve the foreigner in any conversation. Audrey could be awfully spiteful.

The procession had reached the gate to the playground now and someone handed a portable microphone to the smiling mayoress, who turned towards the crowd. Reg and the local MP remained resolutely at her side, but Max hung back a bit, the smile still pinned to his face, his gaze firmly on the horizon.

'Welcome, everyone,' the mayoress said. She wasn't reading from any notes. 'It's wonderful to see so many of you here and to witness the grand opening of our brand new playground.'

At this, the crowd gave a little cheer.

'We are, of course, honoured to have Mr Max Maier with us.'

She swivelled in his direction and he gave a modest nod.

'As many of you know,' she went on, 'it is thanks to Mr Maier that we have been able to save the land from development and preserve it as a play park for the children of Tremarnock to enjoy. Hopefully their children and their children's children will benefit, too, for many, many years to come.'

After this, she gave a brief summary of the moving story of how Max's grandfather had come to Tremarnock as a prisoner of war in the nineteen forties and how he had taken the village and its people to his heart.

She mentioned the message in a bottle that he had thrown into the sea when he finally left England to go back to Germany, and how it had been discovered only recently by local schoolgirl, Rosie Broome. Thanks to some clever detective work, she had managed to track

Max down and he had decided to buy the playground and have it refurbished in his grandfather's memory.

All the while the mayoress spoke, a snapper from the local paper took photographs while beside him, a woman reporter with auburn hair and freckles scribbled notes in a pad.

Max, meanwhile, had his head bowed and appeared to be listening attentively to all that was being said, his hands clasped in front of him, his legs apart and feet planted firmly on the ground.

Liz got the impression that this was a bit of an ordeal for him, and that he wasn't enjoying himself but was doing his best to play the part until such a time as he could hurry away.

This made her feel sad and a little guilty, because she knew how much he'd loved his grandfather and how thrilled he'd been initially to forge the link with Tremarnock.

It was her fault, at least in part, that the situation had turned sour. If only she had rejected his kiss; if only she'd never allowed herself to be attracted to him in the first place.

She was still looking at him, safe in the knowledge that his eyes were firmly on the ground, when all of a sudden he glanced up and stared straight at her, just as if he'd been planning this moment all along.

He caught her completely off guard and instantly her cheeks burst into flame, yet she couldn't seem to look away. Instead, he held her gaze for what seemed like an eternity, though in actual fact it could only have been a few moments.

They must have been about fifty metres apart, the length of an Olympic swimming pool, yet the distance between them seemed to shrink to nothing. It was as if they were the only two people in the field, and they were being drawn together as though by some magnetic force.

Instinctively, she took a few steps towards him before stopping herself. He, too, seemed to bend in her direction, while their eyes remained locked.

At last, with some effort of will, she managed to pull her gaze away and stooping low, she put her arms around Lowenna and picked her up. The little girl was still light, so it wasn't hard. Liz found it comforting to bury her nose in her daughter's soft dark hair and inhale the sweet scent of new skin, soap and shampoo.

But her mind was still racing with questions: what did he want? Did he still have romantic feelings towards her, or had they turned to anger? Was he after love, friendship, reconciliation – or some sort of revenge?

She told herself not to be paranoid, but from this distance at least, it was impossible to interpret his motives or guess what he was thinking.

The band stopped playing and the woman MP gave a short speech, before asking Max to unveil a large, rustic wooden sign, which was attached to a post just outside the playground entrance.

In one swift move, he pulled off the hessian sack that was covering it, to reveal a rectangular plaque. From where she was, Liz couldn't see the words that were written on it, but the mayoress read them out:

'Franz Maier Memorial Playground,' she said, adding, 'and then there are two quotes. Max chose them especially, because he thought his grandfather would have liked them:

'"Whoever wants to understand much must play much", Gottfried Benn, and "Play is the highest form of research", Albert Einstein.'

There was a general murmur of interest and quite a few folk nodded, as if they agreed wholeheartedly with the sentiments. Then, at last, it was almost time for Max to cut the red ribbon, which was tied with a rosette around the metal gate that led into the playground.

First, he said just a few short words, alluding to his grandfather's love of Tremarnock and the gratitude that he'd expressed down the years to the villagers for treating him so kindly. After that, he used a big pair of scissors on the ribbon, which fell to the ground, and declared the park officially open.

At that point, the crowd gave an enormous whoop and a host of small children, shrieking excitedly, started to surge towards the now open gate.

'Er, wait a moment please.'

The woman MP looked dismayed, then relieved, when most of the children stopped in their tracks and retreated back to their parents' sides.

'We're going to have a demonstration now from the local gymnastics group, then there'll be a special surprise for our honoured guest.'

The MP grinned at Max, who smiled broadly back, but Liz didn't think that he was being sincere. She believed she knew him well enough by now to recognise when he was genuinely happy, and this was just put on.

Before long, a gang of mostly girls in bright leotards, plus a few boys, had entered the playground. They entertained onlookers with a fantastic display of vaults, handsprings, somersaults, cartwheels, twists and balances.

The crowed oohed and aahed appreciatively and Lowenna, still in Liz's arms, was transfixed.

After about ten minutes, Jean whispered in Liz's ear, 'We'd better get going. We're on next.'

Together with Ruby, the women ushered the choir over towards the playground, and waited just outside until the gymnasts took a bow.

'And now,' said the mayoress, taking the microphone again, 'it's time for our special event. Please welcome the Kernow Kids, Tremarnock's newly formed sea shanty choir. All the children attend the local village primary school and they've been practising hard in the past few weeks. So, ladies and gentlemen, a big round of applause now for THE KERNOW KIDS!'

The crowd duly obliged, clapping enthusiastically while the children, along with Liz, Jean and Ruby, assembled in front of the ship. They were soon joined by Alex, with his accordion, and the mayoress handed the microphone to Liz.

She had been prepared for this and knew that she was to say a few words but even so, her legs felt like jelly when she started to speak. She deliberately avoided looking at Max, for fear that she'd lose her nerve entirely.

'We know that Mr Maier's grandfather loved the sea, and he also loved Cornwall,' she said, 'so we thought – what better than to get the children to sing a few famous sea shanties? We hope you enjoy them, and please, those of you who know them – and lots of you will – please feel free to join in.'

Turning her back to the crowd, she nodded to Alex to play the first note and led the children with a 'one, two, three' into the first line of the song, 'The Robbers Retreat':

Come fill up your glasses and let us be merry!
For to rob and to plunder it is our intent.

The children, all in their white sailors' hats, put their hearts – and lungs – into the performance and sang with great gusto.

There was much chuckling, cheering and clapping at the end, before they launched into 'Drunken Sailor', 'Mingulay' and 'Spanish Ladies', complete with rousing hand gestures and lots of 'heave-ho's'.

For the grand finale, they performed 'The Song of the Western Men' about the brave Cornish patriot, Squire Trelawny.

It was the unofficial Cornish anthem and when they reached the refrain, the hairs on the back of Liz's neck prickled.

Here's twenty thousand Cornish men
Will know the reason why!

She had sung the song to Max, in the car going back from the airport on the very first day that they'd met.

By the time they reached the final chorus, he had the words off pat and was joining in lustily. She could still recall how very much at ease she'd felt with him, this virtual stranger. He'd teased her and they'd laughed a lot; it was almost as if she'd known him her entire life.

Did he remember those few moments, too? Back then, she hadn't given them any significance, but after what had happened subsequently, she'd viewed them rather differently.

After all, it wasn't every day that you met someone with whom you felt a strong affinity and it wasn't as if she'd been looking for it, either. She was a married woman, for goodness' sake, with two daughters, a home and a tortoiseshell cat.

Yet it had happened with Max, and since then she'd been doing her best to make it un-happen, or at least to convince herself that it had been just a silly little flirtation. She and Robert had been going through a bad patch, she'd got briefly carried away with the excitement of it all and ultimately, it had meant nothing.

Yet the hairs on the back of her neck told a different story. The sooner this was over and she could go home, the better, she thought. She just had to get through the next couple of hours, then she could breathe once more.

When the singing was over, the mayoress announced that all the other children could now use the playground. Immediately, a gaggle of youngsters and their mums and dads flocked towards the entrance and before long, you could hardly see the climbing frames, swings, slides and roundabouts through the sea of bodies.

While Lowenna and a little friend were occupied in the sandpit, Liz found a bench nearby and plonked down, relieved to have a moment to herself.

'Hello, Liz.'

A deep voice behind made her jump and her heart seemed to pole vault into her mouth, threatening to land, with a splat, on the ground in front.

She knew exactly who it was, of course.

'Hi,' she said, twisting around to find Max standing right beside her and forcing her mouth into a tight, painful smile. 'How are you?'

It was a fatuous question, but she couldn't think of anything else. She wasn't surprised when he didn't respond to it.

'I got your email,' he said instead. 'I thought you weren't coming. What made you change your mind?'

No sugar soaping, no niceties, nothing. He was straight to the point.

'They asked me to lead the choir. I felt I couldn't say no.'

He laughed, loud and humourlessly.

'And there was I, hoping you just couldn't keep away. How disappointing!'

His voice was heavy with sarcasm and she writhed uncomfortably on the bench. She'd far rather have kept things light, pretending that nothing had happened, but she should have known that small talk wasn't his thing.

'Max...' she started to say, and his body stiffened, every fibre on alert. 'I can't...'

He gave a low, hollow groan, which hurt her, too, like a blow struck deep into her gut.

'It's OK,' he said, swallowing. He was trying to compose himself, she could tell, and he was speaking more to himself than her. 'I'm going to go and mingle. They'll wonder what I'm doing.'

And with that, he turned and walked off. She didn't try to stop him. Instead she watched him retreat, his shoulders square and head held high, until he melted into the crowd and was no longer visible.

She had a hard lump in her throat and her eyes stung, but at the same time she was grateful that he'd gone. As long as there was enough space between them, she felt protected. It was when he came too close that her foundations weakened, her defences started to crumble.

'I just saw your husband.'

When Liz looked up, Chabela had taken Max's place. She was wearing a white T-shirt with three-quarter-length sleeves, a bright red, swishy skirt that ended just below the knee, and red sandals.

Smiling, she pointed towards the entrance and Liz caught sight of Robert, coming in her direction. He looked tall and handsome and immediately, the lump in her throat dissolved and her pulse started to relax.

'Hey!' he said, bending down to give her a kiss. His lips felt warm and reassuring. 'I'm sorry I missed the ribbon cutting. How did the sea shanties go down?'

Liz smiled. 'They were a big success. The kids made a few mistakes but no one noticed. I think we got away with it.'

'Well done!' Robert turned to Chabela now and shook her hand. 'How are you finding the Secret Shack? I hope Loveday's not making you do all the work?'

He arched an eyebrow.

'Oh no,' Chabela replied, rather too quickly. 'She's being really helpful. I'm enjoying myself, actually. It makes a change from marking essays.'

'Good.' Robert gave a thumbs up and she responded with a dazzling smile.

Liz was momentarily taken aback; everything about the Mexican was glossy, she thought: shiny hair, gleaming eyes, even her skin looked as if it had been polished and buffed to a sheen, like a piece of valuable walnut or mahogany, yet she didn't seem like the type to spend hours primping and preening; it must be natural. Lucky thing. Liz wondered why she hadn't noticed before.

'Are you hungry?' Robert offered Liz his hand and pulled her up to standing. 'I think the food's ready but I'll have to leave you to it. I have to go back to work, I'm afraid.'

'But you've only just arrived!' Liz protested. 'Can't you at least stay for half an hour?'

She was still feeling shaken and wanted some backup. Besides, she knew if Robert were with her, it was less likely that Max would try to speak to her again.

But Robert shook his head. 'Too busy, sorry.'

Chabela must have sensed Liz's disappointment, because she touched her arm.

'Don't worry, we can have lunch together.' She hesitated. 'That is, if you want to...'

Liz did her best to pull herself together. 'Good idea.' She made a mock-tragic face. 'That poor hog must be well and truly roasted by now. It smells delicious.'

Robert said goodbye and the women headed for the food area, with Lowenna trotting by their side. After loading their plates with meat, apple sauce, cold potatoes in mayonnaise and salad, they sat on a corner of rug on the grass beneath the oak tree.

The rug belonged to Tabitha, who had just opened a bottle of wine when she saw the threesome approaching.

'Good timing!' she said, grinning. 'I've got extra glasses. Come and join us!'

After they'd eaten, Danny got out his mouth organ, Tabitha her guitar and they started to play some folk songs. The pair sounded very good together and soon they had quite an audience as folk gathered around in a circle and a fair number joined in with the singing.

As Liz glanced around the field, she could see different groups of people eating, just chatting together or playing frisbee. There was even a game of rounders under way. This involved some quite elderly grannies and grandpas versus children, which didn't seem very fair, but they were all clearly having a lovely time and no one minded.

You could feel people's happiness; it was palpable, and Liz found herself thinking how lucky she was to live in such a beautiful village, among kind people who looked

out for each other and who – most of the time, anyway –
seemed to have each other's best interests at heart. To
her, it was more than just a place, it was a state of being.

She had discovered Tremarnock long before she'd
found Robert, and initially it was the village and its
inhabitants that had helped her and Rosie back on their
feet. Little by little, they'd built a new life for themselves,
then she and Robert had fallen in love, Lowenna had
come along, and their joy had seemed complete.

That she, Liz, would do anything at all to jeopardise
this hard-won happiness seemed unthinkable – yet she
had.

'Hey! You look like you're a million miles away!'

She was brought back to the present by a nudge in
the ribs from Tabitha, who had put down her guitar
and was squatting beside her. The music and singing
had stopped and Liz hadn't even noticed.

Tabitha, who was of mixed race, had long, wavy, jet-
black hair, brown skin and soft brown eyes, which were
now fixed on Liz.

'I was just thinking how lucky we are to live here,'
she said, smiling. 'I'd rather be in Tremarnock than
anywhere else in the world.'

'Me too.'

Just then, a group of people standing around and
talking a little way off moved apart and Max came
into view. He was in the middle of them all, the centre
of attention, moving his hands and arms in a way that

suggested he was in the process of trying to explain something rather complicated.

He hadn't seen Liz yet, but she stiffened all the same. It was all she could do not to cry out in surprise.

Tabitha must have sensed something. Looking from Liz to Max and back again, her eyes widened and she cleared her throat self-consciously.

'He seems a bit different from the time he came before,' she commented, watching Liz rather too closely for comfort. 'He seems tense and uptight.'

'Does he? I haven't noticed.' Liz tried to act casual but her voice came out as a bit of a squeak.

She leaned forwards to scratch an imaginary itch on her ankle and when she glanced up, he was staring at her again. His look was intense and a bit wild, almost desperate, perhaps, as if he were trying to plug a gap in a dam with nothing but his finger, like the Dutch boy in the famous story.

She wasn't sure how to respond. Without realising it, she held her breath for several seconds, convinced that Tabitha would hear her heart pounding in her chest.

Half of her wanted so much to dash over and throw her arms around him, just as if he *were* that little boy by the dam who needed comforting. The other part wanted to run – fast – the other way.

'What's up, Liz?'

This time, Tabitha's tone was concerned and urgent. 'You can talk to me, you know.'

Liz opened her mouth and for a split second, she thought that she might tell her friend everything. She trusted Tabitha and valued her judgment. And after all, what were friends for?

Instead she said, 'Nothing.' Shifting her gaze away from Max, however, she knew that he was still looking at her. She plucked a daisy from the grass and started to pick off the delicate petals, one by one.

'Nothing at all.'

Chapter Thirteen

IT WAS ONE OF THOSE lazy summer Saturdays that seemed to go on for ever. The combination of warmth, sunshine, food, music, plenty of bonhomie and even more alcohol meant that no one was in any hurry to leave, and indeed, there was no need.

Most people didn't have work the next day and there was no school for the children. When Danny suggested fetching the portable outdoor speaker from his pub, he received numerous offers of help, and soon there was a bit of a disco going on beyond the oak tree.

At any other time, busybody officials or, indeed, the police, would no doubt have been summoned to quash the noise and close the party down. However, as most of the officials and even some of the local cops were here enjoying the fun, it was unlikely that the celebrations would be interrupted.

There wasn't anybody to complain anyway. Practically all the residents from round about who might have been disturbed by the noise were in the field, too. The only possible objectors were the squirrels, hiding in trees, or the rabbits in their burrows, and they were sensibly keeping well out of it.

By about four o'clock, Liz felt that she'd done her bit, shown her face for long enough and could quite justifiably slip away with Lowenna without causing any raised eyebrows.

The little girl, however, had other ideas.

'Me, me!' she shouted, tugging at her mother's dress and pointing in the direction of the blaring music.

Liz could see Rosie standing at the edge of the makeshift disco floor, chatting to a school friend, while Rafael was showing off nearby, doing a worm dance.

'It's time to go home now,' Liz said, but Lowenna shook her head and tugged even harder.

'I'll come over with you,' Tabitha suggested, taking her own son, Oscar, by the hand. 'We can gawp at the teenagers. That'll annoy them!'

It would have been difficult to say no, and as they got closer to the action, Liz could tell that something was up with Rosie. She was smiling at her friend, but she looked strained and her eyes were sad. Liz knew her so well.

She hadn't clocked Chabela from where she'd been sitting, but she saw her now, standing to one side with Rick, Alex and Jesse. They were an unlikely foursome and Liz felt slightly uneasy, though she wasn't sure why. Loveday was nowhere to be seen.

The men were watching Rafael and laughing. Suddenly Jesse broke away and started doing his version of the Milly Rock hip-hop dance, complete with hand swoops and circles.

Chabela, who'd been quite still, resting one leg in front of the other, uncrossed her arms, clapped her hands, tossed back her long black hair and laughed unrestrainedly. She had a big, wide mouth, strong white teeth and the smile, so spontaneous and free, seemed to fill her entire face. It was very infectious.

'*Muy bien*! *Magnífico*!' she cried delightedly, which seemed to spur Jesse on, because his movements became more and more exaggerated. Meanwhile, Rafael switched to walking on his hands, which looked quite dangerous on the uneven grass. Liz hoped he wouldn't fall.

Lowenna was clearly enchanted and tried to copy, bending down to put her hands on the ground and raising one leg in the air. Everyone laughed louder, and this made Oscar go all silly, rolling around and pulling daft faces.

As she watched, Chabela took hold of the edges of her bright red skirt and swished it back and forth whilst jiggling in time to the beat. She looked beautiful and carefree and Liz couldn't help noticing Rick inching ever closer, as if he couldn't bear to be too far from her orbit.

Then, without warning, Jesse stopped what he was doing, took a few steps towards her, grabbed her hand in one of his and wrapped his other arm around her waist. Straight after, he proceeded to whisk her away from Rick onto the makeshift disco floor, whirling her around in a somewhat clumsy version of a waltz.

Chabela laughed again, before breaking off and doing a twirl, followed by a sort of solo salsa, twisting her hips in a sultry fashion and moving her arms fluidly in time to the beat. She was a natural dancer and clearly loved it. So lost was she in her own rhythm that she didn't seem to notice all eyes were on her.

Jesse stopped moving completely at that point and simply stared, with a slightly stupid grin playing on his lips. Meanwhile, Rick seemed thoroughly agitated, shifting from one foot to another. It was as if he didn't know what to do with his body and was having some difficulty holding back and preventing himself from charging onto the dance floor to claim Chabela for himself.

As if this wasn't enough, Rafael then pushed forward with a sort of swagger, and the folk around the edges, including Felipe, who was taking a well-earned break, took a step back. The others were either jigging desultorily, as if aware that the entertainment was happening elsewhere, or had given up altogether and joined the audience.

Rafael, who was tall, thin and athletic, ran a hand through his Mohawk – a bright green strip of hair that stuck up at right angles to his scalp and bristled down the centre. The rest of his head was shaved.

He knew that he was a causing a stir and milked it for all it was worth, flexing his muscles and cracking his knuckles to show off the thick silver rings on his fingers and thumbs.

He was wearing his trademark black T-shirt and jeans and had large round holes in both earlobes, lined with silver rings, like flesh plugs, off which hung substantial wooden crosses.

Some of the villagers had found him rather intimidating at first, but now that he'd settled into village life, they'd grown used to him. They knew that he was a bit of a softie, really, and wouldn't hurt a fly.

Besides, his school didn't allow the Mohawk or flesh plugs so he only ever showed them off at weekends, which meant that everyone got some respite from them.

Raising his arms above his head, he clapped a couple of times like a swaggering male flamenco dancer, then, watching Chabela all the time, he started to mimic her moves, snaking his hips in an outrageously sexy way while his feet strutted back and forth, seemingly independently of the rest of him.

She appeared to remain in her own world but she must at least have been aware of his presence, because sometimes she would mirror his shapes, rather than the other way around. And although no part of them was touching, it was as if their bodies were at one, entirely in tune and synchronised, like a pair of courting swans.

It was rather as if the villagers were being treated to their own, personal Latino dance performance and they seemed entranced. However, when Liz checked on Rosie, she could see that her daughter was very upset, biting her lip and trying to hold back the tears. After all, Rafael was *her* boyfriend, sort of, anyway, though he seemed to have forgotten it. Plus, Rosie was shy and sensitive, which was hardly surprising, given her history. He really should have known better.

On the other side of the dance area, Loveday had appeared now, too, and was standing with her hands on her hips, glaring at her boyfriend, Jesse, who was like a lovesick fool. Liz didn't even dare look at Audrey, hovering in a proprietorial fashion near Rick, but thought that she could sense disapproval emanating from the older woman's every pore.

Liz's heart sank. Chabela was clearly enjoying herself immensely, pouring her heart, body and soul into the music, and seemed to have no idea of the upset she was causing.

She couldn't be accused of leading Rafael or Jesse on because she was barely looking at them, so absorbed was she in her own rhythm. Indeed, she looked almost as if she were in a trance. But Liz guessed that this would be no consolation to Rosie, or Loveday, for that matter, and it wouldn't stop Audrey from gossiping, either.

'Encore!' someone shouted, when the music came to an end and Rafael stayed where he was, eager for more. He was so young and fit that he probably could have gone on dancing for hours.

For a moment it seemed that Chabela would continue, too, but during the pause, she glanced up, scanned around the audience for the first time and a shadow fell across her face.

Perhaps the penny had dropped and she'd realised the attention that she was attracting. Whatever the reason, she smoothed her wild hair, tucked it behind her ears as if embarrassed, and frowned in dismay.

'I'm tired,' she said, wiping a lower arm across her brow with an exaggerated sweep. 'Thank you, *señor*.' And with that, she gave Rafael a mock curtsy and melted, apparition-like, into the crowd.

Liz turned back to Rosie. She was about to ask if she wanted a drink or an ice cream but didn't get the chance, because the girl put her hands over her eyes and started to half limp, half run across the field towards the exit.

'Rosie!' Liz called, and, 'Darling!' but it was too late, because the girl was already out of earshot. She could move fast when she wanted to, despite her disability.

'What eez the matter? Is she sick?'

It was Rafael who spoke. He had left the floor to the other dancers, who were beginning to stream back now that the music had started again, and he'd clearly spotted Rosie racing off.

Liz was too angry with him to reply. Turning instead to Tabitha, she said, 'I have to go after Rosie. Would you mind dropping Lowenna off on your way back?'

Tabitha nodded. She'd seen what had happened, too.

'I don't think we'll be long after you. I won't let Lowie out of my sight.'

As Liz bent down to explain to her youngest where she was going, she was distracted by an angry voice. Glancing up, she saw that Loveday was standing right in front of Jesse, alternately jabbing a finger in his direction and shoving him in the chest with the palm of her hand.

'You tart!' she was shouting. 'You fucking bastard!'

Liz winced. You could see the spit spraying from Loveday's mouth and she was bright red in the face.

She was a couple of inches taller than Jesse in her heels, and he looked thoroughly intimidated. He didn't even attempt to retaliate but just stood there with his head bowed and shoulders hunched, his arms hanging limply at his sides.

'Now, look here—'

Rick stepped forward to intervene, but Audrey grabbed his shoulder.

'Don't you dare get involved!' she hissed. 'You've caused quite enough trouble as it is.'

Rick muttered something but Liz didn't wait for Audrey's reply.

'I have to go!' she whispered to Tabitha, before jogging across the field in the direction of Rosie, hoping that she wouldn't be too late to catch her up.

Whatever else was going on, Rosie took priority. Liz could never bear to see her daughter upset and felt right now that if given the chance, she would gladly strangle Rafael with her two bare hands.

The gate that led into the field was wide open and the road outside was clear. Turning right, she was hoping to spot Rosie heading down Fore Street towards home. Liz was concerned, however, that instead of making for Bag End, her daughter might go up onto the cliffs, or into the woods outside Tremarnock, where she could stumble and fall on her wonky leg and it would be difficult to find her.

Even if she didn't hurt herself physically, isolation wasn't good for anyone and bottling up her feelings wouldn't help either; she needed to talk and Liz wanted to be there to listen.

The car park was still packed with vehicles. She could see them through gaps in the laurel hedge, stuffed together like sardines with barely enough space to open the doors and climb inside.

Feeling out of breath, Liz slowed to a fast walk for a few moments, intending to pick up the pace again once she'd recovered. As she passed the entrance, however, something made her turn and she caught sight of Max, on his own on the other side of a bright blue hire car, preparing to climb into the driver's seat.

Her guts turned to mush and her brain swam. His head was bent and he mightn't notice her. Should she tiptoe by? But then he glanced up and she knew that all was lost.

'Liz!' he said once more in a hollow voice, as if they'd been separated for years. 'What are you doing?'

Never before had she felt so torn, between going after her daughter and staying with this man who seemed to hold such power over her. Should she try – yet again – to resolve once and for all this conundrum that she found herself in with him? If she didn't do it now, he'd have gone back to Germany and it would be too late.

Then she pictured her daughter's distressed face and imagined her running for the woods.

'Rosie,' she said. 'I must—'

'Where is she? Is she all right?'

Max's concern sounded genuine. He seemed to have switched in an instant into a different mode and at that moment, Liz forgot all about their differences and found herself gabbling about what had happened. It was a relief to share her worry and she felt instinctively that he, being a father himself, would understand.

'She was really upset... she was crying... I must find her...'

Liz was crying a little herself now, too.

'Where d'you think she's gone?'

In seconds, they'd hatched a plan. He would run down to the beach and if Rosie wasn't there, he'd take the path up to the cliffs. Meanwhile, Liz would check the house first, then call Rosie's mobile before picking up the car and making for the woods.

'Text if you find her,' Max said. 'I'll do the same.'

Without more ado, he sprinted off down Fore Street. Liz hurried back home, thinking only that she was profoundly grateful he'd been there to help and it was lucky that she'd stumbled across him in the car park after all.

IT WAS STRANGE, LIZ THOUGHT, how you could often sense that a house was empty even without looking around. The moment that she entered Bag End, she just knew that Rosie wasn't here.

It was true that her shoes weren't lying abandoned in the hallway and she hadn't slung her jacket or sweatshirt across the banisters, as usual, instead of hanging them neatly on the coat rack.

The carpet runner was still firmly in place, not scuffed at the edges, there were no sounds of music coming from upstairs and the kettle wasn't boiling in the kitchen.

Mitzi the tortoiseshell cat slunk out of the room next door, yawning, and draped herself around Liz's feet, a sure sign that she hadn't been fed.

But none of these clues would have totally persuaded Liz of her daughter's absence. Rather, it was the stillness in the air, as if the atoms and molecules, the protons, electrons and neutrons that were in a state of constant agitation when the house was occupied, were enjoying a well-earned rest.

Even so, Liz called out her daughter's name and checked each room to be absolutely sure, and no one was present. When she tried Rosie's mobile, no one answered, and it was then that her imagination really began to run riot.

Disturbing images flashed before her eyes: Rosie lying in the forest at the roots of a tree with a broken leg; Rosie at the foot of a cliff, with the tide lapping over her.

Liz told herself not to be silly, but it didn't work too well. There really was no need for her to watch scary films or TV drama series; her mind was quite capable of conjuring up terrifying scenarios all by itself.

Next, she tried Robert's phone, but he didn't pick up either. Then she remembered that he'd told her he'd be running the Secret Shack single-handed for a few hours before closing, as the temporary staff weren't able to stay on that long. No doubt his mobile would be off or on silent. She sent him a quick text, asking him to get in touch, but had little hope of a speedy answer.

Sitting on the end of their bed, she could hear the seagulls stomping overhead, probably preparing to roost, and she found herself gnawing at the corner of a fingernail and frowning. Where was he when she needed him most? Not here, that was for sure.

She had phoned the local council about the gulls the morning after Robert claimed he'd almost been attacked by them outside the house. Unfortunately, an officious-sounding man from the Environmental Health department had confirmed that anyone killing or otherwise harming the birds could pick up a £5,000 fine or a six month prison sentence.

As neither Liz nor Robert wished to fork out or go to jail, the birds, it seemed, were sitting pretty. It would have been comforting to have Robert around right now, however, even if only to bang a broom handle against the ceiling and shout at them.

A loud buzzing brought her back to the here and now. Max's name flashed up on her phone and she quickly swiped to answer.

'I've got her,' came his voice and she exhaled deeply.

'Oh thank God. Is she OK? Where was she?'

'She's fine, yes. She was on the beach – right at the other end, beyond the rocks.'

There was a pause when he offered the phone to Rosie and Liz could hear the two of them talking. Rosie sounded upset still. Her voice was cracking and she let out a sob, so he came back on the line.

'She can't really speak.' His tone was apologetic, as if it was somehow his fault, which of course it wasn't. 'I'll bring her back now. We won't be long.'

Liz went downstairs to fill the kettle and it was only then that she began to feel nervous about seeing Max again. As she fetched three mugs and a half-eaten walnut cake from a tin in the cupboard and set them on the kitchen table, she gave herself a stiff talking-to.

Whatever had happened in the past, she must put her own unease to one side and show Max how thankful she was for his help. Also, it was crucial to act normal around him in front of Rosie. She had taken a strange dislike to the German the last time he'd visited. Liz never had discovered why, but feared that her daughter was no fool and might have suspected that something was going on between him and her mother.

The mere thought that Rosie might be suspicious made Liz feel sick and when someone knocked on the door, she was so on edge that she almost cried out. After quickly smoothing her fringe and straightening her skirt, she hurried to answer. On opening the door, Rosie ran into her arms and buried herself in Liz's chest.

It was a long time since she'd wanted a hug like this and Liz held her daughter tight. Rosie felt thin and vulnerable, she was crying softly and her tears started to soak through Liz's dress, leaving a damp patch on her breastbone.

'There, there,' she was saying, 'it's all right,' all the time stroking her daughter's hair while her chin rested lightly on Rosie's head.

Some moments passed before Liz even looked at Max, standing right behind, and when she did, she was struck by the softness in his eyes and the gentleness of his expression. He seemed quite different from the tense, hard, inscrutable man of earlier in the day.

'Thank you so much,' Liz managed to say, with a steady gaze. She wanted to convey her heartfelt gratitude.

'Glad I found her,' he replied, with a small smile.

There was a slight pause when Liz opened her lips to speak. She noticed his brows lift, as if he were hoping for an answer to a question that had long been troubling him, but then she closed her mouth again. She hadn't known what she wanted to say anyway.

'I'd better go,' he said with a sigh. 'My flight leaves early tomorrow.'

'Won't you have a cup of tea first? I've just boiled the kettle.'

He glanced down the hallway and seemed to hesitate before shaking his head.

'You two need to be alone. I don't want to get in the way.'

Rosie made a snuffling noise and Liz couldn't argue with him; she really did need to talk to her daughter.

She was about to thank him again but he stopped her.

'Liz?'

His tone was urgent and she felt herself stiffen. Rosie did, too.

'Will you write and tell me how she is? I'd like to know everything's OK.'

Liz's heart seemed to sink and rise simultaneously because she knew that she couldn't refuse. Now, she had a perfectly good reason to be in touch, which was both negative and positive at the same time.

She shouldn't be in contact, of course, she should ask someone else to do it for her. But she'd be kidding herself if she didn't admit that she dreaded the thought of never seeing or hearing from him again, and even more so now that she'd set eyes on him once more.

'Of course,' she said, attempting a polite smile, but she must have given something more away because the corners of his lips seemed to curl up like the fronds of a young fern or the scroll of a violin handle.

'Good,' he said, nodding slowly, as if he needed time to absorb the information.

They were still at the open door and Rosie had scarcely moved, but she shuffled now and broke the spell.

'I guess it's goodbye then,' said Liz. 'Safe flight tomorrow.'

Max turned his back and raised his right hand high above his shoulder – perhaps in thanks or recognition or simply to say goodbye, she wasn't sure. He kept it raised, with all five fingers spread wide, as he walked down the garden path, then when he reached the gate, he waved it from side to side a few times without looking back, as if he knew that she'd still be watching.

She smiled, because the gesture was funny and a bit flirty at the same time, a moment shared between just the two of them.

'Mum!' Rosie's voice brought her crashing back to reality.

'Come on, you,' Liz said, closing the door and leading her daughter towards the kitchen. 'I'll put the kettle back on. There's no problem in the world that can't be solved with a cuppa, a cuddle and a good old chat.'

Chapter Fourteen

CHABELA WAS ANXIOUS TO GET away from the playground, the field and, suddenly, the village itself. As she hurried from the makeshift dance floor she felt guilty, as if she'd done something wrong, but she wasn't sure what.

It had been ages since she'd danced like that at a gathering, and she'd enjoyed it so much; it had felt wonderfully freeing, and the fact that she'd been joined by someone who, like her, really knew how to salsa, had made it all the more entertaining. She'd always loved dancing, ever since she was a little girl, and could never understand people who didn't.

To her, it hadn't mattered who Rafael was, only that he clearly adored music and movement just as much as she did. But when the song had stopped she'd suddenly become aware of a peculiar atmosphere and when she'd glanced around, she'd realised that some people were staring at her in a not entirely friendly way.

This wasn't unusual. She'd attracted attention, good and bad, all her life, or ever since she'd grown up, anyway, and had managed to ignore it most of the time. However, she'd felt so safe and comfortable in Tremarnock up to now, so welcomed by the whole village, that it was a shock to think she might have upset anyone, male or female. It was the very last thing that she would have wanted.

It crossed her mind that it might be considered bad manners in Tremarnock to dance with a younger person, or maybe people had a problem with the fact that Rafael and Rosie were boyfriend and girlfriend. But Chabela hadn't meant anything by it; it had just been a bit of fun.

She bit her lip and swore that from now on, she'd do her best to steer well clear of all the local boys and men, including Rick; she wouldn't even look at them if she could possibly avoid it.

It was still only five thirty and she wondered what to do with herself until bedtime. She'd seen Bramble and Matt by the playground, with drinks in hand, chatting to friends, and it didn't seem as if they'd be going home any time soon.

Chabela didn't fancy rattling around Polgarry Manor on her own with just painful feelings for company. As the weather was still beautiful – warm and sunny – she decided to go for a stroll along the cliff top. Hopefully, she'd wear herself out and be ready for a long sleep when the time came. She had work tomorrow and wanted to wake up fresh.

Strolling along Fore Street towards the seafront, she passed the Hole in the Wall, which belonged to Tabitha's partner, Danny. The door was open and there was a young woman standing behind the bar, but otherwise the place was silent and empty.

She had to walk carefully on the uneven cobbles, and just a little way past the steeps steps that she'd taken to reach Simon's house, a small, sharp stone slipped into her espadrille.

'Ay!' she squealed, limping a couple of paces before she had to stop.

Leaning back against the wall for support, she crooked one knee, resting her foot against the other leg, and tried to tease out the stone from beneath her instep with a little finger.

When she put the foot back down, however, the pebble was still there. It was only tiny but it hurt a lot. Damn! There was nothing for it; she'd have to take off the whole shoe.

Bending over, she started to untie the laces around her ankle. She was aware that she didn't look exactly ladylike with her bottom in the air, but fortunately the street was deserted. Or so she thought. It was a bit of a surprise, therefore, when she was startled by a noise nearby, like someone clearing their throat, and then a man spoke.

'Er, can I help?'

The sound of the voice made Chabela jump. The shoe was off by now and there wasn't time to put it back on, so she hopped around clumsily on one foot to find out who it was.

'Oh!' she said, when she saw Simon hovering just behind. He would have been subjected to the sight of her prominent posterior, all the more obvious in the red skirt, of course, and she could feel her face heat up. 'What are *you* doing here?'

She instantly regretted her words because his palm shot up and he slapped his forehead several times, before shrugging his shoulder and jerking his chin in that nervous way of his.

'Sorry,' she said quickly, hoping to calm him down. 'That sounded rude. It's just that you made me jump. I had a stone in my shoe.'

As she pointed unnecessarily to the red espadrille lying on the cobbles, he followed her gaze. For a moment the two of them just stood there, gawping, as if neither had ever come across such an extraordinary sight before.

She was pretty good at standing on one leg, flamingo-like, but after a while, her balance started to go. Wobbling precariously, she grabbed with both hands onto the nearest thing that she could find – which happened to be Simon's shoulder.

Her sudden weight made him lurch to one side and it seemed likely that they might both tumble like dominoes into a heap on the ground, but he managed to save himself in the nick of time.

Now that she had support again, she, too, returned to an upright position, with both feet firmly on the cobbles. The only problem was that with just one sandal she was lopsided, listing like a drunken sailor.

Simon didn't seem to notice. 'Here,' he said, bending down to retrieve the other espadrille, which he turned upside down and shook vigorously, to get rid of the stone. Then he gave the sole one final slap to be absolutely sure, before passing the shoe over.

'That should be all right now. You can put it back on.'

'Thank you,' she said, setting it down with heel and toe pointing in the right direction, but for some reason, she couldn't slide her foot into place. By the time she realised that the bag on her shoulder was upsetting her equilibrium and she should put it down, it was already too late.

Letting out a scream, she tumbled backwards and landed with a bump on her buttocks.

'Ouch!' she hollered, as bits of gravel sank into the palms of her hands and her bottom started to throb. '*Que duele*!' That hurts!

'Oh dear! Oh dear me!' Simon was clearly horrified. Hurrying to her aid, he squatted down, tucked his hands beneath her armpits and without more ado, he literally heaved her up just as if she were a sack of coal – or potatoes, perhaps. It wasn't exactly dignified.

He must have had strong muscles because she was no featherweight and soon she was standing again. Straight away, he stepped behind her and proceeded to give her an energetic brush down, rather as if she were a dusty rug hanging on a washing line. Back, hips, thighs and calves, they were all swept and patted clean of debris, but he was careful to avoid her bum.

'There!' he said at last, moving around to face her again. 'You're all back to normal. How are you feeling?'

'OK – I think.'

The truth was that she was hurting a bit, and her pride had received a blow, too. It occurred to her that she hadn't exactly stuck to her vow to keep well away from the village men, either. In fact she'd messed up quite spectacularly by practically falling on top of one of them. But then Simon did something unexpected, which took her mind right off the pain and shame.

Crouching down again, he reached for her hands and placed them on his upper back. She had no idea what was happening but she didn't object. After that, he picked up her bare foot ever so gently and rested it on his knee. Her toes, with their pale pink painted nails, looked small, wiggly, and really rather vulnerable against the roughness of his dark twill shorts.

There were a few specks of dirt, which he dusted off lightly and methodically with his fingertips before slipping her foot into the espadrille.

Touched by his gentleness, she didn't wish to offend and let him finish. Finally, he carefully tied her laces in a surprisingly neat bow before setting her foot back on the ground.

'I feel like Cinderella,' she said with a laugh, while he was still squatting at her ankles. 'Thank you.'

This was his cue to spring up and take a few steps away so that he was no longer occupying her personal space.

'My pleasure. I was on my way to the cliffs.' He glanced at the sky, which had turned ominously grey in the short time they'd been there. 'But I might not bother.'

'How funny! I was going there too.'

It was only now that Chabela had the chance to look at him properly and take in what he was wearing: a dark grey T-shirt, stiff, practical-looking cargo shorts (brown, of course) with lots of pockets, and thick black socks tucked into big brown walking boots. There was a black backpack at his feet, which he picked up and pulled on, along with a slightly silly beige floppy hat.

The ensemble was comfy, no doubt, but not exactly elegant. Chabela couldn't help remembering Alfonso's summer wardrobe, which consisted of well-cut linen suits for work and slim-fitting chino shorts with fine cotton tailored shirts for weekends.

He always wore suede loafers in hot weather; he had several pairs in different colours. And she'd never, ever seen him in walking boots. He wasn't remotely sporty and hiking definitely wasn't his thing.

As far as she knew, he liked to spend his vacations reading and relaxing by a pool or the sea. When his children were younger, he'd told her that he paid for them to have lessons in surfing, tennis, horse riding or whatever was their particular passion at the time. That way, he barely had to move from his sun lounger, except for meals, which his wife or maid would cook.

Simon was fiddling with the cord of his hat beneath his chin, adjusting it for a secure fit, and she found herself thinking that she rather admired his lack of vanity. At least if a woman went out with him, she wouldn't have to compete. Not that he was ever likely to have a girlfriend, of course. Sometimes, when she'd been on a date with Alfonso, she'd clocked him checking out the other women to make sure they'd noticed him. He loved the fact that she was admired wherever they went, but he wanted his own place in the sun, too.

'Well, goodbye then.' Simon had finished adjusting his hat and put out his hand as if to shake hers.

Chabela pictured the rain lashing down as she wandered alone on the cliffs, then she thought of her isolated room at Polgarry Manor, which was elegant and comfortable but seemed awfully big for just one person, especially on a Saturday night when the rest of the world was out partying.

'I, um...' She wasn't usually reserved, quite the opposite, in fact, but the hostile response to her dancing earlier had made her unsure of herself. 'Would you like...'

The exact same words slipped from his mouth simultaneously and they both laughed in surprise.

She paused, waiting for him to go first, but he shook his head, insisting on letting her.

'I was going to say...' she began again, licking her lips. 'I wondered... if you're not doing anything, that is... shall I cook us some dinner?'

Never in her life had she found it so difficult to be direct; perhaps some of his English awkwardness was rubbing off on her.

'I don't have any ingredients, obviously,' she went on, 'but if you've got eggs, I could make an omelette?'

'Plenty of eggs – and potatoes. I imagine you need those, too?' He gave a small, tight-lipped smile, which she'd come to realise was his way of showing considerable pleasure. 'Thank you, that would be nice.'

In the face of such restraint, Chabela had an insane urge to throw her arms around him, just to see what he would do. She was learning the hard way, however, that exuberance didn't seem to go down too well around here, and she managed to rein herself in.

'*Bueno*,' she said instead, rubbing her hands together. They were still smarting from her fall. 'Is the local shop open? Shall I go and get us some wine?'

She was thinking that they'd both need alcohol to oil the wheels of conversation; he could be hard work, unless she could get him on one of his pet subjects, which seemed to be education, semantics – and Mexico.

He insisted that he had wine already and in any case, the stuff they stocked in the general store was mostly unpalatable.

Chabela wasn't dressed for a hike over the cliffs to his cottage at this time of day. It would no doubt be quite late by the time she left, and she hadn't brought a sweatshirt, cardigan or waterproof. She wasn't about to point this out, however. The prospect of not having to spend the evening alone far outweighed any potential future discomfort, and if the worst came to the worst, she could probably borrow something of his.

'Off we go,' he said cheerily, bounding up the steep steps like a mountain goat, while Chabela trudged behind. He was exceedingly fit and she was only halfway up by the time he'd reached the top. He didn't even look out of breath.

Thankfully the rain held off until they reached Karrek Row, when the sky, which had been getting progressively darker, suddenly turned almost black. A flash of lightning was followed almost immediately by a crack of thunder, then the heavens opened and water slashed down, quickly drenching them right through. It was as if they'd stepped into the shower.

'Run!' Chabela shouted, and she was aware of Simon by her side as they hurtled past the row of cottages – Gwel Teg, Seabank, Wild Rose, Crafty and Farthing. When they finally reached Kittiwake on the end, she didn't think twice before opening the gate and rushing up the path first to his front door.

It was a tremendous relief to step inside the dry porch, which smelled of roses and rubber boots. Water streamed down the back of her neck, off her clothes and onto the stone floor, leaving a sizeable puddle at her feet.

'Oh dear!' Simon muttered as he hurried in behind her. He was soaking wet like her and panting heavily and she smiled, comparing his mild exclamation with the much stronger words that she'd just used under her breath.

It was quite a squeeze for them both to fit under the small porch roof and she could feel him scrabbling around in his pocket for the key. Then he leaned forwards to put it in the lock, opened the door and she was just about to rush in when he stopped her in her tracks.

'Er, wait a minute,' he said, in an abrupt, schoolmasterly sort of voice. 'Please take off your shoes first.'

Duly reprimanded, she bent down obediently to untie her laces and he did the same, before removing his boots and shuffling around to get in before her.

'I'll fetch some towels. I suggest you undress in the cloakroom downstairs. I'll dry your clothes while you have a bath.' He sounded as if he were planning a military operation. 'Wait there. I don't want the floors getting soaked.'

And with that, he disappeared, leaving her standing and shivering inside the entrance like a wet dog.

She might have felt offended, but actually it wasn't a bad scheme. She could understand why he didn't want his wooden floor drenched and her spirits lifted when he returned soon after, clutching a big, soft beige towel and a white towelling bathrobe.

By the time she'd removed her soggy garments and slipped the bathrobe on, he was upstairs running her bath, into which he'd poured a few drops of delicious, lavender-scented oil.

It was strange to see him standing over the tub, whooshing his hand around in the water to test the temperature. The room was hot and steamy, and she felt tired suddenly and longed to immerse herself in the bubbles.

He had changed, too, into a rather strange, long tan kaftan, made of rough cotton and complete with ethnic stitching around the sleeves and neck. It looked like something he might have picked up on travels in North Africa, perhaps, or the Middle East.

For a moment, she felt slightly uncomfortable. What was she doing in a strange house and foreign country with a man in an odd, long tunic, who was possibly naked underneath, and whom she barely knew? But she needn't have worried. He turned off the taps and straightened up.

'There you go,' he said in an efficient sort of way without so much as a whiff of suggestion. 'I've put some clothes for you on the chair.'

She glanced at the wicker seat in the corner of the room and saw that there was, indeed, a pile of folded-up garments, which was very thoughtful of him.

'They'll be too big, but you can use the cord to keep them up,' he went on. 'Your stuff shouldn't take long to dry.'

Then he turned and left the room, closing the door firmly behind him.

As Chabela sank into the soothing water, which was just the right temperature, she found herself thinking how silly she'd been to doubt him for one second. He was far too involved in work and his books to be interested in her as anything other than a friend or, more accurately, an acquaintance. After all, they'd only just met and besides, he wasn't the sort of man to get close to anyone.

No, with him she was perfectly safe and she needn't even fret about the villagers gossiping, because he didn't seem to mix much with them. Self-contained, that's what he was. For some reason, she found it really rather appealing.

The bath was a smooth, comfortable shape and as she lay back and rested her head on the rounded edge, she scanned her environment to see what, if any, light it shed on the owner.

The room itself was pleasingly square and cosy, with clean white walls, blue shutters on the little window, and blue and white patterned tiles in places that might get splashed with water.

There was a narrow shelf facing her, on which were set a number of green glass bottles in different shapes and sizes, each with a cork stopper and a handwritten label.

She could just about read the words from where she was: Apple Cider Vinegar Detox Bath; Seasalt Detox; Chamomile and Rosemary – Headache; Lavender – Calming; Peppermint – Fatigue.

She recognised the writing as being his, and guessed that he'd probably made the concoctions himself. It rather amused her to think of him grating and grinding herbs and plants and infusing them into delicious-smelling potions, like an old-fashioned apothecary. He was quite unlike any man she'd ever met.

The tub was positioned underneath the window, looking out over craggy cliffs, sea and sky. Through the open slats of the shutters, she watched the rain descending in perpendicular sheets, until gradually it began to ease off and the sky brightened again briefly before darkness began to fall.

She was so comfortable that she could have stayed there for ages, but then she noticed the water starting to cool and felt guilty for taking so long.

Simon might want the bathroom himself and furthermore, she'd offered to make supper and he was probably ravenous. The thought of food made her own stomach rumble; it was hours since she'd eaten.

Heaving herself up out of the water with a sigh, she noticed that her skin had turned wrinkled and pink like a baby's. After reaching for the towel, she dried herself down quickly before climbing rather tentatively into the clothes that Simon had left for her.

They were, of course, mostly brown: brown corduroy trousers, which she had to roll up and tie at the waist with the piece of cord that he'd kindly put out for her; thick brown socks, which felt extremely cosy; a white T-shirt in a man's size medium, and a very old, holey, heathery-coloured, round-necked woollen sweater, which was a nice touch, as it was probably the only vaguely colourful item in his wardrobe.

When she checked herself in the mirror above the washbasin, she thought that she resembled one of the scarecrows you see in the countryside outside Mexico City, with dark, glittery buttons for eyes, red cheeks and a knotty black wig on top. As she had no comb, there was nothing whatever that she could do about her hair, so she decided to go downstairs just as she was, first letting the water out of the bath and giving it a cursory wipe down.

Simon was laying the table in the kitchen. He'd obviously showered in her absence because his hair was wet and he'd changed into a new pair of trousers and a buff sweater.

His face was slightly pink, like hers, and when she apologised for looking a mess, he seemed surprised, as if her appearance was of absolutely no significance whatsoever.

'Are you warm enough?' he asked. 'I can put the heating on if you like? Or get you an extra layer?'

Chabela said no, she was fine, and she walked over to the worktop, where he had put out a carton of eggs, milk, an onion, potatoes, some fresh parsley, butter, olive oil, salt and pepper and a big wedge of cheddar cheese.

Alongside were a frying pan, a wooden chopping board and a sharp knife, and there were some fresh green salad leaves soaking in the sink, along with baby tomatoes, a cucumber, radishes and a bright yellow pepper.

'They're from the garden,' he said, noticing where she was looking. Then he smiled. 'I've checked them for slugs. Don't worry, they're completely safe.'

There was everything here that she needed, and she proceeded to mix the eggs with milk, salt and pepper and chop the potatoes and onion into small chunks. Then she warmed some butter in the frying pan and watched the vegetables start to sizzle, giving off delicious smells.

Meanwhile, Simon opened a bottle of red wine and passed her a glass, before fixing one for himself.

'Do you have any music?' Chabela asked, stirring the onions and potatoes with a wooden spoon.

'What would you like to listen to?'

'You decide.'

Before long, she recognised the deep, soulful voice of Aretha Franklin wafting in from next door. She took a sip of wine, which trickled down her throat and seemed to warm her right through, then she and Simon stood side by side while he prepared the salad and she kept an eye on the omelette to make sure that it wasn't burning underneath.

By now, it was dark outside and the room was lit by under-cupboard lights, spaced apart at regular intervals above the worktops. Simon hadn't bothered to pull down the blinds, and through the window you could see the knobbly outline of the gnarled old apple tree in the garden, while overhead shone a crescent-shaped moon, surrounded by bright stars twinkling like jewels in the clear night sky.

There was no external noise, only Aretha's voice and the spitting pan. Chabela realised that she hadn't felt safe and cosy like this for years, possibly ever. From where she was standing, she couldn't see the neighbouring house or any other signs of life; she and Simon could have been on their own on a desert island, for all she knew, with everything they needed right here: food; wine; music; books – and each other for company.

'It's ready,' she said, checking herself, for she could sense her thoughts starting to run away with her.

She sliced the omelette into two, put each half on a plate and then they sat down opposite each other with a basket of French bread, the open bottle of wine and a big bowl of salad in between.

The food tasted good and after wolfing down a few mouthfuls, she helped herself to a big portion of greenery, with a generous amount of Simon's home-made vinaigrette on top, sprinkled with rock salt.

'*Muy rico*!' she said, picking up her wine glass and taking a big slurp. Delicious! There was only an inch left in the bottom, so she gave herself a refill before offering to do the same for her host.

'Not yet, thank you,' he said stiffly, placing a hand over his glass, which still had a few inches of wine in it. 'I'd better pace myself.'

'Really?' Chabela was unaccustomed to such self-discipline and raised her eyebrows. 'You don't have to work tomorrow, do you?'

He shook his head.

'Then have more, go on!' Without waiting for an answer, she filled his glass to the brim. 'If you don't help me out, I'll drink the whole lot!'

He seemed to loosen up a little after that and she noticed his features starting to relax, the lines on his forehead beginning to smooth out, as if someone had pressed it with a hot iron.

Knowing that he wouldn't like personal questions, she decided to tell him more about herself instead. She mentioned her childhood, her mother, her schooling, her life at the university and the research projects she was doing. He was particularly interested in them. The only subject that she didn't touch on was Alfonso.

'A few years ago, I spent the whole summer in Paracho,' she said, taking another forkful of omelette. 'I was doing some research on rural schooling. I stayed with a local family; they were very kind but the house was pretty basic.'

Simon said that he'd visited the small town in Mexico's western highlands, which was famous for its guitars.

'I bought one for myself, actually, from a market stall.'

It was quite a coincidence, as few foreigners knew about the place, and Chabela was delighted. She asked if he could play anything, and when he said that he was teaching himself, she insisted that he fetch his purchase.

The instrument was handsome and cream in colour, with pearl and wood details around the sound hole and on the head.

'Let me hear something!' Chabela cried, clapping her hands in excitement, for it was a large bass *guitarrón* of the type favoured by the mariachi bands popular all over Mexico.

'Really?' He looked uncertain. 'I'm not much good.'

But she was adamant and at last he sat down again, pushed back his chair, rested the guitar on one knee and began to strum.

He chose a rousing, patriotic ballad called '*México Lindo y Querido*' ('Lovely Beloved Mexico'), which she knew well and it took her right back to her childhood. He had a good voice and she closed her eyes, allowing her thoughts to drift away.

About halfway through, however, he struck a discordant note and the music stopped dead. Chabela, who had been in another world, jumped in surprise and her eyelids sprang open.

Without any explanation, he handed her the guitar, which she took without a murmur; she was far too dazed to ask why. Then he left the room again and when she looked around a few moments later, she let out a cry – 'Oh!' – and burst into laughter.

For there, standing in the doorway, was her host as she had never seen him before, with his shoulders thrown back, his head held high and a fake-haughty expression on his face. The most extraordinary thing, however, was what he had on his head: the most enormous, wide-brimmed sombrero that could barely even fit through the entrance.

He looked absurd, of course, especially with his tortoiseshell glasses on, and he twirled a pretend moustache, which made Chabela laugh again. So he did have a sense of humour after all!

This time, when he started to play, she joined in the chorus:

México lindo y querido
Si muero lejos de tí
Que digan que estoy dormido
Y que me traigan aquí

My beautiful and beloved Mexico
Should I die far from you
Let them say I'm asleep
And bring me back to you

On the very last word, she stood up and howled soulfully, like a dog baying to the moon. This made him laugh out loud, too, and he roared again when she plonked herself back in her seat, knocked back the last of her wine with a dramatic flourish and turned the finished bottle upside down in the empty salad bowl.

'I'd better get some more,' he said doubtfully, propping his guitar on the edge of the table. 'Or would you prefer coffee?'

'No! Wine!' she cried, shaking her head and slapping her fist on the table. She was enjoying herself immensely and didn't want the evening to end.

He duly topped them up before starting on his next song, another mariachi classic called 'Volver Volver' ('Going Back, Going Back'). This was followed by a flamenco tune, which he messed up but it really didn't matter.

'Encore!' she shouted, when he came to the end, but he shook his head, insisting that he couldn't play another note.

'That's it! You've heard the full repertoire.'

He got up to prop the guitar in the corner and when he came back, he'd put his glasses down and was flapping his hands and blowing on his fingers.

'They get sore after a while. It's the metal strings. They're quite hard and stingy.'

By now, they were about halfway through the second bottle of wine and Chabela, who wasn't especially shy in the first place, seemed to have lost any of her remaining inhibitions.

'Here! Let me do it,' she said, leaning forwards, grabbing his hands and rubbing his fingertips, which were red and dented from the hard guitar strings.

She would have done the same for a friend or family member, even without the wine, but not for an acquaintance – and an uptight English one to boot.

He stood stiffly while she massaged but didn't tell her to stop, and when she looked up to check that he was OK with what she was doing, he gave her a real, proper smile that lit up his whole face.

It was strange seeing him without his glasses and she was taken aback by the warmth and playfulness of his grin as well as the gentle candour in his eyes. Now that she could see them properly, she noticed a depth and steadiness behind the hazel irises. It was quite a revelation.

He looked like someone that she could trust and she glanced away quickly, afraid that she might reveal some of the hurt and despair that she carried around with her wherever she went. She didn't want anyone, least of all him, to see that.

He must have noticed something, however, because the atmosphere seemed to change and he removed his hands and started to clear away the supper dishes.

'It's getting late,' he said quietly, filling a washing up bowl with hot, soapy water and stacking the dirty dishes. 'You can stay here tonight if you like? In the spare room,' he added quickly. 'The bed's already made. You shouldn't drive anywhere now; you're almost certainly over the limit.'

It was after ten o'clock, she had indeed had a fair amount to drink and was grateful for the offer, but she didn't want to put him out. Besides, her head was muzzy and as it had stopped raining, she decided that she could do with some fresh air.

'Thanks, but no,' she said. 'I'll get a taxi in the village and pick up my car in the morning.'

When he realised that her mind was made up, he fetched her clothes from the dryer and told her to change again in the cloakroom. Then he dug out an old jacket for her to borrow and insisted on bringing his torch and walking with her to the bottom of the steps. This time, she didn't argue; she didn't fancy trying to find a path across the cliffs in the dark on her own.

They went in silence most of the way, but it didn't feel uncomfortable. Chabela was thinking that all the while she'd been at Kittiwake, she'd virtually forgotten about the hostile looks she'd received earlier in the day when she was dancing, and they seemed less important now, rather as if it was all a bad dream. She'd even temporarily forgotten about Alfonso.

She was quite sorry when they reached the bottom of the stairs that led down to the village and spotted the old-fashioned lamp that lit this section of the street with a warm, yellowish glow. She could see her way to the end of the road perfectly well now, and told Simon that she'd ring for a taxi when she reached Humble Hill; there really was no reason for him to linger.

She started to unzip the jacket that he'd lent her, but he urged her to give it back to him next time.

It was only when they said goodbye and he kissed her, lightly on the cheek this time, that she realised they hadn't even mentioned James Penhallow or any of her other Cornish ancestors. Which was strange, considering they were the only reason she and Simon had met.

'Thanks for a lovely evening,' she whispered, checking for the mobile in her bag. She was standing in a circle of lamplight, while he hovered a few feet away in the shadows.

'No, thank *you*,' he murmured back.

Chapter Fifteen

As she strolled along the dark, deserted street towards Humble Hill, Chabela replayed the evening in her head. The thing that stood out most of all, she realised, wasn't the food and wine, the warm atmosphere, Simon's surprising appearance in a sombrero or even his guitar playing.

No, what she couldn't put out of her mind was that smile – the real, proper one when she'd taken his hands in hers. And the gentle, steady look in his eyes.

She was reminded of the way Alfonso used to look at her, and how it had changed during the course of their relationship. At first he'd seemed amused, almost mocking, because he could tell she was smitten and that he could twist her around his little finger.

Later, his gaze had become soulful, fiery and obsessive. When they were together, his eyes followed her constantly and he could hardly bear it when she left the room.

Towards the end, however, a strange cloudiness had crept in behind the irises. Sometimes, when she looked at him, it was almost as if he were wearing dark glasses, because she could no longer read his thoughts.

It troubled her, but she put it down to stress at work and issues with his eldest son, who was causing some anxiety. She tried to help by being extra loving and not making too many demands.

In her heart of hearts, though, she must have known that something was wrong. How she wished now that she'd listened to her gut! She could at least have saved herself a little heartache and slightly lessened the pain of her rejection.

It had all been so different a few years previously, when Alfonso's passion and jealousy were at their peak. She was in her mid-thirties then, and beginning to come to terms with the fact that she might not have children.

She had always felt ambivalent about becoming a mother, perhaps because of the poor example set by her own, but it was unsettling to know that before too long, the choice would be taken out of her hands altogether.

Alfonso said he didn't particularly want more kids, though he didn't rule them out, but he wanted her and so she didn't look around for anyone else. It wasn't as if she was without other admirers, but most soon gave up when they realised that her heart lay elsewhere.

There was one, however, who stuck around for longer and who might possibly have been in with a chance, had not Alfonso sent him packing.

Juan Raoul was a postgraduate student at the university where Chabela taught. They got to know each other one summer, when Alfonso was out of the country with his family and Chabela remained in Mexico City on her own.

Most of the university was closed and the majority of staff and students were away, but Juan Raoul had stayed behind to complete his thesis. Meanwhile, Chabela was working on a book proposal and the pair kept seeing each other in the almost empty library, until finally he plucked up courage to come over to talk to her and they quickly became friends. To be honest, to start with Chabela was just lonely and grateful to have someone to go for coffee with.

Juan Raoul lived quite near her apartment and soon he took to dropping by with a bottle of wine in the evening when they'd both finished work. She began to look forward to his visits because he was clever and interesting and they talked a good deal about work, but had a laugh, too. They both enjoyed watching a silly, long-running, late-night TV soap and sometimes they'd play cards to unwind.

He was a little younger than her and at the time she assumed that he wasn't interested in her romantically.

Looking back, though, she was pretty sure that he had hopes of something more.

But it wasn't to be. When Alfonso returned from holiday and found out about the friendship, he put a stop to it immediately. Like some old-fashioned Knight of the Round Table, he turned up unexpectedly at Chabela's flat one evening when he suspected that the young man would be there, and virtually claimed her as his own.

She could still remember how he kept putting his arm around her, stroking her hand and hair and calling her '*mi amor*' and '*corazón*' (sweetheart). He'd never behaved like that in front of anyone before and she found it embarrassing.

She knew that his wife would be expecting him at home, but he hung around all the same, pretending to be interested in Juan Raoul's academic work whilst subtly undermining him.

He was clearly in awe of the Great Professor and seemed to wither before Chabela's very eyes. She felt sorry for him and tried to intervene, to no avail. Her lover was ruthless and in the end, Juan Raoul sloped off home, probably to rethink his entire thesis. He never visited her again. Alfonso could have that effect on people; he could destroy them with one swift blow. She recognised that now.

He stayed with her that night – what he told his wife, she had no idea – and she could still recall his words the morning after.

'Don't ever make me suffer like that again, Chabelita,' he said, holding her face gently but firmly between his hands and pressing his forehead against hers. 'I thought I was losing you. I'd be a wreck without you. You must never, ever leave me.'

Of course she assured him that she never would, safe in the knowledge, as she thought then, that it was only a matter of time before they'd be together for ever...

She'd arrived at the end of the street now, which was deserted, though she thought that she could still detect the presence of the crowds who had walked this way earlier in the day, en route for the playground festivities.

After calling for a taxi, she stood outside Liz's darkened house, her arms clasped around her, waiting for the purr of an engine coming in her direction. There was a burst balloon lying in the gutter at her feet and as she picked it up and felt its rubbery softness through her fingers, she thought of Alfonso's son Enrique's surprise eighteenth birthday party last June, just over a year ago.

He was the youngest and, she guessed, favourite child, and Alfonso had talked a fair amount about the celebrations that his wife, Pilar, was planning for the big day.

She had reserved an entire restaurant for the evening and invited more than a hundred guests, including aunts and uncles, friends, godparents and neighbours.

The cab arrived surprisingly quickly and Chabela climbed into the passenger seat. She watched while the

driver did a three-point turn before heading back the
way that he'd come. The road was clear and by now
she knew the way to Polgarry Manor so well that she
didn't need to keep checking whether they were on the
right route. Her mind was thus free to return to the
party.

There were to be speeches, dancing, a big cake, a
steel band and a giant, brightly coloured, papier-mâché
piñata, suspended from the ceiling and stuffed with
sweets and gifts.

Chabela had her own reasons for looking forward
to the event, even though she hadn't been invited, for
Alfonso had always said he'd leave his wife when Enrique
turned eighteen. At last the time was almost here.

She kept hoping that her lover would raise the issue
in the run-up to the party but he didn't, so in the end
she decided to take the initiative herself. It was a week
or so before and he was in her apartment on one of
their appointed afternoons together.

They'd just made love and she was lying in bed beside
him, his arm around her waist while her fingers played
lazily with the soft, curly hair on his chest. The window
was ajar and a slight breeze rustled the open curtains,
as the late-afternoon traffic rumbled by.

Now seemed as good a time as any to speak up.

'Would you rather wait till September to tell Pilar?'
she asked. 'It might be easier when Enrique's away at
university?'

She noticed her lover tense, but only for a second.

'Sure,' he said carefully. 'It would be best to get him settled in first.'

'How do you think she'll take it?' Chabela asked then, and Alfonso carefully removed his arm from around her middle and sat up against the pillows.

'Badly.'

She noticed his frown and tried to cheer him up.

'She mightn't be as upset as you think. I mean, deep down she must know your marriage is dead and has been for years. She'll probably be relieved. Once you go, she'll be free to do whatever she wants – travel, meet someone new, buy as many clothes as she wants without having to hide them from you...'

It was only a joke, but Alfonso's frown deepened. 'You don't know her. She likes security and stability. She'll be lost, angry and frightened.'

Never before had he spoken with any real concern for his wife and his words played on Chabela's mind. Even so, she didn't believe that he was having second thoughts and just assumed he needed longer to prepare.

The party was a huge success, and then the whole family went on holiday as usual. It wasn't until mid-September, when Enrique had begun his new course, that she broached the issue again.

'It must be the right time now, surely? How about tonight, when you get home?'

They were side by side on the sofa in her living room, her head resting on his shoulder, a half-drunk bottle of wine on the coffee table in front.

'I know it's going to be painful, but you can't keep putting it off for ever.'

Alfonso let out a sigh. 'It's impossible just now, *mi amor*. She's not well.'

'What's wrong?' It was the first that Chabela had heard of it.

His wife was suffering from insomnia, he said. 'She's got sleeping pills, but she doesn't like taking them because they make her tired and forgetful. She's afraid to drive in this state, so she's stuck in the house all day.'

'Can't Bertha take care of her?' Bertha was the maid. Chabela didn't like the hardness that had crept into her voice, but felt confused and a little afraid.

'It'd be too much responsibility. Pilar's not herself at all. On top of everything else, I think she's missing Enrique. A lot of women find it difficult when the last one goes, so I'm told. Empty nest syndrome, you know?'

They looked at each other and Alfonso slowly shook his head.

'Of course you don't. Why would you? You haven't got children.'

His words stung and Chabela bit her lip. It was all she could do not to bite back.

Soon after that he went home, leaving behind a chilly atmosphere and a great deal left unsaid. Alarm bells rang, but Chabela decided not to mention the subject again for a few weeks, by which time she hoped that Pilar might be on the mend.

As it turned out, however, the question didn't have to be repeated. After all those years of waiting, the answer came so suddenly and unexpectedly, it was like an earthquake or tsunami.

Chabela could remember the moment of truth as clearly as if it were yesterday. She and Alfonso had been having an early evening drink in her apartment when he received an SOS call from his older son. He had twisted his ankle playing tennis and needed a lift to the hospital. He was clearly in a lot of pain and his father rushed out in a panic, leaving behind his jacket.

After washing the wine glasses, Chabela went around the apartment, turning on lights and closing blinds. Finally, she got around to plumping the cushions in the living room and it was only then that she spotted the jacket on the back of an armchair.

She picked it up, intending to hang it in the cupboard, and for some reason felt compelled to dip a hand into one of the pockets; she'd never done that before. Inside, she found a wodge of folded up paper, consisting of several sheets of A4 stapled together. Feeling slightly guilty, she pulled the papers out and opened them up.

At first glance, they didn't look remotely interesting. As she flicked through, however, she began to feel as if someone's hands were in her guts, swirling them around and wringing them out like bits of washing.

It soon became clear that she was looking at details of luxury retirement villas for sale near the city of Mérida, on the sunny Yucatán Peninsula in south-eastern Mexico. There were quite a few to choose from, all accompanied by glossy photographs and elaborate floor plans, but one in particular caught her eye.

The property was called Hacienda Masul, which apparently meant Birdsong in the ancient Mayan language, and someone had put a ring around the name with a heavy black pen.

She could see why, because it was undoubtedly the most beautiful home of the lot: large, light and airy, with giant windows overlooking a garden filled with lush jungle plants. There were four big bedrooms with en suite bathrooms and a swimming pool, as well as a white sandy beach just a stone's throw away.

The blurb also highlighted the fact that the villa, although secluded, was not far from a shopping mall, complete with a cinema and theatre complex, and there were two golf courses and a thriving bridge club in the area, too.

The words 'Golf' and 'Bridge' were underlined in the same black pen as before, with a giant asterisk alongside. On seeing this, Chabela's hands started to shake and goose flesh chased up and down her spine. Alfonso loved golf, he always said that he hoped to play a lot more when he retired, and she happened to know that his wife was a big fan of bridge.

She tried to persuade herself that all this meant nothing. Alfonso had probably been handed the leaflets by a random estate agent in a shopping mall, or perhaps Pilar had been house-hunting and passed the details to her husband, little knowing that he was on the point of leaving her.

But why, then, keep them folded up so neatly in his pocket? Why not throw them away? And what about the underlining and asterisks?

In her heart of hearts, the answer was obvious, but Chabela needed to be a hundred per cent sure and when Alfonso arrived back at her apartment later that evening to pick up his jacket, she was waiting.

At first, when confronted, he tried to deny everything: of course he wasn't intending to retire and move to Yucatán with Pilar! Of course he wasn't specifically looking for somewhere with a golf course and a bridge club. What a ridiculous notion!

But she could tell that he was lying and in the end, with tears in his eyes, he admitted the truth: he couldn't leave his wife because she wouldn't cope without him, and the children would never forgive him either.

He also said that he was tired of working, but wouldn't dream of trying to drag Chabela away from Mexico City and the job she loved.

'The age gap between us is just too big,' he said plaintively. 'We're at different stages in life. We want different things.'

Implying that he had her interests at heart, too, was the last straw. For once, Chabela lost all control and flew at him, punching and slapping with all her might while he tried to defend himself, until she ran out of energy and slumped to the floor.

'Go,' she said wearily at last. 'Take your stuff and don't ever come back or contact me again.'

He did as he was told, all apart from the last bit. A couple of days after the debacle, he tried to call but she blocked his number. Later, he knocked on the door of her shared office at the university, but she asked a colleague to turn him away. He sent a letter, too, a long, heartfelt one, begging her to try to understand his point of view. She wasn't sure if he was hoping she would keep the bed warm for him in Mexico City once he moved away or if he simply wanted to assuage his guilt. In any case, she tore the letter up without replying.

For a few months, she went about in a sort of dream, seeming on the outside to be functioning normally, but inside she was falling apart.

She lost a lot of weight, felt permanently exhausted and often went to bed as soon as she returned from work. But she only felt more tired than ever the following day.

Colleagues started to comment on her gaunt appearance and urged her to see a doctor, but she denied that anything was wrong. Then one morning, she arrived at the lecture theatre to give a talk to third year students, only to discover that she couldn't think of a thing to say or even what topic she was supposed to be discussing.

For what seemed like an age, she just stood there, eyes wide with panic and her heart racing. Eventually, one of the female students stood up and asked if she needed anything, at which point Chabela burst into tears, rushed from the room and barely stopped crying for a month.

Still, she didn't tell anyone, not even her closest friends, what was happening and in the end it was a neighbour who came to her rescue. Concerned that she hadn't seen Chabela for a while, the elderly woman knocked on her door and insisted that she see a doctor.

The pills that he prescribed helped to get Chabela back on her feet, but she was a mere shadow of her former self. All the joy and curiosity seemed to have been sucked out of her and she could see no point in anything.

For several more months, she just went through the motions, getting up, going to work and returning to her apartment to eat and sleep. It was more like existence than living.

Gradually, her appetite and sleeping did start to improve and she began to feel a little stronger, but still, she didn't think that she would ever recover from the

grief, heartache and betrayal. She had given everything
to Alfonso and felt as if there was nothing left.

The seasons passed and spring arrived again, which
always seemed to bring with it the promise of fresh
beginnings. Still stuck in her rut, however, Chabela
began to wonder if she needed to do something drastic,
like quit her job and move cities or even countries.

She started looking at job ads for other universities
and putting out feelers, but nothing appealed. Then
Simon's letter arrived and before she knew it, she was
arranging a business visa and booking her trip to the UK.

Friends thought she was mad. Why Cornwall, for
goodness' sake? Why not Paris or Rome instead? As a
single woman, wouldn't she be safer in a big city – and
wouldn't she have more fun?

But they couldn't see inside her heart or know how
badly she was hurting. So here she was, on a dark
night in faraway Tremarnock, weaving in a taxi along
narrow country lanes that seemed as different from
the highways and byways of Mexico City as you could
possibly imagine.

It wasn't long before they reached Polgarry Manor
and passed through the heavy iron gates. About
halfway up the drive, she spotted a welcome light on
in Bramble's and Matt's bedroom window and guessed
that they must be home.

After leaving the cab and paying the fare, she headed
towards the front door. Her feet scrunched on the gravel

and the sound seemed to echo around the silent cliffs. Not so long ago, the unfamiliar quietness might have troubled her, but now, she found it comforting. The air felt soft and warm on her skin, like being wrapped in black velvet, and not far off, an owl hooted and seemed to say that she wasn't alone; she was surrounded by friends that she just couldn't see.

Never before, she realised, had she felt so connected to a place, so at one with her surroundings. It must be the Cornish blood surfacing in her veins.

This thought amused her and laughing silently to herself, she tiptoed up the stone steps to the old oak front door and used the spare key that she'd been given. For all she knew, Alfonso hadn't even heard of Cornwall, and he'd certainly never visited. Hope fluttered its delicate wings.

Here, she was forging real memories that he had nothing to do with. She scarcely dared think, far less believe it, but perhaps, just perhaps, slowly but surely, with baby steps and inch by inch, she was beginning to move on at last.

Chapter Sixteen

WHILE CHABELA SLEPT SOUNDLY IN her grand, first-floor bedroom high up on the cliff, residents in a particular part of downtown Tremarnock were having a restless night.

As it was warm, most of the windows were open in the small flat that Jesse and Loveday shared in Towan Road. This meant their neighbours could hear pretty much everything that was going on, and it wasn't pleasant.

'I saw you!' Loveday screeched. It was after midnight and she'd been shouting, off and on, for at least half an hour. 'You were staring at her chest!'

Jesse protested loudly, but his girlfriend was having none of it. 'Stop trying to deny it! I'm not stupid, you know!'

'Oh, for fuck's sake,' Jesse ranted. 'How many times do I have to tell you – I DO NOT FANCY THAT WOMAN!'

This clearly didn't cut any ice with his girlfriend, however.

'You're playing with fire!' she went on, as if she hadn't heard a word of what he'd just said. 'She's not this nicey-nicey person you think she is. She's a man-stealer. Don't tell me I didn't warn you.'

The pair descended into loud bickering for a while, until Jesse's voice rose once more above the hubbub.

'WHAT THE HELL ARE YOU TALKING ABOUT?' he yelled, and at this point, his girlfriend leaned right out of the window, cupped her hands around her mouth and began to holler.

'THAT MEXICAN COW! WATCH OUT, EVERYBODY! SHE'S A MARRIAGE WRECKER! SHE'S AFTER YOUR MAN!'

If the neighbours had been in doubt about what or who was the cause of the couple's argument, they weren't any longer. As far as anyone knew, there was only one Mexican currently residing in Tremarnock – and that was Chabela.

The rowing quietened down after that and most folk were able to doze off at last. Unfortunately, however, the damage had been done, the genie was out of the bottle and it wouldn't go back in.

News travelled fast in the village and by noon the following day there was scarcely a soul who hadn't heard the gossip about the sexy foreign visitor. Some said they didn't believe it, others shook their heads and condemned prevailing 'petty bourgeois' attitudes, but 'There's no smoke without fire,' seemed to be the general consensus.

Robert was one of the few prepared to defend Chabela, even after Liz told him how upset she'd made Rosie.

'She's Latina,' he said. 'Dancing's in her blood. I doubt she even noticed Rafael was flirting with her, or Jesse for that matter. And even if she did, and she encouraged it – and I bet she didn't – it would only have been a joke. They're young enough to be her sons.'

Liz was inclined to agree, but still, loyalty lay with her daughter, who had wept bitterly last night and insisted that she and Rafael were finished. Chabela should have known better, Liz thought, and her behaviour seemed like a double betrayal, given that Liz was the one who'd introduced her to Robert and helped her get the job.

Of course Chabela had no idea what was going on behind her back, and was a little surprised by the cool reception she received at the Secret Shack the following morning from staff and customers alike.

'Are you OK?' she asked Loveday at one point, because the girl looked shattered and was scarcely speaking to her. Rosie seemed distinctly frosty, too, and Rafael was monosyllabic.

'I'm fine,' Loveday replied, swishing her hair and marching over to the other side of the kiosk.

But something was clearly up and Chabela did fear that her salsa dancing yesterday might be to blame. It seemed to make no sense, however, because she hadn't done anything wrong. Was it her, or had the world gone mad?

The beach was usually packed on a sunny Sunday, even before the official start of the tourist season, and today was no exception. For several hours, Chabela was so busy serving teas, coffees, ice creams, cold drinks and snacks that she had no opportunity to delve further into the strange behaviour going on around her.

To her dismay, even Liz, who came at lunchtime with Lowenna, Tabitha, Danny and Oscar, was offish. In fact the only person who seemed, if anything, friendlier than ever, was Rick.

He turned up at around five p.m. having closed his shop early, and hung around at the kiosk for a while drinking a bottle of mineral water. When he'd finished, he made a great to-do about the fact that he was going for a swim.

'Anyone care to join me?' he quipped, glancing sideways at Chabela, who pretended not to notice. 'The water will be cold, but there's nothing like the hot shower after. You feel fantastic.'

He made it sound vaguely suggestive, and Chabela picked up a damp cloth and started vigorously scrubbing the work surface.

'No takers?' Rick went on. 'Shame.' And with that, he proceeded to strip off down to his trunks right in front of the open serving hatch.

Chabela tried not to look but couldn't help noticing that he had a very big body and an awful lot of stringy grey hair on his chest and shoulders.

'OK if I leave my stuff here?' he asked, plonking his clothes in a bag on the ground by one of the tables before anyone could object. 'I'll be back in a jiffy. Won't be long.'

'Like we care,' Loveday muttered under her breath, but he didn't hear. She really was in a foul mood today.

He set off for the seashore, picking his way through the groups of people still on the sand, soaking up the last rays of sunshine. The wind had picked up a bit and parasols and coloured towels were flapping. Quite a few folk had donned sweatshirts or cardigans but seemed in no rush to pack up their things and leave.

Rick wasn't deterred by the breeze either. The tide was coming in and Chabela watched his large, bulky frame in bright green shorts arrive at the water's edge. Without any girly dithering, he launched himself in with a terrific splash, forcing onlookers into a hasty retreat, and proceeded to crawl quite far out, stopping only once to look back and adjust his goggles.

Chabela couldn't help being impressed and was even more awestruck when she spotted the tall, statuesque figure of Audrey striding down the beach in bare feet, a towelling robe and white swimming cap. Before long, she'd shed the robe and was doing a stately breaststroke towards Rick, though she'd have a devil of a job to catch up with him.

'Are you *sure* they're not dating?' Chabela asked Loveday, who was standing nearby. She had temporarily forgotten that the girl wasn't speaking to her. 'They seem to get on so well.'

'What's it to you?' Loveday said nastily, which made Chabela flinch, as if she'd been stung by a wasp or bee.

'Please,' she said, mustering all her courage and looking steadily at Loveday. 'Will you tell me what I've done wrong? I really don't know, but I want to put it right if I can.'

Loveday chewed her lip. For a moment it looked as if she might just be considering opening up, but then she tossed her hair again in that haughty fashion and turned the other way.

'I don't want to talk about it.'

There was nothing more that Chabela could do, and she was still smarting when Robert arrived unexpectedly with boxes of fresh supplies. He smiled warmly at her and she felt like kissing him because the atmosphere had been so cold all day.

'How're you doing?' he asked, setting the boxes down in the corner; they didn't look heavy.

Chabela failed to notice Loveday's scowl or Rosie's gimlet eyes, but Robert did.

'I hope you two are pulling your weight?' he said fiercely. 'Why do I get the impression Chabela's doing most of the work round here?'

'That's not true!' The last thing she wanted was to seem like the class swot. She was in bad enough odour as it was.

She must have looked rather desperate because without any warning, he reached out, put an arm around her shoulder and gave her a friendly hug.

Grateful for his kindness, she inclined her head towards him and allowed herself to sink a little into the comforting embrace. She was only there a moment, but it was long enough for Liz to see.

Having got up from where she was sitting, she was making her way towards the kiosk, holding Lowenna with one hand and carrying a heavy basket in the other. On spotting the pair, she did a sort of double take, then tried to cover it up by bending down to adjust her flip-flop.

It didn't fool Chabela, however, who quickly broke away, fearing that Liz might get the wrong end of the stick. Sure enough, she approached with a stony smile and laid claim to her husband by asking if he wanted her to record something for him on TV.

'Is the restaurant full tonight?' she said then, and he told her there were a few empty tables.

'We might get passing trade,' he added, scanning around the beach. 'I reckon there are quite a lot of people down for the day.'

Just then, Rafael dropped a tumbler on the floor and it smashed into pieces. Everyone turned to look.

'Shee-it!' he yelped, staring helplessly at the broken bits of glass.

He had had his back to Liz while he was loading the dishwasher, but he glanced at her now, and Chabela noticed the other woman purse her lips menacingly.

As he hurried away to fetch a dustpan and brush from the cupboard, it dawned on Chabela that her worst fears had probably come true: it must be because of her that Rafael and Rosie had fallen out; Rosie was upset with him for salsa dancing, which meant that her mother was too, and also with Chabela by association. Loveday was furious with her as well, because Jesse had been showing off in front of her.

None of it was her fault, but no one would believe it. How on earth could she remedy the situation?

In normal circumstances, she would have hurried over to help Rafael clear up the mess he'd made, but she feared it might only cause further trouble. And she was scared of looking at Robert with Liz close by, so she stared at her feet instead.

To add to her woes, Audrey and Rick returned dripping wet from their swim and Rick seemed absolutely determined to attract Chabela's attention.

'Señorita Penhallow!' he said, in a voice so loud that neither she nor anyone else could ignore him. 'You should have come in with us! The water's gorgeous!'

She felt obliged to give a weak smile in return, which unfortunately, he seemed to interpret as encouragement.

'Next time!' he added, with a wink. 'I look forward to it!'

Loveday made a scoffing sound, Liz narrowed her eyes again and Audrey growled like a cat with a mouse in its sharp little teeth.

'Oh dear!' Chabela muttered under her breath, wondering which way to turn. 'Everything's going wrong. I wish I was back in Kittiwake with Simon!'

ROSIE WAS WEEPY AND DISTRESSED when she returned from her shift at the Secret Shack and claimed that she couldn't go to school the next morning.

Despite all Liz's best efforts to dissuade her daughter from being too hasty, she'd gone ahead and dumped Rafael by text before work, and then they'd barely exchanged so much as a glance all day.

Rosie said she couldn't face seeing him at school or having to tell friends that they'd split up.

'Why don't you call him and suggest going for a walk or a coffee?' Liz said reasonably, as they sat at the kitchen table eating supper. 'Go on. Do it now. Wouldn't it be better to talk things through?'

'I don't *want* to talk to him,' Rosie replied miserably. 'I never want to see him again. I thought he really liked me. I really, really liked him. Everything's ruined.'

Before Liz could reply, her daughter got up and half limped, half ran upstairs and slammed her bedroom door shut.

'Oh dear.' Liz was on the bottom step, clutching the handrail and staring helplessly after her daughter. That saying – you're only as happy as your unhappiest child – never rang more true, because right now, she felt truly and utterly dejected.

Instead of going to bed, she paced around the cottage late into the evening, waiting for Robert to return. She wanted him to listen and be comforting, not to solve her problems, but he was weary after his long shift and tried to brush off her concerns.

'Rosie's overreacting,' he said, bending down to take off his shoes in the hall before giving his wife a kiss. 'She's a teenager. That's what they do. It'll blow over.'

His face was pale, almost grey, and he had dark circles under his eyes. He worked so hard. Liz knew that what he needed now was sleep, but she had needs, too, which weren't being met.

'That bloody woman,' she said viciously, meaning Chabela. She was being deliberately provocative but couldn't seem to stop herself. 'I wish she'd never come here. She'd probably be gone by now if *you* hadn't given her a job.'

By now, they were in the kitchen. Robert had his back to Liz, pouring a glass of water from the tap, and he swivelled around, eyes flashing.

'So it's my fault now, is it? And who was it who introduced her to me, exactly?'

Normally even-tempered, he was running on empty tonight.

'I didn't interview her, though, did I?' Liz bit back. 'I suppose she pulled the wool over your eyes and charmed you silly, just like she does with everyone.'

The implication that Robert had been hoodwinked by a Jezebel type seemed to annoy him even more, but still, he did his best to try to defuse the situation.

'Look,' he said quietly, 'it's late. You're tired and down because Rosie's in a bad patch. Don't take it out on me.'

He tried to walk past her with the glass in his hand, but short as she was in height, she managed to bar the way.

'Why is it always me who has to pick up the pieces? I feel like I'm a single parent most of the time.' She could hear the resentment and self-pity in her voice and hated herself for it.

He reeled, as if he'd been punched in the solar plexus.

'Do you?' he said. 'Do you really?'

She wanted to tell him no, it wasn't true. He was always there when she needed him most; it's just that he worked slavishly hard and worried about his businesses. He had such a deep fear of financial insecurity, which probably went back to childhood, and providing for his family was his main priority. Rather than berate him, she should try to help him find more balance.

Even as all this whizzed through her mind, a set of very different words were taking shape in her mouth. It was as if all the fear, excitement, guilt and confusion that she'd been feeling over Max these past few months had suddenly crystallised into a giant, multi-surfaced glass ball.

This wasn't to do with Rosie and Rafael any more, or Chabela. It wasn't even to do with Robert's long absences at the restaurant. It was about them as a couple, their marriage and whether they were meant to stay together.

'We need to talk,' she said heavily. 'I've got something to tell you.'

Her mouth felt dry and a sense of dread crept through her body, from her toes right up to the top of her head. Robert could clearly tell that she was serious, because he slumped down on a kitchen chair, his back rounded and shoulders hunched.

'What?' he asked in a dull, anxious voice.

There was still time to row back; she could have made something up, anything to avoid the inevitability of what was to come. But she didn't.

'I-I think I might be in love with someone else,' she stammered. 'At least, I'm attracted to him – and he is to me.'

The air between and around them seemed to freeze. Nothing moved. Their chests stopped rising and falling with their breath; they scarcely blinked. It was as if time stood still.

Then all at once Robert put his head in his hands and groaned, long and loud. It was an animalistic sound, primitive and scary.

'What do you mean, Lizzie?' he asked. 'What are you talking about?'

She couldn't look at him, she just stood there beside him and told him about Max, about how they were just friends at first, but how over the course of the last few months, their feelings had deepened into something more.

'I didn't want it, I still don't,' she said. 'I told him not to contact me when he went back to Germany the last time. I wasn't even going to go to the playground ceremony, but then Jean roped me in and I felt I couldn't say no.'

Tears sprang from her eyes and dribbled down her cheeks, but she didn't bother to wipe them away.

'Part of me never wants to see him again...'

Robert looked up at her now, with hollow eyes and sunken cheeks. His face seemed to have deflated, like a beach ball.

'And the other part...?'

She swallowed. 'I don't know. I'm sorry. I don't understand. I still love you and want to be with you. Why did I even look at him? It makes no sense.'

Robert snorted then, a nasty, sneering sound.

'Oh my God! Don't you think I notice other women? Of course I do. I get attracted to people all the time. It's normal. The difference is, I value our marriage so I don't do anything about it. Obviously it doesn't matter to you the same way.'

This hurt more than he realised, and she was dreading the next question, which she knew would come.

'So, how far has this gone? Have you slept with him?'

'No!' she cried. That much was true.

There was a pause and he gave an almost imperceptible nod.

'Do you *want* to sleep with him?'

This was more difficult. She didn't know what to answer so she shrugged and shook her head at the same time.

He sighed and it was such a sad sound that she wanted to hug him, but she'd forfeited that right. She hated to see her husband in so much pain, and knowing that she was the cause made it infinitely worse.

'What else has happened? You'd better tell me everything. Did you snog?'

Of course he'd chosen the playground word deliberately, and it worked. She felt foolish, immature and ashamed. She deserved it.

'Yes,' she said, and then he wanted to know the details – such as where it had taken place and when.

As soon as she'd finished, he pushed back his chair and rose quickly. She had no idea what he was thinking.

'I'm going to get my stuff and sleep at the flat tonight.'

The two-bedroom apartment above A Winkle in Time, which Robert managed for the owners, was empty at the moment, awaiting a new booking.

He sounded determined and she didn't try to argue with him. She didn't blame him. She deserved to be punished and probably would have done the same to him under similar circumstances. It still hurt, though.

'Can we talk about this properly – another time, I mean?' she asked in a small voice as she trailed after him up the stairs.

'I don't know,' he said in a way that made her stomach twist and her legs start to give way, so that she had to hang onto the banisters to stop herself from falling. 'I'm not sure there's anything more to say.'

She should have known that he'd react like this. He was very black and white when it came to relationships. After all, he'd been messed around by a previous girlfriend, his fiancée no less. It had taken him years to believe in love once more, and now Liz had shattered his trust all over again.

The fact that she and Max hadn't been to bed together was almost irrelevant. The feelings that she'd admitted to were enough of a betrayal and she wasn't sure that Robert would ever forgive her.

Hovering by the window, she watched him as he wordlessly threw his toothbrush and a change of clothes into a backpack before going downstairs and opening the front door.

'What shall I tell the girls?' she called helplessly after him as he strode towards the gate.

He stopped for a moment and turned his head.

'No idea. You should have thought of it before you got involved with *that* man.'

Straight away, he marched on long legs out of the garden and up Humble Hill towards South Street. There was a lump in Liz's throat that had become so painful, she could hardly bear to swallow. But she didn't cry.

Instead, she stood in the hallway for a few minutes, savouring the bitter and all-too-familiar taste of isolation.

It had been the same when her previous partner, Greg, had left, and she'd experienced it many times subsequently, when she and Rosie had lived alone. Somehow, though, she didn't think she'd ever felt quite as bad, or as bleak, as she did now.

The knowledge that she'd brought it on herself didn't help, but more importantly, she'd never truly been in love with Greg. Robert was different. When she finally met him, she believed that she'd found her soulmate.

Panic rose up from her belly into her larynx, causing her to choke. Blind with tears and fear, she stumbled into the sitting room and stood before the fireplace, taking deep inhalations and trying to calm herself down.

Of course Robert was angry and upset, he had every right to be, but it would blow over. Tomorrow was another day and with luck, they'd both see things more clearly in the cold light of morning.

But what of Max? Strangely enough, she'd scarcely thought of him for the past couple of hours. He seemed almost an irrelevance. This house, the hearth, her girls asleep upstairs and Robert around the corner, they were what really mattered. How could she ever have thought otherwise?

Chapter Seventeen

THE DRUMMING OF SEAGULL FEET on the rooftop sounded positively melancholy when Liz woke at around five the following morning.

She'd slept on Robert's side, breathing in his comforting scent on the pillow, but she'd been aware all night of the cold, empty space next to her.

Now, as she looked at his things on the bedside table – books, mostly, and a wonky glazed pot that Rosie had made for him one Father's Day – she felt a profound sense of regret and sorrow.

She could only begin to imagine how much he was hurting and half wished that she could take back what she'd said. Deep down, though, she knew that she couldn't have lived with her guilty secret for much longer. It had been slowly growing in the dark, like a cancer, and she suspected that only the light of exposure could destroy it.

Tormented by her thoughts, she decided it would be better to get up and distract herself until the girls woke. She was anxious that Rosie might still be refusing to go to school and decided to try to coax her down by making her favourite breakfast pancakes.

Fortunately all the ingredients were to hand, and a choice of toppings, including blueberries, raspberries and chocolate spread. Liz also made rolled oat granola with walnuts and seeds, which she toasted in the oven, hoping that the tempting smells would waft upstairs into the bedrooms.

She wasn't hungry herself in the least, but she put on the radio and made herself a pot of coffee, all the while hoping that Robert would magically appear at the door, give her a big hug and tell her that she'd just had a bad dream. She didn't want to call him in case he was still asleep and besides, something told her that it would be wise to let him cool off for a bit longer, though in truth, he wasn't usually one to fester or hold grudges. He'd come about; he always did.

This thought kept her going until Lowenna came downstairs at around six thirty with her favourite teddy under one arm and a thumb wedged in her mouth like a cork.

Her eyes were still sleepy and her dark silky hair was tousled. Feeling a rush of love, Liz picked her up and kissed her on one soft, warm cheek after another. She smelled sweet and faintly grassy, like full fat milk. The

scent reminded Liz of wheat fields, of new-born lambs –
and heart-breaking innocence.

'Where's Dadda?' was the little girl's first question,
while she was still in her mother's arms.

The hard, scratchy lump reappeared in Liz's throat
and she put her daughter gently down.

'He's at work,' she said, crossing her fingers that there
wouldn't be a tantrum. Lowenna adored her father,
she was a real Daddy's girl, and most mornings they'd
have a tickling match, or play 'thumb wars' in Liz's and
Robert's bed.

Fortunately, the little girl was distracted by the sight
of Mitzi poking her round head through the cat flap,
quickly followed by the rest of her furry body. She had
her eye on her bowl of food, but Lowenna grabbed her
before she could get there and hung on tight.

Mitzi didn't look too happy. Letting out a pathetic
miaow, she struggled a bit and tried to jump down, but
Lowenna only tightened her grip.

'Come on, puss-puss,' she said in a strict, motherly
sort of tone. 'Do you want a nice ride in your pram?'

It was no doubt the last thing that Mitzi fancied,
but the pair disappeared into the front room where
Lowenna kept her doll's pram, and Liz could hear
her daughter trying to tuck the poor cat in. It had
become a fairly regular ritual, but it never lasted long.
Usually, Mitzi hopped out of her blankets the moment
Lowenna's back was turned and made a run for it,

scarpering through the cat flap before her mistress could nab her again.

Rosie appeared with a scowl on her face, but she was dressed in her uniform, her hair neatly brushed, and Liz breathed a silent sigh of relief. She was going to school after all, then. That was one thing to be grateful for.

'How did you sleep?' she asked her eldest.

'OK.'

Rosie plonked down on a kitchen chair and poured herself a glass of orange juice.

'Would you like some pancakes? Or I've made granola.'

'Pancakes,' she said, taking a big slurp.

It was like trying to get blood out of a stone, but Liz didn't complain. She thought that she could put up with anything this morning, so long as Rosie got to class on time at least.

Lowenna had playgroup at the Methodist church hall from ten to twelve o'clock. Then, and only then, could Liz start to think properly about how she was going to try to piece her marriage back together.

'Have you heard anything from Rafael?' she asked Rosie, as she poured some of the pancake mixture into a frying pan and watched it begin to sizzle.

To her surprise, Rosie revealed that he'd sent her a text late last night.

'What did he say?' Liz held her breath, fearing a sharp rebuff, but Rosie nonchalantly twizzled a strand of hair around her finger and told her mother that he'd apologised.

'How nice!' Liz couldn't disguise her relief and pleasure, which clearly annoyed her daughter enormously.

'No it's not! He shouldn't have done it in the first place. Then he wouldn't need to say sorry, would he?'

'Of course not,' Liz replied quickly, lowering her head and flipping the pancake over to cook the other side.

She wanted to ask if Rosie had accepted the apology and if she and Rafael were back together again, but was scared of having her head snapped off. At least the signs were optimistic, though.

Liz had a feeling that relations between the two would be restored by the end of the school day. She certainly hoped so; they were good together and seemed to make each other happy – most of the time, anyway.

Rosie left promptly and after dropping Lowenna at the church hall, Liz made her way to A Winkle in Time. Not having heard a squeak from Robert, she decided that the best course of action would be to face the situation head on and request a meeting.

She was still praying that he'd have softened up and would be keen to sort things out. Her heart sank, however, when she arrived at the restaurant to find the door shut tight and no signs of life inside. Robert usually got to work first, at around nine a.m., unless he had something else to do beforehand, and now it was ten twenty.

There was no separate entrance to the flat and Liz didn't have a key anyway, so she had to ring the bell. Presently, Robert opened the inner door that led from the apartment into the restaurant. When he saw his wife peering through the bevelled glass, he hesitated for a moment before opening up.

'Can I come in?' Liz asked, noticing how pale and drawn he looked. He clearly hadn't shaved or combed his hair either.

He stood aside to let her pass and then she waited, expecting him to lead her upstairs. Instead, however, he pulled out a chair for her at one of the wooden tables and took the seat facing it himself.

'Why have you come?' he asked, scanning around the room as if he were searching for something, before resting his gaze on an invisible spot on the wall.

It wasn't a good start and it knocked her off balance, but she mustered all her courage and asked if they could please talk about what happened last night.

'Go on, then,' he replied, still refusing to meet her eye. 'What do you want to say?'

'I-I'm so sorry,' she stuttered. She wasn't used to this new, hard, unflinching Robert. It threw her completely.

'Sorry for what?' he said coldly. 'For falling in love with another man, or for telling me about it?'

'Darling—' She was hoping to take the edge off his pain, to soothe the troubled waters, but it didn't work.

'Don't call me that,' he snapped, quick as a flash. 'I'm not your darling any more.'

Tears sprang to her eyes and she found that she couldn't speak, so he filled the silence.

'I'm going to stay here for the time being,' he said heavily. 'I'll come round later to pick up some stuff. You'd better tell the girls we've had an argument, you don't need to say what it's about. I'll visit them every day and Rosie can call at the flat whenever she wants. I'll get an extra key cut for her. I want her to feel she can come and go.'

A sense of dread settled in Liz's stomach, like murky, stagnant water. He'd clearly thought it through; he probably hadn't slept all last night for planning; he looked exhausted.

'Won't you—' she pleaded, but he shook his head and raised a flattened palm.

'Stop!'

She'd been poised to beg him to come home, but he halted her in her tracks.

'Would you consider going for some marriage counselling?' she tried now. 'I've heard it's really helpful.'

'Absolutely not.'

Feeling beaten and desperate, she lowered her head and picked at the corner of a fingernail.

'When will you be willing to discuss it?' she went on, in a small voice, and his look made her insides shrivel.

'I don't know,' he said, shrugging. 'I've got no idea. Quite frankly, right now I just want you to go away and leave me alone.'

WHAT TO DO? WHERE TO go? For a while Liz wandered around the village in a sort of trance. She ended up on a bench on the seafront, staring out at the glassy ocean and wondering how her life had come to this.

The sun was shining, which seemed like an affront, when her carefully constructed world was falling down around her. For a split second, she contemplated walking out to sea and never coming back, until she thought of her girls and knew that she couldn't do it to them.

There was still an hour to go before she had to pick up Lowenna, and all of a sudden, Tabitha popped into her head and she knew that she had to see her.

Tabitha, Oscar and Danny had recently moved into a cottage close to where Tony and Felipe lived with Rafael, and Liz made her way there as quickly as she could, hoping that she wouldn't meet anyone she knew on the way.

Fortunately Tabitha was at home, watching the clock. Like Liz, she didn't want to be late for playgroup pick-up time, as Oscar went there, too.

'Come in!' she cried when she saw her friend on the doorstep. 'You look terrible!'

This made Liz, who was already fragile and slightly nauseous, immediately feel ten times worse.

The tiny two-up two-down cottage was only rented, as Tabitha and Danny were looking around for somewhere to buy. You walked straight into the sitting room, which was pleasantly furnished with modern, Scandinavian-style furniture, wooden floors and brightly coloured rugs and cushions, while the newish, mainly white kitchen was at the back.

Although most of the furniture belonged to the owners, it still had Tabitha's stamp on it. She'd finally put a few of her own colourful pictures and prints on the wall, which Liz recognised from the previous home she'd shared in the village with her ex.

There was also an eye-catching, zebra-print throw on the sofa now and a dusty pink velvet chair with a scallop-shaped back, that looked as if it had come straight out of a nineteen thirties silent movie. In fact it probably had. Tabitha loved buying old furniture and getting it restored, especially anything art deco. In a perfect world, she'd probably sing professionally and own an antiques shop on the side.

The women sat side by side on a boxy blue sofa, facing a bay window that looked out onto the narrow, cobbled street, and Tabitha asked what was the matter.

It didn't take long for Liz to fill her in on everything that had been happening, including her feelings for Max and the terrible bust-up with Robert.

Tabitha listened quietly, without showing any emotion, right up until the moment when Liz told her that she thought she and Robert might be getting divorced.

'Don't be silly,' Tabitha said, giving her friend a spontaneous hug. 'He must be really, really hurt, but he adores you. Everyone's allowed one mistake. You just have to convince him you're completely over Max. He needs to be sure you bitterly regret it and it'll never, ever happen again.'

Her words brought some comfort, but she wasn't letting Liz off the hook entirely. Tabitha said in no uncertain terms that Liz had been a fool, and she had to agree.

'Why on earth would you risk your marriage?' Tabitha asked incredulously. 'You must have known you were playing with fire?'

Liz bit her lip. 'I know it sounds mad, but I didn't think it through. I suppose I got swept away in all the excitement. I really did like Max; it wasn't just some silly crush. I know he has strong feelings for me, too.'

Tabitha looked unimpressed. 'I had a hunch something was going on. I wish you'd talked to me sooner. What did you imagine the outcome would be? A quick shag with him? Then what? You didn't really imagine you'd have a future together, did you?' She crossed her arms tightly over her chest and frowned. 'Sure, he's cute-looking, but you live in different countries and you're from completely different backgrounds. Besides, you don't really *know* him. Not properly. If you spent any time together you might find you don't have that much in common, really.' She fiddled with the corner of her sleeve. 'Does he have other girlfriends?'

Liz's eyes opened wide. 'I haven't asked him.' She realised that this sounded silly, but it was the truth.

'Well you should,' Tabitha went on firmly. 'He doesn't strike me as the type of man to be on his own for long. Actually, I wouldn't be surprised if he's a bit of a player.' She peered at her friend critically. 'Surely you didn't think you'd walk off into the sunset with him, hand in hand?'

Liz shrugged, and Tabitha let out an exasperated sigh. 'Well *that's* never going to happen!'

Liz swallowed nervously. For some strange reason, the thought that Max might be a smooth operator had simply never occurred to her. He'd always seemed quite serious and genuine, rather than flirty, and she'd been so anxious not to mess him around that it had never crossed her mind she might be vulnerable to being treated badly herself.

'I don't think he's a womaniser,' she said quietly, but Tabitha had cast doubt in her mind and Liz knew now that she'd have to ponder the matter further.

A tinkling sound outside the window made them both glance up as Nathan, the postman, cycled past, giving a cheery wave. A few minutes later, a pile of mail plopped through the letter box and landed on the doormat.

'He's late today,' Tabitha commented, getting up to fetch the mail and putting it on the little table beside her. Then she examined Liz again.

'What are you going to do?' she asked seriously. 'I don't mean about Robert. I mean, how are you going to occupy yourself while he's away? You need to find something to get your teeth into, otherwise you'll over-think things. I know what you're like, you'll go mad.'

Liz knew that her friend was right. Moping around wasn't an option, she'd be better off upping her hours at the South East Cornwall Five Fishes Project, which used volunteers to provide hot meals for the poor and vulnerable, or looking for paid employment.

'I'll get a cleaning job,' she said suddenly. She didn't fancy trying to resurrect her own business right now; she'd rather work away from home and not have to think too much, either. 'It shouldn't be difficult at this time of year.'

Tabitha raised an eyebrow. 'Really? That sounds a bit grim. Isn't there something else you'd rather do?'

Liz shook her head. 'I like cleaning. I'm good at it. I find it therapeutic.'

She paused for a moment and took a deep breath.

'You know, it's ages since I had a proper job. I never imagined I'd be a kept woman, but that's what I've become. It's not good for me, I don't think. It's time I got out and earned a living again. I need to stand on my own two feet.'

'Well done!' Tabitha said with a smile. 'I'm sure Robert will respect you for it. I can always have Lowenna, if needs be. Oscar will be delighted.'

The church clock chimed three times, indicating a quarter to twelve, midday. The time had flown. Tabitha rose, smoothing her white top as she did so. 'I need the loo, then we'd better get going. You know what they're like if we're late.'

They strolled side by side towards the Methodist hall, commenting on their favourite cottages as they went. Most had hanging baskets and window boxes stuffed with glorious blooms – red and white geraniums, midnight blue lobelia and trailing pink fuchsia. In fact the entire village was a riot of colour now, thanks also to the jolly summer bunting strung across lamp-posts and attached to shopfronts in the main streets.

The recent rain, followed by hot sunshine, had turned the lawns particularly lush and green, and daisies poked their heads through the blades of grass while bees hummed around purple stocks and lavender bushes.

Quite a few folk passed by in the other direction and nodded or said hello. Liz didn't recognise everyone and guessed that some were holidaymakers with grown-up children, perhaps, taking advantage of the relative peace and quiet before the schools broke up and the place became jam-packed.

As they continued up the hill, heading out of the village in the direction of Polrethen, in the distance they saw a very tall man with dark brown hair leave someone's house and start to climb into his car.

Liz's heart skipped, because for a moment she thought it was Robert. But then she realised that this man was chunkier and he was wearing shorts and a dark green T-shirt that she didn't recognise. Besides, Robert didn't know anyone in that cottage and didn't drive an electric blue car either.

She realised with a stab that she was missing her husband already and the reality of her situation hit her once more like a juggernaut.

Lowering her head against a powerful, imaginary force, she told herself that this wasn't the first time she'd faced a crisis and most likely it wouldn't be the last. She'd made it through before and somehow she'd survive now, too. She'd have to.

Chapter Eighteen

THE SUMMER SEASON STARTED FAIRLY slowly, but Tremarnock began to fill up in early July and by the end of the month, it was heaving. Come early August, all the bed and breakfast accommodation was taken, and the nearby camp and caravan sites were packed.

Often, the same families would come back year after year and they knew exactly where to go, how to behave and which places to eat in. It was the newcomers, however, that you had to watch out for. Unused to local ways, some of them strode around as if they owned the place, parking inconsiderately, talking in loud voices, dropping litter and generally drawing attention to themselves.

Most of the villagers managed to tolerate these ill-manners, knowing that without the 'emmets', as they called them, and the cash they brought in, the village would surely die. Some, however, made a habit out of sitting and watching their antics from a distance with either amusement or horror, depending on the circumstances, rather as if they were animals in a zoo.

Later, they'd recount to each other what they'd seen over a pint or a half of cider in the pub, keeping their voices low, so as not to be overheard.

Audrey, in particular, reckoned that she could spot the ne'er-do-wells a mile off. These were the types who would leave the beach with their families at the end of the day looking like lobsters, not having realised how strong the Cornish sun could be, even when the sky was cloudy. Or, even worse, they'd give their children flimsy inflatables to play with in the water, and then express surprise when the wind and tide dragged them out so far that they had to be rescued by the poor, overworked lifeboat men and women.

Audrey was careful never to offend these hapless holidaymakers to their faces, for fear of putting them off the pricey swimsuits and fancy cover-ups on sale at her clothes shop in South Street. When it came to Chabela, however, she had no such scruples and would happily speak ill of her to anyone who cared to listen. This behaviour had finally caused a rift between Audrey and Rick, who were scarcely talking to each other.

Rick's soppy idolisation of Chabela, as Audrey viewed it, absolutely infuriated her, as did his constant search for excuses to get close to the Mexican. He had even put himself in competition with Simon to see who could discover more about her Penhallow connections. Audrey found this pathetic, and wasn't afraid to say so, but it seemed to have no effect on Rick whatsoever.

Not that Simon realised it was a contest, of course. In fact, when Rick tracked down and managed to purchase some books about the Cousin Jacks in Mexico, which included several mentions of James Penhallow, Simon said he was delighted because it saved him a job.

However, Chabela was less than pleased when Simon invited her and Rick over to peruse his findings, though she wanted to see Simon, so she accepted. When Rick suggested that she meet him at his shop and they walk together, she felt that she couldn't refuse.

It was a Sunday evening at the beginning of August when she left her car on Humble Hill and strolled along South Street towards Treasure Trove. On her way, she passed by A Winkle in Time and peered through the steamy window. It was humming inside, every table was taken, and loud voices and laughter were drifting through the open door.

Robert was in his usual position behind the bar; she recognised his tall frame and gave a wave, but he didn't notice. He was now officially renting the flat upstairs himself and he'd changed so much since the split. Everyone had noticed it, including Chabela, and she felt sorry for him.

He seemed to have withdrawn into himself and rarely spoke to anyone, other than to issue instructions. He'd got thinner, too, and appeared to have lost interest in the Secret Shack, which he visited far less these days.

Luckily, Chabela was a quick learner and could pretty much run the business day to day on her own now. This was just as well, because Loveday often showed up late and left early. She and Jesse had recovered from their argument and she was no longer snubbing Chabela, but they weren't exactly friends. Chabela missed the chats and laughs they used to have.

Meanwhile, Rosie, too, was still playing it cool. Chabela gleaned that the relationship with Rafael was on again, though not official. He must have been under strict instructions not to look at Chabela, far less engage in conversation, because he avoided getting too close and they barely exchanged a word.

One afternoon, Chabela overheard Rafael and Rosie talking in the cloakroom. Rosie was in tears about her parents' split and he was trying, in his slightly clumsy way, to reassure her that things would work out all right in the end.

'They love each other,' he said simply, as if that were enough.

'Well, I *hate* my mum,' Rosie replied angrily. 'It's all her fault.'

Chabela had no idea what she meant by this and tiptoed away. When she saw Rosie again, she'd calmed down, but the truth was that most of the fun had gone out of the job; it simply wasn't the same.

If it weren't for the fact that Chabela had no desire to return to Mexico City, she might well have booked a flight home. However, she didn't feel ready to say goodbye to Simon yet, though she wasn't sure why.

At the bottom of South Street, she was slightly dismayed to see Rick on the pavement outside his shop with a pink rose in his hand, which he said he'd picked for her from his back garden. She tucked it in her thick hair, pretending to be pleased, but as they set off on their stroll, she maintained a discreet distance and tried to keep the conversation as light as possible.

When he started to talk about his previous romances, she deftly steered the subject on to her professional relationships with university students. And when he mentioned that his house was a bit big for one person, she extolled the virtues of singledom and insisted that she could never live with anyone else.

Unfortunately, he wasn't to be put off quite so easily and kept trying to initiate a deeper and more meaningful tête-à-tête, right up until the moment when they reached Kittiwake, some thirty minutes later.

Grateful to have arrived at last, Chabela marched ahead and when Simon came to the door, in a funny, friendly old checked shirt with a frayed collar, she opened her arms wide and rushed in to give him a big hug.

It was completely spontaneous, born out of relief and, frankly, desperation, because Rick had been getting heavier by the minute. If the walk had lasted much longer, she feared that he might actually have lunged at her or, even worse, got down on his knees and proposed.

Simon tensed slightly at first but then relaxed, put his arms around her and returned the hug. As her nose brushed the collar of his shirt and his neck, she became aware of his scent. It was a pleasant, slightly earthy smell, like burning wood or wax myrtle. His body, close up, felt neat, strong and strangely alert, too, as if he were biding his time, waiting for something to happen.

The moment was only brief, but it was long enough for her to sense a slight shift, as if something between them had almost imperceptibly altered. She didn't think that she could have been imagining it.

'Erm, mind if I join in the cuddle?'

Rick's voice broke the spell. It was supposedly a joke but you could tell that he was miffed and Simon dropped his arms and took a step back.

'Sorry,' he said, reaching over Chabela's shoulder to shake the other man's hand. 'Come on in! I hope you remembered the books?'

Rick said that he had and soon they were in Simon's front room, leaning over the coffee table, their heads virtually touching, while Rick flicked through page after page of writing. Every now and then he'd read out little sections and point to photographs of random Cornishmen and women in Mexico, going about their mining work above and below ground.

Finally, towards the end of one of the books entitled: *Cousin Jack: A Brief History of Cornish Miners in Mexico*, Rick stopped at a black and white photo of a group of men in football gear, all crouching down, arms around each other's shoulders, smiling at the camera. Most looked British or European, but there were some darker Mexican faces, too.

Beneath the picture were the names of each of the men, including one James Penhallow. On seeing it, Chabela's heart gave a little flutter and Rick nodded triumphantly.

'That's him.' Placing an index finger on a small figure to the left of the shot, he glanced sideways at Chabela. 'There's your relative. See? I found him for you. What do you think about that?'

She scrutinised the photo, which was a little grainy, but still distinct. James was in shorts and a striped shirt, like the others, and he had a handlebar moustache, which was fashionable at the time.

He was probably in his twenties and it was impossible to tell much more from the image, but she did note his smooth, high forehead, straight nose and amused smile. He looked as if he might have had quite a sense of humour and she decided that they would have got on.

'He looks kind,' she commented, feeling the same catch in her throat that she'd experienced when Simon had told her about James Penhallow's untimely death.

'I wish he'd jump out of the page right now so I could talk to him. There's so much I'd like to ask.'

Rick puffed out his chest and looked extremely pleased with himself, as if the compliment had been just for him.

'You can ask *me* anything you like,' he said, stroking his bushy beard, 'and I'll endeavour to find the answer. I'm almost as intrigued about the Penhallows now as you are.'

They were both distracted by a strange noise – like a harrumph – coming from Simon, and when Chabela glanced around, she could see that he was frowning.

'Aren't you researching your own family tree, Rick?' he said. He looked really quite annoyed. 'I should have thought you'd have enough to do with that.'

He seemed to have forgotten that it was he who approached Rick for help in the first place, and Rick appeared slightly taken aback.

'Aye,' he replied, 'I *am*, but it's not every day a charming Mexican lady comes to my village, wanting help, is it?' He winked at Chabela, but she pretended not to notice.

'My family tree can wait,' he went on. 'I'm happy to put myself at the señorita's disposal while she's here.'

And with that, he gave her a sort of mock bow from his seated position, like a true Spanish caballero, which only made Simon's frown deepen.

'"My" village?' he echoed, with an uncharacteristic sneer. 'Since when has Tremarnock belonged to you?'

There was an uneasy pause, and Chabela chewed on the corner of a nail. Simon seemed to be trying to pick a quarrel with Rick – but why? It crossed her mind that he might just be a teensy bit jealous, because Rick was muscling in on what had been *their* project.

The idea amused her but it did seem unlikely. Simon was a loner; he didn't need people and had only a passing interest in her. But he had pricked her curiosity and now that she might have had a glimpse behind the mask, she wanted to know more.

'Thanks, both of you, for all your help,' she said quickly, in an attempt to take the heat out of the situation. 'I'm very lucky to know you.'

Simon glowered at Rick, but fortunately his skin was thick and the scowl didn't penetrate.

'Shall I make us some tea?' Chabela suggested, rising and striding towards the door, without waiting for an answer. 'I think I know where everything is.'

She would have loved Rick to decline the offer and leave, so that she and Simon could be alone. Rick, though, had been so helpful that she wouldn't want to hurt his feelings and she reminded herself to be kind, however annoying he might be.

When she returned with the mugs of tea, she was relieved that the atmosphere seemed to have mellowed somewhat. The men were talking perfectly amicably about a recent biography they'd both read of Hernán

Cortés, the Spanish conqueror who overthrew the Aztec empire in the early sixteenth century.

Chabela had read it, too, and soon she and Simon got caught up in an involved discussion about the relative merits or otherwise of Aztec law and order.

'Can we talk about something else?' Rick said tetchily at last, as this was clearly a subject about which he knew very little. Then he turned to Chabela. 'I love hearing Spanish spoken but I don't know any myself. This might sound a bit strange but – would you mind reading me a poem? Tell me one you like. I'll find it on my phone.'

She could hardly refuse and Rick gazed at her mistily while she recited several verses of Mexican poet Octavio Paz's 'Piedra de Sol' ('Sunstone').

Not to be outdone, Simon got up the minute she'd finished to fetch his guitar. Soon, he was serenading her with several of what he now knew to be her favourite songs while Rick bristled quietly in the corner.

After that, Rick asked if Chabela would give him Spanish lessons, which he'd be happy to pay for. Before she had the chance to answer, however, Simon snapped back that she was far too busy and what on earth was Rick thinking? She was a university lecturer, not a language teacher, and besides, she already had a temporary job in Tremarnock. One was quite enough for anyone.

Rick looked daggers at Simon, who pretended not to notice, and as the tension mounted and threatened to become unbearable, Chabela decided that it was time she left.

Immediately, Rick sprang to his feet and offered to walk with her back to the village.

'I'll come, too,' Simon said, quick as a flash. 'I'll get my walking boots.'

Rick looked less than pleased.

'There's no need—' he began to say, but Simon interrupted.

'I've been in most of the day. I'd like some fresh air.'

It looked as if there might be a squabble, and Chabela clapped her hands in a bid to break it up.

'Great!' she said. 'We can carry on with our interesting discussion as we go.'

The light was dying as they set off, and the colours of the landscape seemed to have faded into a murky blend of browns and greys. Chabela was careful to give equal amounts of time and attention to both men, so that she couldn't be accused of favouritism. It was like having to deal with a couple of school kids.

She couldn't help suspecting that Simon was only coming along to annoy Rick, but she was grateful, nevertheless. It would save her from having to fend off any unwanted advances. And perhaps when Rick saw how she treated both men in exactly the same way, he would finally get the message that she wasn't interested in him romantically – or anyone else for that matter. She fervently hoped so.

When they reached the bottom of the steps leading down into the village, she looked at each man in turn.

'Thank you for a lovely evening.'

Rick tried to insist on walking her to her car, but she wasn't having any of it.

'I'm quite capable of getting there on my own. I'm very independent, you know.'

They exchanged kisses and Rick turned first and started to walk off in the other direction. Chabela caught Simon's eye and smiled. For one brief moment, she thought that he might be about to ask her something, but he didn't.

IT WAS IFFY SORT OF weather the following day: hot and sunny one minute, cloudy and overcast the next. The temperature was high, however, and the lack of constant rays didn't stop folk flocking to the beach to swim, surf, paddleboard, kayak and windsurf.

Chabela was rushed off her feet in the café, where she had become a dab hand at making teas and coffees, filling sandwiches, pulling cold drinks out of the fridge, collecting money and chatting to customers, all virtually simultaneously.

She finished work exhausted but didn't mind. She knew it meant that she would sleep soundly that night and wouldn't brood. Indeed, Alfonso's memory seemed to be fading a little into the background. Every day was so busy and varied and her old life seemed so far away that at times, she could scarcely remember what it was like. This was good, she decided, despite the continuing frosty atmosphere between her, Loveday, Rosie and Rafael. It was what she needed.

She was driving home one evening along the main road from Polrethen towards Tremarnock when she spotted Liz on the right. She was outside one of the big holiday homes on the edge of the village, weighed down with what appeared to be an enormous bag of laundry. Indeed, she seemed to be having some difficulty trying to heave it into the open boot of her white Audi.

She didn't notice Chabela, who would have driven by without any acknowledgment. Just as she passed, however, she glanced in the mirror and saw Liz stagger, drop the bag and the contents spilled out onto the road. Her hands flew up to cover her face, and although Chabela couldn't hear anything, she was convinced that the other woman was crying.

They had seen very little of each other since the salsa dancing debacle back in June. To be honest, Chabela was relieved, as it had been so awkward the last time they'd met that she'd done her best to avoid another encounter.

Nevertheless, she knew that Liz and Robert were having a hard time and hated to see anyone in distress. Noticing a big space in front of the Audi, she slowed down, reversed and got out.

'Can I help?' she asked, walking back to Liz, who was bent double, stuffing sheets and towels into the laundry bag. She glanced up, surprised, and her face was smudged with dirt and stained with tears.

'Oh,' she said. 'It's you!'

Chabela didn't reply, but squatted alongside and helped cram the laundry into the giant yellow sack. There were heaps of pillowcases, facecloths and towels, and several bulky duvet covers that had to be refolded.

It didn't take long with two of them and when they'd finished, they took a handle each and swung the bag into the boot.

'That's a lot of washing,' Chabela commented, thinking that it would take most of the next day to get it cleaned, dried and ironed. 'Whose is it?'

Liz wiped the hair off her forehead with the back of an arm. She'd stopped crying now but still looked upset and pale. She explained that she'd got a job with a local cleaning company, which specialised in holiday lets.

'I prepare the houses for new guests and clean up afterwards. I usually go in at least once midweek, as well, just to check everything's OK and give the place a quick tidy. You'd be amazed how much mess they make.'

It sounded like hard work and Chabela was surprised. She wouldn't want to do it. She guessed, though, that the job had something to do with Liz and Robert's split and resolved not to probe.

'How's Lowenna?' she asked instead, and Liz said the little girl was with Tabitha and Oscar.

'It's lucky the children get on so well. They're a bit like brother and sister.'

Sensing that Liz's hostility towards her had started to fade at last, Chabela decided to try to rebuild some bridges.

'I'll be seeing Rosie at the café tomorrow,' she said brightly. Since school had finished, Rosie and Rafael had been working part-time during the week as well as at weekends.

At that moment, Liz choked and her hands flew up to cover her face once more.

'What is it?' Chabela inhaled sharply and instinctively reached out to put a hand on Liz's shoulder. 'What's the matter?'

Liz shook her head, unable to answer, and made strange spluttering sounds. At a loss to know what else to do, Chabela rootled in her bag and pulled out a clean tissue, which she passed across.

Liz blew her nose loudly and gasped a few more times before finally looking up.

'Thanks,' she said, giving a small, embarrassed laugh. Her eyes were red and her face was still damp. 'Sorry. I needed that.'

Whether she meant that she'd needed the tissue, the nose blow or a good cry, Chabela wasn't sure. In any case, she was clearly in a lot of distress. Chabela didn't like to think of her driving back alone, perhaps to an empty house and so, having no plans herself, she suggested a drink in the pub.

'Go on. It might cheer you up.'

She fully expected Liz to say no, but to her surprise and pleasure, she accepted. They went in convoy to the top of South Street, before parking and continuing the rest of their journey to the Lobster Pot on foot.

Jenny was outside Gull Cottage, chatting to Ruby Dodd. She waved and smiled over Ruby's shoulder as the other women strolled by, but they didn't stop. A little further down, outside A Winkle in Time, a group of strangers were studying the menu in the window, but there was no sign of Robert. In any case, Liz turned her head the other way.

It was a warm, dry evening and folk were spilling out of the pub on to the seafront. They were a colourful sight in bright shorts, dresses and sweatshirts. There was a row of wooden shelves attached to some metal railings in front of the beach, for people to put their glasses on, and quite a few were leaning over the barrier, enjoying the view.

Behind them, all the chairs around the little round tables were occupied, and more customers were just standing about. Further along, some children were sitting on the sea wall, clutching packets of crisps and fizzy drinks, their bare feet dangling over the sides.

'What would you like to drink?' Chabela asked, going inside and elbowing through the crowds to get to the bar, while Liz lagged behind.

They both opted for a gin and tonic, which they carried out again, settling on a public bench, which had recently been vacated, a few metres along from the pub.

It was almost eight p.m. and the tangerine sun was low in the sky, although it wouldn't set for another hour or so. It cast a golden glow across the smooth water, and some way off, a couple of dark fishing vessels were chugging slowly and silently towards the horizon. No doubt they wouldn't be back till morning.

The children on the sea wall had finished their drinks and the two women watched the bigger ones leap down on to the sandy beach some way below. Soon, they were running around in circles like mad things while their younger siblings looked on enviously. Chabela found herself hoping that they wouldn't be tempted to jump, too; she didn't fancy having to rescue them.

She swirled the chinking ice and lemon around her drink before taking a sip and Liz did likewise, visibly relaxing a little as she did so.

'Thanks for suggesting this,' she said. 'I mustn't be too long, though. I have to pick up Lowenna.'

Chabela paused for a moment before deciding what to say next. She hoped that Liz would feel able to open up if she wanted to, but was afraid of overstepping the mark.

'It must be tough for you right now,' she said carefully at last. 'I've heard things are a bit difficult.'

Liz nodded. Of course everyone in the village knew about her and Robert, so Chabela's comment wouldn't have come as a surprise.

'It's hell, actually,' she said honestly. 'Robert moving out was bad enough. I'm devastated. On top of that, Rosie blames me for everything. It's toxic at home. Half the time she won't tell me where she is or when she'll be back. I'm convinced she's drinking and smoking, I can smell it on her clothes. I'm worried sick about her.

'I'm anxious about the effect it's having on Lowenna, too. I'm trying to keep things as normal as possible for her, but it's not easy. I'm sure she picks up on my upset and Rosie's. She's not stupid. The other day she refused point-blank to go to Jean's house. She used to love going there to play, but she clung to me like a baby. She screamed so much I had to take her home. She's terribly unsettled, poor lamb.'

Liz's small hands trembled slightly as she lifted the glass to her lips again. Her situation did, indeed, sound miserable and Chabela wished that she could think of something comforting to say.

Now that she was more fully in the picture, she thought that instead of avoiding Liz, she should have tried to talk to her sooner. Not that there was anything much she could do apart from lend a friendly ear.

Sometimes, of course, people didn't want to confide anyway. Chabela had rarely shared her feelings about Alfonso, after all.

'Are they seeing much of Robert – the girls, I mean?' she asked tentatively, and Liz nodded.

'He pops in and out and Rosie goes round to his flat quite a lot, but it's not the same. Lowenna misses him like crazy. She used to climb into our bed most mornings and they'd read stories together. She still keeps asking where he is, even though I've told her lots of times – not the whole truth, of course, a watered-down version.'

Chabela made a sympathetic noise. Despite having no children herself, she could imagine how hard it must be for Liz, trying to hold everything together for her daughters' sakes.

'Have you and Robert spoken much?' she wanted to know now. 'Do you think you'll be able to sort things out?'

At this, Liz's eyes filled with tears. 'I'm not sure. He's very angry with me.' She swallowed. 'He has every right.'

Chabela would have left it at that, but without any prompting, Liz went on to explain a little about the background to the break-up, including her flirtation with Max, though she didn't go into details. She was clearly in the mood for talking and it helped that the women were side by side on the bench, instead of facing each other; it felt less intense.

'Things had got so bad between me and Robert,' Liz said quietly. 'He was always working and we hardly ever had any time on our own. I know I should have been brave and told him how I was feeling, instead of messing around with Max. Hindsight's a wonderful thing.' She gave a sad smile. 'Robert was never going to take it well, after what his former girlfriend did to him.'

She glanced sideways at Chabela, her eyes full of fear. 'You must think I'm a really bad person. Especially now you know Robert. He's such a good man, and you know how considerate he is as a boss. He's probably wondering what on earth he married.'

She was being very hard on herself, but Chabela knew a great deal more than most about the lure, potency and pitfalls of forbidden love. Feeling it would be hypocritical to stay silent or worse, seem to judge, she, in turn, revealed something of what she had been through with Alfonso. It wasn't easy, but it seemed the right thing under the circumstances.

Liz listened quietly while she spoke, nodding occasionally and making supportive comments: 'Go on'; 'Oh my God!'; 'What a bastard!'

Time was marching on, but so caught up was she in the story that she seemed to have forgotten all about Lowenna; perhaps the little girl would end up sleeping at Tabitha's.

When Chabela finally finished, Liz shuddered before letting out a sigh. 'That explains such a lot.'

Chabela, puzzled, asked what she meant.

'I mean, it explains what you're doing here in Tremarnock and why you had to get away. It's not easy, trying to mend a broken heart.' She shivered slightly, as if she knew what she was talking about. 'I'm sorry for misjudging you.'

After some persuasion, she then admitted that she, along with quite a few others, had suspected Chabela for quite some time of being a femme fatale, or a man-stealer.

This wasn't entirely surprising, but Chabela was hurt nevertheless, particularly as it couldn't have been further from the truth. The thought that villagers had been gossiping about her behind her back was upsetting, and both women agreed that cultural differences probably played some part.

'I'll salsa with anyone and everyone,' Chabela insisted, referring to her dance with Rafael. 'He just happened to be nearby.'

When Liz explained the full extent of the trouble it had caused Rosie and her boyfriend, however, as well as Jesse and Loveday, Chabela felt embarrassed and a little ashamed. She understood better now why Liz had cooled towards her, and resolved to be more sensitive in future.

Both women had long since finished their drinks, but neither had wanted to interrupt the conversation by getting up and going back to the bar. Tired after so much deep talk, they were silent for a few moments and gazed out to sea, realising that the sun had set without their even noticing.

Now that it was dark, the streetlamps had been lit and were casting a soft, yellowy glow. The children from earlier had left the beach and gone home, and a slightly different crowd had appeared, in smarter evening clothes – long trousers for the men and, in some cases, strappy summer dresses for the women.

A slight breeze was coming off the water but the air was still warm and there was no need for a sweater.

'Have you spoken to Max recently?' Chabela asked at last, and Liz said that she'd texted him a few days after the plaque unveiling, just to say that Rosie was all right.

'He replied straight away and we messaged a bit after that,' she went on. She was still holding the empty glass between her hands, her shoulders hunched and knees pressed close together. 'To tell you the truth...' She swallowed, as if mustering courage to say what she wanted to. '...He mentioned that he'd seen his ex-wife a few times. I'm sure it was deliberate. I think he was trying to make me jealous, but it seemed to have the opposite effect.

'He said they went for a meal together and she showed him round her new flat. I don't know if he wanted me to imagine that they slept together, but you know, it made me realise I didn't care that much if they did. Well, only a bit.

'I can't be bothered with silly games. It just reminded me how honest Robert's always been. He never once messed me around when we were dating. I'm the one who's behaved so badly. I felt like saying that to Max but I didn't. I haven't talked to him about the fact Robert's moved out, either. I don't want him to know, actually. It seems quite telling, don't you think?'

Chabela touched her lightly on the arm and nodded. 'You don't need to mention anything to him if you don't want to.'

'When do you plan to go back to Mexico?' Liz wanted to know next. She was keen to change the subject.

Chabela admitted that she wasn't sure.

'I'm due back at work at the end of August, but I might ask for more time off. They like me and I've never had a day off sick while I've been there. I think they'll say yes, especially if I tell them I'm having personal problems. It's the truth, after all.'

Liz agreed. 'I hope you can stay here longer. Up until Christmas, maybe. It's lovely in winter – much quieter. I'm not sure when Robert's planning on closing the Secret Shack, probably at the end of October. But I expect he could find you some work at the restaurant if you want it. He always needs people.'

Chabela was touched, particularly now she knew that Liz had been so wary of her motives. She was quick to forgive and forget, clearly. After that, they somehow got on to the subject of winters in Mexico City and Liz said that she'd love to visit the country one day.

'I've never been. It's on my bucket list. I'd like to see Frida Kahlo's house, and the ancient pyramids.'

Her enthusiasm seemed genuine and before Chabela knew it, she was inviting Liz to stay.

'We could go for a week or two? You can use my apartment. I've got two spare bedrooms. I'd love to show you around.'

Liz looked doubtful.

'Rosie can come, too,' Chabela went on, warming to her theme. 'It'd be a good opportunity for her to practise her Spanish. And bring Lowenna, if you think she's old enough.' She frowned. 'When's the next school holiday?'

Liz told her about the October half-term and the two-week Christmas break.

'October's a perfect time to visit,' Chabela replied. 'It'll be warm then but not too hot – around twenty-three degrees Celsius. There's not much rain, either. Sometimes a bit in the afternoons, but only for an hour or so, then the sun shines again.'

Clearly taken with the idea, Liz asked how much the flights would be. The answer made her wince, but Chabela pointed out that she wouldn't have to pay for accommodation. Moreover, food, drink and entrance tickets to museums and so on were cheap.

'Come!' she urged, conscious that Liz was buckling. 'I'll be ready to go back then, at least for a short while. It'll be good to see a few people and I'll probably have some admin to catch up on. You deserve a holiday, and it would be nice for you and Rosie to have some time away together.'

Still, Liz hesitated. 'I don't know. Everything's so bad at the moment, and what would Robert think?' She paused. 'He'd probably say he doesn't care what I do, though he'd want to know about the girls. I've never been to North America, never mind Mexico,' she added in a small voice. 'In fact I've hardly ever been out of the UK, to be honest.'

Sensing that victory was close, Chabela went in for the kill. 'All the more reason to say yes,' she said with a grin. 'You'll regret it if you don't. And it would be an amazing experience for Rosie. We can ask Rafael, too, if you like, or another school friend, to keep her company. She'll come home speaking Spanish with a Mexican accent!'

This finally swung it for Liz. If she had been invited on her own, Chabela suspected that she would have said no.

'All right,' she said finally. 'I'll talk to Rosie and check out dates and flights. If you're sure...?' She was looking for reassurance, and Chabela duly obliged.

'I'd be so happy to show you my country,' she said warmly. 'I was sad and desperate when I arrived here, I didn't know which way to turn. You picked me up, dusted me off and made me feel so welcome. It would be an absolute honour to return the favour.'

Chapter Nineteen

LIZ FELT BETTER AFTER THE chat, and the prospect of a trip to Mexico helped lift her mood, too. She and Robert rarely went on holiday with the girls, mainly because he didn't like to leave his businesses, and in summer they always had the beach, anyway.

But she was curious about the world and wanted to see more. There wasn't much money around when she was a child so she didn't travel far with her parents, mostly just to Sussex or Dorset. Max had invited her and the girls to Munich and she'd been sorely tempted, but had turned the offer down, fearing at that time that she couldn't trust herself – or him.

Chabela's suggestion, however, was fraught with no such dangers. It would undoubtedly benefit Rosie and perhaps be good for Liz and Robert as well. Who knew? He might find that he missed her when she was away and feel more inclined to come back home.

EMMA BURSTALL

By October half-term, she'd be eligible for some leave from her job, and there were no obstacles in Rosie's way, either. The only problem was Lowenna. Liz felt that it was probably too far for her to travel and besides, she'd cramp their style. The little girl wouldn't want to be climbing pyramids or mooching around art galleries, she'd much rather be at the local play park, messing around with her friends.

It was almost ten p.m. by the time Liz reached Tabitha's house, and she was full of apologies for being so late. She needn't have worried, though. Lowenna and Oscar were still wide awake, running around making a racket, but Tabitha seemed perfectly relaxed about it.

'They haven't got playgroup, so it doesn't matter how grumpy they are tomorrow,' she said reasonably. 'Anyway, they both napped in the car this afternoon.'

'No wonder they're so full of energy,' said Liz, who had stepped inside and could hear the children through the open back door, tearing around her friend's small garden. 'Lucky things.'

Tabitha, who was in rolled up jeans, bare feet and a baggy white man's shirt, presumably Danny's, examined her friend anxiously.

'You look knackered,' she said, taking a red scrunchie off her wrist and pulling her curly black hair off her neck into a high ponytail. 'Have you been working all this time?'

Liz said no, and as she followed Tabitha into the sitting room next door, she started to explain about her chance encounter with the Mexican.

'You know, I think I got her wrong.' She was careful not to break any confidences or mention Alfonso. 'She's been through a lot recently. She doesn't want any trouble; she's genuinely just come here to research her family history and recuperate.'

Tabitha nodded. 'I never saw her as some sort of cougar or man-eater, but I always thought there was more to her story than meets the eye.' She settled on the sofa next to Liz. 'I'm glad you had a chat. Did you tell her about you and Robert, too?'

Liz glanced at the delicate gold watch on her wrist, which her husband had given her, and fiddled with the strap.

'Yes,' she said, before mentioning Chabela's suggestion about a holiday. 'She offered to show Rosie and me around. It's a nice idea, but not exactly practical right now.'

Tabitha was quiet for a few moments, staring at the pink scallop chair, seemingly lost in thought, and Liz wondered what was going through her mind. Then all of a sudden, she leaned forwards, rested her elbows on her knees and propped her hands under her chin.

'I can have Lowenna,' she said. 'She'd be happier here than anywhere else – when she's not with her dad, that is.'

'What?' Liz was bewildered; Tabitha had lost her.

'When you and Rosie go to Mexico,' she said patiently, leaning back against the sofa once more. 'You *must* go. It'll be amazing. Lowenna and Oscar are like siblings. They'll love it. I'll keep them really busy and she'll be fine for a week or two. If there are any problems, Robert will be just round the corner.'

It was an incredibly generous offer and Liz thanked her friend profusely, reflecting on the fact that now, with the problem of what to do with Lowenna seemingly sorted, all the other barriers that she'd mentally erected seemed to be melting away, too.

She could really think of no reason why she shouldn't go, not even cash.

After all, what was money for if you never spent it? You couldn't take it with you, that was for sure. She was naturally quite frugal and had saved enough over the years to fund the whole trip; she wouldn't need to ask Robert for a penny.

'I'll have a proper think about it – and talk to Robert and Rosie,' she said. 'I'd only go for a week, though. That'd be quite long enough for Lowenna – and you!'

'Fair enough,' replied Tabitha, 'though I wouldn't mind doing ten days or two weeks. But that's the spirit. Seize the day! If you don't go, I will, so you'd better hurry up and book!'

At that moment, Oscar and Lowenna shoved open the door and tumbled into the room like a couple of overexcited puppies. Straight away they threw themselves on the floor at their mothers' feet and rolled around, play-fighting.

'Careful,' Tabitha said. Oscar was bigger and rougher; he didn't know his own strength. 'Don't hurt Lowie.'

Right on cue, the little girl let out a yelp, because he'd accidentally pulled her hair. She jumped up, ran over to Liz and buried her face in her lap while Oscar looked on, perplexed; he had no idea what he'd done wrong.

It seemed like the right time to leave, but Liz suddenly felt a little lonely saying goodbye to Tabitha and driving back to Bag End: Robert wouldn't be coming home tonight; she thought she'd never get used to it.

Although he had always worked long hours, he'd sometimes gone in later or returned between the lunchtime and evening shifts, and she'd looked forward to his occasional days off.

Now, when he popped in to see the girls, he hardly spoke to her and she had the feeling that her very presence made him recoil, as if she had bad breath or an infectious disease. As a result, she did her best to stay out of his way.

In any case, it was preferable for Lowenna not to be exposed any more than necessary to the hostile atmosphere between them. Quite often, Robert would leave without Liz even knowing and she'd only find out when her youngest came searching for her.

The little girl was half asleep by the time they entered the house. Liz carried her upstairs and put her straight to bed, fully clothed. The sole items that she removed were her daughter's sandals, and she barely even stirred when Liz dropped one accidentally on the floor.

Afterwards, she tiptoed along the landing to Rosie's room and knocked on the door, but she wasn't surprised when no one answered. She had guessed that her eldest must be out because the cottage was so quiet and there were no telltale shoes, bags or sweatshirts in the hall.

Back downstairs, she checked her phone and was relieved to find a message from Robert saying that Rosie was with him at the restaurant and he'd make sure that she was home by eleven p.m.

There were no kisses, or indeed any kind words, just the bare facts, but Liz was grateful for them; at least now she had one less thing to worry about.

For some reason, she didn't feel sleepy at all and after filling the kettle, she wandered aimlessly around downstairs, checking each room for something, though she wasn't sure what.

Everything was exactly where it had been when she'd left that afternoon, which was only to be expected, as there was no one else to tidy up. Lowenna had tipped out all the plastic bricks from her toy box and strewn them across the sitting room floor, while the dining table was covered in bits of wooden puzzle. Liz couldn't be bothered to clear them away now; they could wait till morning.

She realised as she glanced about that it wasn't so much Robert's stuff that was missing, for he'd left plenty of things behind. Rather, it was his presence, an ill-defined feeling of his actually having *been* here, doing the normal things he always did.

Usually, she'd find the novel he'd been reading lying face down on the coffee table, and she'd pop a bookmark in the right place and close it for him. Or he'd take off his shoes and deposit them by the armchair, along with an empty mug and a half-eaten packet of biscuits, and leave behind a dent in the cushion when he'd got up.

It wasn't that he was particularly untidy, just that sometimes he forgot to put things away and she was exactly the same. She'd leave sewing on the kitchen table, or a dirty plate in the sink instead of putting it in the dishwasher.

Robert's absence seemed to have damaged the atmosphere, like a hole in the precious ozone layer, and it dawned on her that even if he came back now, the house would probably never feel quite as safe again.

The sound of a key in the front door brought her back to the present. The lock was a bit sticky, and the person on the other side was having trouble opening up.

She went to help but before she could get there, the door flew open and she was confronted by the sight not just of Rosie but of Robert, too, standing right behind, towering over her.

Liz's heart fluttered. He looked handsome and a bit wild, she thought, and strangely unfamiliar. His hair was uncombed, his pale blue linen shirt crumpled, and his hazel eyes were darting hither and thither, like leaves tossed about in a storm.

She tried to attract his gaze, but couldn't, and for a moment, she was overwhelmed by the urge to run into his arms, forcing him to focus all his attention on her. But then she reminded herself that he and she were separated and it was her fault, and she managed to hold back.

'Hello!' she said, giving her daughter a kiss on the cheek as she pushed past and dumped her bag on the bottom stair. Then, to Robert, 'Come in!'

At first it looked as if he would refuse, but then he changed his mind.

'Just for a moment,' he replied, tersely. 'I need to talk to you about something.'

It sounded ominous, and Liz led him into the kitchen where he settled slightly stiffly on a wooden chair around the old pine table, scored with marks through years of use. Rosie had already gone upstairs.

'Tea?' Liz asked, pointing to the kettle, but he shook his head, so she pulled out a chair opposite and sat down herself.

'How's it going tonight?' she asked, meaning the restaurant. 'Are you full?'

She was hoping to lighten the atmosphere but he ignored her small talk, running a hand through his messy hair and frowning.

'I think you should know, Rosie's asked if she can come and live with me.'

His words went off like an explosion in Liz's head and seemed to bounce around the four walls and ricochet from corner to corner. She stared at him blankly and her stomach rocked and rolled, making her feel sick and dizzy.

'I explained to her why that wouldn't be a good idea,' he went on, still avoiding eye contact and focusing on the darkened window behind his wife instead. 'I'm not around much and Lowenna would miss her.'

Liz couldn't seem to process what he was saying.

'Anyway, there's more room here and she's got all her things...'

His voice tailed off and Liz felt herself sway. Had it really come to this? Never in a million years would she have believed that her beloved girl would want to leave home so young. The sense of rejection that Liz experienced in that moment was so strong that Rosie might just as well have stamped in hobnail boots on her face.

Her mind darted back to their earliest days together: Rosie's difficult birth, the joy of holding the tiny bundle that was her for the first time in her arms, those worrying days and weeks when it became clear that something wasn't right, Greg's abandoning of them, the move to Tremarnock and that unbreakable bond between mother and daughter that had sustained them through so many trials and tribulations. What had happened? Where had it gone?

'Are you all right?' Robert's voice brought her back to the present and she realised that she must be pale. Her forehead and upper lip felt sweaty, too.

'Yes, yes I'm fine,' she lied. 'Can I have some water?' She didn't want to risk trying to stand herself.

He fetched a glass and filled it up from the tap before passing it to her. After a couple of sips she felt a little better and he returned to his seat. This time, however, he leaned across the table and looked into her eyes.

'She'll be OK, Liz,' he said seriously. He was trying to reassure her, which she appreciated, but there was only anger, regret and pity in his gaze, not love. 'She's really upset about us and she's a teenager, which makes everything seem much worse. But she knows we love her and she loves us. She needs time to adjust to the new situation, that's all. She'll calm down.'

Liz nodded miserably. The sweat now drying on her skin made it prickle and all of a sudden she felt deathly cold. Robert must have noticed her shivering, because he gave her the pink sweater lying on the seat next to him, which belonged to Rosie.

'Thank you.' Liz pulled it on and crossed her arms over her chest, as if that would warm her more. The situation felt unreal, as if she'd made a mistake and walked into someone else's life. This wasn't how things were supposed to be.

'Did Rosie agree to stay here?' she asked now. She was frightened of the answer; she almost didn't want to hear it.

'Grudgingly,' Robert replied. 'I suggested she could maybe spend weekends at the flat and stay here during the week. But I said I'd talk to you first. I won't do anything about the children without running it by you beforehand. I trust you'll do the same with me.'

He fixed her with a piercing look, the kind that means business, which made her shiver again.

'Of course,' she said quietly. Were they really behaving in such a cold, formal way with each other? This must be what divorce was like, when love had flown and all that was left was anger, hurt and grim practicalities.

'Does that mean she'll spend *every* weekend with you?' she asked now, trying to imagine how it would feel, saying goodbye to her eldest on a Friday afternoon and perhaps not seeing her again until Sunday evening. Robert would be out working much of the time, Rosie would have free rein and Liz would have no control over her bedtimes or homework.

Far more importantly, however, she'd miss her.

'I guess,' said Robert, and then, as if reading Liz's thoughts, 'We'd better have a conversation about curfew times and so on. She can't stay out till all hours just because you're not watching over her.'

This reassured Liz somewhat, and they agreed that they'd discuss it more the following day.

'I-I wanted to ask *you* something as well, actually,' she stuttered, feeling as shy and unsure of herself as if they'd only just met. 'It's not really relevant now, though.'

She was thinking about Mexico, but regretted her words almost immediately, wishing that she could take them back. It was foolish even to mention the idea, under the circumstances. Of course Rosie wouldn't want to go; she didn't even want to live with her mother any more.

However, Robert wouldn't let it drop. 'Go on,' he insisted, 'it's better to air things straight away.' So Liz explained about the meeting with Chabela.

'I thought it might be good for Rosie's Spanish. And I've always fancied going there myself. It wouldn't work, though.'

'Why not?'

Liz swallowed. 'Well, for a start Rosie will say no. And Tabitha's offered to have Lowenna, but—'

'I'm her *dad*, Liz,' Robert interrupted, sounding slightly exasperated. 'If anyone's going to look after Lowie, it'll be me. I'll take some time off. I'm due a break. I might need a bit of help from Tabitha, but not much. The staff will manage without me; they'll have to.'

His comments came as a surprise to Liz, who thought he'd never trust anyone but himself to run the restaurant and café, although it would be October by then when things would have quietened down.

'Rosie—' she started to say, but he stopped her again.

'Leave it with me, I'll have a word with her. She won't say no, trust me. It'll do her...' he paused, 'it'll do you both good.'

Liz was touched. Perhaps he did still care about her, just a little, anyway, and it was so typical of him to put others first. He'd always been kind and unselfish; it was one of the reasons why she'd fallen in love with him.

'Are you sure?' she said, but then she frowned. 'It's not right, going away now. Not with all that's happening. Even if Rosie agrees to come, we wouldn't be able to enjoy it.'

'Rubbish.' Robert was adamant. 'You'll have a great time. But seriously,' he said more softly, 'life has to go on, you know. Just because...'

She glanced at him and he looked away.

'Just because we're not together any more doesn't mean we can't do things. We just have to learn to do them separately. We must.'

He was right, of course, but still the idea of split parenting and divided holidays sounded horrible. A painful lump appeared in Liz's throat, which she tried to swallow down.

'Use the credit card to book the flights,' Robert went on, matter-of-factly. They had identical cards attached to their joint bank account, and the bill was settled each month by direct debit.

Given the circumstances, he might have told her to use her own money, but Liz knew that this wasn't his style. His generosity made her guilt even sharper; it hurt almost like a physical pain. When she told him that she intended to use her savings, he shrugged, as if it didn't matter either way. They had never argued about money; they hadn't needed to.

'Leave Rosie to me,' he repeated, 'and don't mention anything till I've spoken to her.'

There was silence for a short while then Liz again offered him something to drink. She was hoping to detain him but he wouldn't be persuaded, and he rose and said goodbye.

She wanted to follow but he wouldn't have it.

'I'll let myself out.' He didn't wish her goodnight.

When he'd gone, he seemed to have left behind a cold, empty space. Alone at the kitchen table, Liz felt chilly and desolate and had to remind herself once again that she was strong; she was a survivor and a grafter and it wasn't in her nature to give up.

Otherwise she might have curled herself into a little ball in the corner of the room and cried herself to sleep.

*

SOMETHING PINGED AGAINST HER WINDOW, and then again, only this time louder. Liz kept her eyes shut, thinking that she must still be dreaming.

Then there was a shout – 'WAKE UP!' – followed by a deafening thud overhead and a loud squawking.

'WAKE UP!' the person called again from outside in the street, and this time, Liz's eyes sprang open. She'd know that voice anywhere – it belonged to Jean.

The alarm clock by the bed said that it was 6.17. No wonder the first flush of light was only just beginning to peep through a chink in the curtains.

Jumping up, Liz hurried to the window and peered out. At first, she couldn't see anyone but then, as she lowered her gaze, she spotted Jean's blonde head and familiar round face. She was standing in the centre of Liz's tiny front garden, staring up at her with a clenched fist and one arm raised, clearly about to throw something.

'STOP!' Liz cried, quickly pushing up the sash window and leaning out. Luckily, Jean lowered her arm, opened her fist and a pile of gravel fell out. That explained the pinging, anyway.

'What's happened? Are you all right?' Liz called now.

Straight after, there was a flurry of wings and feathers and two fat gulls flew down from the roof, virtually hitting her on the nose as they flapped past.

They landed in the corner of the garden near Jean's feet, soon to be followed by two more birds, then started hopping around, screeching aggressively.

Puzzled, Liz glanced at Jean again and it was only then she noticed that her friend was rather oddly dressed, in wellington boots, though it wasn't raining, and a large beige mac.

'A baby's fallen out of your nest. It's right there,' Jean hollered, pointing to where the gulls had congregated. Her mac flew open to reveal a floral nightie underneath. She'd clearly dressed in a hurry.

Liz tried to see the chick through the throng of adult birds, but couldn't.

'Oh dear!' she cried, wondering how on earth she could help. 'Hang on a moment! I'm coming down.'

She was about to abandon her spot at the window when she saw another neighbour, Debs, leave her cottage, followed by her husband, Des. They were both in nightclothes, too, but hadn't bothered with the mac and wellies.

By the time Liz had thrown on her dressing gown and flip-flops and joined the others, four more folk had appeared, including Tony and Felipe, inexplicably, as they lived in the parallel street behind Humble Hill. They couldn't possibly have heard the commotion from there.

They all gathered around, keeping a safe distance from the adult birds, which looked big and very fierce. It was hard to spot the chick, cowering beneath a butterfly bush, but Liz did eventually, and she could tell that it was still quite young. From her limited knowledge of all things avian, she guessed that it was probably a nestling, partially covered in splotchy grey feathers while the rest was fluff.

It couldn't yet fly, it seemed, but at least it appeared uninjured and fairly robust.

'It'll die! It'll get eaten by a cat!' Jean said, pulling a distraught face. 'What can we do?'

Liz thought of Mitzi, whom she'd last seen indoors, curled up at the foot of her bed. She'd looked a picture of soft, furry innocence then, but she'd be licking her lips if she knew about the chick; in fact it was a wonder that she wasn't prowling around already, waiting to pounce.

'We could try to put it back in its nest?' Tony said doubtfully. He'd gained even more weight recently and was bulging out of his navy tracksuit top and jogging bottoms. He didn't look fit for scrambling up ladders. 'Felipe can do it, he's very agile.'

Tony was good at nominating his partner for tasks that he didn't fancy doing himself and normally Felipe didn't seem to mind. Now, he looked doubtful, though.

'I do not know if that is the right thing,' he said, in his strong Brazilian accent. 'I do not think the baby's parents will like it.'

At that moment, one of the adult birds opened its large wings and took off with a screech, making everyone jump back in surprise. It flew above their heads and circled around a few times, before landing right on the edge of Liz's roof, from where it stood surveying them menacingly.

This alone was enough to make Liz think that it would certainly be difficult, if not impossible, to get to the chick now, without risking serious injury and possible hospitalisation oneself.

'Why don't we give it something to eat? It might be all right,' said Debs, a large lady in her sixties who had moved to the village with her husband a couple of years ago when they both retired.

Tony rubbed his unshaven chin. 'I think I've read somewhere that parents come down and feed chicks that have fallen out of the nest. Maybe it's best if we don't interfere.'

He popped the brown paper carrier that he'd been holding on the floor and Liz saw that it contained some milk and a newspaper, no doubt just purchased from the village store; he was probably keen to get home and read it.

Jean, however, was having none of it. 'That's a terrible idea!' She looked outraged. 'It won't last five minutes out here on its own. We'd be condemning it to a horrible death!'

They were in danger of having a row, but luckily Felipe had the bright idea of checking the Internet for advice on what to do in a situation like this. Before long, the group were chewing over the relative size and maturity of the chick, its percentage of fluff to feathers and the likelihood of its parents being able to fend off predators like Mitzi if it were to remain on the ground.

In the end, it was agreed that if they possibly could get the creature back in its nest, this would be its best chance of survival. However, they would have to wait till the parents flew off before attempting any sort of rescue mission, or someone might get seriously hurt.

Liz was conscious of a certain irony in the fact that not so long ago, Robert was trying to frighten the birds off the roof by firing at them with a BB gun, and what's more, she'd encouraged him. She wasn't hard-hearted, however, and now that she'd seen the cute, fluffy chick, she felt just as invested as the others in its survival.

'All right,' she said decisively, 'you'd better all come inside. We'll get out the ladder and take it in turns to keep watch on the baby. When the parents go away, someone can go up on the roof and pop it back.'

No one replied for a minute and the word 'someone' seemed to hang in the air like an armed drone seeking its unsuspecting target.

'I'll do it!' Liz had forgotten that Deb's husband, Des, was a former military man who kept himself in very good nick. There was a collective cheer.

'Good show!' Tony cried, slapping Des on the back and Felipe looked relieved. He was super kind and helpful and would do anything for anyone, but climbing very tall ladders clearly wasn't his forte.

'Well done!' he echoed. 'I will hold the ladder at the bottom to make sure it doesn't wobble.'

Liz had thought to go somewhere with Lowenna today, maybe to a different beach or to the animal petting zoo five miles away, but it seemed that plans had changed.

It didn't really matter, though. On a Tuesday morning like this in term-time, the little girl would be at playgroup. But the days seemed to merge one into another in the holidays and arrangements could easily be altered or abandoned.

Soon, Liz was filling the kettle and making mugs of tea for everyone. Lowenna came downstairs in her pink pyjamas and was delighted to discover that they had a houseful. Liz didn't dare risk showing her the chick in situ, in case its parents launched an attack, but Jean found some pictures of baby gulls on the Internet and pointed through the window to the spot where it was hiding.

'Poor baby,' the little girl said several times. She seemed to find the idea of a chick separated from its mummy deeply distressing. 'Baby go back to its nest.'

By the third mug of tea as well as toast and jam for everyone, also made by Liz, there was quite a jolly atmosphere.

'It must have been like this during World War Two,' Debs said brightly from her spot on the sofa. 'Everyone huddling in an air-raid shelter, cracking jokes and keeping up the Dunkirk spirit.'

'We're not being bombed, my dear,' Des replied slightly tetchily.

'No,' said his wife, 'but we've battened down the hatches, haven't we? It feels like we're under attack, only not from bombs but belligerent birds!'

'Do you think they know what we're up to?' Jean asked nervously. 'They might be plotting something, too.'

For the next hour or so there was quite a lot of activity in the garden as the chick's parents flew back and forth. Eventually, however, they got bored, hungry, tired or all three, and when Liz glanced out of the window for the umpteenth time, she noticed that the chick was finally on its own.

'Quick!' she hissed, rising as quietly as she could, for she didn't want to alert the feathery squatters on her roof. 'Des, the parents have gone. Now's your moment.'

He was a big, sturdy chap with broad shoulders and strong, capable-looking hands. Even so, he seemed quite alarmed when he realised that his moment had finally come and he would have to venture outside again.

Liz had dug out Robert's leather gloves and thick, green, military style jacket. It was a bit tight on Des, but he managed to squeeze into it somehow, and stuck the yellow hard hat firmly on his head.

'Lord!' said Jean. 'Now you really do look as if you're off to war.'

'Best of British!' joked Tony, but Des couldn't see the funny side and gave him a stony stare.

They all watched with bated breath as Des left the cottage and crept across the garden on his hands and knees, glancing up anxiously every so often to check if he was about to be dive-bombed.

As he neared the place where the chick was hiding, he went right down on his belly and slithered like a snake, dragging himself along by his elbows. It was a good job that he was wearing his long striped pyjamas or his knees would have got grazed.

Fortunately, it was still early and there were no passers-by to disrupt the operation in progress. Liz had also taken the precaution of locking Mitzi in the utility room, or she might well have got to the chick before Des.

'He's almost there,' whispered Felipe, whose nose was virtually pressed against the windowpane. 'Only a few more centimetres...'

Just then, Lowenna jumped up and tried to scramble on to the window ledge, knocking over a ceramic vase in the process. Thankfully, Liz caught it just before it hit the floor; it would have made a terrible noise if it had smashed into pieces.

'Lowie,' she hissed, 'get down!'

The little girl did as she was told, but not before Des, who had clearly heard something, turned and glared at them, waving his arm angrily in their direction as if to say, 'Go away, you fools!'

Liz held her breath for a few moments, terrified that the birds would have heard, too, but it seemed not. Soon, Des had his head under the butterfly bush and was reaching out with both hands, presumably to grab the chick.

'I hope he can get it,' said Debs, and Liz crossed all her fingers.

Des seemed to be under the bush for an eternity, but at last, he shuffled backwards on his knees, holding something carefully between his hands, and everyone let out a silent cheer.

'Thank God!' Jean exclaimed, only to be slapped down by Tony, who pointed out that this was only the beginning.

'The hardest part's going to be shinning up that ladder. Beats me how he'll manage it without alerting the parents. Maybe all their friends and neighbours, too.'

The thought of her husband being set upon by a swarm of angry birds was too much for Debs, who made a choking sound and her hand flew up to cover her mouth.

'Don't worry,' said Liz, patting Debs on the back, 'I have every faith in Des. He'll be fine.'

She scowled at Tony; she really thought she could strangle him at that moment. After all, he was the one who had initially volunteered Felipe for the task. Either he was exaggerating the risks of the ladder part of the mission, or he was extremely cavalier with other people's safety.

By now, Des was fully upright, tiptoeing across the garden towards the ladder with the chick still safe between his palms. This was Felipe's cue to creep outside and join him.

Liz had managed to find another of Robert's jackets for the Brazilian, as well as some woollen gloves and a baseball cap. The get-up wasn't as protective as Des's, but at least Felipe wasn't the one potentially coming face-to-face with the nesting gulls.

As soon as Des reached the ladder, he began to climb. Without the use of his hands, he had to use his elbows again to steady himself. Meanwhile, Felipe put one foot on the first rung and took hold of the rails on either side.

Des's progress was slow, especially in tartan carpet slippers, and the others watched nervously from within the cottage.

'I hope he doesn't squeeze the chick so tight he kills it,' said Debs, and Jean let out a squeak.

'Oh don't! That would be terrible!'

At last, Des climbed so high that they could no longer see him any more, not even his slippers. They had to rely for information on Felipe, who gave a thumbs-up when things were going well, and a flattened palm accompanied by a so-so wrist wiggle when he wasn't sure.

At one point, he was craning his neck so hard to try to see what was happening that Liz feared his neck might snap.

'What's going on?' Debs asked, when several minutes had ticked by and he had failed to update them with any kind of gesture. 'Do you think I should call an ambulance – or the police? Maybe Des is hurt.'

They all made reassuring noises, but Debs wasn't convinced. She became so agitated that Liz feared she might rush out at any minute to try to help her husband, which would most likely only make his situation worse.

She was contemplating the feasibility of grabbing Debs by the arm and pinning her to the sofa – not easy, given their size difference – when Felipe turned to them with a wide grin on his face and raised both thumbs triumphantly in the air.

'He's done it!' Debs cried, doing a little jig on the carpet in her long blue nightdress, and the others clapped and cheered. Jean, clearly the most moved of them all, went around giving everyone a hug, just as if they'd survived the Blitz.

'I hope my husband isn't hurt,' Debs said when they'd all started to calm down a bit.

'At least you've still *got* a husband,' Tony replied, rather waspishly Liz thought.

When Des himself came into view – feet first and then the rest of him – everyone cheered again, including Lowenna, who also did a celebratory roly-poly. Des was beaming from ear to ear when he came back into the house and Debs dutifully helped him take off his protective gear, just as if she were a medieval lady and he her knight in shining armour. They made a rum sort of Queen Guinevere and Sir Lancelot in their nightclothes, but everyone was full of admiration just the same.

After that, they all wanted a blow-by-blow account of the operation, which seemed to have gone remarkably well. Des explained that when he got on to the roof, he could see the mother in the nest with her other chicks, but not the scary dad.

The mum squawked a bit and ruffled her feathers as Des approached, but he went very slowly and cautiously and managed to plop the baby back in with its siblings without any trouble.

'I was afraid the father would come back and go for me,' he said grimly, 'so once the chick was in, I got out of there as quickly as I could.'

'You're a hero!' Debs said, smiling proudly at her husband.

'It was nothing,' he insisted modestly, but Liz could swear that his chest expanded and he'd grown a couple of inches in height.

'How many chicks did you see?' she wanted to know, and Des said he'd counted five.

'Just think how many more rescue operations that'll mean,' Tony quipped, grinning wickedly. 'Liz, you and Des had better set up a hotline. I'm sure Felipe will volunteer for more ladder-securing duties if you ask him nicely.'

After that, everyone wanted more tea and when they finally left, it was almost lunchtime. Rosie had stayed in her bedroom throughout the commotion, but she emerged now, presumably because she was hungry.

Liz, who was still in pyjamas, offered to make her a sandwich but she wanted to do it herself. Then she said she would go over to the restaurant to see if Robert needed any help; she wasn't working at the Secret Shack that day.

'I thought I'd take Lowie to the beach this afternoon, fancy coming with us instead?' Liz asked hopefully, but Rosie shook her head.

'Don't feel like it.'

Her cold response, though predictable, still managed to upset her mother, who felt tears prick her eyes. She turned away quickly, so as not to be noticed, and stacked the dirty mugs and plates from earlier in the dishwasher.

'Robert told me you wanted to go and live with him,' she said now. She hadn't meant to; it just slipped out.

'Yes,' said Rosie.

'I feel really sad about it,' Liz said truthfully.

'Yeah, well, I'm sad too,' came the curt reply.

Liz looked at her daughter now, and her greeny-grey eyes were hard and pitiless. Shocked, she glanced away; she barely recognised Rosie any more.

'Darling,' she pleaded, 'I know you're angry with me, but please can we talk about it? I can't stand it when you're like this, it breaks my heart.'

She let out a small sob and something in Rosie seemed to soften at last, like snow melting in spring.

'Don't cry, Mum,' she said, walking over to the dishwasher and giving Liz a hug.

She was so surprised and relieved that she burst into tears and it was her daughter who had to comfort her, rather than the other way around.

The show of sympathy didn't last long, however.

'I *am* angry with you,' Rosie said at last, pulling back, but at least her voice was a bit gentler than before. 'You've hurt Robert so much and broken up the family. I can't forgive you but you're still my mum and I still love you. Maybe one day we can be friends again.'

Chapter Twenty

A HEATWAVE STARTED AT THE weekend and as the barometer rose, the tourists seemed to multiply in numbers, too. Some days, it was hard to find a spot on the beach even to lay your towel, and Chabela was so busy in the café that she barely found time to go for a pee.

Fortunately, Robert had drafted in extra staff as promised – mainly local students back from university – but they needed quite a bit of supervision and weren't as efficient as the regular employees.

Chabela found herself agreeing to lots of extra shifts to help Robert out. She didn't mind; it wasn't as if she had much else to do. It meant, however, that there was little opportunity for more research on the Penhallow clan and she went for days without seeing or even speaking to Simon. In fact at one point she wondered if he were away, until someone mentioned that they'd spotted him in the village.

Rick, however, was another matter. He seemed to find countless excuses to visit the café before and after work, and sometimes, during. Chabela began to wonder if he could be making any money in his shop, because he closed it so often to come to Polrethen Beach.

She would chat to him when he stood around at the serving hatch, sipping tea or coffee, but was careful not to give him any encouragement. He was remarkably tenacious, however. Perhaps he thought that, in the end, she would get so tired of fending him off that she'd finally capitulate and go on a date with him.

Friday was particularly sweltering. By lunchtime, the mercury had hit thirty-five degrees centigrade and Loveday complained of feeling sick and had to go home.

The others soldiered on, constantly sipping cool drinks to prevent dehydration. Although the shack was shady inside, it seemed to heat up like an oven as the day progressed and the fans only worked if you stood right next to them.

The lunchtime rush was crazy; at one point there was a queue stretching halfway along the beach and they ran right out of lobster rolls and ice cream. Chabela was accustomed to scorching weather, but wasn't used to no proper air conditioning, and when the queue finally lessened, she had to drag a chair into a darkened corner and sit down.

Her feet were throbbing and she had a pounding head. One of the temporary staff brought her a glass of water, which she took gratefully, along with a painkiller. Then she closed her eyes and waited for the thumping in her temples and across her brow to subside.

Gradually, the sounds of the other staff at work started to fade, and she found herself focusing instead on the distant hum of folk on the beach and the cries of seagulls overhead.

She would have given anything to lie down somewhere quiet and go to sleep. Indeed, she must have nodded off for a few moments where she was, but jerked awake again when her head slumped onto her chest, causing a sharp pain in her neck.

It was only when she opened her eyes that she realised someone was watching her through the side door of the café, which had been left open in the hope of catching even the slightest breeze.

'Simon!' she said groggily, for she was still only semi-conscious.

His face broke into an amused smile and he took a step forward.

'Hello! Did I wake you? Sorry! I didn't know you were having a nana nap!'

She grinned sheepishly and wiped her mouth with the back of her hand, fearful that she might have dribbled in her sleep.

'I was feeling sick, to be honest,' she said truthfully, 'and I had a headache. I took a pill, though, and it seems a bit better.'

'It's the heat,' Simon replied sympathetically. 'Boiling, isn't it?'

He pointed to a blue rolled-up towel tucked under his arm; she hadn't noticed it before.

'I'm going for a swim. Would you like to come?'

She was about to say no, she couldn't leave work, but one of the students, Martha, had overheard their conversation and chipped in.

'Go if you want,' she said kindly. She and Chabela had struck up quite a rapport. 'It's not so busy now. We can manage till you come back. A swim might make you feel better.'

Chabela hadn't had a break yet and the prospect of a dip was very appealing. She'd brought a swimsuit and towel to the café on her very first morning and kept it in the cloakroom. So far, however, she'd only ventured into the water once.

Simon raised his eyebrows hopefully and she didn't like to disappoint him.

'OK,' she said, rising from her chair. 'I'll get changed. Give me a moment.'

It didn't take long to remove her clothes and put on her swimsuit – a bright red halter-neck with high legs and a plunging bosom. It felt strange appearing in front of him with so little on, but he didn't seem to notice.

As they picked their way through the countless bodies down to the ocean's edge, she was aware of attracting a few stares, but Simon looked resolutely ahead.

When they were almost at the shoreline, he threw down his towel, stripped off his shorts and T-shirt, removed his tortoiseshell glasses and peered at her short-sightedly. 'Come on then!'

She was about to say that she'd rather take her time and get in slowly, but he reached out and took hold of her hand. She was surprised, but his hand felt warm and secure and she trusted him completely; she didn't try to let go.

Without more ado, he pulled her gently to the edge of the waves, clasping her all the time. When her toes made contact with the water, she squealed; it was much colder than Acapulco or Cancún, but he tightened his grip a little, encouraging her to go on.

In they went, deeper and deeper, until the water was up to their thighs, then their waists. Despite the warmth of the sun, the chill almost took her breath away.

Their hands were still linked, but it didn't feel unnatural. In fact she liked it. Although she hadn't had a proper look at him in his bathing shorts, she could see his neat, strong torso in the corner of her vision and his smooth, powerful shoulders and arms.

She insisted on holding her arms high in the air to keep them dry, which meant that he had to do the same, until an icy wave leaped up unexpectedly, almost to their necks.

Chabela gasped again and was tempted to turn back, but Simon wasn't having any of it.

'It's no use,' he laughed. 'You can't put it off any longer!' And with that, he launched himself head first into the brine, dragging her with him.

It happened so suddenly that Chabela took in several gulps of salty water.

She was a good swimmer, though, and after ten or so strong strokes, her body acclimatised. Simon had let go of her hand by now, and she was aware of him finning along beside her.

They resurfaced almost at the same time and looked at each other while treading water. Simon's wet, dark hair clung smoothly to his head and he made a snorting sound, like a seal, and blew water out of his nose, which made her laugh.

His face broke into a smile, too. 'Good, huh?' he said, turning around to look at the shore. He seemed more relaxed in water than on land; he was clearly in his element.

They were just out of their depth and had left behind most of the other bathers, who were splashing around in the shallows. A man in a mask and snorkel passed by, followed by a woman paddleboarder with a very long pole, and then they were alone again.

'Shall we swim to the cove?' Simon suggested, pointing to some rocks a little way off to his left, which were jutting out to sea. 'There's a beach on the other side. Most people don't bother to go there. It's only small but very pretty.'

'Good idea.'

Soon he was doing his strong, speedy crawl towards the rocks, making quite a splash, while she followed behind. The tide was against them as they swam parallel to the shore, and it was quite hard work. He stopped every now and again to check that she was OK and give her time to draw breath; it was further than it looked.

She'd forgotten all about the café and by the time she remembered, they were such a long way away, and it would have taken so long to get back, that there was no point worrying. In any case, she just about trusted Rosie, Felipe and Martha to take care of things until she returned.

At last they reached the craggy grey rocks, which were covered in seaweed and barnacles.

'Careful you don't get scratched,' Simon warned, as he started to heave himself out of the sea. 'They're quite sharp.'

The rocks weren't particularly high, but still he clambered on all fours for a short way, before straightening up and turning to Chabela, who was just beginning to get out of the water herself.

'Need a hand?' he asked, bending down and extending an arm.

'I think I can manage, thanks.' She wished that she were wearing a different swimsuit. This one, with its plunging neckline, wasn't really made for scrambling and she hoped that her boobs wouldn't fall out.

The barnacles were, indeed, sharp and pricked like needles, but she managed to avoid any injuries. Slowly, she picked her way over the peaky stones, following in Simon's tracks and taking care not to lose her balance.

He stopped again when they reached the highest point of the promontory, so that she could admire the small, crescent-shaped cove, which was sheltered on all sides by tall rocks and pitted with caves. The thin ribbon of fine yellow sand running between each outcrop looked extremely inviting and what's more, they would have the whole place to themselves.

'It's lovely!' she cried, blinking in the bright sun.

'Told you!' he replied with a grin.

It was quite steep on the other side, and Chabela dropped to her hands and feet and crawled sideways, like a crab, until the very last bit, by which time Simon, who was ahead of her, had reached solid ground again.

Now, when he extended both hands, she took them and he held on firmly while she hopped safely onto the beach.

Beneath her feet were numerous little shells, broken up and bleached almost white by the sun and tide. At the very edge of the water, bits of driftwood wrapped in stringy seaweed bobbed lazily on the foamy surf.

'Shall we sit down?' said Simon, nodding towards the boulders on the other side.

She followed him across the cove – it was only a few paces – to the flatter rocks and they settled down, leaning their backs against the warm granite.

For a few minutes they didn't speak but closed their eyes, enjoying the sensation of the warm sun on their faces and the gentle breeze fanning their cheeks.

As Chabela breathed in and out slowly, it occurred to her that right now, she felt totally content and at ease. Perhaps it was the friendly endorphins whooshing around her body, or maybe the soporific sunshine. In any case, she didn't feel at all awkward in Simon's company and he seemed equally comfortable with her. There was no sign of his nervous twitch, and his breathing was as steady and relaxed as her own.

Her knees were drawn up to her waist and her hands placed, palms down, on either side of her body. After a while, she stretched out her legs to loosen the muscles and became aware of his thigh and calf, alongside. He was very close, but he didn't try to move and nor did she. The fingertips of her left hand and his right were almost touching, too.

She wanted to open her eyes to see what he was doing and also, truth be told, to have a sneak peek at his body, which was surprisingly buff. But she didn't dare. She had a feeling that he was looking at her, though she couldn't be sure, and she didn't want him to catch her at it, too.

The tips of her fingers seemed to tingle, giving off electric flashes, and she hoped that it wasn't too obvious. There again, she sensed that his skin was also sparking, but she might have been imagining it, of course.

She couldn't quite believe that the feelings she was having for him were real, yet at the same time they seemed quite natural, as if she'd known all along that she thought this way about him. But then she checked herself, doubting her gut. Simon had never shown any interest in her, other than as a friend, and besides, she wasn't looking for romance; she wasn't over Alfonso.

His image swam before her and immediately her eyes fluttered open and the sparks in her fingertips died, just as if someone had flicked an off switch.

Simon shivered, as if he'd felt it, too, and pulled up his legs, as if preparing to rise.

She wanted to say sorry for having ruined something that might have been really special, but she'd have felt silly.

'Chabela?'

The sound of his voice startled her and she turned to look. He was sitting very upright now, facing her, and he had a strange expression, almost as if he were in pain.

'What—' she started to say, but before she could finish, his head moved really close, so that their brows were almost touching, and there seemed to be a question mark right in the centre of his round, black pupils.

Instinctively, she raised her chin just a little and before she knew it, his mouth was on hers, his lips pressing gently against her own. He smelled of the ocean and tasted of salt and sea.

At first the kiss was shy, tentative and slow, each drinking in the other in little sips, savouring the newness. Then, to her surprise, he nibbled her lower lip, pulling at it slightly. She bit back playfully and when he nudged her cheek, butting it softly with his nose, she opened her mouth wider and allowed his tongue to slip in.

He made no attempt to touch her anywhere else; the only point of contact was the lips. Deeper and deeper went the kiss, until it became so intense that it was almost unbearable, and she longed for him to explore other parts of her, but he held back.

Everything was concentrated in just that one place and the kiss seemed to say it all; nothing more was needed. So wrapped up were they in each other, they might have been the only people left on the planet.

When they finally drew breath, Chabela looked at Simon again and could see that he was smiling. They were both still sitting up, resting against the granite, and without speaking, she laid her head on his warm chest and curled into his side, allowing him to wrap an arm around her.

She was filled with a sense of wonder, remembering the shy, awkward man that she'd first met. She'd never have believed him capable of a kiss like that; truly, it had blown her away.

'There's something you should know,' he said at last, pulling her in even closer, as if afraid that she might get up and leave.

'Tell me,' she replied. She didn't think there was anything he could reveal that would put her off now, but she sensed that he wanted to speak.

'I'm a bit, well, odd,' he blurted, and she laughed, she couldn't help it.

'I know *that*. I like eccentricity, it's more interesting.'

He shuffled uncomfortably. 'No, you don't understand. I've never had a proper relationship. I mean, I've had a few girlfriends, not for a while, though, but I didn't love any of them, not really. I'm not sure I'm capable of it.'

'Why not?' Chabela could tell that this was important. She straightened up and his arm dropped away. They were still touching, though, her knees pulled in and resting against his thigh. She didn't want to lose all contact with him.

'I don't know,' he said, staring into the distance, deliberately avoiding her gaze. 'My father was a loner and he and my mother didn't get on particularly well. They never did anything together, just the two of them; they led quite separate lives. I guess I don't know what a normal relationship looks like.'

Chabela frowned. 'Are you saying you don't want a relationship with me? If so, I need to know now, before...' She bit her lip.

'Before what?' he asked urgently.

'Before this goes any further.'

He twisted around so that he was fully facing her again, his whole body tense and on alert.

'Do you *want* this to go further?' He sounded nervous and eager at the same time.

It was a very direct question, but she didn't mind. It was better to sort this now, rather than risk future hurt; she wasn't sure that she could stand any more suffering.

'Yes, but I'm afraid. How about you?'

'Afraid of what?'

'Rejection, sorrow, pain.'

This made him wince. 'Chabela, I'd never deliberately hurt you. Not in a million years. You see, despite what I just said about not loving anyone, I... I think I might be able to fall in love with you.'

She started. She was so surprised that she thought she must have misheard. 'What did you say?'

He repeated the words and this time she knew that it was true.

At that moment, she would have thrown her arms around his neck and snogged him senseless, but he stopped her in her tracks, raising a flattened palm.

'I'm scared,' he went on in deadly earnest. 'I'm afraid I can't give you what you need and deserve. Because I've never had a real relationship, because I'm weird...'

His honesty and sincerity melted her heart.

'I don't care,' she cried, meaning it. 'I'm useless at relationships, too. We can learn together!'

He smiled, reaching out to take her face in his hands and staring into her eyes. The look was so intense, so full of longing, that it seemed to burn right through her.

'I should tell you about Alfonso,' she whispered reluctantly. His name seemed to sully the atmosphere and she could have sworn that the sky darkened briefly.

'Go on then,' said Simon. 'I'm ready.'

He held her tight while she rested her cheek on his chest. They remained like that for a long time while she explained the situation as well as she could. She didn't put all the blame on Alfonso or try to exonerate herself, she just gave the facts and explained her feelings as clearly as possible.

If Simon were shocked that she had been someone's mistress, he didn't show it. Nor did he suggest that she'd been a fool for believing all the promises of marriage.

In the end, he said simply, 'This doesn't change anything, Chabela, but I'm glad I know. I'm sorry you've been unhappy.'

Her cheek felt sticky and hot against his skin, but she didn't want to move it. Instead, she snaked an arm around his waist and squeezed.

She realised that it was a relief to have revealed her story at last, warts and all. The shame and misery that she'd carried around for so long felt less intense, now that Simon seemed to accept her for what she was without criticism. It was wonderfully freeing.

'He must be quite something, Alfonso, to have kept you waiting all this time,' Simon said then.

Chabela thought about this for a moment.

'He's very clever, he's got an amazing mind,' she agreed. 'And I certainly found him attractive. A lot of women do.'

'The only thing that puzzles me is why you hung around so long?'

Simon sounded genuinely perplexed; she didn't blame him. She didn't understand it herself.

'I was obsessed, I suppose. No one else seemed to match up to him.'

There was a pause, as if Simon needed time to absorb the information.

'And are you still obsessed?' The question seemed to hang in the air between them, heavy with significance.

'I don't think so, I don't know.' She was determined to be as truthful with him as he had been with her. 'Some days I think I'm over him, and others, well, I realise he's still on my mind. I don't want it to be like this. We're finished. There's no going back. It's just, well, sometimes I can't seem to get him out of my head.'

She feared Simon's response, but she needn't have worried.

'Thanks. I think I can live with that for now.' He left it there.

They must have been in the same position for ages, though she had no idea of the time. At last, conscious of having abandoned her job, she said that she'd better get back.

'I hope the others are managing. It's really bad of me to have been away so long.'

As they set off again over the rocks, she mentioned that she might return to Mexico in October with Liz and Rosie and maybe Rafael, too.

'Just for a week or two, if Liz decides to come. I'd like to stay in Tremarnock until Christmas, if I can. I don't feel ready to go back to work yet and have to face Alfonso.'

By now, they'd reached the other side of the promontory and Simon plunged into the sea, followed by Chabela. It felt extremely cold after being in the hot sun and they swam fast at first to get used to the temperature.

Presently, they stopped for a rest, floating on their backs and gazing up at the sky. The sun was just beginning to dip, changing slowly in colour from bright yellow to a more orangey hue. As they got closer to the beach, they could hear the distant shouts of people, which was strange after the quietness of the cove.

'Why don't you come, too – to Mexico, I mean?' Chabela said tentatively. 'Only if you'd like to, of course.'

She'd been mulling it over ever since she'd told him that she was going. She didn't think it would seem too forward, given that she knew he loved the country, but still, it had taken a while to pluck up the courage to ask. She explained that it would be a bit of a squash in her flat, but she could just about accommodate everyone. They'd probably spend most of their time in Mexico City but might visit Hidalgo as well.

'It'd be interesting for Liz to see the place where the Cornish miners settled, and I could look up the Penhallows, too.'

He waited a moment before replying; he must have been mulling, also.

'I think I'd like that,' he replied at last. 'Thank you. I've never been on holiday with a woman before. I guess it's about time I did.'

He was joking, but she could tell that the prospect unnerved him somewhat.

'If you change your mind—'

'I won't,' he said firmly, and the subject was closed.

Their towels were still on the beach where they left them, and Simon pulled his shorts and T-shirt over his wet trunks and replaced his glasses. When they finally arrived back at the café, Chabela was convinced that the others were looking at her slightly oddly.

'I'm sorry we've been so long,' she said, conscious of her wet, tangled hair and slightly flushed cheeks. They must wonder what on earth she'd been up to.

Simon looked a little sheepish, too, shuffling awkwardly from foot to foot and clearing his throat rather too often.

Luckily, there was no queue now and only a few of the outside tables were occupied with people finishing their drinks and snacks. Most looked almost ready to pack up and leave; it must have been gone six p.m. and the sun was less intense, although the air was still warm.

'I'd better get changed,' Chabela said, relieved that there was only an hour to go before she could legitimately lock up.

'Me too,' said Simon, but he seemed reluctant to head off.

'Well, goodbye then.' Chabela was conscious that the others were still watching and didn't want to give anything away.

He bent down and fiddled with his flip-flop, before standing up and deliberately catching her eye.

'I enjoyed our swim, thank you. It was a most interesting cove. We should go there again soon.'

Rafael stared at them both and Martha looked confused. Chabela bit her cheek and tried not to laugh.

'As soon as you like,' she added cheekily.

Chapter Twenty-One

To Liz's delight, Robert managed to persuade Rosie to go on the Mexican trip with her mother and before long, it was all fixed. They were to fly from Bristol to Mexico City, leaving on Friday night at the beginning of the October half-term and returning just over a week later. Tony and Felipe were happy to pay for Rafael, so he was to go, too, along with Simon and Chabela, of course.

Many of the villagers were quite relieved when August came to an end and the place calmed down, not least of all, Liz. As far as she could tell, the last of the seagull chicks had finally flown the nest and the parents must have moved on. She was no longer being woken every morning by drumming feet, which was a blessed relief, and she'd been in touch with the British Pest Control Association about installing deterrent measures, so that the birds wouldn't return next year.

The streets were much quieter, too, but partly thanks to the good weather, a new, smaller crowd, of those without school-age children, arrived in early September and the beaches remained busy.

For this reason, Robert decided to keep the Secret Shack open, which was good news for Chabela. By now, the university students had returned to their studies, and often it was just her and Loveday manning the place during the week, with Rosie and Rafael helping out at weekends.

The autumn term is a demanding time for most teachers, and Simon was no exception. Chabela saw next to nothing of him between Monday and Friday, but he'd often visit the café on Saturday or Sunday and they'd go for a dip during one of her breaks.

When the temperature started to drop towards the end of September, he persuaded her to buy a wetsuit from Rick's shop. This made getting in the cold water much less of an ordeal and to her amazement, she developed quite a passion for wild swimming.

Simon refused to wear a suit himself, insisting that he liked plunging into freezing temperatures and it was beneficial to his health. In certain ways, she found this even more eccentric than his other habits, but he certainly seemed very fit, so maybe there was something in it.

Often, the pair would go back to Kittiwake for supper afterwards, or they'd eat out at the Lobster Pot or the Hole in the Wall. Dining at A Winkle in Time would have felt too much like a busman's holiday for Chabela, with Robert there, so they avoided it.

Villagers began to spot them out and about and of course, word spread. Rick must have heard the gossip, or even spied Chabela and Simon together, because he finally gave up on her and went back to online dating, much to her relief.

The more she saw of Simon, the more she liked him. They seemed to have a lot in common and she ceased to notice his involuntary spasms, which were becoming less pronounced anyway. He still wore a lot of brown, but he'd relaxed his diet and would now happily scoff scones and cream with her on a regular basis or drink too much wine. She even got him into her home-made churros, dipped in melted chocolate. He complained that he was putting on weight, but she couldn't see any evidence of it.

She adored hanging out with him in Kittiwake, watching the sun go down over the cliffs, listening to music and helping him cook tasty meals using some of the herbs and vegetables from his garden.

They'd kiss and cuddle, but he was the perfect gentleman and never tried to push for anything more. Indeed, she began rather to wish that he would, but was afraid of making a move herself for fear of frightening him off. In any case, Alfonso would keep popping unbidden into her head at odd moments, so it wouldn't have felt quite right.

Then, one evening after supper, they were side by side on the sofa listening to music when lust grabbed them with both hands, gave them a shake and it just sort of happened. It wasn't how Chabela would have planned it, or Simon, probably, but somehow it felt just right. No fuss or embarrassment, no awkward asking each other if they liked it this way or that, just messy and glorious, leaving behind a sense of deep satisfaction and fulfilment. Perfect.

The deal had been sealed, so to speak. Neither needed to pretend any more that they didn't fancy the pants off each other, which was tremendously freeing. So much so, in fact, that they were both keen to repeat the experience as often as possible thereafter.

In the meantime, Liz put together a sort of itinerary for their Mexico trip, and Chabela telephoned her cleaner, Verónica, asking her to prepare the apartment for their arrival. She wired Verónica some cash to buy two airbeds, one for Rosie and the other for Rafael, and got her to make them up, along with two others, for Liz and Simon.

As the day of their departure drew near, Chabela started having butterflies in her stomach and realised that it was excitement and nerves. Certainly, she was looking forward to seeing her home city and tasting some real Mexican food again. The main reason for her agitation, however, was Simon. She couldn't quite imagine how it would feel to be with him in her own country, to hear him speaking with locals and to show him some of the places that she loved most. It seemed almost too good to be true.

Deep down, she hoped that his visit would go so well that it would finally expunge her last lurking memories of Alfonso. With luck, she would return to Tremarnock with a clear head and a completely fresh slate, so to speak, all ready to begin the next chapter.

Just two days before they were due to leave, she was in her bedroom at Polgarry Manor, starting to put things in her suitcase, when she received a call from Simon.

It was Tuesday night at around eight o'clock when he'd normally be busy marking homework. He was never one just to phone for a chat, so she knew that something was up.

'Hello,' she said tentatively, and the heaviness in his voice only confirmed her concerns. He explained that Ralph, the head teacher at the secondary school where he worked, had gone down with shingles. That very afternoon, Ralph had been at home with his wife recuperating when he'd developed complications and had had to be admitted to hospital.

The deputy, Marion, was beside herself with worry because no one knew how long Ralph would be off work. The school was due an inspection by Ofsted, and Marion had reason to believe that the assessors might arrive soon after half-term.

'She was expecting to spend the holiday preparing, but she thought Ralph would be sharing the load,'

Simon went on. 'It's most unfortunate. I can't leave her to do it all alone. She was stressed even before he fell ill; this might tip her over the edge.'

At first, Chabela couldn't quite believe what she was hearing, then she tried to persuade Simon to bring his work with him.

'You can have my study all to yourself. It's nice and quiet in there. You won't be disturbed.'

But Simon said that he should be around in person for Marion, and besides, he'd need to pop in and out of school to check on various things.

'Can't some of the other heads of department help her?' Chabela asked next, but according to Simon, two were brand new to the school and the others hadn't been there anything like as long as him.

'I'm the only one who knows where all the records are kept, apart from Ralph and Marion, that is. I'm afraid I'm the obvious choice. No one's more sorry than me, Chabela,' he added. 'I'm gutted.'

She tried to hide her disappointment as best she could. 'What a shame! Another time, perhaps,' she said, fake-brightly.

As soon as she hung up, however, she threw herself on the bed and wept bitterly. Although on one level she understood his reasoning perfectly, on the other, she couldn't help feeling desperately hurt and rejected. If he really wanted to come, surely he would find a way around the problem? She wanted him to move heaven and earth for her and instead, he'd cancelled what would have been their first ever holiday together for a highly strung woman called Marion.

All of a sudden, the trip, which she'd been so looking forward to, seemed much less like fun and more like hard work. She'd do her best to make sure that the others had a good time, but as far as she could see, there was nothing in it for her; she didn't even fancy revisiting Mexico City any more.

There was no going back, however, and once she'd stopped crying, she got up and continued packing as if nothing had happened. When Bramble tapped on her door later on and asked if she'd like to join her and Matt for a drink downstairs, she'd never have guessed that there was anything amiss.

ROBERT DROVE THE FOUR TRAVELLERS to Bristol airport. Liz sat beside him in the car and Chabela noticed that they barely exchanged a word for the entire two and a half hours. He dropped them outside the departures gate and left immediately; Jean was kindly looking after Lowenna and he'd promised that he'd be back to collect her by nine-ish.

Liz's eyes were damp as she watched her husband go and she was quiet for a while, but didn't say why. She perked up a bit when they got to the duty-free lounge and she bought some make-up for her and Rosie. Meanwhile,

Rafael wandered around the alcohol section, looking longingly at all the labels on the bottles, knowing full well that he wouldn't get served.

They had something to eat and drink and before they knew it, it was time to board. It was the first time that Liz and Rosie had flown since they'd gone to Oklahoma for Rosie to have life-saving proton beam therapy treatment. Liz felt a bit strange, remembering how frightened she had been, wondering if the treatment would work.

She checked on her daughter a few times, but she seemed perfectly happy, chatting with Rafael and flicking through the in-flight magazine to find a film. Perhaps, at that age, you had a shorter memory, or maybe she had blanked out the experience. Either way, Liz was pleased that she was so relaxed.

The journey took about thirteen hours and they arrived in the dark at around three a.m. Mexican time. They were weary and hardly spoke in the taxi from the airport to Colonia del Valle, but they livened up when they finally stepped out of the lift on the fifth floor, and spied the door to Chabela's apartment right across the hallway.

'Here we are,' she said, opening up and beckoning them all in. 'Your home for the week. Welcome!'

It felt strange to be back in the apartment, seeing it partly through her visitors' fresh eyes. Verónica had closed the blinds and put on the air conditioning so that it was cool and dark, and seemed very quiet after the hustle and bustle of the airport and motorway.

Chabela dumped her bag on the floor, switched on a few lamps and looked around. Everything was exactly the same, but also different somehow. The soft, sandy walls, dark wood furniture, green cushions and terracotta sofas and chairs reminded her of the Mexican desert on a sultry summer's evening just before sundown.

The main room where they were was wide and spacious, with a high ceiling and large windows, though the kitchen and guest bedrooms were smaller. Even so, the proportions could hardly have been more different from Kittiwake, with all its nooks and crannies, and, of course, there was no salty smell or view of the sea.

After showing the others to their rooms, Chabela strolled into her own and felt a stab of regret, grief and longing deep in her guts. Her big bed, with the dark wooden headboard and green satin cover, had been her haven with Alfonso. It was where they had laughed, argued, eaten, drunk, put the world to rights, listened to music and made love.

She couldn't help thinking that if Simon were there with her, the regret wouldn't be nearly as sharp, the grief not half as deep. As it was, she was alone with her difficulties and sorrow.

Liz knew about Alfonso, of course, but Chabela didn't want to spoil her holiday by going on about him, and besides, the poor woman had her own problems. For the next seven days, Chabela would just have to don her happy mask and get on with it.

Verónica had left milk, bread, cheese and various other items in the fridge, and there was plenty of tea and coffee. They all ate toast around the kitchen table, which was really only big enough for two, then went to bed for a few hours. Because of the time difference, however, no one could sleep and as soon as it was light, Chabela rose again and popped to the local shops for fresh fruit, croissants and jam.

By about nine fifteen everyone had showered, dressed, had breakfast and they were on the road again in Chabela's white Volkswagen Atlas, which she kept in the car park beneath her block of flats.

They had already planned to hit the ground running and spend the day at the magnificent ancient city of Teotihucán, some fifty kilometres south of Mexico City. Built more than a thousand years before the arrival of the Aztecs, it was home to the magnificent Temple of Quetzalcoatl and the great Pyramid of the Sun and Pyramid of the Moon.

It was the ideal day to visit because the jet lag made it easy for them to set off early, and they managed to beat the crowds and walk around the whole city before the sun got too hot. There were plenty of willing, English-speaking guides on site but they didn't need one, because Chabela knew the place and its history like the back of her hand.

Later, they ate tacos in a bar and returned home exhausted but happy at around seven p.m. and almost ready for bed.

The following day, Chabela had organised a visit to the city centre, taking in Zócalo (Constitution Square), the Metropolitan Cathedral and the Education Ministry, to see the famous murals of the artist, Diego Rivera. They ate ice creams and drank cool lemonade on the terrace of the Café Don Porfirio, overlooking the Palacio de Bellas Artes with its sturdy façade and ornate art deco interior.

In the evening, Chabela booked a restaurant in the quirky neighbourhood of Colonia Roma, where they ate *chiles en nogada* – chillies filled with chopped meats, fruits and spices and covered in walnut cream – and chicken with mole poblano, a rusty red sauce made with plain chocolate.

Rosie, who wasn't particularly adventurous with food, had some difficulty, but picked her way around the things she didn't like and filled up any remaining corners with bread.

By day three, everyone had settled nicely into holiday mode, and Chabela was pleased to see Liz looking happier and more relaxed. She was clearly getting on all right with Rosie, and Rafael kept them amused with his clownish behaviour and silly jokes.

That morning, they got up quite late and visited the Frida Kahlo Museum, also known as the Blue House on account of its cobalt-blue walls, in the district of Coyoacán. When they were starting to flag, Chabela suggested a movie. They chose a Spanish language film with English subtitles in one of the city's luxury theatres, complete with reclining leather chairs and service brought to your seat. Chabela and Liz ate sushi, washed down with white wine, while Rosie and Rafael opted for sandwiches and French fries.

The week was whizzing by so fast and they were so busy that Chabela had little time to brood. Frequently, however, she did find herself fervently wishing that Simon were there, too. It was hard not to feel resentful, when she'd looked forward to being with him so much. She knew that it was unfair to blame him in any way but still, she didn't feel like getting in touch and he didn't make contact, either.

On Thursday morning, they set off for the little mining town of Real del Monte, which was up in the mountains and about a two-hour journey by car from Mexico City. The Tremarnock connection failed to interest Rafael much, but Rosie and Liz were keen to find out more about the Cornish migrants who travelled all that way to settle there.

Chabela had only visited once, and that was long before she knew about her Cornish ancestry. As they drove through the narrow, cobbled streets to their small hotel, she had a strong sense of déjà vu, for the brightly painted houses on either side with their sloping roofs, low doors and colourful gardens were reminiscent of Tremarnock and all the other little fishing villages round about.

They parked the car and, after depositing their bags in their rooms, strolled back to the town centre, where the main square was home to a famous clock tower, built by Francis Rule. Originally from Camborne, he became known as the Silver King, having made a fortune from his numerous mining interests.

They also made some enquiries and managed to locate the grand hacienda, which James had lived in with Jacinta and their children. Unfortunately the current owners were away, but Chabela in particular enjoyed looking around the outside and trying to imagine the Penhallow family in situ.

Little shops selling *pastes*, or Cornish pasties, abounded, only these ones contained unfamiliar ingredients such as chilli and pineapple, sweetened rice, avocado and mole. The general consensus was that Cornish ones were better, but that it was good to experiment with different flavours, too.

They all wanted to see the square on the edge of town where Cornish miners used to play football. When they got there, however, they were surprised to find that it was nothing more than a rather shabby car park, with a metal plaque on the wall proclaiming: 'Here, football was played in Mexico for the first time.'

Nearby was a run-down football museum, basically just a couple of rooms containing old photographs and some dusty memorabilia.

Rafael was a bit disappointed, having expected a more impressive display. Chabela, however, was fascinated to see the faces of the football-playing Cornish miners and to imagine her ancestor, James Penhallow, setting eyes on Jacinta for the very first time in more or less this exact same spot.

As dusk approached and the temperature cooled, they drove to the Panteón Inglés – the Cornish cemetery – located in a forest on a hilltop overlooking the town. After parking the car, they strolled through the vast, wrought-iron gates into the tranquil, leafy graveyard, overhung with fir trees and abundant with wild flowers.

Here, the group split up and Chabela found herself wandering alone among the graves, amazed to learn that all but one had been carefully aligned to point in the direction of distant England.

There were literally hundreds of dilapidated Victorian tombstones, featuring Gothic monuments such as angels, wreaths and broken pillars, all dotted with moss and stained with lichen. The epitaphs were in English, and she was touched to read the names of the brave Cornishmen and women who risked their lives to get here and never made it back to their native land.

Each epitaph seemed to tell its own story of courage, toil, suffering and love. One in particular caught her eye, that of Robert B. Noble, from St Hilary, Cornwall, who passed away in 1875, aged forty-two. Buried with him were his two infant sons, James, age four months, and Robert, seven months. Chabela could only begin to imagine the grief of the surviving mother; her poor babies had scarcely lived at all.

Other names sounded very English, too – Pengelly, Skewes, Rule, Ough, Pratt and Richards. Many had died in childhood, adolescence or their twenties. Only the lucky ones, it seemed, had made it to their fifties and beyond.

Most of the tombs were neglected and overgrown with weeds. However, Chabela was touched to see some recently scattered sweets and flowers on that one of a man named Richard Bell. Clearly he was still remembered by someone.

It was only when she went around the cemetery a second time, enjoying the sense of stillness and breathing in the scent of fir, that she took a look at some of the more modest tombstones, some of which were listing at an odd angle or had actually fallen to the ground.

At the far end of the cemetery, where the graves seemed to preside over the town below, her gaze fell on a small, square stone, which was bleached with age and covered in ivy.

For some reason, she decided to rip off some of the ivy tendrils with her fingers and wipe away the soil beneath. The writing, when it emerged, was quite hard to decipher but the more she stared, the more convinced she became that her eyes weren't deceiving her. For there, in faded black lettering, was a name that had become extremely familiar to her of late: JAMES PENHALLOW.

Shivers ran up and down her spine and she felt a sudden surge of energy, as if someone had just joined the broken wires of an electric circuit back together again. All of a sudden, the Cornish link felt properly real. The same blood that once ran through the body buried beneath her coursed through her veins, also.

She wondered what genetic traits might have been passed down the generations. Had she inherited the same-shaped nose or mouth as James, for instance? Or was she prone to the same illnesses and allergies? He might have lived more than a hundred years ago, but if you stood them side by side, would you be able to tell that they were related? It seemed fanciful, but she'd noticed enough resemblances between different generations of the same families to know that certain physical features did seem to reproduce themselves ad infinitum.

Below James's name were his dates, which tallied with those that Simon had told her, and the words, 'Rest in Peace', but nothing more. There was no mention of how he'd died, or of his beloved wife or children.

Chabela felt a pang of sadness that his life should have ended in this way, commemorated only by a mean, stark tombstone, which gave no clue as to his hopes and desires, his achievements and character.

There was no sign of Jacinta's grave, either, but Chabela was certain that they would have wished to be buried together. Perhaps, one day, she or some other relative would be able to put this right but for now, the former lovers remained separated in space and time.

So lost was she in her own thoughts that she didn't hear Liz come up behind and when she tapped Chabela on the shoulder, she jumped.

'What have you found?' Liz asked, and Chabela pointed to the tombstone.

'Wow!' Liz exclaimed. 'That's amazing! How weird that you've managed to locate him. What are the chances of that?'

She urged her friend to take some photographs, and also insisted on snapping Chabela herself by the epitaph.

'I think there's something rather lovely about stumbling across him here,' Liz went on. 'I hope he's looking down on you from somewhere up there.' She pointed to the sky. 'Sending loving thoughts.'

Chabela smiled. 'I hope so.' Then, without thinking, she crouched down and planted a kiss on the stone.

'Thanks for leading me to Tremarnock,' she whispered. 'If it wasn't for you, I'd never have known it even existed.'

She was silent as she drove the group back to their small hotel, reflecting on the strange paths down which life could take you, the curious twists and turns of fate. Rosie fell asleep on Rafael's shoulder and Liz looked out of the window, gazing at the sun sinking slowly over the baked hills and fields of cacti.

They had supper in a traditional, family-run Mexican restaurant with yellow tablecloths and wooden beams, which had once been a grocery store selling *pastes* and home-made bread. Afterwards, they went for a drink in an old-fashioned cantina with wood panelling and saloon bar doors, which sold every type of tequila under the sun.

By the time they returned to their rooms, they were so tired they could barely speak. Chabela hopped into bed and was about to turn out the light when her phone, which was on charge, pinged on the table beside her.

Immediately, she jerked upright and her tummy fluttered. Simon? She'd sent him one of the photos of herself by James Penhallow's grave from the restaurant. She'd had a feeling that he was waiting for her to contact him, rather than the other way around, but it was the first time that she'd felt like doing so all week.

To her dismay, the name that flashed up on the screen wasn't Simon's, and her heart started to thump and the veins in her temples throbbed.

Should she answer? She was under no obligation, but she knew that she was going to and gave a silent groan.

'Alfonso?' she said, after swiping right. 'Is that you?'

'Chabelita,' came the velvety reply. 'A little bird told me you're in town. I have to see you. Can I come round now?'

Chapter Twenty-Two

THE CHEEK OF IT, THE sheer nerve! After all that had gone on between them, she couldn't quite believe it. If he thought that he could click his fingers just like that and she'd come running, he was very much mistaken. He'd nearly broken her heart but she'd picked herself up and dusted herself off. She wasn't the same person that she'd been before she left Mexico. Tremarnock had changed her and she'd moved on.

'I'm not in the city,' she said coldly, 'I'm in the country. And don't call me Chabelita.'

'Whereabouts are you?' he asked, ignoring her last comment.

Once again, she bristled. He had no right to ask such a question; it was none of his business. She nearly told him so, but then his tone changed.

'I've missed you so much,' he said plaintively. 'I wanted to call you. I picked up the phone every day when you were away and started to ring your number, but somehow I always managed to stop myself. I didn't think it would be fair.'

'How uncharacteristically kind of you!' she said sarcastically. 'Where's your wife, then? Is she better now?'

'Not really, no.'

'I'm sorry to hear that,' she lied. 'Perhaps a change of air will sort her out. Have you bought your luxury retirement villa in Mérida yet? When do you move in?'

She hated the sneer in her voice but couldn't help it; hurt could come out in a myriad different ways.

'I've made an offer,' he replied heavily, 'but it might all fall through. You know how these things are.'

'Not really, no. Why would I?' She wanted to remind him that she had no husband with whom to buy a gorgeous pad by the beach, that she'd never have one, probably, because she'd given her best years to a married bastard. She didn't, though.

'Don't be like that,' he said. 'Look, I know you're angry, you have every right to be, but can we at least talk – please?'

She was sitting on the edge of the bed now, her feet resting on the cool floor. She didn't realise that she'd been biting the nail on her right thumb but when she looked down, she saw that it was ragged and torn.

'What's there to talk about? You told me you'll never leave Pilar. End of...'

To her dismay, there was a wobble in her voice and a lump appeared from nowhere in her throat. She hated him for upsetting her, and hated herself even more for letting him do it. She should never have answered his call.

'You know it's more complicated than that,' he persisted.

'Is it?'

A sob escaped from her mouth and her hand flew up to her chest, to where her heart was. She hadn't wanted him to know that she still had feelings for him, but it was too late.

'I wish you were here. I want to hold you and comfort you.'

'Well I'm not – and you can't,' she snapped, suddenly jolted out of sorrow and into anger. Childish wasn't the word for the way it came out, she thought; she sounded like a baby.

He sighed. 'Oh, Chabela.' And then she heard a noise, which sounded to her very much like a snuffle or a moan. Was he crying? In all the years that they'd been together, she'd only ever seen him do it once, when his mother died.

She could feel her defences weaken, her resistance start to crumble. She should have hung up there and then and she knew it.

'Please can I come and see you when you get back? Just one more time. I won't stay long, I swear. Call it closure, if you like. We finished in such a bad way. We never even properly said goodbye.'

She thought of Simon and Kittiwake, of his guitar playing and his cooking, of the lovely evenings they'd had together and all those glorious snogs. He kissed like Romeo and made love like Casanova, but he hadn't been in touch, even just to see how she was. He couldn't feel the same way about her as she did him; not really.

'All right,' she said, squeezing her eyelids tight to shut out the lamplight's glare. 'I'm back tomorrow night but I've got guests staying. I'll meet you in the bar just across from my apartment. Eight p.m. If you're late, you've had it. I won't be waiting around for you. I'm not doing that ever again.'

SHE DIDN'T SAY ANYTHING TO Liz about the phone call when they met for breakfast the following morning. Deep down, she suspected that Liz would only tell her to cancel the arrangement with Alfonso, and she knew that she wasn't going to do it.

Rosie and Rafael were subdued as they ate their *huevos divorciados* (divorced eggs), which consisted of two fried eggs served on a flour tortilla topped with red and green sauce. They both complained of being tired, and Liz looked weary, too.

'Shall we have an easier day today?' Chabela suggested, and everyone agreed. It was decided that they would pay a visit to the historic Acosta silver mine,

THE GIRL WHO CAME HOME TO CORNWALL

which was built in the typical style of Cornish mines and was now a museum. After that, they would make their way slowly back to Mexico City, perhaps stopping to buy food en route that they could prepare and eat at home.

Chabela explained that she would have to go out briefly later to meet a work colleague, and no one asked any further questions.

'I imagine I'll be back by about ten. You could watch TV if you like. It'd be good for Rosie's Spanish.'

It was interesting to go down the mine, which was so similar in many ways to the one that Chabela had visited with Rick. The British-built engine house and high chimneys seemed to preside over the surrounding lush green countryside, acting as a powerful reminder of Cornish influence in the area.

Meanwhile, black and white photographs displayed the smudged faces of Cornish miners, side by side with their Mexican counterparts. Any one of the fair-skinned men could have been the young James Penhallow, before he made his fortune, but they were unnamed and Chabela would never know the truth.

All day long, her thoughts kept returning to last night's conversation, though she tried to hide her distraction as best she could. In her mind's eye, she had an image of herself in the bar, looking perfectly composed as she told Alfonso that she was over him, and there was no going back.

'You could have had all of me, everything,' she would say. 'I was completely and utterly in love with you. But you're not the man I thought you were.'

His face would fall as the devastating realisation of what he'd lost sank in. He would be thinking that from now on and for ever more, his fate would be to dwell on what he'd lost. Trapped with his shallow wife, Pilar, inside their luxury villa, he would be like a bird in a gilded cage, condemned to spend his remaining days gazing wistfully out of the window, speculating on what might have been.

She took time to get ready that evening, having a shower, washing her hair and putting on the red dress that she knew he'd always liked her in. When she checked herself in the mirror, she was quite surprised by the strong, confident woman who stared back. Her eyes seemed to burn with anger and determination, but then she touched the gold earring in her left earlobe and realised that it had been a gift from him.

All at once her self-belief seemed to trickle away, like water from a sponge, and she had to take a deep breath to shore herself up again.

'You can do this,' she told herself. 'Go there, see him for half an hour, say what you have to say, then leave.'

'You look lovely,' Liz commented when Chabela emerged from the bedroom and she smiled gratefully; she needed that boost.

'Thank you,' she replied.

She looked left and right as she crossed the street, half expecting to see strangers watching, as if the world somehow knew that she was on a vital mission that would change the course of her life. But it was getting dark and folk were going about their business quite unaware of her movements, wrapped up in the drama or boredom of their own existences. No one knew how nervous she was feeling, and probably no one cared. She was on her own.

Alfonso was sitting at a small wooden table with his back against the wall, facing the door. He spotted her immediately and she him, and their eyes met in recognition and apprehension. He looked intelligent, handsome and for once, slightly unsure of himself. She felt her knees wobble as he rose to greet her and she hurried to the chair opposite, anxious to sit before she fell.

'Hello, Chabela,' he said, leaning across the table to kiss her lightly on one cheek.

She felt the slight pressure of his hand on her shoulder and caught a whiff of his aftershave, but it wasn't the same as the one she remembered. He must have changed brands.

He had already ordered her a drink – a margarita made with tamarind, which he knew was her favourite.

'How have you been?' he asked, as she took a sip.

She opened her mouth to launch into the speech that she'd prepared in her head, but to her surprise, something quite different came out.

'All right, pretty good, I suppose, all things considered. What about you?'

'An absolute mess.' He took off his glasses and rubbed his eyes, leaving red rims around the edges. 'I've missed you so much,' he went on, 'I've made a terrible—'

'Don't!' she interrupted. 'Don't you dare pull that one on me. I'm not going to fall for it again.'

She sounded more certain of herself than she felt and he looked deeply uncomfortable, running a finger around the edge of his glass and frowning.

'I know I hurt you,' he said quietly, 'I'm desperately sorry. I wish I could turn back the clock. I was confused. There was so much going on with the kids, Pilar being unwell, my work. I thought I was ready to retire. There were a lot of problems in the department, some of which you know about and some you don't. But they're sorted now and I realise I'm not ready to leave my job; I love it too much.

'In short, Chabela, what I'm trying to say is...' he looked at her now, his brown eyes pleading, 'I want you back. I need you, I love you. I can't do without you. Please,' he went on, reaching over to touch her hand, which she quickly slid away, 'at least consider it. Give me a second chance.'

She was shocked, dumbfounded and, for a moment, lost for words. His speech was eloquent and he seemed genuine. Perhaps it was all true; maybe he had had second thoughts.

But then she remembered the estate agency details about the house in Mérida and something in her hardened again.

'What about Pilar?' she said coldly. 'I thought you could never leave her and she'd fall to pieces without you.'

His face looked odd, slightly red and blotchy and he nodded his head sadly.

'I just can't do it to her, it's hard to explain. I don't love her but I feel responsible. She's always been a bit vulnerable, as you know. Before we married, I promised her parents I'd look after her. For a long time when I was with you, I thought I *would* be able to leave her eventually, but then I realised I couldn't. We've been together so long and she's the mother of my children. What kind of shit would leave his wife of thirty-odd years when she's unstable and can't take care of herself properly?' He sighed. 'I'm trapped. I found the love of my life – you – but I can't be with you. It's hell.'

His eyes filled with tears and his hand trembled as he raised his glass to his lips and took a sip. Seeing him like that made Chabela's heart hurt but still, she needed to protect herself.

'Why didn't you tell me before?' she asked. 'As soon as you'd made the decision to stay with her? Why did you string me along, allowing me to believe we'd be together eventually?'

He placed his elbows on the table and rested his head in his hands, as if it were too heavy to support unaided.

'Fear,' he said sadly. 'I was scared of losing you; I didn't think I could live without you. I've made such a mess of things,' he went on, staring hard into the distance. Then he laughed humourlessly. 'So you see, I'm not the great professor after all. I'm just a weak man, groping around in the dark like everyone else looking for answers.'

She was silent for a moment, processing the information. Finally, it all seemed to make sense. She'd held him on a pedestal for so long and then he'd toppled from it spectacularly. He'd gone from angel to devil in her mind in the space of a few short hours and yet, in truth, he was neither. He was somewhere in between.

Alfonso wasn't all good or all bad. Just as he said, he was flawed, like most people, a typically imperfect example of that great species, homo sapiens. It was as if a veil had slipped from her eyes and she had him right-sized at last.

'I do really, really love you,' he repeated in a small voice, reaching out again for her hand across the table. This time, she left it there, allowing his fingers gently to caress hers.

Inside, an internal battle started to rage. She could feel Tremarnock – and Simon – pulling her one way, while Mexico and Alfonso dragged her the other. She'd worked so hard to get over her obsession with him and she'd almost succeeded; it would be madness to slip backwards. And yet...

The prospect of one more night with him was hard to resist. She felt some guilt about Simon, but his failure to contact her seemed to outweigh this; it had made her doubt him and the future of their fledgling relationship. Plus, there was unfinished business with Alfonso. She needed closure and she deserved it, surely, after all those years of waiting for him? This time, she would be calling the shots; she'd be the one finally to walk away.

Over another drink, they talked about the university, his latest book and her time in Cornwall. He wanted her impressions of the place and people and she told him how much she loved being there and about the Penhallow link. She was careful not to mention Simon, though.

Afterwards, they went out into the darkened street. It was almost eleven p.m. and the streetlamps had been lit. The air was still warm and she felt more relaxed than she had been all evening, all day, even. Ever since he'd phoned, she'd been on edge, but now she felt as if she had a handle on things.

'So, is this really goodbye then?' he asked softly.

'I guess so.'

He pulled her gently towards him, putting his hand around the back of her neck, beneath her hair. It felt very intimate but still, she wasn't sure when he placed his face close to hers if he intended to kiss her on the cheek or the mouth.

In any case, this time it was going to be her decision and she raised her chin and kissed him hard instead, like she really meant it. Out of the corner of her eye, she checked her apartment windows and could see that the lights were off.

'One more night,' she whispered, taking his hand firmly in hers and leading him back across the street towards home. 'For old times' sake.'

He laughed softly. He was putty in her hands.

'For old times' sake – if you insist,' he replied.

THERE WAS NOTHING WRONG WITH their lovemaking but when she woke to find him in her bed and saw him again in the cold light of day, she knew that it really was over.

He was still asleep. Propping herself up on her elbow, she gazed at his peaceful, familiar face and grief hit her again, but it was a longing for what had been, not for what they might have had in the future. And mixed with loss was a sense of relief, because she felt as if the slate really had been wiped clean. Now, her life was a blank sheet of paper to fill with whatever she chose.

This time, she was gentle and not angry when they said goodbye.

'I wish you well, Alfonso,' she murmured, as he got dressed. 'I really do.'

'Can't we at least see each other when you get back again?' he asked, zipping up his trousers. 'Just as friends, if that's what you want.'

She was certain that he believed he'd be able to win her around again, no problem; she knew him so well.

'Maybe – as friends,' she replied, and she noticed him smiling to himself as he laced his shoes, and he was cheerful when they kissed goodbye.

'See you at Christmas,' he said, sounding very self-assured. 'Enjoy the rest of your sabbatical.'

'Goodbye, Alfonso,' she replied, watching as he entered the elevator and waiting until the doors swished shut. There was a whoosh as the lift went down and she heard it ping at the bottom. Over and out.

As soon as she was sure that he'd left the building, she went back inside, picked up her mobile and rang Simon. It was three in the afternoon there and she had no idea what he'd be doing or whether he'd even have his phone with him, but he answered almost straight away.

'Chabela!' he said eagerly. 'It's so good to hear you! I loved that photo you sent me. What an amazing discovery! How are you? What else have you been up to?'

'I'm OK,' she replied. 'We've been all over the place. How are the preparations going at school?'

He made a grunting noise. 'Lots to do, not enough time, but we're making progress. Marion couldn't possibly have managed on her own. I'm sorry I haven't been in touch,' he went on and her ears pricked. She needed to hear this. 'I felt sick about not being able to come. It's been easier to bury myself in work and I've been so busy. Plus, you know I'm not very good at chat. I'm glad you rang me, though. I was worried you were furious with me.'

'Disappointed and hurt, yes, furious, no,' she replied honestly.

'I'm sorry. I hope you'll invite me to Mexico again,' he ventured. 'I hope I'm not persona non grata now.' This made her laugh, despite herself.

'You can come whenever you like.' She swallowed. 'The only thing is... I think I've had enough of Mexico City for the time being. I'm missing Tremarnock – and our swims.'

'Are you?' She could hear that he was smiling. 'It's not the same without you. Not at all.'

She paused for a minute, mustering courage.

'Simon?'

'Yes.'

'I need to ask you something.'

'Go ahead.'

'If I said that I might pack in my job here and move to Cornwall permanently, or at least for a year or so, would you be pleased, horrified or indifferent?'

He was silent for what seemed like an age, but in actual fact it was only a few moments.

'Very, very pleased,' he replied warmly at last.

There was a song in her heart when they hung up and she was still humming it when Liz and the others joined her in the kitchen for breakfast.

'You look cheerful,' Liz said, putting on the kettle and making herself a cup of tea.

'I am,' Chabela replied, smiling at Rosie, who looked about twelve with tousled hair, and Rafael, who was still half asleep. 'I'm in a very good mood. The best, in fact. It's taken me a long, long time, thirty-nine years to be exact, but I think I've finally worked out what I *really* want.'

Chapter Twenty-Three

THE NEXT FEW DAYS PASSED by in a pleasant sort of blur as they hurried from one place to another, keen to see as much of the city as possible before it was time to leave.

On their return to the UK, Simon drove to Bristol airport to collect Chabela, while Robert came with Lowenna to take home Liz, Rosie and Rafael. As soon as Chabela saw Simon waiting for her behind the barrier in the arrivals lounge, she knew that something had changed.

Gone was the stiffness, that feeling she'd always had that he was holding something back, keeping something in. His whole demeanour was more open and vulnerable somehow, and his eyes were soft and a little bit wary. It was as if he knew that he was exposed and was afraid of getting hurt.

She understood it so well because she felt it, too.

'Hello,' she said, gazing steadily into his eyes, wanting to reassure and be reassured at the same time. 'Thanks so much for driving all this way.'

She was aware of the others, walking around the barrier to meet Robert, and hoped that they weren't looking.

'Thank God you're here,' he said, in a deep voice. 'I thought I might never see you again.'

'I was always coming back,' she replied with a smile.

He looked so defenceless, almost naked, that she wanted to throw her arms around him right there and then, but there was a metal fence between them and besides, her friends might be watching.

'Do you want to go straight back to Polgarry, or come to Kittiwake first?' he asked, as soon as she joined him.

She didn't hesitate. 'Kittiwake please.'

He took her bag and started to wheel it towards the exit while she walked alongside.

'Bye, Liz, Rosie and Rafael!' she called, once they reached the car park. 'You've been fabulous travelling companions.'

They all hugged and Liz said that she'd had one of the best times of her life.

'Thank you for showing us your beautiful country and looking after us so well.'

Chabela did most of the talking as they headed back to Tremarnock while Simon listened. He made the odd comment, but seemed a little distracted. She put this down to the fact that he had a lot on his mind with the school inspection looming.

The head teacher had just come out of hospital and it didn't look as if he'd be fit to return to work anytime soon. This meant that Simon and Marion would most likely have to manage on their own, and there was much at stake. A bad report would cause a lot of upset and it could take years to restore the school's reputation. They simply had to get it right first time.

He left her bag in the boot of the car after parking, and they walked the final stretch across the cliff top to his cottage. As soon as she spotted the familiar whitewashed walls and slated roof, with patches of rough, orangey lichen, her pulse seemed to slow right down and a sense of calm washed through her.

Although it was autumn and the sky was grey, the grass in the front garden was newly mown and the lush spiky plants in tubs on either side of the front door had been cut back. She was amused and really rather relieved to see a line of mostly brown washing flapping in the wind. Simon had been busy.

Before going inside, she told him that she wanted to admire the view. They stood on the edge of the grassy headland for a few moments, gazing at the restless waves, the curved beach and Old Charley at the far end, looming large, dark and formidable, stretching his bony fingers out to sea.

'He looks a bit grumpy today,' Chabela commented.

'He's been like that ever since you left. Must be catching.'

She smiled at the joke and he told her that he'd made something for lunch, just in case she decided to stay. She was expecting to sit down straight away as it was gone two p.m. and she guessed that he must be hungry. She was, too.

As soon as they entered the house, however, he grabbed her around the back, pulled her to him and kissed her on the mouth with such ferocity that it almost took her breath away.

She was so surprised that her knees went weak and she nearly lost her balance, but he was holding on tight so she couldn't fall. It was almost as if he feared that if he let her go, she would disappear again to Mexico. She hadn't even had time to take off her jacket or put down her handbag!

The heat that he radiated melted something in her and before she knew it, she was tugging at his brown sweater and pulling it over his head. Next, her fingers fumbled with the buttons on his shirt while he dragged off her jacket and sweatshirt.

'Have you been swimming much?' she asked distractedly, while he fiddled with her bra strap, yanked it off and threw it unceremoniously on the floor.

'Not without you,' he murmured, pulling her into him again so that they were skin on skin. Her body tensed as he ran his hands over her back, shoulders and breasts before moving down to undo the top button of her jeans.

'Wait a minute,' she whispered, pushing his hands away. Then she planted little kisses down the centre of his chest to his bellybutton, all the while breathing in his warm scent. She'd wanted to do that again all week.

She was about to undo his trousers but he stopped her.

'Come with me,' he said. Then he led her, half clothed, up the stairs and on to his bed, from where they had a fine view of Old Charley, gazing at them through the slightly open window.

'We can't!' she gasped. 'Not in front of him! Close the blinds! He wouldn't approve!'

Simon laughed. It was a lovely sound – deep, infectious and decidedly naughty.

'Oh, he won't mind,' he said, unzipping her jeans and tugging them off. He stopped for a moment to admire her red lace knickers, but before long, they were on the floor, too. 'I reckon he's seen it all in his time. He's a wise old thing.'

Old Charley looked discreetly the other way.

IT HAD BEEN AN EMOTIONAL reunion for Liz at the airport, not least because she'd never left Lowenna before. The little girl had clung to her like a limpet all the way home, insisting that Liz should sit beside her on the back seat and hold her hand for the entire journey.

Liz had hoped that Robert would stay for a cup of tea at least when they got back to the cottage, but he turned her down.

'I've got too much to do,' he said, giving Rosie and Lowenna a goodbye hug. 'Lowie's been fab. We've had great fun, haven't we, sweetheart?'

The little girl beamed at her dad. She looked very pretty in clean pink dungarees, her dark hair tied in two fat bunches on either side of her head. He'd obviously done a great job with her in Liz's absence.

'Thank you,' Liz said, 'for looking after her so well.' He'd been staying at Bag End with her while Liz was away.

He grunted an acknowledgment. 'I'll pop in later to pick up my stuff. I haven't got time now.'

It was strange walking around the cottage and seeing evidence of him everywhere: his sweater on the back of the bedroom chair; his toothbrush in their bathroom.

She guessed that moving back in temporarily must have been poignant and peculiar for him, too, and she was overcome once again with a sense of guilt and sadness. And yet... she couldn't deny that she'd had these feelings for Max; they weren't made up and at least she'd finally been honest about them. There was some small comfort in that.

She'd hoped so much that Robert might have softened a little in her absence and that he would be ready to talk, but this didn't appear to be the case. Clearly the hurt ran very deep; perhaps so deep that it could never be erased.

She sighed as she opened her suitcase on the bed and started to unpack her things. For one whole week while she'd been gone, she'd mostly managed to put her troubles on the backburner and throw herself into all the new experiences. Now that she was home, though, she could feel the problems starting to crowd back in, making her quite sick and fuzzy.

Rosie shouted up that she and Rafael were going out to see friends.

'When will you be back?' Liz asked, walking to the top of the stairs and looking down at the pair, putting on their trainers in the hall.

'Dunno,' said Rosie in an off-hand manner. She picked up her phone and keys from the table and stalked out of the house, with Rafael trailing behind.

It seemed that she, too, had reverted to what had become her normal self now that they were in Cornwall again. During the holiday she'd been reasonably friendly towards Liz, and sometimes even quite loving.

Still, Liz knew that there was no point feeling sorry for herself. She had Lowie to look after, and friends to check on, and she was back to work on Monday, cleaning houses. There was no time to wallow.

Tabitha popped around with Oscar the following day and the four went for a walk along the coast and had lunch in a little café. Tabitha wanted to know all about the trip, of course, and she filled Liz in on what had been happening in Tremarnock in her absence.

Rick, having given up on Chabela, had wasted no time in finding a new amour through a dating website. Her name was Olga, she had red hair and wore leopard-print shoes. All in all, she seemed highly suitable.

Meanwhile, Tony and Felipe had had a massive argument one evening, which could be heard in the surrounding streets. Tony had stormed back to London, where he had a small flat, leaving Felipe bereft.

He'd been spotted several times wandering mournfully on the beach by himself and everyone had been worried about him. Fortunately, however, Tony had phoned quite quickly, they'd made up, sorted out their differences and now he was back in Tremarnock, behaving as if nothing had happened.

On top of this, Sally the Jack Russell had gone missing, which was a frequent occurrence, and had been found again in a side street, rootling in an upturned bin, much to Jenny, her owner's, disgust. Nathan the postman had got engaged to Annie, the fitness instructor, but other than that, not a lot had changed.

'Phew,' said Liz, when Tabitha had finished. 'Thanks for the update. Sounds like I've missed masses.'

Tabitha gave a wry smile. 'At least it's never dull here, is it? There's always something going on.'

'Too true,' said Liz, thinking of her own dramas. 'There's something about this place; you never know what's round the corner.'

They got on to the subject of Robert next, and Liz said how sad she felt, being in the house again without him in it. Tabitha said that she'd seen him with Lowenna a few times in the village and that he looked pretty bad – gaunt and weary – although he was obviously trying to put a brave face on it.

'You've got to have a proper talk with him, Liz,' she said seriously. 'Being in limbo like this is crippling for you both. You need to sort things out one way or another. Do you want him back?'

She looked at her friend squarely and Liz's eyes clouded over.

'I do,' she said, 'I miss him so much, but I've tried so hard to have a conversation with him and he won't.'

She was staring into the distance as they strolled back along the coastal path, past abundant gorse and wild grasses, with long, spidery tendrils swaying in the breeze.

'Incidentally, I haven't spoken to Max for ages, and I don't want to. He just seems like a flash in the pan, now. I can't believe I was so nuts about him; I must have been crazy. It could never have worked out. Besides, I have a feeling that he's hoping to get back with his ex-wife.

Relations between them seem to have thawed recently. Perhaps it would be for the best. I expect their daughter would be pleased. Apart from anything else, we live in different countries and I don't suppose either of us would have wanted to move.'

'You're not a bad person for having had strong feelings for someone else, you know,' Tabitha commented. 'You and Robert were going through a bad patch and these things happen. But you need to resolve matters with him one way or another now, not least for the children's sakes. Kids need stability and at the moment, you're all over the place. I'm pretty sure Robert wants to get back with you but he's going to need a lot of persuasion.'

Liz nodded. They were wise words and she was grateful for them.

'I'm going to email him,' she said decisively, 'and ask again if we can meet up. You're right, we can't go on like this. Either we try our absolute best to make it work, or it's time to call it quits.'

CHABELA DIDN'T RETURN TO POLGARRY Manor on the night she arrived back in England, she stayed in Kittiwake. Waking up the following morning in a strange bed to find Simon asleep beside her was a surprise to say the least.

At first she couldn't remember where she was, then, when she glanced out of the window through the half-open blind and spied Old Charley keeping watch outside the cottage, it all came back.

Of course! She was in Simon's cottage, with Simon, and they'd made love yesterday afternoon and again in the evening and both times had been glorious!

She gazed at his sleeping face, taking in the thick brown hair, dark eyebrows, straight nose and full lips. Without his glasses he looked younger and there was a light sprinkling of freckles across his nose and cheeks.

She leaned over and pressed her mouth softly against his. He stirred slightly and made a grumbling sound but didn't wake. All of a sudden, she was filled with a deep sense of wonder. Here was a man, she thought, whom she could really love, not in the way that she'd loved Alfonso, like a groupie, looking up to him and hanging on his every word, no – Simon felt to her like an equal, someone with whom she could stand side by side, shoulder to shoulder, each reflecting the exact same amount of light so that neither was forced to lurk in the shadows.

His eyelids fluttered open and when he saw her bending over, gazing at him, his face lit up in a smile.

'Good morning!' he said in a jokey voice, 'Now, who is this very attractive lady in my bed?'

She laughed. 'Your paramour. Had you forgotten you have one?'

'Ah yes,' he replied, grinning, 'I remember now.'

He sat up and took her head in his hands, staring deep into her eyes.

'Are you OK?' he asked softly. His look was tender and searching. 'You don't regret anything?'

She shook her head.

Reassured, he pulled her towards his chest and wrapped his arms around her, before gently kissing the top of her tousled hair.

She breathed in and out deeply, savouring the sense of comfort and safety flooding through her.

'Chabelita,' he whispered, rolling the name around his tongue, as if testing out the sound. '*Cómo te sientes?*' How do you feel?

'*Muy, muy contenta,*' – very, very happy – she replied, meaning it.

They got up slowly and spent the rest of the morning taking a shower and eating breakfast: fresh eggs from the local farm, toast and locally produced honey, tea, coffee and orange juice.

Later, he drove her back to Polgarry, where she finally unpacked and caught up with Bramble and Matt.

'You look different,' Bramble commented, as she sat opposite Chabela on one of the sofas in the grand drawing room. 'All sort of sparkly.'

'Must be the holiday,' Chabela replied. She wasn't yet ready to tell anyone about Simon. In fact, she needed time to process it herself. 'We had beautiful sunshine practically the whole time we were there.'

It was back to work the following day, but she scarcely needed to have bothered to open up the café because there were so few customers.

When she mentioned this to Robert, he agreed that it was time to shut up shop there until spring. He promptly offered her another job as a front of house manager at A Winkle in Time, which would free him up to focus on admin and other tasks.

The restaurant remained quite busy all through October, November and even into December, and with so much to learn, Chabela barely had time to think during the day. At nights, she mostly went to see Simon or had a drink in the pub with Liz, Tabitha and other villagers before going home to bed.

About six weeks after her return from Mexico, she woke feeling nauseous and the sensation persisted throughout the afternoon and evening. It was only when she climbed under her duvet at the manor that night that she realised she hadn't had a period for quite some time.

Checking in her phone diary, she saw that she was two weeks late. Her heart went into her mouth. She couldn't be pregnant, could she? She wasn't exactly young any more and besides, she was on the pill, though once or twice in Mexico she had forgotten to take it at the correct hour.

She barely slept that night, and the following morning before work, she drove into the neighbouring village to buy a pregnancy testing kit. Looking left and right as she left the pharmacy, she fancied that all eyes were on her and felt ashamed and foolish. Women of her age didn't usually get pregnant by mistake, and certainly not by ex-lovers. It simply wasn't the done thing.

She popped into the restaurant cloakroom during a lunchtime lull and opened up the box with trembling hands. Peeing onto the stick wasn't difficult, and she checked the clock on her phone to make sure that she waited a full two minutes before looking at the result.

When a plus sign appeared in the window, Chabela's stomach turned over and she felt faint and had to lean against the wall to stop herself from falling.

She felt scared and at the same time, a little excited. A baby wasn't what she'd had in mind at all, and yet... somehow the prospect filled her with a sense of wonder that she would never have expected. Her own child! A girl or boy who might look like her, sound like her...

All of a sudden, a terrible thought rushed into her head. Was it Alfonso's – or Simon's? When she counted back the days, she decided that it must be the former, given the dates and the fact that she'd missed the correct time to take the pill while in Mexico.

It was hard going back to work afterwards, and Robert asked if she were OK, because she'd gone so quiet. She told him that she wasn't feeling too well, but didn't mention the sickness; the last thing she wanted was to alert him to what was really going on.

As the afternoon progressed, she began to feel increasingly panicky as the reality of her situation started to sink in. Her immediate thought was to phone Simon, but then she realised that she could hardly tell the man with whom she thought she'd fallen in love that she might be pregnant by someone else.

Despair gripped her insides and twisted as it dawned on her that she had thrown away her chance of happiness with Simon for a final, one-night fling. Why on earth had she done it? Partly it was out of childish pique, because Simon hadn't come with her to Mexico, yet she knew that he would have if the head teacher hadn't fallen ill. She ought to have admired him for his work ethic and strong sense of responsibility, not berated him for his virtues.

Revenge had also come into it; she'd liked the idea of finally calling the shots with Alfonso but the whole thing had backfired spectacularly. She was ashamed of herself and also grief-stricken about what she had lost.

Now, she would most likely have to return to Mexico City and her job. Tremarnock and all its inhabitants would fade into a distant memory. She could envisage a scenario of single motherhood, juggling work and childcare, with Alfonso dropping by from time to time when it suited him. She was well and truly trapped.

Of course there was the option of a termination, but she knew without a shadow of doubt that she wouldn't do it. The fact that she was pregnant at all seemed like nothing short of a miracle; she couldn't possibly destroy this new life growing inside her.

The last lunch customers left at three thirty, and she drove home to Polgarry for a rest. It was a whole two hours before she was due back for the evening shift, and she knew that she couldn't put off what she'd been planning any longer.

Sitting in her bedroom on the small armchair beneath the window, she looked out at the distant cliffs and the roaring sea beyond. She was going to miss this view, but most of all she'd miss Kittiwake – and Simon.

There was a lump in her throat as she rang Alfonso's number and her sweaty palms felt slippery against the phone casing. There was no reply at first, just a generic, recorded voice telling her to leave a message. She didn't want to speak to a machine and pressed the off button.

It was hard to know how to occupy herself now, with so much hanging in the air. She tried to read her book, but couldn't focus, and there was no way that she would be able to sleep, although she felt dog-tired.

She was thinking of taking a shower just to kill some time when the phone rang loud and clear on the bedside table and she hurried to pick it up. When Alfonso's name appeared on the screen, she felt her knees give way and she plonked onto the bed, with the mobile pressed tight to her ear.

'Chabelita!' he said in a honeyed voice. 'What a lovely surprise!'

He started to ask what she was up to, but she had no time for such niceties and cut straight to the chase.

'Alfonso,' she said, 'I'm pregnant.'

There was silence at the other end for a few minutes before his voice came back cold and clear: 'Congratulations. Whose is it?'

Chabela was taken aback. 'Yours, I believe,' she said.

'You *believe*?' he repeated. 'You mean you don't know?'

No warm, soothing words, no asking how she was feeling. He sounded harsh and inquisitorial and she was on the back foot.

She couldn't lie, so she told him exactly what had happened.

'I've been seeing someone,' she explained. 'It's early days. But I've looked at the dates and I don't think the baby's his.'

'Well, it's definitely not mine,' came the response. 'I've had a vasectomy.'

Chabela started and her mouth dropped open. 'What? When?'

'Soon after Enrique was born.'

'You never told me.'

'Why would I? It wasn't going to affect you one way or the other.'

Tears sprang to her eyes as the reality of what he'd just said sank in. Although she'd always been ambivalent about having children, he knew that she'd been considering them; in fact they'd talked about it sometimes, and he'd always said they couldn't make any decisions until he'd left Pilar.

'There's still time,' she remembered him saying to her over a glass of red wine in a bar off Mexico City's main square. His youngest must have been about ten. He'd gently pushed a few strands of hair out of her eyes. 'We'll revisit the subject when I'm free.'

But he'd known even as he said it that she'd never have children with him because he couldn't; he didn't want any more. If he'd been truthful with her from the start, she might have accepted his decision. It was the lie that hurt, and the fact that her wishes, hopes and needs hadn't even entered the equation.

'You bastard,' she said. It just popped out, but it came right from the heart and gut.

'What?' He sounded puzzled, as if he thought that he must have misheard. She'd rarely ever spoken to him like that.

'You don't care about me at all, do you?' she went on now. The words flowed freely, gushing forth in a stream of consciousness. 'It was all about possession, with you. You wanted to own me but my happiness didn't matter.'

Even as she spoke, she noticed that she was using the past tense and despite the lump in her throat, a profound sense of relief came over her.

Finally, in a flash of clarity, she knew that she'd made her decision. No more wavering, no more hankering after something with Alfonso that could never be; she'd held this fantasy for so long and her unexpected pregnancy had momentarily relit the flame. But she didn't even want the dream to become reality now. She wouldn't marry him if he asked. He was dead to her.

She heard him inhale and exhale slowly and purposefully, as if he were processing what she'd just said and working out the best response, the one most beneficial to him, no doubt.

She wasn't going to give him the satisfaction of having the last word.

'OK,' she said. There was a wobble in her voice but she managed to keep going. 'Now I know this baby isn't yours, I won't be troubling you again. Good luck, Alfonso.'

'I, um—' he started to say, but she hung up without waiting to hear the end.

Chapter Twenty-Four

CHABELA STOOD WITH HER BACK to the wall for quite a while breathing in and out to steady her nerves. She was deeply shocked, but her dismay turned to joy when she realised that if Alfonso wasn't the father, then it must be Simon.

She was filled once again with a sense of amazement, that a brand new person was growing inside her who had half of her genes and half of Simon's.

How would it look? Would he or she have very dark hair and brown eyes like her, or Simon's lighter hair and hazel eyes? Either way, the baby would be much loved by them both, she was certain. What she didn't know, however, was how he would feel about it.

She barely slept that night, thinking about the implications. Should she move back to Mexico City still or stay here in Tremarnock? It would depend on Simon's response and that would have to wait till he was back from work this evening.

She texted him to ask if she could pop around to Kittiwake later, and he quickly said yes. Then she had to endure another whole day of work until it was finally six o'clock and she could legitimately depart.

After leaving the car in the car park opposite the playground, she walked to the bottom of the stone steps on Fore Street and began the familiar climb. It was already quite dark and she used the torch on her mobile to make sure that she didn't trip and fall.

The journey took longer than usual, because the ground was slippery and she had to walk slowly. When she eventually reached Kittiwake, Simon was already at the door, which he opened wide to let her in.

'*Holà!*' he said, taking her in his arms and kissing her on the lips. 'How are things?'

'OK,' she replied. 'Just. Can we talk?'

Noticing how serious she was, he led her straight into his sitting room, where they sat on the sofa and he put an arm around her shoulder.

His arm felt heavy and soothing, and she rested her head against his chest.

'I've got something to tell you.'

His body tensed. 'Fire away.'

'I'm pregnant,' she said simply. 'You're going to be a father!'

Simon started. 'I beg your pardon?'

She repeated herself.

'Oh my God, I can't believe it!' There was a catch in his throat and his eyes were damp with tears. 'That's the best news I've ever heard.'

'Is it? Is it really?' She needed to be sure that he wasn't saying it just to please her. 'Aren't you horrified? Isn't it too soon? I mean, we haven't exactly known each other long.'

'Chabela, I've been waiting for you all my life,' he replied simply.

Then he gave her a smile, which was like a bright spring flower bursting into bloom. It lit up his eyes, too, and seemed to pierce through all the bad in her life and make it right again. It was the most beautiful, radiant, shimmering, glorious smile that she'd ever seen.

After that, he reached around to hold her tight and they sat in the shadows for a while, listening to each other's breathing. Then, with a sick stomach and fear and trepidation in her heart, she braced herself and did what she had to do: she confessed everything, including her night with Alfonso, the sorrow and regret she felt, how she found out about the pregnancy, Alfonso's response and what she had learned from it about herself, him, and her true feelings for Simon.

She expected Simon to be shocked and hurt, and he was. For a while he said nothing at all, he just stared into the distance, his eyes filled with pain. It broke her heart to witness his suffering and to know that she was the cause made it ten times worse.

For a while, she thought that all might be lost. To her profound relief, however, in the end Simon turned to her and said he believed her when she insisted that her relationship with Alfonso was truly and utterly dead.

'I love you and I want to be with you. I won't let him ruin our happiness.'

His words made her love him even more and profound gratitude surged through her veins.

Before too long, the conversation switched to what hopes and dreams they would have for their baby boy or girl. Light from the twinkling stars shone into the room, casting a silvery glow over walls, floor and ceiling and the only sound between conversations came from the branches softly tap-tapping against the darkened windows.

He rose at last and turned around to face her, taking her hands in his.

'Chabela,' he said, 'Señorita Penhallow, You're more to me than life itself. I would do anything for you – climb mountains, fight sharks, even sit on cactuses.'

This made the corners of her mouth twitch and rise.

'I want you in my world for ever and ever,' he went on. 'I want to have lots of fun with you and raise a family and grow old together. Please will you marry me and be my wife?'

Chabela's heart leaped. It was as if all the pain, humiliation and loss of those long years with Alfonso melted away and in their place were warm summer raindrops and sparkling sunbeams. Everything was going to be all right now. She had Simon and he had her and they need never be alone again.

'Señor Hosking,' she replied, her heart full to bursting, 'I'd like that more than anything in the whole wide world. I want to live with you here in Kittiwake and eat ice cream and drink red wine and grow vegetables and go swimming every day in the sea. What I'm trying to say is...' she went on. 'What I really mean is... in other words – yes, yes, YES!'

ONCE THE MARRIAGE HAD BEEN decided upon, Chabela and Simon wasted no time in booking the church and reception venue – which was to be none other than the Secret Shack. They settled on the date of 23 December, which was only a few short weeks away, and the ceremony itself was to take place in the Methodist church.

It was to be a smallish, relaxed, casual affair and Bramble, who had lots of experience of running events, agreed to help with the arrangements. Robert was to walk Chabela up the aisle, while Rosie and her friend, Mandy, were to be bridesmaids. Chabela was determined to hold her celebrations on the beach. After Kittiwake it had become her happy place, the place where she felt most alive. Of course it might be blustery or even raining, so at Bramble's suggestion, she organised a giant white tepee to go alongside the café, which would give plenty of shelter, and there would be outside caterers – namely Audrey and her team of helpers – providing food and drink.

They invited fifty guests, including Simon's family from Camelford, and two of Chabela's closest girlfriends from Mexico City. Other than that it was all villagers, plus Sally the Jack Russell in a purple bow.

Chabela, who prided herself on being unconventional, looked stunning in an avant-garde, off-the-shoulder, wine-coloured velvet dress. Her baby bump was hardly showing yet, and the gown was fitted on the waist and hips and ended with a flamenco-style ruffle just below the knee. The back, meanwhile, was in the shape of a swishy mermaid's tail, which fell all the way to the ground.

Simon had bought a very dashing velvet suit that was black, not brown, and he had a crimson silk tie. In fact, for once, he didn't have a single brown item on him, save his wallet, which was hidden anyway.

The bridesmaids were in pale pink, with scarlet rosebuds in their hair and silver shoes, and they carried posies of red, white and blue polyanthus. Meanwhile, Chabela's bouquet was made of rich red hellebores with silver foliage that seemed to sparkle in the dimly lit church, and she had nude sandals with glass heels on her feet.

Most of the guests had on Christmassy colours also – red, white, green, silver and gold, and the church was filled with garlands of white winter roses and dark green ivy, which coiled around the stone pillars and rambled over the edges of the wooden pews.

The ceremony was at eleven thirty and everyone was seated, listening to Pachelbel's Canon in D on the organ, when Chabela arrived on Robert's arm, ten minutes late. Rosie and her friend, both with big smiles and flowers in their hair, were just behind.

Immediately the music stopped and started again with '*El Son de la Negra*', which was often played at Mexican weddings. This caused a number of raised eyebrows among the congregation, who were not used to such foreign imports, but they took it in good part and soon relaxed into it.

The service itself was conducted in English, with a nod to Mexican tradition when the bridesmaids placed *lazos*, two flower leis tied together in the middle with a bow, over the bride's and groom's heads during a special prayer, before they said 'I do'.

There were quite a lot of tears shed when they made their vows, not least from Liz, who always blubbed during weddings. Simon couldn't take his eyes off Chabela the entire time, and she gave him smiles back that would melt the hardest of hearts.

Once or twice Lowenna, who was sitting on her mother's lap in the front row, shouted, 'What are they doing, Mummy?' and had to be shushed. But no one minded; it just seemed to add to the joyful atmosphere.

As soon as the rings had been exchanged and the final hymn, 'All Things Bright and Beautiful', had been sung, the newly-weds went to sign the register, witnessed by Robert and Liz.

The pair stood stiffly side-by-side, their hands clasped in front of them, their eyes fixed on the marriage licence. As she looked up from the page, however, Chabela couldn't help noticing Robert casting a furtive glance in Liz's direction, and she gave a small, shy, half-smile back.

The moment was so brief that most people would have missed it, but not Chabela, whose heart fluttered with hope. Then she and Simon walked out of the church into the watery December sunshine, where they were sprayed with dried petals.

The biggest surprise was when a mariachi band in white suits popped out of the bushes with their guitars to entertain everyone while photographs were being taken. Chabela had found the musicians through a specialist hire company online and on discovering that they lived not far away in Exeter, she had wasted no time in booking them.

Most of the guests left first for the reception on Polrethen Beach, then Simon drove Chabela. As they travelled, the sky clouded over and she feared that it might rain. However, once they arrived at the Secret

Shack, the December sun had peeked through again and was casting a cold, watery glow over everything.

Chabela giggled as she teetered over the sand in her high heels, hanging on to Simon's arm. She was wearing a white faux-fur shrug over her dress though it wasn't particularly cold, and they stopped for a moment before they went inside to admire the view. The crescent-shaped beach seemed much wilder in winter. It was flanked by giant granite boulders on one side and rocky mounds on the other.

Ramshackle wooden breakwaters stretched some way out to sea on which perched seagulls, preening their feathers and pecking at barnacles. Further out, a number of fishing boats bobbed friskily in the choppy silver-white waves, while a long way away, they spotted a battle-grey warship, which had probably come from the royal naval dockyard in Plymouth.

'I love it so much here,' said Chabela, closing her eyes for a moment and breathing in the scent of salt and seaweed.

She was holding her husband's hand, which felt large, warm and comforting.

'And I love *you*,' he said softly. 'I can't quite believe this is true, can you?'

They turned around after that to admire the tepee, which was open wide at the front and already buzzing with people inside. The wooden poles that stuck out of the top had jolly flags on them and there was brightly coloured bunting around the entrance too, so that it all looked very festive.

It was lovely and warm inside, owing to the giant brazier in the centre, filled with burning logs that licked and crackled enticingly. It was quite safe, because the cone-shaped tepee had a hole in the top, which drew the smoke upwards like a chimney, allowing it to escape into the outside air.

Large ceramic pots filled with lush green ferns stood at intervals, and the slatted oblong tables with wooden benches underneath were positioned around the edges, leaving room in the middle for dancing later.

Fairy lights twisted around the tepee's internal lodge poles and industrial-type light bulbs hung from planks that were suspended from the roof poles.

Chabela herself had done the floral arrangements, which were glass jam jars filled with rich, dark greenery and seasonal wildflowers – hebe, japonica and winter honeysuckle, which gave off a heady perfume.

The whole effect was casual, pretty and rustic, and very soon the mariachi band struck up again and the guests listened and chatted while the waiters and waitresses – mainly local teenagers – passed around champagne, margaritas, soft drinks and canapés.

Most of the fare was Mexican, but there were a few traditional British recipes for those with less adventurous palates or who simply couldn't cope with anything spicy.

When they finally sat down to eat, the numerous dishes included *pozole* – a hominy stew served with chicken – *chiles rellenos* – poblano peppers stuffed with fried cheese and tomato sauce – *chiles en nogada* – chillies filled with chopped meats, fruits and spices and covered in walnut cream, which Liz and the others had eaten in Mexico, and savoury tamales, or pieces of dough steamed in banana leaves and filled with meat, cheese and vegetables.

Each table had on it a good bottle of tequila, for those who wished to indulge, as well as jugs of water flavoured with hibiscus or orange and lime. There was also as much beer and wine as anyone wanted, and there were plenty of soft drinks for the children.

Chabela and Simon sat with Robert, Bramble and Matt, Loveday and Jesse, Rosie and Rafael, Tony and Felipe. They would have liked to ask Liz, too, of course, and Lowenna, but for obvious reasons, felt that Liz and Robert would want to be apart.

There was so much food that folk couldn't possibly eat everything, but everyone did their best, especially Tony, who was always hungry, and Rick, who had brought along his new squeeze, Olga, in a purple frock.

By now, the mariachi band had gone silent, and the tepee was filled with only happy voices and laughter. As Chabela gazed around, the faces of all those she had come to know and love in the past six months seemed to smile back at her, and she had to pinch herself to make sure that she wasn't dreaming.

They had *tres leches*, or three milks cake, for dessert, with a soft, melt-in-your-mouth texture, as well as cookies made with pecans and butter, and hosts of special candies made of chocolate, coconut, amaranth and molasses.

When at last people started to slow down and Tony could be heard exclaiming, 'I can't eat another thing!', Robert rose, pinged a spoon against his glass and declared that it was time for the speeches.

The day had already been so unconventional that no one batted an eyelid when he said the only speakers were to be the newly-weds themselves.

Chabela rose first, her cheeks flushed with happiness and tequila.

'I was sitting in my office at the University of Mexico City,' she began, 'feeling blue about the end of a relationship and wondering what to do with my life, when I noticed a letter in my in-tray with unfamiliar writing on the envelope...'

She went on to explain about Simon's correspondence, his family's link with the Penhallows, and her spontaneous decision to book a flight to Cornwall to come and meet him.

'I didn't think we'd have anything in common, apart from the possible historic ties between our ancestors,' she explained. 'At that stage, though, I didn't even know if James Penhallow and I were related.

'The first time I set eyes on Simon,' she went on, with a smile, 'he was exactly what I expected – middle-aged, intellectual, a bit awkward – in other words, a typical English eccentric.'

Simon pulled an abashed face then shrugged, as if to say, 'What can I do? It's just the way I am,' which made everyone titter.

'But I quickly realised there was more to him than met the eye. He spoke great Spanish, played the guitar and was a brilliant cook. What's not to like?'

This prompted an outburst of laughter.

'Soon, I was making all sorts of excuses to find out more about the Cornish tin miners who moved to Mexico. He must have thought I was passionate about genealogy.' She gave a cheeky grin. 'But seriously,' she continued, 'isn't it amazing? I came here to get over a break-up and I found a husband. When I married my darling Simon, we brought together the Penhallow and Hosking families once more and reforged the historic links between Cornwall and Mexico's Little Cornwall!

'*Viva la entente cordiale!*' she cried, to rapturous applause. Then everyone raised their glasses. 'Long live the entente cordiale!'

Simon's speech was shorter but by no means less heartfelt. He spoke of his love for Chabela and all things Mexican, as well as her new-found enthusiasm for wild swimming.

'And now we have a baby on the way,' he said, putting an arm around her shoulders and pulling her close, 'we'll have our very own James or Jacinta.' He was referring, of course, to the love affair between James Penhallow and the young Mexican who became his wife.

'Whether he or she will prefer clotted cream teas or tortillas, only time will tell. Hopefully, both!' he added, with a flourish, to cries of 'Hear! Hear!' and 'Definitely both – if you two have anything to do with it!'

After that, staff cleared away the dishes, packed up the tables and the area became a dance floor, with chairs dotted around the edges for those who wanted to sit.

By now, it was getting dark outside and the fire in the centre of the tent was still orange and smouldering. It was giving out so much heat that one of the door flaps had to be kept open, letting in the night sky, and the numerous fairy lights coiled around the wooden poles twinkled merrily.

Rafael had offered to deejay and music blasted out of the speakers and seemed to hurtle headlong onto the beach before roaring out to sea. It didn't matter that it was loud; there were no houses nearby.

Little by little, people began to spill out of the tepee onto the sand, kicking off their shoes and dancing their hearts out. Their internal thermostats were turned up high enough to keep them warm, and there were colourful blankets on hand for those who preferred to remain still.

At first, Liz seemed to hang back, watching the others rather wistfully from a distance. A little later, however, Chabela, who was dancing on the beach with Simon, looked over his shoulder and saw that her friend was now twirling Lowenna, while Robert jiggled slightly uncomfortably nearby.

Before long, the little girl ran over, grabbed her father's arm and literally tugged him towards her mother, plonking her hand in his and forcing their fingers to intertwine. Both Liz and Robert looked awkward, but neither tried to pull away.

Esme, who didn't normally do dancing but was making an exception tonight, sidled over and whispered in Chabela's ear.

'It's such a shame, what happened to those two.' She, too, was gazing in their direction. 'They're so good together. I do hope they can work things out.'

'Me too,' Chabela replied warmly, then she nudged Esme in the ribs. 'Look!'

The music had changed to a softer, bluesy number and both women couldn't help gawping as Robert turned to face Liz full on. For a moment, she gazed questioningly into his eyes, before melting into his body. Meanwhile, his arms snaked around her shoulders, hugging her so tightly that she couldn't possibly break free even if she wanted to.

Despite her young age, Lowenna seemed instinctively to know when she wasn't needed and she sidled away to join Rosie, who was dancing with Rafael. Rosie, too, must have noticed her mum and Robert because Chabela saw her whisper something to her boyfriend, who gave a furtive grin.

The next thing Chabela knew, Mr and Mrs Hart were in a steamy, passionate clinch, completely oblivious, it seemed, to everyone and everything around them. They might have been the only people on the planet.

'Thank heavens!' Esme exclaimed, before discreetly turning the other way. Chabela and Simon did likewise, smiling to themselves and each other as they sidled off in the other direction, putting, they hoped, enough distance between themselves and the lovebirds so as not to interrupt their moment.

'What's happening with you and Caroline? I hope *you* can find a way to be together again,' Chabela remarked at last, once they were well out of earshot.

Esme's long thin nose seemed to quiver slightly, and her mouth drooped at the corners.

'It's Philip,' she began, referring to Caroline's husband, who was becoming increasingly afflicted by his Parkinson's disease. 'She can't—'

'I know,' Chabela said, reaching out to touch the older woman's arm. 'But don't give up hope. I nearly did when I split up with Alfonso, and look what's happened to me!'

At that point the music slowed again and Simon gave her a gentle pull, as if he were jealous and couldn't bear her focus to fall on anyone but him. His arms, which were already on her back, crept further around and she dropped her head on his chest, against his heart.

She could feel his breath rising and falling, and their bodies seemed to move in synch, as if they were one and the same person. Meanwhile, the black velvety sky seemed to wrap itself around them like a soft blanket, keeping them warm and safe.

Chabela caught some of the voices of nearby guests, including Audrey's shrill tones and Lowenna's giggle; it was astonishing that she was still awake, really. The excitement must have been keeping her going.

Although the tide was out and the ocean was some way off, Chabela fancied that she could hear it murmuring to her. It spoke soft words of long voyages and joyful returns, of families past and present, with all their hopes, fears, triumphs and disasters, and of the generations to come that would plant their feet on this very sand and live and love and grow old, just like her and Simon.

That she had finally sunk her roots into Cornish soil seemed suddenly so very obvious that she almost laughed out loud. Hadn't Alfonso always said that she had far to go? She'd always thought that he meant she was destined for great things in terms of her career. Now, however, she decided that even back then, he'd recognised something in her that she hadn't even been aware of herself: the need to find out where she really belonged.

Well she'd found it now, in Simon and Kittiwake, in the sun, sea and sand of these shores, in Liz, Robert and her other new friends and, of course, in darling Tremarnock.

Acknowledgements

Big thanks to my gifted editor, Rosie de Courcy, and my equally brilliant agent, Heather Holden-Brown. Also to the fantastic team at Head of Zeus.

I'm grateful as well to Stephen Lay and Gill Rifaat of the Cornish-Mexican Cultural Society, for providing me with so much colour and invaluable information.

It was my friend Yael Brown who first tipped me off about 'Little Cornwall' in Hidalgo in deepest Mexico, and it was a huge thrill to visit the village with her and her family. Their warmth and hospitality were second to none.

Finally, a big thank you to my precious family, whom I love very much.

About the author

Emma Burstall studied English at Cambridge University before becoming a journalist and author. *Tremarnock*, the first novel in her series set in a delightful Cornish village, was published in 2015 and became a top ten bestseller.